CAROLIN

A SONG OF MANGE AND POISON

FAMILY DYNAMICS CAN BE FATAL

A Song Of Mange And Poison.
Copyright 2023 by Caroline Noe
All rights reserved.
No part of this book may be reproduced, distributed, or transmitted in any form or by any means, without the prior written permission of the author, except for the use of brief quotations in a book review.

This is a work of fiction. Names, characters and events, other than those in the public domain, are either a product of the author's imagination or are used in a fictitious manner. Any resemblance to actual persons, living or dead, events, or locales is purely coincidental.

This book, in its entirety, was written by a real human: a cranky, middle-aged woman with a penchant for wolves.

*For the mixed up, united packs of the world.
We are family and refuse to be separated.*

*This book is written in the English version of English,
since I am English.*

By the same author

Firestone Key

Canellian Eye: Prophecy
Canellian Eye: Rebellion
Canellian Eye: Chosen

The Ezekiel Factor

A Wolf So Grim And Mangy
A Song Of Mange And Poison

ACKNOWLEDGEMENTS

My grateful thanks to my cover designer, Olly at More Visual Ltd. Yet again, you've taken my weird ideas and produced something stunning. There's no-one I would commission before you.

To Janice Mackenzie, who trawled through most incarnations of this book, your care and hard work are an inspiration. More than this, your friendship is what most in their right mind long to have.

To my sisters Penny and Heather, our Mum and Dad are proud of us all.

To my brothers and sisters at Sudbury Hill Community Church, you're the true definition of found and diverse family.

To my book buddies at Instagram, your support means the world to me. A mixed up pack indeed.

And last, but never least, my Jesus, who saved my life, soul and sanity. It's been some wild ride.

CHAPTER 1

The Madcap Recap

Hah, got you. I've called it Chapter 1, but it's actually (whisper) a recap, a prologue of sorts. See, I know there's a twitchy pile of you, lurking out there, who won't read the dreaded p word, so I'm sneaking it in under the radar. Probably should change that recap subtitle, but I've never been accused of subtlety.

If you thought you'd heard the last of Edi(th) Breaker-Smith when the magic book went on the bonfire, think again. Granted words jangle around inside my cavernous skull, rather than zap onto mouldy pages on their own, but I suspect a further story cries out to be told, so here we are. For all I know, that book might have risen from the ashes like a leathery phoenix and winged its way back to the frozen library in the snakes' vacated castle, but I digress to Book 3.

So, this morning, having fed Mr G, the obese, bucktoothed gumwhat, before he could chew my fingers off, I gracefully sashayed into our lodge, tripped over Curt – who was lying on the floor, apparently trying to clean wolf hair out of my rocker – and nosedived into the stew, which was, thankfully, still lukewarm. None of this may seem relevant, but bear with me.

My life thus far…

I was pushing sixty, well into the dry misery that is the menopause, suffering from sciatica, disappointment, loneliness and a snarky attitude, when the teenage colleague from the hell pit of officedom gifted me a leatherbound book for Secret Santa.

A bit of magical faffing about resulted in nearly freezing to death in snowbound Turea, where I was rescued by a limping scrag end of male who morphed into a mangy wolf – as you do.

Turns out, Curt, said grotty wolf, once held the exalted title of pack Alpha, until betrayed by bears who ruined his hip. After which he went AWOL up the mountain and wasn't happy about having to cart this old baggage back down again.

The new Alpha, Curt's younger brother, kindly let me stay in his village, despite the objections of his nanny bald eagle, Wings. I'd been there five minutes when Dulcis, Alpha's teen daughter, adopted me as her surrogate nana, which makes me sound like the dog from Peter Pan, if not as lovable.

Curt threatened to head back up the mountain, but stayed when a delegation from the ruling Snake Empire arrived to broker a truce with the wolves' arch enemy: the bears. It went pear shaped, of course, ending up with a snarling free for all that only ceased when I launched into a rendition of YMCA. (Which is probably the only bit you do remember.)

When the snakes scarpered, along with their eagle guards, the furry packs figured out they were lying through their fangs and Wings took off like he was guilty. We all ended up in the bear camp, plotting how to rescue missing wolves and bears from the snakes' mountain top castle.

Curt and I were finally getting our groove on, when a homicidal bird I'd nicknamed Broken Beak, after having smashed him in the mush, kidnapped me, dumping my freezing posterior in the castle.

Wings winged back to the good guys, dropping Curt and the bears' teen prince, Adamo, on the ramparts. I got rescued, Dulcis got rescued, the missing fur got rescued, but the all powerful Snake Empire turned out to be dying from mould infestation.

We all ended up in a battle with monstrous serpent, King Serpen, but his ambassador, Anguis, took him out with a stranglehold and we all went down the mountain – even Serpen - to form one enormous dysfunctional family, living happily ever after – whatever that is.

Which leads me back to where we came in, to wit, nosediving into the stew, because no matter how idyllic it appears, life always finds a way to dump you in the brown stuff, head first.

Anyway, suitably primed, you can now tackle Chapter 2, which is actually Chapter 1.

Here are the players to date:

Only Human

Me (Edith Breaker-Smith): Gorgeous silver vixen. I wish. Unless your type of vixen sports an ample posterior, hot flushes and sciatica.

Wolves

Curt(us): Mange ridden former Alpha, now getting it on with me every chance he gets.
Alpha: Curt's younger brother, carrying the mixed up pack like a concrete straightjacket.
Dulcis: Alpha's teen daughter, wolfing about in the undergrowth with Adamo.

Bears

Prince Adamo: Redheaded teenage ruler of the bears, accident prone, tad dim.
General Ursid: Scarred, wide as a bus warrior, soggy hearted.
Mama Bear: Self appointed matron of the sick. No idea what her actual name is.
Mama's short, but stout-hearted mate, Friddie.
Their spitting, snarling, teeth laden, homicidally adorable cub.

Snakes

Serpen: Former King, ruddy great serpent, slithering out of depression.

Anguis: His once ambassador, handsome bit of alright, so Curt keeps an eye on him.
Sospa: Serpen's diddly heir niece, trouble in the making.

Eagles

Wings: Flapping old nanny, sings like a constipated parrot. Love him.
Broken Beak: Miserable toerag, actually named Gulid, but I don't care.

CHAPTER 2

Howls, Growls And Rows

"I'm going to miss you, my sweet boy," I tell him, lovingly stroking soft licks of hair curling around his ears. "Being with you brings me peace. Please come back to me. I need you."

Those doleful eyes peer back at me, but no word does he utter. Well, he wouldn't, would he? Being a ram.

Roger's woolly rump swings jauntily from side to side as we wander down the valley, following the bleating crowd of sheep on their mass winter exodus. It'll be spring before I get to chat to my silent friend again. I feel teary, which is ridiculous when you think about it. Curt calls me a nutter, but then, that crazy old wolf should know.

The snow's falling heavily now, coating the town in a blanket of sparkling white and reminding me of when I arrived here, a year ago. So much has changed, I can barely remember my old life. Who am I kidding? Of course I can. It was miserable and lonely. Here, I'm neither. Annoyed, flummoxed, tired and confused on occasion, but not miserable and certainly never lonely. Chance would be a fine thing. Between the wolves, bears, snakes and a grumpy old bird (Wings, not me), there's hardly a quiet moment. It's why I appreciate these glorious chats with my woolly friend Roger; he never talks back.

"Well, Rog old bean, this is it, methinks."

I sniff as I come to a halt and watch Roger forge ahead, snowflakes sticking to his fleece and camouflaging his rump within the snow globe landscape.

"Bye, good boy," I whisper, as though I'm losing a faithful labrador, and wave a hand coated in thick woollen gloves, courtesy of the fluff from his wandering pack. Curt would wet himself laughing, if he saw me now.

Whistling wind carries the promise of a big freeze and it's chilly standing here, even coated in wool and leather layers from head to toe, like a middle-aged marshmallow. I'm about to head back to the mansion, with its roaring fire, when Roger turns, stares straight at me and delivers a reverberating, plaintive bleat. I'm so moved, I actually sob.

A hefty thump on the back of the bonce knocks the sentiment right out of me. A follow up missile inserts snow straight down my ear canal. The accompanying snorted laughter reveals exactly which assailant is about to get his face pummelled into the dirt, if I get my mittens on him.

"Oi, Mange, you better start running," I holler, bundling towards him like a sumo wrestler on stilts.

"Come and get me, Big Bum," Curt yells back, dancing about like a limp boxer.

Two minutes later he lets me catch him, since we figured out the grappling bit is far more fun than the chase. I throw myself at him with a muffled squelch, knocking him backwards into a dune.

"Mind the hip," he grumbles from beneath my bulk.

Rolling in the snow, we're happily exchanging warm breath and tongue suction when I briefly open my eyes to spot Roger fading into the distance. Hey ho, the ram's gone. Back to old people snogging. (If that bothers you, you're in the wrong book. Just saying.)

"I'm soggy," Curt announces, hauling himself up to a seated position by clamping my buttocks. "Let's creep back to our room. It's cold out here."

"Why are we creeping anywhere?" I ask, happily perched on his warm thighs. "Oh wait," I add, riding a brainwave, "shouldn't you be chairing the community meeting?"

"I've taken all of them since we joined. Look how much I've aged," Curt grumbles, lifting his woolly hat. "I'm losing my hair. Or it's where you've been rubbing it."

I give his head a vigorous rub for good measure.

"Anyway," he continues, swiping my hand away and replacing the hat, "I'm supposed to have given up being Alpha, remember?"

"Give over. You love it when your brother wants you to help him."

Curt snorts. "He won't like me now. I told him I was going to get something I needed and didn't go back."

I clamber off his legs and glare down at him. "You did a runner? Not very mature of you."

He drops back, lying flat on the snow with a grunt. "I couldn't stand any more complaining. The wolves are howling too loud all night. The bears keep scratching the woodwork. Everyone insists everyone else has given them fleas."

"Not the snakes," I point out.

"No. They moan 'I'm too cold and I don't like the food.' The bears want a bee farm and I sat through a whole morning lecture on the medicinal benefits of honey. Then some miserable, flea infested bear complained about Wings' singing waking him up."

I can't help but laugh. "Well, too be fair, it is pretty bad. And first thing in the morning it's traumatising."

"Oh, it's horrendous," he agrees. "Gave me nightmares as a pup. But given what the old bird has done for us all, he can sing what the hell he likes, whenever he likes." He sits back up and grabs me around the waist. "Come here, Big Bum. I'll let you squeeze my biceps."

"Oh, well then…" I drop onto him, grabbing those fabulous arms. A stray hand makes it underneath all the layers and he's manoeuvred my trousers around my knees when raised voices interrupt our X rated fun.

Honestly, I could hear them a mile off. Two teenage lovers, who spend half their time arguing these days, are stomping through the snow.

"All I asked was what colour you wanted?" Her Highness the Alpha Daughter Dulcis yells, in far from royal tones.

Clearly Adamo, The Ginger Prince of Bears, trailing along behind her, has managed to stick his two left feet in it, again.

"I don't care," mumbles Adamo.

"What did you say?"

"It's not my room," he shouts. "You've got to live with it."

Hmm. He could probably do with a few more lessons in diplomacy from our former snake ambassador, Anguis.

"Fine," the wolf princess snarls, tossing wavy black hair over her shoulder. "We'll keep it all pink."

"You hate pink," Adamo growls, not knowing when to shut up.

"My dad did it for me."

"Keep it then," he replies, running out of patience.

"Why are you being such an arse?" Dulcis hollers.

Oh dear. We've resorted to name calling.

"Bear arse?" says Adamo and chuckles at his own joke.

"You're not funny," she screeches.

I thought it was a bit funny.

"Why are we screaming about your horrible room?" screams Adamo.

"I hate you!"

Dulcis storms off, directly towards me and the ruffled wolf. Curt pushes me off him and I shuffle behind the nearest tree, desperately hauling my trousers and knickers over my icy nether region to his silent amusement. He's just yanked me out of view when Adamo catches up with his angry girlfriend.

"You might hate me, but I love you," the honey bear insists.

I can't help but 'aww' behind the tree. Curt points down his throat and mimes gagging.

"Look, I know this isn't about your pink room," Adamo says.

No kidding.

"Much as I want to, we can't officially be mates because I'm a prince and you're the Alpha Daughter, unless decreed by your father, who's not going to accept it this young. Especially me. Since I'm a bear. You have to let him get used to the idea. The mixed pack is still new, let alone us."

"It's been a year," Dulcis argues. "Maybe I should tell him we're already mating."

"I wouldn't," Curt whispers, wide eyed. Me neither.

"Great," Adamo laughs. "Your father can kill me in my sleep and then there'll be a war."

Dulcis delivers the theatrical sigh of the drama queen. I know it well.

"I'm tired of sneaking around," she exclaims, her words echoing down the valley.

"Me too," Adamo agrees, quietly. "But if you shout much louder everyone will know."

That sounded like a muffled thump. The 'ow' tells me she hit him.

"Everyone already knows," she proclaims. Her voice suddenly drops. "Except Daddy. I don't know if he doesn't trust you or me. I'm still his little cub in his eyes."

I peep around the tree, catching the ginger prince wrapping his arms around Dulcis and resting his chin on top of her head.

"Give me a chance to convince him I'm a worthy mate," Adamo pleads.

"I'll die of old age and mange before then," she mutters.

An annoyed Curt huffs in my ear and I grin.

"I'll convince him," Adamo insists. "I promise. I convinced you."

She giggles in response.

And that's when the squelchy making out begins and this old couple cringe. If we move, we give ourselves away, but there's no way we're staying here like pervs. Yuck. I'm gesturing at Curt to get moving, when he starts waving his hands and hollers, "Alpha! There you are!" down my ear, triggering my annoying tinnitus.

The teens hear the bellowed warning and scarper into the trees, disappearing just before her father arrives, luckily for them, since he's sporting a thunderous scowl.

"What do you mean 'There you are'?" the pack's frazzled leader snarls, glaring at his brother. "I was there, at that meeting, where you were supposed to be, the whole time."

"It was almost over," Curt responds, his huge grin not placating the miffed Alpha.

"Over?" Alpha splutters. "Over? You missed Mama Bear demonstrating her ideas for mould treatment. She called it Mould Throttler. Squashed fobly bugs. And the stench. Every window in the mansion's now wide open. The snakes are burning half the forest to keep warm."

Curt guffaws. "Serves you right. Now you know how I felt all the other times."

Alpha's clothes go flying and a mass of brown fur, with a jaw full of teeth, flashes between us. I sit heavily in a wet patch of snow and scramble clear of the homicidal monster as it clamps down on the heel of Curt's right boot and snaps its head back and forth, like a pup with a chew toy – which is exactly what he is.

"Alpha, for pity's sake," I moan, taking three hefty rolls back and forth to lever myself to my feet. "Not his boots, again."

Paws slip clear of the ravaged footwear as His Mangy Grey Wolfness reappears, leaving his over excited brother to fling the boot straight at me. How I manage to duck in this get up, I'll never know. Practice, I guess, being as these two have been regressing back to their puppydom with every passing season. Wings, their old bald eagle nanny, struts around the town tutting, pretending to be ashamed of them, but we all know he's as happy as a gumwhat with a custard cream.

There's a shed load of snarling and snapping going on as the wolf brothers spar in the flying snow, trampling all over their discarded clothes. They end up standing on their heads, feet flailing in the air, tugging on each other's tail.

"Hey, no tail pulling."

Alpha duly drops the appendage, but Curt's worrying away for all he's worth, complete with a snarling chorus. I try yanking Alpha's tail out of Curt's jaws, but he's got a fair grip going on. When "Let go," doesn't work, I resort to shoving a handful of snow up his nostrils. A gigantic sneeze expels the tail and a string of snot right up the arm of my coat.

"Yuck. You're disgusting. You know that?"

Curt lets loose a howl and turns to shovel snow at me with his back legs. Two good scrapes later and the howl turns to a painful yip.

"See. You've hurt your hip," I point out, without much trace of sympathy. "Serves you right."

Delivering a heart rending whine, Curt rolls sideways and thuds heavily into the snow with eyes as wide as a cartoon puppy. I've seen this trick on many occasions and I'm wise to it but, bless him, his soft hearted brother falls for it every time. Alpha shuffles next to his sibling and gently noses his leg. Quick as a flash, Curt flicks his foot like it's on a spring, bouncing his paw off Alpha's nose, before haring off, barking with joy. Alpha lets rip with an ear shattering howl and takes off after his brother.

"Don't stay out too long," I holler after the idiot brothers, collecting up their discarded clothing.

I've barely taken a couple of steps towards the mansion, when a call of nature of another variety afflicts me, since it's cold out here. During my early days in the pack, I discovered that the changers tend to exercise their toiletry needs in animal form, burying their business in the woods. As any constipated menopausal madam will impress upon you, crouching in the undergrowth every time you need to strain a number two isn't a viable prospect.

To be fair the snakes were also pretty shocked, being as they were used to medieval style holes in the castle, but they got used to slithering in the forest.

Me, I moaned about the lack of privacy, the weather and the distance until Curt got sick of me waking him up three times a night (on purpose) and built me a toilet cubicle, well two, one up at the lodge and one down here in the town. Both of them are portable to prevent stink, since I moaned about that too. I seem to have some unholy connection to portaloos in this fantasy.

Every few days, he digs a hole, trundles the lightweight wooden cabin to that new location and sets up my wolf's head toilet seat, before heading back and filling in the old hole. The price of my convenience is that I have to fill his bath and get in it with him any time he wants. I still moan, but boy did I get the better end of that deal.

It might take me a bit of searching to spot my beloved toilet, since the bear and wolf cubs have the nasty habit of trying to hide it, for the fun of watching me race around, knees together. Thankfully, on this occasion, 'The Poopy Hut,' as they like to call it, is still where I left it.

I'm settling down with a gratified sigh, when a mini snake dangles from the ceiling and I scream the place down, before opening the door and lobbing the offender into the snow, to a chorus of amused barks and howls. The flying snake wraps itself around a warm bear cub and they make off before I can give them what for. After roughly slamming the door, I'm giving the cubicle a quick scan, in case they left any other nasty presents, when I hear the faint echo of weeping and an intermittent rumble. Now what? I can't even go in peace.

After finishing my business and washing my hands with snow, I head off in the direction of the distress, wolf clothes and my gloves tucked under my armpit, blowing warm air onto frozen fingers. Nearing the outskirts of the town, I spot a pigtailed little girl, face in her hands, slumped on a log, skinny legs kicking against the wood. Beside her, perches a brown bear, his huge paw gently patting her shoulder. A weird image, you might think, but I'm not surprised. Despite his massive girth and scarred face, everyone has cried on the warrior bear's shoulder at some point during the past year.

"What's happening, General?" I ask.

"Grrr," Ursid growls, in response, shrugging furry shoulders. He rises up on his back legs and waves a paw over the girl's head.

"Shall I take over?"

He nods and flings his paws wide open. I love a good bear hug. Only our resident Matron of the Sick, Mama Bear, gives better squeeze.

"Grrr." The walking carpet releases me and points his nose in the direction of the forest.

"Going to check the boundary?" I guess.

"Grrr." He pats the girl's head, then takes off at a bouncing pace, keeping us safe from whatever's out there.

As I settle beside her in the still warm vacated space, a tear stained face emerges from mittened hands and peers at me with sapphire eyes, just like her Uncle Serpen.

"Now then, Sospa," I begin, "tell Auntie Edi what the matter is."

The seven year old, ice blond heir to the former snake king throws herself against my padded chest, wailing, "Auntie Edi, you have to help me."

That sounds ominous.

"With what?"

"I done something really bad."

"You'd better tell me then."

"I've killed Uncle Wings."

CHAPTER 3

The Eagle Is Frozen

"You what?"

She flings her arms around my legs and buries her head in my stomach, from whence she howls a muffled, "He's dead."

"How did you manage that?"

Alright, I know how that sounds, but I doubt she's actually gone and killed him. That poison parrot is indestructible and probably immortal.

Her head pops out as she cries, "I looked at him."

I smother a belly laugh. "You looked at..?" Oh. I get it. The penny drops. "Sospa, were you trying to mesmerise him? You know what your Uncle Serpen said about that."

"Uncle Serpen will hate me now," she cries. "Please don't tell him."

Hmm. I don't know about that.

"How do you expect me to deal with him? I've no idea…" I trail off in the wake of a horrendous, eardrum quivering wail. "Alright. Fine. Show me. Where's Wings?"

"The mansion." She gulps. "I hid him behind a curtain in the study round the back."

"How did you manage that?" I know I'm repeating myself, but she's a tiny thing, not yet come into her full serpent heritage, which is the problem, partly.

"He's on wheels."

Uh huh. "Of course he is." Did I say that out loud? What the heck? This place is nuts. "Wipe your face and we'll go look."

The mansion used to sit in the middle of a picturesque little village, which is now a ruddy great town stretching all the way up to Curt's lodge and heaving with an array of wolves, bears, snakes and one dead eagle, apparently. It's pretty much impossible to sneak anywhere, so Sospa gives her nose a wipe on her sleeve, lifts her head and we march through the packed dwellings, doing our damnedest not to look shifty. We're approaching the back door, congratulating ourselves on our success, when the voice rings out…

"What are you two up to?"

The tallest woman I've ever met looms over us, tapping a finger against crossed arms. Adamo did tell me her real name but, to be honest, I can't remember it and she loves being called Mama Bear.

"Heading inside / Going for a walk," me and scrawny say at exactly the same time.

Nothing suspicious to see here. No sirree.

A sharp pain in my ankle comes courtesy of Mama's homicidal cub who's currently sinking his teeth into my flesh. He's pranked me ever since he dropped out of a tree onto my head.

"Get off you little horror," I yell, waving my foot in the air.

"Drop," commands Mama and her sprog complies with a snuffle. Her face might not crack a smile, but she can't douse the twinkle in those eyes.

After scowling at the bundle of fur, I turn back to his mother with a cheery grin. "Must be going, Mama. I'm sure you've got patients to see."

"I have," she agrees, her eyes narrowing. "But I'm watching you two."

"You sound like Wings," I say, mentally kicking myself in the flabby bum for bringing him up.

"Yes," says Mama, eyes fixed on mine. "Where is he, by the way? Wasn't Sospa supposed to be at her lessons?"

"That's where we're heading," I lie, without missing a beat, ignoring my conscience. "See you later. Must rush. Sospa's late."

I can still feel Mama's suspicious gaze burning into the back of my head as we march through the back door and get slapped in the face by the lingering remains of a stench from hell. We leg it down the corridor as soon as we're out of watering eyeshot.

"Ewww. It still stinks," the midget announces, holding her nose.

"You know I shouldn't have said that to Mama," I tell Sospa, being as I'm a responsible adult. Mostly. "It's not right to lie."

"I know," she states, "but it's better than being yelled at."

Quite.

Before I can dredge up a lecture in morality, she yanks on my hand, whispering, "In here."

We tiptoe over the threshold of the tiny study and quietly close the door behind us. It's so tight you can barely fit the two of us in here, even though it's only decked out with a heavy wooden desk and a couple of chairs. It's also freezing, being as the windows are wide open to the elements.

"Where did you say you put him?" I ask, squeezing my woolly padded bulk around the desk and jamming my posterior between a drawer and the wall.

She points at the window and, sure enough, a strange shape lurks behind winter's hefty woollen drapes. I finally pop free of the desk like a cork from a bottle and gently hike the curtain to one side, resulting in a hefty leap backwards and Curt's boots hitting the floor with a thud, his and Alpha's clothes fluttering down around them.

Yeeesh. It's enough to give me nightmares for the rest of my life. That and Curt's dodgy digestive system.

Right in front of me teeters Wings, balancing on one leg like a stork, body bone rigid, hands hooked into claws, eyes crossed and a homicidal scowl frozen to his face. Gargoyle isn't the word. He reminds me of one of those hideous snake statues at that cursed castle.

Oh and he really is on wheels. I kid you not. The little monster must have shuffled him onto the roller skates Curt made for her at my behest.

That's it. I can't hold it any longer and a huge guffaw pours forth.

"Ssshhh, Auntie Edi," pleads Sospa, pounding on my arm. "They'll hear you."

"Sorry," I splutter, trying to swallow a belly laugh and choking instead.

I'm retrieving Curt's apparel from the floor when the door opens and Dulcis barrels into the room, tripping straight over me. That stops me laughing.

"Glad you did that, for once," says Adamo, lurking in her shadow.

"Were you following me?" I ask, peering at her.

"Saw you both creeping about. Then heard you laughing. What's so funny?" Dulcis asks, parking her backside on the floor and staring at me. I point and she follows my digit up to Wings' face. "Grojat's armpit! What happened to him?"

"Mini snake," I answer, pointing over my shoulder with a thumb.

Sospa cries, "I didn't mean to," punctuating with a hiccup and a gigantic snotty sniff.

"You are so for it from Serpen," Adamo chants, like a five year old.

Her quivering lip immediately gives way to a thunderous scowl, reminding me of her uncle, right before he turned serpent.

"Shut the door," I tell Adamo. "And hush up."

He nearly flattens Dulcis as he squeezes it shut behind him. There are way too many people cushioned in winter layers in this room. Dulcis pops up and parks herself on the edge of the desk, pulling the girl into her arms. "It'll be fine. Edi will fix it. Won't you Edi?"

Great. Why's it always me?

"Won't you, Edi?" Dulcis repeats in a voice full of gravel.

Conscious that three pairs of eyes are staring me down, I dump Curt and Alpha's now filthy clothes on Dulcis' lap and turn back to the iced eagle, whose gaze currently takes in both sides of the room at once. Well, he might be locked in place, but he's still breathing.

"You haven't killed him," I tell our mini assassin. "He's still in there."

"Should I hit him?" Adamo offers.

What an idiot.

"Only if you want to be kicked into next spring when he comes round."

"Right," mutters Adamo, leaning against the door and crossing his arms. "What now?"

How do I know, twit?

"Erm, I'm going to try a mild shake," I say, knowing full well it won't work. And it doesn't. If anything, he looks even more cross-eyed. "What did your uncle say about breaking this mind thing?" I can't believe I haven't asked Sospa this before.

"That's the next lesson," she wails.

Of course it is. Right. Well.

"Adamo, go and get Anguis," I tell him. "Quietly. And try not to fall up the stairs."

He throws me a scowl as he squeezes back out the door and closes it. Two seconds later a muffled thud is followed by, "Ow."

"Are you alright?" asks someone, words coming in counterpoint with approaching footsteps.

Bugger. I know that voice.

"I'm fine, YOUR MAJESTY," Adamo positively bellows, another one never accused of subtlety.

"It's just Serpen now, Adamo," the former king replies.

"Right, have to go. Bye," Adamo yells, followed by a thumping stampede that sounds like he's doing the Charleston out there.

"Strange boy," Serpen mutters to himself.

Meanwhile, inside our tiny room, there's a flying mad scramble to hide. I fling myself under the desk, hauling Sospa down beside me. Wait a minute, I've forgotten something...

I pop up, whispering, "Wings," and madly gesticulating.

Dulcis yanks the curtain across him and lays herself over the desk, splaying out her coat like she's at a glamour fashion shoot, just as the door opens.

I wedge myself back under the desk, ending up with my left knee sticking in my right ear.

"Sospa?" calls her uncle as he pokes his blond head into the room and gets an eyeful of the lunatic teen.

"Dulcis," he says.

"Serpen," she replies, wafting her coat.

Silence.

For goodness' sake, could she be more suspicious? And I've just spotted Wings' one foot on wheels, poking out from under the curtain.

"What are you doing?" Serpen asks, understandably.

"Hiding," Dulcis replies.

"From...?"

"Adamo."

"Didn't he just leave this room?"

"Did I say Adamo? I meant Wings."

Sospa rolls her eyes at me, but my attention's taken by screaming sciatica.

"Actually, I'm looking for Sospa," Serpen continues. "She should be with Wings."

"He's not with us at the moment," says Dulcis.

How true.

"Whose clothes are those?" Serpen asks.

"Uncle Curt's, I think."

Silence.

"Are you sure you're alright?" Serpen asks, probably because she's exhibiting all the vibes of the overly medicated.

"Fine," she replies in a squeaky voice, then coughs it out. "Fine. Just resting in peace and quiet for a bit."

"I can understand that," he replies, sadly. "Well, stay hidden. If I spot him, I'll point him another way."

"Who?"

"Wings."

"Right."

Good grief. Any moment now Wings will topple through the curtain to a drum roll.

Finally, the door opens and closes. Footsteps move away as my head pops out from under the desk to stare at the jibbering idiot.

"What?" Dulcis exclaims, peering back at me. "I thought that went well."

"I'm so dead," Sospa mutters.

Muffled footsteps have no sooner faded away than a chaotic clatter ends with a reverberating thud. Dulcis and I exchange a glance, neither of us entertaining the slightest doubt as to who that was.

"Did you hurt yourself?"

I also recognise the asker of that muffled question: Anguis.

Dulcis heaves open the door and hisses, "Get in here, both of you," through the gap.

A shamefaced Adamo enters, brushing himself down.

"Are you alright?" I ask him. It takes him a moment to spot my disembodied head behind the desk.

"Fine, thank you," he replies. A brief neck stretch delivers a solid crunch.

"I don't think there's room for me in there," Anguis points out, hovering on the threshold.

Adamo grabs the front of his neatly ironed shirt and yanks him inside, squeezing the door shut and removing a couple of layers of skin. I crawl out from under the desk.

"What are you doing down there?" Anguis asks, brushing his shirt back into its immaculate position.

"I was… never mind." Way too long a story.

Sospa reappears, her eyes avoiding her former ambassador.

"Hmm, your uncle's looking for you," says Anguis, before switching his gaze to my face. "I might have known you'd be making trouble."

I take umbrage at that.

"For your information, retired reptile ambassador, I haven't done anything, thank you. This is all snake business." And with that I whip away the curtain, proclaiming, "Tada."

"Well… that's… disturbing," Anguis remarks, barely raising an eyebrow.

"And…?" I prompt.

He takes a determined step towards me. "Wings appears frozen."

"I know that, genius. And get off my foot."

He steps back, straight into Adamo, who gently pushes him forward again.

"Don't you start on me," Anguis says, with mock pomposity, flinging his ice blond hair over his shoulder. "I shall take myself elsewhere."

Right on cue, Sospa whimpers and tears gush from her eyes. If I was the suspicious type, I'd say we're being played.

"Alright, I'm joking," says Anguis, giving her a swift hug, before peering closely into Wings' eyes. "Well done, Sospa; he's totally mesmerised," is the verdict. "If you can't get him back, then it's down to Serpen, I'm afraid."

"No," the midget wails. "He'll make me take singing lessons."

"That's not so bad," I say.

"With Wings."

Oh. Right. Nightmare territory.

"There's nothing for it, Sospa," I decide. "We can't leave him like that. Adamo, please fetch Serpen back."

"Why me?" he asks, still rubbing his neck.

The look Dulcis gives him is as scary as frozen Wings.

"I'm going," he mumbles, squeezing past Anguis.

He levers open the door, comes face to face with Mama Bear glaring at him and screams.

"I knew you were up to something," she says, peering past the quivering prince straight at me. Apparently, nothing gets past her.

"What are you glaring at me for?" I grumble. "And you can't come in."

Mama Bear's eyes narrow to slits. "Are you going to stop me?"

"Lack of space is going to stop you," I point out. "There's no room for any more in here."

"Breathe in Your Highness," she orders and thrusts open the door, mashing Adamo into the wall.

And... standing in her vacated place in the corridor is the chief snake himself. Absolutely nothing gets past Mama Bear.

For fear of being suffocated, I scramble on top of the desk, swiftly followed by the somewhat less weighty Dulcis.

"Look what they've done to poor Wings," the matron bellows, straight down Anguis' ear. "Get out of the way."

Adamo's had enough squashing and joins us on the desk, stamping all over Curt's clothes, leaving a razor thin path for Serpen to squeeze down. The snake king gives us all a longsuffering look that makes me feel like I'm standing on an elevated naughty step.

"Sospa, we will be talking about this later," he tells her.

"Yes, Uncle," she replies, giving him the sad eye and blinking lashes treatment.

He stands on tiptoe, staring directly into Wings' eyes, and relaxes.

Nothing. Not a sausage. Not the tiniest squeak.

The bird is still frozen solid.

"Erm..." says Adamo.

Wings rockets back to life, screaming like a banshee.

Everyone jumps in shock, including the trio on the desk, which creaks, groans and shatters in a shower of splintered wood, dumping us in a pile. The old bird's arms and legs pummel in all directions cracking Serpen in the eye, Anguis up his nose and bouncing off Mama Bear's ample chest. The one standing leg does a wheelie, flying into the air and upending him, which finally brings the onslaught to an end, leaving a room full of the groaning.

The only escapee from pain and suffering is the monstrous perpetrator herself, standing there large as life and twice as shifty. When Wings sits up, Sospa flings herself at him, wailing, "I thought you were dead."

He cuddles her and glares at me as though this is all my fault.

That's it. I've had enough.

I squeeze out the open window, plopping through the gap and landing in a pile of snow below. Standing up brings me nose to nose with a strange woman and we both scream.

"Who are you?" she hollers.

"Who are *you*?" I shout back.

"I am Decipa Longfang, the official messenger wolf of the celebrated southern pack, trusted voice of the Alpha of Alphas."

"Oh. Hi. I'm Edi."

CHAPTER 4

Purgatory's Herald

"What's an Edi?" the stranger demands, her tone giving the impression she would scrape it off her boot.

"It's my name," I reply, clenching my fists. "Edith Breaker-Smith. Adviser to the Alpha, the King, the Prince, the Ambassador and Servicer to the Curt."

General Ursid, who happens to be standing right next to her, rumbles with bear laughter.

"Get away from me, you filthy bear," she snarls, taking a massive side step in her heavy duty snow boots.

Tolerance is clearly her middle name. Not.

Ursid circles the messenger, his prowling keeping her from wandering. She's dressed for lengthy travel in layers of wool peeping out from underneath a hooded leather coat, cut to allow swift movement, and sports a multipocketed backpack.

"Did you find her on your boundary check?" I ask the general and get a rumbling growl in the assertive.

"This scum has no right to threaten me," she says, baring her teeth at him. Any moment now she'll turn wolf and they'll be blood on the snow.

"Watch your mouth," I snap. "General Ursid is a fine bear and an even finer man."

Ursid rumbles gently. Miss Diversity isn't having any of it.

"I demand to speak to your Alpha."

"He's not here, right now," I tell her, hands firmly locked to my hips.

"Are you a bear too?" she asks, her eyes narrowing and nose upturning to an ugly sneer.

"No," I state, a little too vigorously. "Not that I wouldn't love to be," I qualify, glancing at Ursid, "but I'm human."

"And...?"

"And what?"

"Human and which animal?"

"Just human."

"Oh," she replies, injecting every ounce of condescension she can muster into one syllable. "What are you doing here then?"

I've been around this maypole before and I didn't care for it the first time.

"I live here."

Before she can sneer at me again, I turn back to the open window to find a motley array of faces peering at me, clearly earwigging the entire exchange. A sudden flurry of movement sees them climbing over each other to get to the door. Strangely, Anguis decides to follow me out the window, which is a surprise, given that the former ambassador is usually so fastidiously graceful. Mind you, he lands like a ballet dancer, rather than my sack of spuds.

I turn back to Ursid. "General, would you fetch Alpha, please?" He rumbles and peers at the messenger. "I'll be fine."

He growls and thunders off in search of the wolf brothers, leaving Decifor Smartfang, or whatever her name is, staring at her surroundings with unabashed horror. Apparently, the sight of bear cubs bouncing in the snow is an anathema to her wolfy sensibilities.

Then she spots Anguis' blond locks and murmurs, "Snake." Wide eyes drop to his polished shoes in a deep bow.

"This is Anguis," I tell her, "former Ambassador to the Snake Empire." Her gaze rises to meet his and I swear it carries a challenge. "Anguis, this is Dec..."

"Decipa Longfang, the official messenger wolf of the celebrated southern pack, trusted voice of the Alpha of Alphas," she repeats, cutting me off in mid flow. "I've met the Ambassador before, when I was young."

I can see the cogs turning in Anguis' mind as he weighs what to say, but he never gets to deliver it, since Serpen jogs around the corner of the mansion to join us.

"And this is King Serpen," I trumpet.

He arrives out of breath, just as the messenger prostrates herself at his feet, singing, "Your Majesty honours my humble adoration," in full soprano vibrato, if somewhat muffled with her face in the snow.

"The greeting used to be sung," whispers Anguis, seeing my shock. "His Majesty put a stop to it."

"A greeting delivered from flat on your face?" I reply, manifestly not whispering. Serpen throws me a glacial glare. Haven't seen one of those for a while.

"Please rise," Serpen tells the messenger, holding out his hand as she leaps to her feet. She briefly shakes and drops his hand as though it's a hot coal. "That time is over," he continues. "The Empire is at an end and has no need of a king. We live as one pack now." Her expression proclaims her disgust at that news, but she speedily wipes it off, along with a little pile of snow on her nose, when he asks, "Who might you be?"

Here we go again.

"Decipa Longfang, the official messenger wolf of the celebrated southern pack, trusted voice of the Alpha of Alphas. I come with a message for the ears of this pack's Alpha alone."

That's new, and fairly ballsy, given that she was on her face a moment ago. I wonder if she's ever seen a snake in serpent form.

"And I am the Alpha Daughter," announces Dulcis, wading through the snow, Adamo slipping and sliding beside her. "You can give the message to me."

"That would make you Dulcis," Decipa states.

"It would," the teen replies. "I didn't see you last time your Alpha came here with his stink, er revered son. His messenger was – what was his name? – He had a really singsong voice," she chirps, demonstrating.

"Rupert."

"That's it. How is Rupert?"

"Dead. He fell over his backpack."

"Oh dear. I am sorry."

Lord help me, hysteria's going to break out any moment.

"I bring you greetings from my Alpha, his honoured mate, Audira, and sons, Alpha Alpha and Fidus," Decipa announces.

"That's nice," Dulcis replies with a face like a stewed prune. When nothing else is forthcoming from the tight lipped herald, she asks, "Is that the message? You came a long way for that."

"I come with a message for the ears of this pack's Alpha alone," Decipa repeats, like a stuck record.

Whoops, showing my age there.

Earth juddering thuds thankfully announce the return of General Ursid, hurrying along two sodden, bedraggled, mud coated wolves, reminding me of my office rave on a Friday night. They proceed to shake themselves down, splattering everyone. I doubt the 'Alpha of Alphas' would find them terribly impressive from the look on his messenger's face as she wipes mud splash off her cheek.

I get in there before she can reel off her spiel again. "Alpha, Curt, this is Delifa Lingfan." It's a cheap shot, but hey. "The official post wolf of the pack down south."

The scruffy wolf brothers exchange a look that reads 'uh oh.' Curt starts scratching like crazy with his back leg, which he always does when he gets nervous. One of my 'looks' stops him, but I've already seen the trace of panic in his eyes. If he's that agitated, I'm keeping a close eye on this messenger.

"I'm Prince Adamo, by the way," pipes up ginger bonce. "Since nobody bothered to introduce me." Silence. "I'm a bear."

"Really," says Decipa, simultaneously sounding disgusted and entirely uninterested.

"Father, Uncle, perhaps you should change," ventures Dulcis. No kidding. "Decipa, please join us inside where it's warmer." And off our princess stalks, the rest of us trailing in her wake.

I hang back to walk beside Curt. "Is there something up?" I ask my wolf, receiving a baleful glance and a short whine in the affirmative. "I'll stay with Dulcis, but hurry." Curt yips at his brother and they take off at a run, Ursid on their heels.

The mansion's great hall feels warm as I enter, despite the windows being wide open. It's usually far too hot for this menopausal madam and too cool for the snakes, so we compromise with a temperature neither cares for. I peel back my multiple layers of padding and by the time I've lost half my sweaty width in woollens, Decipa has already stripped off the hooded travel kit. She sits bolt upright in my favourite rocking chair, warming her frozen character by the fire and sniffing imperiously. Dulcis gives me a stare, silently pleading for me not to kick up a fuss. I suppose I could be magnanimous. For now. But don't push me.

The messenger turns out to be much younger than I was expecting, early twenties at the most, even given her hard eyes. She's also staggeringly beautiful, encased in leather and wool layers that seem to hug her curvy figure without restricting movement. Dulcis' eyes light up at her more modern apparel, brain already calculating how to emulate the look. That is, until she spots Adamo staring at the newcomer with his eyes on stalks. If young Decipa didn't have an enemy before, she does now.

The silence is deafening, broken only by the annoying squeak of the rocking chair on its backward swing. I don't know if Decipa's trying to be irritating or is merely oblivious to our discomfort.

Anguis gently tugs on the cuffs of his jacket. "Perhaps it would be best if we left the wolves…"

Dulcis cuts him off with, "You're staying," delivered in the polite purr of a homicidal kitten.

"Very well," he agrees, parking himself next to Serpen.

This leaves only Adamo standing, rising up and down on the balls of his feet. I reach out a hand and yank hard on his arm until he's forced to bend his knees. "Sit down," I whisper.

A door opens and footsteps clatter across the hall, belonging to none other than the Berserker Bird himself, apparently recovered from his mesmerising ordeal and minus the rollerskate.

"Ah, Wings, this is Deliba Shortfin," say I, "messenger of Pack South." Turning back to the annoyed messenger, I add, "Wings is an eagle."

When she scowls, he asks, "What happened to Rupert?"

"Deceased," I stage whisper. "Don't ask."

"That's a pity," Wings responds. "I liked his juggling."

He's so deadpan, I can't tell whether he's serious, so it's best not to laugh.

Finally, the wolf brothers deign to make an appearance, heading down the stairs tying back soaking wet hair. At least they're changed, clean and clothed. Ursid trails behind them with all the gravitas of a sledgehammer.

"What did you do with my jumper?" Curt whispers as he reaches my side.

"Long story," I reply.

"Greetings Delifa," says Alpha, pausing before her.

"Decipa Longfang," she replies, glaring straight at me.

"Sorry, my bad," I say, lifting up a palm.

Alpha holds out his hand. "I'm Alpha and this is my brother, Curt."

She rises, leaving his hand hanging for an awkward moment before clasping it. "I come with a private message from the Alpha of Alphas."

"Since when has he been Alpha of Alphas?" slings a miffed Curt.

"Since he united all of the southern packs, Curtus," replies Miss Leather Knickers, insisting on using Curt's hated full name.

Curt says nothing, but I know that look and it's not good. Alpha pauses just a smidgen too long before he replies.

"Well, that's impressive, but I keep no secrets from my brother or my pack. Please deliver the message here."

"With bears, snakes and the human present?" Decipa qualifies.

"Don't forget the eagle," I add.

"They're all my pack," states Alpha.

Her look of horror speaks volumes, but she swiftly wipes it away as she announces, "The Alpha of Alphas formally requests a meeting with this pack's Alpha in situ."

"Agreed," Alpha replies.

Decipa nods and grabs her coat.

Is that it? The whole message? I own to a thundering anticlimax after all that build up. What was the big secret? And why bother to take her coat off?

"Are you not staying for rest and refreshment?" asks Dulcis, watching the messenger layering up once more.

"No, thank you," she replies. "I'll relay your agreement."

And with that, she's flouncing out the door and off before you can say Bob's your uncle, leaving us all a bit stunned.

"That's odd," Curt observes.

I'll say.

"Which part in particular?" I ask.

"I get she didn't like us much," Dulcis replies, "but it's usual to accept hospitality from the host. Not dash off like her tail's on fire."

"And her pack is a long way to go without rest," Curt adds.

"Maybe they're on the way here already," I suggest, giving myself the jeebies for some reason.

Alpha shakes his head. "No, that's not how this works. The messenger visits a full season before the Alpha's arrival. It'll be spring before we see him."

"Are you sure?"

"That's how it's always been," he insists.

"Until it's not," I mutter to myself.

"I hope he's not bringing that horrible son of his," Dulcis moans. "I thought we were rid of him last time."

Something's not right here. My spidey sense is twanging big time.

"All the same," I suggest, "I'd maybe post a lookout. Follow old Decipants for a while."

Everyone stares at Alpha, who sighs and glances at his brother.

"Can't hurt," Curt offers. "If we're discreet."

The general heads for the door, his heels clacking in the silence.

"Ursid," says Alpha, making him pause in mid step, "send a wolf. Just in case."

CHAPTER 5

Ridiculous Surnames And Quivering Nerves

It's still only afternoon, but Curt and I legged it up to our borrowed room in the mansion to make out like a pair of threadbare rabbits. We waited a long time to find each other, so we're at it every chance we get. Probably not something you need to know, but I'm having fun and it's about time.

"They all know we're up here," I point out, when I finally get my breath back.

"So what?" Curt throws me a lascivious grin, nibbles my neck and rolls onto his back with a grunt. He then looses a deep sigh and scratches behind his ear with a vengeance. That's usually a signal he wants me to ask about his state of mind.

"What's up?" I'm nothing if not dutiful.

"Nothing," he mumbles. Another sigh.

"You're scratching."

"I don't have mange, or fleas."

"Of course you don't."

To be honest, he's been doing much better since Mama Bear sneaked one of her 'special' creams to him. He thinks I don't know. She gave me a cream too. It's my business what for.

"Curt, something's bothering you," I insist. "I knew that when you didn't rush me back to our lodge, instead of staying here."

"You know me too well," he replies, blowing out a third sigh.

"Enough with the sighing and the scratching." I carefully straddle his hips and peer down into his face. "Talk. Now."

"I'm reluctant to leave my brother," he says.

"If you're bothered about Decipa's lot, it'll be next spring before they're here, according to Alpha. We're not staying in this room 'til then."

"It's just..." His eyes wander from mine. He really is worried.

"Out with it." I lean right over and kiss his forehead. That nasty crack was my spine, adjusting.

"I've... I've been too happy and..."

"You're worried it'll all go away?"

He nods as his gaze returns to mine.

"You know I'm not going anywhere, right? I burnt that book."

He wraps both arms around me, pulls me down on top of him, head to toe, and whispers in my ear. "I can't shake the feeling something's going to upset us all."

Pulling one of his straggling grey hairs out of his eyes, I ask, "You like the mixed pack?"

"I do. Who'd have thought it?" He snorts and follows it with another sigh.

"Look, I get it," I tell him, kissing his tufty eyebrows. "We were both miserable, remember? Now we're just creamed. In every sense of the word."

He guffaws, but soon sobers. "Edi, if their Alpha has managed to unite the entire south, it could spell big trouble."

"Could your brother have said no to a meeting?"

"No Alpha has ever denied a formal meeting called by another pack Alpha," he replies.

That's a no then.

"Do you know why they're coming here?"

Curt shivers and wraps us both in a blanket as though hiding us from evil.

"Probably because we've joined with the bears, their enemies, *and* the snakes. If they've heard of the collapse of the Snake Empire, they may think the way's open for expansion, or revenge on the bears."

I tuck my head beneath his chin. "The bears and snakes must be nervous then."

"If they've got any sense and they have. Especially that damned poncy snake."

His grip on my back tightens in reflex.

"Stop with the name calling. I'm not with Anguis. As you well know."

"He wants you though."

I admit his mild jealousy makes me smile, which is naughty. "He's never made a single move on me," I point out, giving his ribs a tickle.

He snorts, huffs and wriggles.

"There's more, isn't there?" I prod.

"If rumour of Dulcis and Adamo's relationship has reached them, that may be even worse than a mixed pack in their eyes."

I sit up and turn towards him. "Dulcis is not being forced to mate with Stinky."

"Who?"

"The son. He smells, apparently."

Curt makes a face at me. "How do you know all these things? Anyway, no, she won't be forced into anything. My mother's not here anymore. Thankfully. But…"

Uh oh. "But?"

He sits up and pops the blanket around my shoulders.

"The Southern Alpha. His mother is Yelena. My aunt. My mother's younger sister."

"Frozen Hell's sister?"

He laughs. "You do hear everything."

"Sorry," I tell him, "inappropriate. What's Yelena like?"

"They call her Yellfire."

It's my turn to splutter laugh. "Oh, wow. Yikes."

"She came from harsh times, Edi. Being obeyed swiftly saved lives."

"Do you think she's coming here?"

"I don't know," he replies, back to nibbling at my neck. "Hope not. She'll not be happy to spot me, the defective, that's for sure. She's hated me since Kallosa had to mate with my brother."

"Kallosa?"

"Dulcis' mother."

It strikes me that I never asked her name.

"And their Alpha's sister," Curt continues.

I'm confused, so I'm pretty sure you must be.

"So, your mum Helena and Yelena were sisters. Yelena's children are the Southern Alpha of Alphas and Kallosa, which makes her your cousin... and our Alpha's."

"Yes."

"That's cosy," I say, with a grin. "In a mate your cousin sort of way."

"Don't start."

Which reminds me...

"By the way, do you have a surname?" I ask.

"A what?"

"A second name. She called herself Decipa Longfang."

He looks mighty nervous and starts scratching his hip.

"You do, don't you? It can't be as bad as Breaker-Smith. Come on, tell me."

Curt hauls himself to his feet and my lovely warm blanket goes with him.

"Bear in mind," he begins, wandering over to the window, "I was meant to be Alpha, not Curtus and certainly not Curt."

"Uh huh. This is going to be good," I venture, yanking back the blanket, leaving him shivering on display.

"I'm not telling you," he announces with a dramatic sniff.

"Oh, please," I beg. "Or I'll tickle you to death. And you know I'll do it."

Big, big sigh from His Wolfness.

Wait for it.

Another sigh.

"Furtletooth."

Stunned silence, whilst I take it in.

"Curt Furtletooth," I finally say, right before guffawing like a bear.

If looks could kill, I'd be wolf kebab.

I'm saved from the consequences of my mirth by a thundering crash from below stairs, sounding like the door just came off its hinges, followed by a scream and a muffled thud. Either Adamo fell over the threshold, again, or something's going on down there.

Curt and I exchange a swift glance before heaving on our clothes at top speed. I hold his trousers for him, since it's quicker and he's less likely to fall over. Whilst this song and dance act takes place, the downstairs racket escalates into random running, door slamming and over-heated shouting, though I can't make out anything coherent yet.

Now dressed, to a fashion, we peer over the banister at a crowd surrounding a changing wolf, whose naked human arrives panicked and out of breath. I'm legging it down the stairs when he finally gets the words out in a screech.

"Hundreds of wolves... coming up the valley!"

CHAPTER 6

I Hate to Say I Told You So, But…

Just as well I pushed for a lookout, if I do say so myself, mainly because nobody else is. Although, standing here, gazing at what's coming, I'm not sure knowing in advance makes it any better.

Once Alpha had finished staring at the frazzled wolf, sporting a look of total disbelief, he raced off to see the impending doom for himself, followed by the rest of us, constituting the entire mixed pack and an over-excited set of pups and kids. He did try to insist on going on his own, but good luck with that.

So, a ton of concerned townies now teeter on a slippery slope overlooking the bend in the valley, hustling and shoving to get a decent view over the shoulders of the front row. Nobody, except Curt, dares get too close to their stunned, silent Alpha. Pursed lips remain welded shut, whilst Curt glances back and forth between his brother's thunderous frown and the unfolding scene below.

Roger and his sheep friends shuffled around that bend not so long ago, heading in that very direction. I can only pray they didn't run into the colossal mob of fur and fang tramping along the valley towards us. Hundreds of wolves, in an array of colours and sizes, snarl, snap and howl as they turn the corner, some harnessed to carts, filled to the brim with wooden chests. The lupine flow keeps on pouring. The atmosphere surrounding me grows thick with anticipation and not a little dread.

"That's some pack," I comment, since someone has to say something.

"That's not a single pack," Wings whispers, sidling up beside me. "That's all the southern packs together."

"Seems the messenger was telling the truth," Curt mutters. "They have merged."

"What's to stop them wanting to merge with you?" Adamo asks Alpha.

Ursid shakes his head at his former charge. Now's not the time for this discussion. Too many quivering ears about, including mine.

"I have no intention of merging with anyone," Alpha snaps. "There's been well enough of that lately."

Ouch. I'm not the only one shuffling in the snow after that jibe.

"And if they insist?"

Adamo has a point. Weight of numbers could make any dissent moot.

"Wolves don't fight wolves," Alpha replies, steel running through his tone as though he's trying to convince himself.

"There's always a first time," I mutter.

Curt throws me a sharp glance, clearly reading, 'Not now, Edi.'

I catch a glimpse of the wide-eyed, tight faces around me and shut my big mouth. I feel a set of warm fingers intertwining with mine: Dulcis grasping my hand. I give it a squeeze to reassure her. No stinky son of an Alpha gets to have my girl. He'll have to get past me first.

A large wooden carriage rumbles into view, wheels juddering through the snow, and I catch a glimpse of a face peering through a window before it rounds the corner. It's difficult to tell from this distance, but it seems more ornate than the rest of this travelling circus. If I had to hazard a guess, I'd say that's where the Southern Alpha and his family are lurking.

"What's that carriage about?" Curt grumbles, voicing my thought exactly. "Four paws not good enough anymore? Is he too good to pad at the head of his tribe like a true Alpha?"

Our Alpha stares at his brother, but says nothing.

"What's our plan?" asks Serpen, gliding through the crowd, Anguis following silently on his heels.

Alpha glances at Curt. The look on both faces telegraphs the fact that they don't have one, yet. Bummer.

"Alpha?" rumbles Ursid, nodding in the direction of the massed wolves. "We need to talk. Fast."

"You need to let me think," Alpha snarls back.

"That's all very well," says Adamo, nervously jigging up and down on the balls of his feet. "They might not fight you, assimilate you or even have a problem with your wolves. Who knows, maybe they've come for a great big party, but now they know the rest of us are here."

"My father is our Alpha," Dulcis interrupts, poking Adamo in the chest. "If he says he's thinking, let him think."

"And how much thinking time does he need?" Adamo replies, swatting her hand away. "Since they'll be on our doorstep in time for dinner. That is, if they don't rip us all to shreds first."

Ursid rumbles, but Adamo's on a roll here and an old mentor's growl isn't stopping him any time soon.

"You might trust us, to some extent, but to them we're the enemy. There's hundreds of them. What if they decide the war with bears is still on, as far as they're concerned? And then there's him." Adamo points at the former King Serpen. "He ruled an empire that enslaved everyone. Why would they trust him?"

"Thank you," Serpen says, ramrod straight.

Sospa, being a tad more volatile, kicks the ginger prince in the shins.

"Ow. I'm only telling it from their point of view," Adamo says, finally grinding to a halt. "I like you snakes, but these wolves don't know any of us."

"Unfortunately, they do know me," adds Anguis.

"Let me guess," says Curt, "the Ambassador fed them as many lies as you fed us."

"Yes," Anguis agrees, deciding not to elaborate or apologise.

"What do you suggest we all do?" I ask, yanking my fingers free of Dulcis' paralysing grip. "Go play hide and seek behind the trees?"

Curt flaps out a snort, then morphs it into a sigh.

"I say we get together a 'welcoming committee' to head them off before they get here," Adamo suggests, crossing his arms and delivering a stiff nod to emphasise how serious he is.

Every time he does that I expect him to start rapping.

"No." Alpha delivers his emphatic verdict without turning to look at the bear.

Silence.

"Is that it?" Adamo probes, his voice dialling up through the range of tones. "No. Just, no. Are you still *thinking* or have you gone blank?"

"Hey…" a scowling Curt begins.

Alpha spins on his heel, so fast, I take an involuntary step back.

"You're my pack," he hollers, his words flying over our heads to those at the back of the huddle. "You are all my pack now. I am your Alpha. That's what we decided when you came here. Adamo and Serpen made me responsible."

He marches forward and the crowd duly parts like the Red Sea before Moses. Curt gives me a pointed stare before hurrying after him.

"I will keep you safe," Alpha's word travels back. "All of you."

That little speech is heartwarming, I'm sure. But Adamo pretty much speaks for us all when he says…

"Really? How?"

CHAPTER 7

We're Going To Need A Bigger Town

Striding like he's on military parade, Alpha disappears inside the mansion. His limping brother isn't so lucky and gets waylaid before he can escape over the threshold by a scowling general, an uptight retired king of snakes and a singularly unimpressed prince of bears, not to mention the huge crowd relocating from the slope.

"What are…? Where will we… What if they…" The questions bounce off my mangy wolf like rubber balls.

Ambassador skills abandoned, Anguis hovers beside me, having given up trying to be heard over the din. Wings, being a bright old bird, scarpered round the back as soon as the riot of questions began. The chaotic mob swarms around its victim and all I can catch is the odd word, puce coloured faces and a lot of arm flinging gestures. I can still spot Curt, so they haven't trampled him yet, though if they don't stop soon, I'm going to hit someone. Or inflict YMCA on them again.

"What's the point of asking you?" a woman screeches, high enough to trigger dogs' barking, as she shoves Curt in the chest. "You ran off up the mountain at the first sign of trouble."

I'm about to stalk across the snow and smack her right in face with a snowball, when Curt's temper gives out and his rarely exposed dark wolf persona finally emerges.

Drawing himself up to his full height, eyes on fire, he thunders in a rasping werewolf voice, "Take a step back from me, RIGHT NOW."

He's scary like this. It's easy to see the Alpha he was raised to be, before the injury. I never met Frozen Hell, but I bet she sounded just like this.

"Quiet. Listen to me," he continues, as the tumult shrinks away from the menacing wolfman. "Panic and fear will not help us."

"Neither will pretending it's not happening," Adamo replies, from a safe distance. "I have my bears and cubs to protect."

He's right, of course, and at this rate, the advancing wolf mob will be here before they quit screaming at each other. "Dulcis."

"What?" she replies, lurking behind me.

"Find your bleedin' father before they flatten his brother and do the wolves' job for them."

"Don't bother, I'm here," says Alpha, rounding the corner, having utilised the back door to avoid the crush. Wings follows in his wake like a penguin on hot coals.

"Good of you to show up," grumbles Adamo, drawing a glare from Dulcis.

"I've come to a decision," Alpha states.

"Hallelujah," I mutter.

"Wonderful," growls the ginger prince of bears. "What are we doing?"

"Nothing."

And just like that, all racket ceases. You could hear a pin drop. Well, not in the snow, but you know what I mean. There's only one sound and it's Curt, furiously scratching his hip.

"Listen to me," Alpha continues. "There's no other choice."

"I can think of a few," moans Adamo.

Alpha rounds on him. "And all of them end with blood on the snow."

I hate to say it, but he's probably right. No doubt he'll mansplain for those at the back.

"Number One…"

And we're off on the lecture. I hope he makes it fast, since I can already hear howling getting closer.

"We stop them before they get here and probably end up in a battle, massively outnumbered.

"Two: you all hide. But they already know you're here, so it just makes us look cowardly and shifty, playing into every prejudice they've got.

"Three: The bears go get every bear they can find. It's too late for that and would still result in a fight.

"Four: the king goes serpent and all the snakes reptile up. That'll scare them, but they've still got weight of numbers…"

"And I've no intention of killing anyone," Serpen interjects, quietly, but we all heard him.

"The only way to avoid bloodshed, it seems to me, is to talk. Have a meeting, just as they've asked for and show them the truth of our new pack."

"Risky," says Anguis.

"Yes," Alpha snaps. "What else do you suggest?"

"Risky, but probably the best way," Anguis qualifies.

"I agree," states Curt, moving to his brother's side. "We talk."

"And if they turn on us?" Adamo asks, resting his hand on Ursid's shoulder as if to draw strength from the gnarly general.

"Then I stand with you," Alpha states. "We will not be separated. One pack."

Alpha glances at his brother, who nods his assent. "One pack, indeed."

"One pack," Adamo repeats, after staring at the brothers for a moment. He holds out his knuckles for Alpha to fist pump.

"One pack," Serpen adds, raising his voice so all the snakes follow the shout.

"One pack," we all holler at the top of our voices. "ONE PACK!"

Rumbles of rolling wheels and intermittent howls grow louder as the massed wolves enter our valley, catching sight of the town's mixed folk, awaiting them. We all stand in row after row of family, heads held high, our Alpha at the arrow's point.

I'm shuffling into place somewhere near the middle when Curt waves at me like he's swatting a manic bee. I guess he wants me beside him, despite what his southern relatives will make of it. As I'm edging through the nervous crowd, Anguis slinks up beside me and whispers, "Edi, if this goes wrong, remember I'm still a fearsome snake and Serpen a true serpent. Stay near me at all times."

Curt, having wolf hearing, catches every word and scowls hard enough to break his forehead. When I arrive beside him, he glares at Anguis and ushers me round to his other side, next to Dulcis.

The southern wolves pick up the pace as they head towards us, growling all the way in a clear attempt to intimidate. It's working. Only Curt resists the urge to shuffle backwards.

"Which one's their Alpha?" I ask Curt, scanning the mass of fur.

"He's still not there," he replies.

"In that nasty carriage then?"

Curt grins at me. Close up, that rolling monstrosity appears covered in hideously misshapen wolves' heads. Clearly the 'artist' doesn't possess the carpentry skills of my mangy wolf. Either that or they're into modern art on the lines of half a wolf in formaldehyde.

I do recognise one wolf at the head of the arriving crowd. It's not hard, being as she's the only one still in human form and Decipoop Longsnout is already infamous in my mind. Here she comes, striding like she owns the place, heading straight for our Alpha. Her wolves shimmy into straight lines, like an army in formation. Now there's a simile I didn't need.

Every line does a nifty four paw crossover sidestep as the coach rolls through their ranks and pulls to a halt behind her.

"Wolves at ease," she trumpets and every wolf rump hits the deck at the same time with a muffled thud, leaving us staring at a field of Anubis statues. A mass of wolf cubs sit at the very back of the arrivals, discipline keeping them surprisingly subdued in comparison with our wriggling sprogs.

"Salute your Master," is the next, disconcerting order.

The wolves obligingly deliver a united howl, rising in pitch until I expect blood to start oozing from my ears. I must be squinting from the tinnitus because Curt gives my hand a swift squeeze to calm me. Since when does that work? The howl finishes with an ultrasonic wheeze.

"Alpha of the Cetorn Valley, we are honoured to be your guests." Decipa sweeps her arm in the direction of the coach, which remains resolutely closed. "I, Decipa Longfang, have the honour to introduce the Alpha of the United Southern Pack, Master of the Belch, Pelch, Mortledong, Fangrease and Grissolling territories, Ruler of the True Wolfdom and Alpha of Alphas. Hail, Alpha King."

All their wolves howl at such a decibel level the ground quivers with the vibration, muffling the squeal of iron hinges as the carriage door finally swings open and a human foot emerges.

Decipa drops to one knee as her majestic Alpha steps down from his carriage and promptly slides sideways when his feet hit the snow. My first thought is that we've got another Adamo style, clumsy great man on our hands, but the sudden appearance of a woman, flinging herself out behind him to steady his wobbly legs, tells me there's something very wrong here. She might be pretty in a nondescript sort of way, but he's a mess.

His skin is so pale he would merge into the surrounding snow, if the dark circles under his eyes didn't stick out like a panda's. Unfortunately, he's neither cuddly nor furry, being razor thin and reminiscent of horrendous heroin chic, and it looks as though he's been wiping dust off the furniture with those clothes. He appears a good decade or more younger than his cousins, but it's hard to tell when he's this derelict. Despite swaying as though he's close to passing out, alert eyes still scan those assembled before him, pausing as he takes in the mass of nervous bears and one former snake ambassador.

"Hail Audira. Alpha Mate," Decipa hollers, making both me and the mousy woman shudder. Apparently, I'm not the only nervous wolf lover around here. Audira summons a watery smile, keeping a tight grip on her clearly ailing Alpha mate.

More occupants emerge from the carriage's hardly roomy interior.

"Alpha Alpha, the Alpha son and heir," greets the next to step down.

I hope we don't have to reel that lot off every time he's asked to pass the salt.

The oldest son, a teen teetering on the cusp of adulthood, actually looks rather presentable to middle-aged me, being clean, handsome and sporting a nice shiny quiff, but since our teenage princess, Dulcis, is leaning backwards, I'd guess this is Stinky himself. I can't smell anything at this distance, but I'll wait and sniff. Assuming nobody attacks anyone in the meantime.

The 'may or may not smell' princeling catches Dulcis' eye and delivers a formal nod of greeting which she returns. Adamo's behind me, so I don't see his reaction, but I'm pretty certain that snort and rumble isn't good.

Stinky paces over to his father with the uptight gait of a tin soldier and yanks the illustrious king up by the armpit. "We're fine, Mother," he tells Mousy, peering down his nose. I'd dislike him, if he wasn't also rubbing his daddy's back to aid his breathing.

Oh, here comes another escapee from the carriage. Goody.

"Fidus," announces Decipa.

That it? Just Fidus? No Lord Shiftypants, Master of Universe, Fidus? If he feels short changed by his lone moniker, he doesn't let on, arriving on snowy ground with a beaming smile on his face. Thank the Good Lord, someone half human (literally). He sports a strong resemblance to his possibly pongy older brother, but seems to have been blessed with a good thumping from the pretty stick. He's a handsome item, that's for sure, jiggling on the spot as though waiting for a starting gun to fire. Maybe Dulcis might have been keener if offered him. Too late now; Adamo got there first.

And finally...

"The Illustrious Alpha Mother, the Lady Yelena."

Here we go. Frozen Hell's younger sister. Yellfire herself. This is going to be good. I can feel Curt wilting onto his bad hip as we wait. Apparently, the big bad wolf is scared of his auntie.

And down she steps.

Now, if you're anything like me, you'll be expecting a wart-faced, hump-backed, millennia aged witch, cackling like a banshee, fingernails poised to skewer your eyeballs.

Damn, she's beautiful: slim and shapely in head to toe bronze leather, stalking across the snow like the wolf she is. Her face reminds me of an older Dulcis, but there are flashes of Alpha and Curt in there too. It's not her grace and beauty that most shock me. I was expecting an ancient crab, but she appears barely older than me and a great deal lovelier.

"Was Dulcis' mother a lot younger than you?" I whisper, scowling right into Curt's face.

"A bit," he splutters.

"What's a bit? That woman, her mother, looks hardly older than you."

"Erm, she also ages well. All our family do," he replies, not looking at me.

I glare at Alpha and Curt. Cradle snatchers, the pair of them.

By now, Yellfire has made her way over to Dulcis, pointedly bypassing her waiting father.

"There you are, my beautiful one," the infamous granny says, wrapping her arms around the quivering girl.

She has a gorgeous silky voice to go with that body. I hate her.

"Welcome, Grandmother," Dulcis replies, pulling back from the embrace like she expects to be eaten alive.

"You're looking more and more like my beautiful Kallosa with every passing year. It's been too long. You should have come and stayed with me. The south is so much warmer."

"It's good to see you, Aunt Yelena," Alpha ventures, choking on his words half way through.

"I doubt it," she replies, barely glancing at him. "The girl needed her mother. She should have been sent to me."

"She also needed her father," Curt interjects, steeling himself not to flinch.

Sure enough, Yelena glares at him as though he's poisonous mould, and we all remember what that was like. Her gaze swings back to Alpha. "I thought The Reject was no longer accepted in your domain."

Now there's the Wicked Witch of the South I was expecting.

"Whomever I so decree is accepted in my domain," Alpha replies with brittle calmness.

Yelena huffs politely. Her gaze wanders to Adamo and a colossal sneer wraps itself around her face. "What is that?"

"A bear," the ginger prince replies, crossing his arms and peering down at her from his greater height. "My name is Adamo. It's thrilling to meet you. I'm a prince, by the way."

"How trying for you," Yelena replies, her icy gaze already slithering along the line until it grinds to a juddering halt at the former king of the Snake Empire.

"His Majesty King Serpen," Alpha announces, "and Ambassador Anguis."

She deigns to half bow, constituting a mild twist of her neck, and Serpen responds in kind, neither breaking the iron eye lock.

Wow, they're either trying to psyche each other out, or there's a seriously warped backstory lurking in the undergrowth. You could cut the atmosphere with a blunt spoon.

"You look so much like your father," Yelena hisses, as though she's about to genteelly spit on him. "Are you like him, Your Majesty?"

"In some ways," he replies, eyes narrowing. "Not in others."

Unfortunately, whilst we adults can all sense the razor-edge of diplomacy, a certain cub with a ready set of choppers thinks this is all a jolly game and comes flying across the snow, his enormous mother in full pursuit. The whirling dervish bounces up to the lines of statuesque wolves, having spent the last year being indulged on every front by wolf, bear, snake, eagle and Edi, only to find himself facing a snarling set of choppers attached to a parked Anubis, snapping right over his sensitive snout.

The wailing ball of fluff promptly rolls across the snow in terror and sinks his teeth into the nearest limb. Unfortunately, that's my ankle.

CHAPTER 8

The Portrait

"Ow, bloody hell. Why'd you bite *me*, you little monster?" I yell, leaping up and down like a hysterical flamingo, clutching my ankle.

Mama Bear thunders onto the scene, scoops up her errant cub, grasps him to her ample chest and glares at the snarling, dribbling wolf who, amazingly, backs down. "Sorry," she whispers to me, not prizing her gaze from his for one second.

"No worries," I reply, thumping my foot back on the ground.

"Perhaps it would be wise to keep the cubs under control," says Yelena.

Part of me hopes Mama will wipe the condescension right off her face and, indeed, the bear's mouth is opening for a rip-roaring reply, when it's drowned out by the Alpha of Alphas honking out a horrendous cough that makes his ribs creak in sympathy. Mousy Audira takes over rubbing his back as the ailing wolf hauls in breath and I catch a look of anguish flash across his eldest son's face.

"That poor wolf doesn't sound at all well," Mama observes and promptly bustles towards the expiring Alpha King, handing off the snarling ball of fluff to me. I thrust him into Ursid's arms before the dear thing's claws puncture my nose. Tufty Monster calms down in the old bear's embrace, tucking his sore nose under the general's chin.

"Mama is our pack healer," I'm in the process of advising, when Decipa steps straight into her path and Mama only just avoids a collision that would blind the young woman.

"Keep away from our king, bear," the messenger orders.

Yelena, oh so slowly extends a perfectly manicured finger and lays it on Decipa's shoulder. The girl freezes on the spot.

"Thank you, Messenger Longfang," is enough to make her skitter back to the lines of wolves with a bobbing bow. Yelena's simmering gaze meets Mama's concerned eyes. "Perhaps our own healers might be somewhat better placed to treat our Alpha, don't you think?"

Mama Bear is a soft-hearted friend, a fabulous healer and a wonderful mother, but she's not a great fan of condescension.

"Really?" she snorts. "You've got a funny idea of healed, if that's what it looks like to you."

"I doubt a bear would have the knowledge or the inclination to care for a wolf," Yelena replies, her tone darkening with every word. "Our experience of your kind has hardly been honourable. Bears are renowned for inflicting injury upon the innocent."

The wolf army grumbles and snarls, snapping in agreement. One or two rise up onto four feet, with more joining every passing second.

"Stay where you are," rings out the deep voice of the Southern Alpha Big Wolf. A coughing fit immediately follows, but the wolves duly settle back into place, albeit displaying far too many shiny sets of teeth for my comfort.

A short, slightly dumpy man pushes through the crowd, collects his cub from a quivering Ursid and sidles up to his towering wife. "Maybe later, my dear," he offers, giving her a pointed look and directing her gaze to the slathering lines of wolves. "Time for the little one's feed?"

"Yes. You're right, Friddie," Mama replies, backing up slowly.

"Aunt Yelena," blasts a nervous Curt, giving me a fright. "Let me introduce you to Edith, known as Edi, my..."

"The Human," she states.

And three syllables are all I get by way of acknowledgement. Not that I expect a warm hug. Wait, she's holding out her hand.

I'm obliged to take it and force myself not to wince under the crushing pressure. She drops my fingers as though I'm laden with bacteria and I resist the urge to count my traumatised digits.

"Perhaps we might go inside," she says, turning to our Alpha, "or do you intend to carry out our meeting in the snow, as of old." The last said with a glance at Serpen.

"Indeed. Yes," Alpha stammers. "Er, no. Not outside. Inside. Please follow me. There'll be room for family, of course, but not…"

"Decipa, take over," Yelena orders, before striding in the direction of the mansion. Audira and Stinky gently support the Southern Alpha Big Wolf as he staggers after her.

I think I'm just going to call him Big Wolf since there's way too many Alphas here, what with Curt being a former Alpha, Parco now our Alpha, Dulcis our Alpha daughter, the Alpha of Alphas, Alpha Alpha Heir – good grief, enough already.

"Wolves erect your shelters," Decipa bellows, like a sergeant major, "and set patrol."

The statues leap to their paws, the majority changing into human form as they head towards the laden carts. Those remaining as wolves prowl through the town, heads swinging from side to side as though searching for thieves and traitors. I catch Ursid's eye. It's not hard to tell we're both concerned.

"I don't like this," I whisper as he pads over to me.

"Me neither," he replies, patting my arm, "but I'm trusting Alpha knows what he's doing."

"For now."

"For now," he agrees.

"Are we supposed to go inside with them?" I ask.

"I don't know. I doubt it."

I'm thinking Ursid's probably right, when Curt gestures for us all to follow him, waving a hand behind his own back.

"I'll stay out here," Ursid tells me. "Keeping an eye on our guests. Adamo can listen to all that endless chatter for once."

I've taken a few nervous steps towards the mansion, when I'm waylaid by young Fidus, trailing behind the rest of his family.

"Sorry about them," he says, leaning in close as we pace, side by side. "They used to be more fun than this. It's been a hard year and doubly difficult since Papa got ill."

"I understand they came here a while back, your father and Stin… your brother."

"Did you almost call him Stink?" Fidus roars with laughter, slapping a thigh.

"No. I'm so sorry. I didn't…" I'm stammering for England here. What an idiot.

"Can't blame you," he continues, chuckling. "He was sick himself then. Smelt like two day old runny poop. He's better now and smells a lot better, thank Grojat."

"Sorry. Really didn't mean to be so rude," I finally get out.

"I'll keep it to myself," he tells me, with a grin. "You should hear the stories they tell about me."

"Oh? A bit wayward, are we?" I enquire, smiling back at him.

"Used to be. My grandmother keeps her eye on me and when she's asleep, Primus stands guard."

"Primus?"

"My big brother does have a name, like most Alpha heirs. It's Primus, but you can't call him that, I'm afraid. Unless you're alone with me, 'cause I don't care. My father used to be called Surdi, a long long time ago. Mama still uses it, when she thinks we're not around."

"May I ask you something?" I venture, taking my chance, since he seems forthcoming.

"Ask away."

"How did all the packs join together?"

He delivers a mild frown. "Bears, I'm afraid. I know they're your friends, but that's not our experience. Far from it. Attacks against the packs were so bad, we joined up or faced dying. My father took over when most of the Alphas got torn to shreds. There's been no bear attacks since."

"Your father's ill?" I ask. "You don't have to answer if it's too personal."

The twinkle drops away for the first time. "I don't know what'll happen if he passes."

"Your brother will become Alpha?" I suggest.

"Should do," he agrees, "but Granny's scarier."

I can't help but allow a snort to escape and he grins at me.

"Fidus!" Yelena calls. There's no doubt it's a summons.

He rolls his eyes and jogs after her, heading inside together. Dulcis loiters at the door, waiting for me.

"Making a new friend?" she mutters, as I arrive. I don't reply.

Inside, Adamo, Serpen and Anguis have already settled themselves by the fire, leaving the wolf contingent milling about as though waiting for battle to commence. Someone's been round closing all the windows and it's heating up to a pleasant warmth.

"Perhaps, as it's rather hot in here, we might have our meeting in a private room?" Yelena asks. Though it's less a request than an order.

"These are also pack leaders," Alpha responds. "I would rather anything you had to say be discussed in their presence."

Adamo swiftly covers his grin, but Yelena sees it. Her scowl could curdle milk.

"Cousin," Big Wolf says, shrugging free from his wife and son's grip. His words arrive in short blasts as he struggles for breath. "I need to speak privately, wolf to wolf, as family. If you then wish to share it, I have no objection. Please."

Alpha glances at the bear, snakes and me before nodding in agreement. "As you wish. Come with me. Curt, Dulcis."

Yelena stares at Curt with surprise.

"He's my brother," Alpha insists, catching her glare.

"Erm, is my presence required?" asks Fidus, leaning nonchalantly against the fireplace as he watches his family move out.

His father barely hesitates, but it's long enough to speak volumes. "Of course," he coughs, finally.

As they pass out of the hall, heading for a meeting room towards the back of the mansion, Yelena's gaze finds two portraits, hanging side by side. The first is of her older sister, Helena, still sporting a hefty tear courtesy of a missile launched by Frozen Hell's son, Curt. Nobody cared enough to mend it.

Yelena pushes a finger through the tear and I'm surprised to spot the ghost of a smile. It flees when she turns to the companion portrait of her own daughter, Kallosa. A wince, laden with the pain and anguish of loss, swiftly morphs into white hot anger that sends shivers down my spine.

I had wanted to be in that room with Curt, but not any longer. Being the last through, Yelena closes the door behind her, catching and holding my gaze as though issuing a challenge. I'm relieved when the lock clicks, separating us.

A leathery arm wraps around my shoulders. I didn't see Wings standing in the corner. His comforting gesture worries me more than all that preceded it.

"Since they don't need me here, I'm off." A miffed Adamo vaults out of his chair and marches upstairs, the woodwork quivering with every stomp. As he reaches the top, he glances at the others and, seeing their attention elsewhere, waves for me to follow him.

What's he up to?

I deliver a hefty fake sigh, announce, "I'll be in my room. Let me know when they're finished," and forlornly wander up the stairs.

Once out of sight, I leg it down the corridor, turn the corner and crash straight into the waiting Adamo.

"What are you doing?" I whisper, poking him in his six pack.

"Listening in, of course," he replies, grabbing my wrist and dragging me after him.

CHAPTER 9

Eavesdroppers United

We've legged it along the upper corridor and are heading down the back stairs when I whisper, "Do you think we should be doing this?"

"No," he replies, and shrugs. We peer at one another, conspirators both. "Which room is it?"

"This way."

I usher him towards an alcove which overhangs the slightly sunken meeting room. Before you think I do this all the time, Dulcis once told me she often used to listen in to her father and grandmother arguing. I told her that wasn't an honourable thing to do, which now makes me a hypocrite.

Today, I don't much care. Shoot me.

Our tiptoed footsteps alter to silent stealth creepage as the ceiling closes in, which isn't easy to accomplish when you're Adamo's height and cursed with two left feet. He's forced to semi-crawl, ducking his head and lifting his knees just short of his chin in a parody of a cartoon villain.

Voices drift up from beneath our feet, but I'm yet to make out the words. No-one's yelling, at least, which is good news. I hope.

Adamo slinks into the alcove and lays flat on the wooden floor in a youthful display of suppleness, right ear pressed tightly to the slats. Ordering my conscience to take a walk, I park myself beside him, posterior stuck in the air, cursing the cracks and groans of sciatica. I shuffle my ear into position with an audible grunt.

We both freeze in place, staring at each other, but there's no sign of my having been heard coming from below, thank goodness. Adamo grimaces at me and I mouth 'sorry.'

"If you're here to negotiate for a mating alliance, we've already discussed this."

That's our Alpha's voice.

"Thank you, no."

Not sure if that's Big Wolf or his oldest son. Definitely not jolly, high-toned Fidus.

"You made it insultingly clear last time that my advances were not welcome."

No cough and he sounds miffed; I'd guess at Stinky Primus.

"At least she can be in the same room as you now," jokes Fidus, "without passing out."

"Fidus, that's inappropriate," scolds Big Wolf, with a cough. "This is serious."

"Apologies, Father."

"I'd like our wolves housed," barks Yelena, forgoing polite introduction to her topic. "It's snowing."

"There's no room," Curt states, with an audible air of belligerence, given he was quivering at the sight of her a few moments ago. "You brought the entire south with you."

"You appear to be housing a multitude of bears," says Yelena. "Can they not share for the duration of our visit?"

"They built those houses," Curt snaps. "We're not throwing anyone out of their own home."

"Are you Alpha now?" Yelena counters.

"You know very well, I'm not. Did you come here to bring discord with my brother?"

Ouch.

"Curt," says Alpha.

"Be careful how you speak to me, nephew," warns Yelena. "Your mother wouldn't approve."

"I'm well aware of that," Curt replies, with a cynical snort.

"Curt," Alpha repeats, a warning edge to his tone.

A tap on my back nearly makes me levitate with shock. Luckily my forehead bounces off the back of my hand in a silent thud of pain. A guilty look over my shoulder reveals a frowning Wings, glaring down at myself and Adamo, arms crossed in terminal judgement. I give him a nasty, wide-eyed stare which he returns with interest.

"What are you…?"

"SSShhh." We both grab at his knees and he staggers.

'Are you earwigging?' he mouths, yanking on his ear lobe in illustration.

Down below, the conversation continues to heat up. "Why are you here?" asks our Alpha, loud enough for his voice to carry clearly.

Wings flashes into motion, knees crunching as he squeezes between me and Adamo. His ear slaps into position, face nose to nose with the prince, leaving me staring at the back of his bald bonce.

"The Southern Packs…" The words cut off in the wake of a lung shredding cough and a muffled retch.

I can't say I'm drawn to his family, but Big Wolf sounds two tail wags away from an early grave to my mind. It's a pity they don't want Mama Bear to take a gander at him. She might be the only hope he has.

"The south has been mercilessly attacked by swarms of bears."

That's Stinky rescuing his father from further speechifying. Scowling Adamo doesn't seem too chuffed, face pressed to the floor, but then he wouldn't, would he, following that announcement? Not to mention the earlier threat to make them homeless.

"When rumour of the collapse of the Snake Empire reached us, the bears attacked all the small wolf packs first," Stinky continues. "It's only because my father took control we were able to stop them as a united pack. Unfortunately, that came too late for most of their cubs."

Oh, Lord. Adamo looks like he's turning green at that revelation. I can't see either him or General Ursid ever waging war on cubs.

A creak along the corridor makes three heads snap in that direction, only to see Serpen and Anguis tiptoeing towards us. This is ridiculous. Twice in one day I'm sandwiched into a tiny space with half the town. The snakes don't fling themselves on top of us, thankfully. Leaning over, far too close, does the trick. If Curt caught Anguis this close to my raised nether regions, there'd be hell to pay, particularly since the snake's eyes sparkle in the gloom like fairy lights.

"We came when we heard a rumour that bears and snakes were living here," Stinky says, drawing my attention back to the floorboards, "and we wanted to be sure they weren't holding you or your pack hostage, as slaves. We came because we're concerned for your safety."

"I'm sorry to hear what's happened in the south," our Alpha replies, "but we have no quarrel with the bears here. Indeed, it's been an entirely peaceful transition."

"And the bear princeling bows to your leadership?" asks Yelena.

"He *agrees,* yes," Alpha replies. "Especially since he's far too young to lead himself."

I can sense Adamo scowling, even hidden by Wings' bald head.

"He'll mature," Yelena points out. "And you'll be sorry."

"So, these bears have never attacked you?" Stinky asks, hitting the target with laser sight.

I doubt I'm alone in flashing back to a blood on the snow free for all, only ended by yours truly singing off key. We were more than lucky no-one was mortally injured that night, or later killed taking out a king turned serpent.

"In the past, there were skirmishes, yes," Alpha's forced to admit. "But not since we joined as one pack."

"Perhaps you could explain why you would place yourself and the wolves in your care in such a dangerous position? Did you ask them what they wanted?"

I can tell it's Yellfire, not simply from her tone, but because she starts every blasted sentence with 'perhaps.'

"I am their Alpha," he states, as though that answers her question.

"You didn't need to bring them here, to your home, even if you did decide to broker a truce," she continues. "From what I understand, you could have left the snakes to perish. Do you not care how they enslaved us all for centuries? Yet you bring them here, despite having no reason to trust any of them, least of all their king, leaving your own wolves in mortal danger.

"And not only the snakes. You're actually living with bears. You know what the bears did to our family: the starvation and violence. I saw it with my own eyes. My little brother, who never raised a paw against a single bear, slaughtered because he was sick and couldn't run away. You never forget it, Parco. Never."

The use of his pre-Alpha name doesn't escape me, or him.

"And if we continue with the hate, it'll all happen again," Alpha replies. "I don't want that for my daughter."

"I didn't want an early death for my daughter, either."

"That wasn't my father's fault," Dulcis insists.

"You never told her the truth?" says Yelena. "Surely she's old enough to hear it now?"

What does that mean?

Adamo's head rises to look at me. I shrug, having no idea what's coming either. Wings turns his forehead to the floor and closes his eyes. I guess he does know.

"If Kallosa had mated with your true Alpha, he might have protected her," Yelena continues, no doubt referring to Curt. "But he was too busy trying to broker a truce with the bears. See what that got him."

"Aunt Yelena, this is all..." Curt begins, but she's not finished by a long shot.

"You relinquished your title, Curtus. Don't speak to me."

"My mother died from an accident," Dulcis states.

"Yelena," growls Alpha. It sounds like a warning.

She ignores it.

"Your mother died from a fall, being chased by a pack of bears."

Oh, Lord, no.

I stare at Adamo. He peers back at me, shaking his head. I believe his confusion is honest, but he would have been a child at that time and might not know the facts.

"Is that true, Daddy?" Dulcis asks. I can hear the tremble in her voice.

"No," he replies, fighting to keep his voice calm. "There were no bear tracks anywhere. I checked, believe me. It was a tragic accident."

"She ran towards the most dangerous drop at night," Yelena continues. "Why else would she do that?"

"I don't know. No-one does," Alpha insists. "Except that she was reckless and wild, doing her damnedest not to be like you."

"How dare you blame…"

"I'm not blaming anyone. Not even her," Alpha replies. "It was an accident."

"Mother," says Big Wolf. I can tell it's him because it's followed by more coughing. "None of that helps now."

"She was your sister and now they make her daughter live with the very bears that killed her. What do you intend to do? Mate her with that red abomination?"

"Nobody's mating with anyone," growls our Alpha.

Wings and I glance at a puce faced Adamo, since we all know that ship has sailed. All except her father, apparently.

"What do you intend to do here?" Alpha asks.

"Nothing," Big Wolf replies.

"Perhaps…" old Yellfire starts.

"Nothing," her son repeats, with more emphasis. Everyone waits for the latest fit to subside. "If you tell me you're content as you are, that your pack is safe, we'll leave after the Howling."

There's a muffled thump. Probably furniture taking a battering. Someone's none too happy down there.

"Do they join you in the Howling, all these beasts?" Yelena asks.

In the silence, my imagination conjures up the naked people, come wolves, dancing around the campfire and I want to laugh. It was some sight when I first arrived in the, what was then only a village.

It's all gone quiet down there. What's going on?

"We haven't had a Howling together," Alpha finally replies.

He's right; we haven't. Not since we all united.

"Really? I wonder why," says Yelena.

That came laden with condescension. I'm waiting for the 'perhaps.'

"And what will The Human do?" she continues, surprising me. "Freeze naked in the snow? Curtus?"

"I thought you didn't want me to speak to you," he snarls, in *that* tone he only uses when I catch him scratching.

"Will she be joining us?"

"I doubt it," he replies.

"Ah, so she isn't your mate."

What?

What did she say?

And why is Wings staring at me with pity?

"But of course she couldn't be, could she?" Yellfire continues, unknowingly twisting a dagger in my heart. "Not being a wolf, or any kind of changer. Though I'm sure she's fun in your... home."

"Mother," mutters Big Wolf. "Enough."

"You have no idea about either of us," Curt snaps.

"Perhaps you could clarify," says Yelena. "Have you passed through the mating ceremony with... I'm sorry, what is her name?"

Fidus replies, "Edith. Edi."

"Yes. *Edi.* So, Curtus, did I miss our invitation to your mating ceremony?"

Silence.

"Well?" she probes.

My heart's hammering so loudly it makes the floorboards vibrate.

"No, of course not," Curt mutters, so softly my clamped ear can hardly pick it up. My heart hears, though. Loud and clear.

Adamo reaches out to me as I push myself to my feet, but Anguis shakes his head. As I stagger down the corridor, mind in turmoil, not caring if my heels clatter, I can sense them all staring at my back.

I don't turn.

CHAPTER 10

The Infamous Howling

Stars twinkle brightly in the night sky. I sound as though I'm about to break into a Christmas Carol, but there's no Jingle Bells in this heart. Not tonight.

I usually love this view, perched on my favourite riverside rock, listening to the tinkle of rushing water, not yet fully frozen. As the winter sun disappeared, taking any warmth of the day with it, my spirits sank into the horizon along with the lengthening rays, but the seething temperature of my blood kept me warm. That and two coats, gloves, five feet of scarf and an oversized beanie.

I've been left to my own devices, since I'm out of view of most of the town and they don't know I'm here. At least, I hope that's the reason. Ever since Yellfire's acidic little revelation, I've been questioning everything about my being here. Perhaps they don't notice my absence at all? Now I'm sounding like a grouchy crab.

A tall shadow weaves through the outer smattering of chalets, heading directly for me. I can't see who it is, as flickering light from the windows doesn't cast that far, but since they're not limping, I know it's not Curt. As my heart sinks into my wool lined boots, I can't tell if I'm sorry for myself or livid. Maybe both.

A touch of starlight twinkles in the gaze of a familiar face as he silently sits beside me. He is ever graceful.

"How did you know where I was?" I ask, when the freezing silence forces me to speak.

The snake turns to look at me, locating my eyes between the wool letterbox of scarf and hat. "You love the stars and this is the darkest place to look at them," Anguis replies. "Besides, I waited forever for you to stop hiding in the toilet and followed you." His gaze rises to take in the starry firmament. "I think you come here to tell stories to yourself."

"Delude myself more likely," I reply. That's cynical. I haven't sounded like that for a long time. Not for a year.

"I'm so tempted to step in here," Anguis continues, after a momentary pause. "To tell you all I see in you. I think you know."

I do. I look away from his piercing gaze before I'm tempted to start overflowing on his shoulder.

"But..." he continues, "don't assume anything without talking to Curt. We're here in our mixed up pack, living together, but we all grew up differently, with far different customs. Let him have a chance to explain, at least."

"Why are you so nice all the time?"

He smiles. "I was an ambassador, remember?"

"You make me feel like the black sheep of the family."

"What's wrong with a black sheep?"

"Never mind."

He leans towards me, with a conspiratorial air. "I'm steering clear of Auntie Yelena though. I truly hope they all head back down south as soon as possible."

"Me too. By the way, do snakes have a mating ceremony?"

He laughs. "We do. It involves rupturing and shedding our skin, so it's done in private."

"Ewww."

"Edi!"

Ah, the dulcet tones of Dulcis, followed by the sound of stomping through the snow. I remind myself she didn't have a fabulous afternoon either. It's no use taking my misery out on her.

"Edi!"

She's ratcheting up the snarl to siren level. Anguis smiles again and nods, eyes wide, before sliding off the rock.

"Here, Dulcis," I call out, holding his gaze as he gently places a hand on my cheek. I mean my face, not... Sorry, killed the mood.

Anguis passes Dulcis, like ships in the night.

"What are you doing out here with him?" the teen demands, staring after him as he merges into the darkness. She turns to glare at me.

"Don't start," I tell her. "It's not been a good day."

"Me neither," she replies, crossing her arms and rubbing them against the cold.

She must be frozen out here, not wearing her coat. I want to discuss her mother's accident, but can't let her know I was eavesdropping.

"Where's your coat?" I ask, opening my cavernous layers of coat and woollies and pulling her into the gap. I'm not her mummy, but it sure feels like it sometimes.

"I'll be changing soon," she replies, snuggling closer. "I came to get you for the Howling."

"What for? I can't join you." Blast; that escaped from an open wound before it seeped through my brain.

Dulcis leans back to take in my expression. I fake a smile, which doesn't convince her for a moment. She knows me too well.

"What's the matter, Edi? Have they said something nasty to you?"

I can't look her in the eyes, which pretty much signals the affirmative.

"Daddy always told me my grandmother's family weren't very nice. What did they say to you?"

I give her a hug, but the question searing my mind won't be kept down. I simply don't have the character to suppress it.

"Why didn't you tell me being mated to a wolf needs a ceremony?"

She jerks back out of my grasp. "They told you about that?"

"I heard it from a wolf, yes." Semantics, but still not a lie. "I thought Curt and I were... but now..."

"Uncle Curt loves you," she says, peering at her toes. "That ceremony is for wolves and you can't..."

Ah.

I don't think I want to hear any more. Apparently, my days of rejection aren't quite as over as I thought.

"Don't worry. It's fine," I tell her, launching myself off the rock, feeling as petulant as I sound.

"Edi, please speak to..."

"We have to go. We'll be late for the Howling."

Plodding through the snow this fast makes my legs ache, but I don't care. I don't want to look her in the eye right now. I don't want to look at any of them. Not that the bears or snakes have anything to do with this. Do they?

I arrive back at the mansion to find Wings waiting for me outside the front door, hands clamped behind his back, doing his best duvet coated butler impression. He opens his mouth, thinks better of it, and closes it again. Instead, he holds out a padded arm for me to take, as though leading me to the dance floor. That simple gesture very nearly undoes me. I haul in a deep breath and clasp his arm like it's a lifebelt.

Alpha's wolves stack more logs and twigs onto the central bonfire and Wings escorts me away from the growing flames. It strikes me that the only sound is the crackle and snap of wood as it catches light. I don't think I've ever heard it this quiet in the town, even up at our lodge. It's eerie.

"Where is everyone?" My head's on a swivel, scanning the empty walkways.

"In their homes," Wings replies. "Adamo and Serpen thought it might be less... confrontational."

"Am I allowed to hide too?" I ask, trying not to shiver under all my padding.

He titters and pats my arm. "Chin up, Human. Don't let them scare you."

"They don't," I lie, partly. "Wings, do you...?"

My question's cut off by the most godawful howling I've ever heard. It's even more nerve-shredding than the music the snakes' trumpeter used to play, and I don't say that lightly.

Around the corner, from the back of the mansion, pads our Alpha as a fully changed wolf, grey mangy Curt at his side. When my wolf lays his yellow eyes on me, he trots in my direction, but I wave him back to his brother's side. Now is not the time. Something's happening here and I don't like it.

Alpha yowls at Dulcis. She glances at me, before stripping off her clothes and changing into her sleekly glorious lupine form. As she pads over to her father and uncle, the pack arrives, following their Alpha in rigid formation, noses held too high and limbs too stiff. I've lived with these wolves for a year and I've never seen them behave like this. As Alpha draws to a halt, his wolves press tightly around him in a semicircle, not a single whine, whimper or yowl escaping closed maws.

The appalling howling, straight out of a horror film soundtrack, isn't coming from them, but it is getting closer.

"They're not starting as human at all," I observe.

"No," mutters Wings, his hand tightening on mine. He's beginning to frighten me.

And then I see it.

Through the town, through every walkway, past every door, beneath every tightly closed window, creep the southern wolves, stalking some invisible prey, howling out a predator's death chant. They join together in front of our Alpha, pouring into one mass like an oil slick on water, flames reflecting off their teeth as they howl and snarl.

"Who's that?" I ask.

"Their messenger," Wings replies.

Up front slinks Decipa Longfang, maw open wide, displaying the truth of her name. Every molecule in my body freezes and I feel the bones of Wings' hand creak under my petrified clutch. The old bird neither moans nor pulls away.

"This isn't like the one I saw before," I mutter, trying to find solace in voicing my thoughts.

Wings glances at me, but doesn't reply. When his eyes widen in horror, my head snaps around to follow his gaze and my racing heart skips a beat.

Through the trees, head held high, teeth dripping saliva, paces the ugliest and most revolting wolf I've ever seen. It's not her black and grey flecked coat, which is as beautiful as that of her granddaughter, nor is she in any way deformed or broken, despite the huge size of those fangs. The horror emanates from the look in her eyes as she takes her place at the head of her battalion. I have no doubt she would eat me raw, in a heartbeat.

As if she reads my thoughts, her gaze swings to mine and stays locked in place until I look away. I peer up at Wings and the fear must be showing in my eyes because he pulls his hand from mine and wraps his arm around my shoulder instead, hauling me close, his instinct to protect me. I've never loved him more.

The front door opens and two young male wolves exit, ahead of their illustrious father. His mate brings up the rear, enclosing him in a protective circle. I can see why. He looks appalling. Not frightening, nor vicious, but fatally ill. If it were possible, the Alpha of Alphas appears in worse condition as a wolf than man, the change having torn all reserves of strength from his body.

Either the southern wolves can't see his condition or, more likely, they ignore it as their heads rise as one and howl a fanfare to the night sky. I'm wondering how he's going to stay upright on those wobbly legs, when Yelena throws herself into the air, snapping at the nearest wolf, who barely pulls clear of her jaws in time. She takes off, hurtling around the campfire and even crashing into stray branches, spraying sparks high into the night sky.

Big Wolf issues a short, sharp bark and chaos erupts like a drug fuelled rave. He remains still, his mate beside him, as his sons join the snarling, snapping melee as it rotates around the fire in a whirling mass of teeth and fur. My Curt's somewhere in the midst of that violence and my heart's terrified for him, and my sweet girl. I can't believe our Alpha led them to this bestial nightmare.

I catch a brief glimpse of Dulcis, finding a modicum of relief in noting that Fidus' wolf runs alongside her, bouncing his shoulder into any who come too close. Bounding from the opposite direction, Decipa's snarl shaves my girl's ear as she flies past. Fidus roars right in the messenger's face and she stops in her tracks with a look of disbelieving shock imprinted on her furry features. Serves her right and good for Fidus.

Pressing closer into Wings' shoulder, I tear my gaze from the roiling darkness and catch a woman peering through the window of her tiny chalet in horror. I follow her gaze up to another window on the upper floor of the mansion, where Adamo stands in witness to it all, Ursid at his shoulder. I've never seen either look so serious, or uncomfortable. I know how they feel.

A wobbly Big Wolf teeters on the brink of passing out when the maniacal wolves finally begin to run out of steam and cease snapping at one another.

"Is it over?" I ask Wings.

"I don't know," he barely whispers. "I hope so."

A familiar chattering above my head reminds me that my chubby, bucktoothed gumwhat friend will be expecting his dinner.

Sure enough, Mr G sits on the mansion's window ledge shuffling snow out of his way.

"Not now," I stage whisper at him. "Shoo. Go. Come back later."

He's busy raising his chatter to the level of enraged honk, when a flash of black and grey fur whips past my ear, yanking my woolly hat clean off my head. Wolf Yelena takes a flying leap at Mr G, jaws wide open, my hat swinging from her canine fang. He yelps and bounds across the ledge, his snapping hunter in full pursuit. She catches up as he flies off the ledge, aiming for the roof, and her jaws clamp shut with my little friend inside.

I leap on the monster's back, yanking on her upper jaw. Her nose bends upwards, but it's like trying to prise open welding, so I punch her in the throat instead. She gags and out flies a spit coated Mr G, bouncing across the snow, shrieking so high it makes my eyes squint and water. I've no idea where he goes after that, since my entire view fills with the snarling maw of a homicidal wolf.

I'm about to lose my head. Literally. I throw up my arms. Not that they'll save me; I'll just be armless when I'm digested.

Yelena gets side swiped with a crunch and she buckles over, smacking her nose on a patch of ice, which cracks under the onslaught. Curt's wolf staggers, his eyes crossing, apparently having just nutted his auntie to save me. There's no time for gratitude as the two of them face off, snarling at each other, teeth barely an inch apart. It takes Alpha, Dulcis and Stinky Primus to separate them by leaping in between.

A flurry of shrinking fur heralds the return of human Yelena, bellowing, "She struck me!"

"You ate my friend," I shout back, peering over the top of Dulcis' wolf.

"What? It's a gumwhat!" she hollers, as Curt changes behind his brother's shielding flank.

"I'm sorry, Aunt Yelena," he says. "I couldn't let you bite Edi, no matter what she did."

That little speech gets a thunderous glare of betrayal from me.

"To protect a gumwhat?" says Yelena, shoving the newly changed Primus to one side before he can intervene.

"He's her pet, sort of," Curt tells her.

"It's a snack."

"What can I say? She's odd."

"Aunt Yelena, please let it go," Alpha pleads, popping upright from the snow. "Please."

Naked Yellfire stamps on the spot, scowling, until announcing, "Fine. But if she ever touches me again…"

"She won't," Alpha says. "I give you my word."

I'm not touching her with a bargepole. Just a minute. Don't speak for me.

"And she apologises," Curt adds. "Don't you, Edi?"

I feel Dulcis' wolf nudge me in the back of the knees and Wings nods from behind Alpha.

"I apologise for punching you in the throat," I proclaim. "Nice teeth, by the way."

"We're leaving," Curt insists, hauling me in the direction of the mansion. "Now."

"You need to get some clothes on." I glance up at the window and catch Adamo giving me a thumbs up. Ursid smacks the back of his head.

"Are you mad?" Curt asks, dragging me over the threshold and up the stairs. "You want to die for a gumwhat?"

"Alright, I didn't think. Ok?" I admit. "Ow, you're hurting me."

"You're lucky you've still got a face."

Once inside our room, he slams the door, rattling the hinges, before rummaging in our wardrobe. A full ensemble of dinner wear gets yanked onto his body with such force, I expect to hear seams rip.

"Do not carry this on over dinner," he commands, grimacing from the pain in his hip.

"Let me help you."

"Get yourself dressed," he snaps. "And for all our sakes keep quiet. I don't need you airing your wit right now."

"Hey. Don't talk to me like that."

He pauses, thumping his socked feet into his shoes and reaching out to clutch my hand. "I'm sorry. I didn't mean that. You know I love it when you make me laugh. But I want them to leave, Edi. Just let them go. No more fights."

I don't know why I say this now. I know it's not the time.

"We need to talk, about us."

"We will," he replies, pulling on his best embroidered jacket, given as a gift by the snake children. "When this is over."

And he's out the door, footsteps echoing down the stairs.

CHAPTER 11

Trout Pout

I'm searching for the long burgundy dress I always wear for best, when there's a tap on the door and Wings lets himself in, carrying stunning sky blue material draped over his shoulder.

"Curt's already vanished," I tell him, trying to ease the creases from my wrinkled dress.

"I passed him, heading for the kitchen to check on the food," Wings replies. "He looked anxious."

"Him and me both." I stare at his concerned face. "And no, we haven't had a chat about mating ceremonies yet. I'd probably kill him, right now. Assuming that woman doesn't bite my head off first. Don't be scolding me. I wasn't going to let her eat Mr G."

"It wasn't the wisest thing you've done," he comments, swinging the material off his shoulder. "But not the most stupid, either."

"Thanks."

"I'm not here to flap."

"And please don't sing. I'm traumatised enough."

He tuts and holds out the sky blue ream. "This is for you. Though after that comment I should keep it."

I take it from him and splay the material, revealing the most beautiful dress I've ever seen. The spun wool feels as soft as

Roger's bottom and the neckline and sleeves carry delicate swirls of gold embroidery.

"This is gorgeous. Where did you get it?"

"I made it for you for… another occasion," he says, running a hand over his bald head. "But I thought you might like it for tonight."

"You made it yourself?" I squeak with uncontrolled incredulity.

"You sound surprised." Those flapping eyebrows meet in a frown and he crosses his arms. "Who do you think makes Dulcis' clothes?"

"You're kidding. And an amazing old bird."

He sniffs. "Anyway, Dulcis helped and Anguis did a bit of embroidery."

"Anguis?" This is getting surreal.

"Yes, why not?"

Why not indeed? Apparently, I'm still harbouring some ridiculous sexist views in my handbag. Can't shake the image of the bird and the snake wearing cloth caps, sitting on a rocking chair and knitting.

"I love it," I tell him, holding the dress against myself in the mirror. "And it's not gumwhat yellow."

"Never thought of that," he says, with his best poker face. "Next time. I'll leave you to try it on. I know it'll fit."

"Wings."

He pauses in the doorway.

"Thank you," I say. "You mean a lot…"

"Hmmph," he mutters and sails out before I can embarrass him.

I'm pretty much dressed when Dulcis arrives, a vision in velvet black, to create a work of art with my thinning grey hair. She twists and pins, furtively glancing at me in the mirror, until I can't stand it anymore.

"Out with it," I tell her. "You don't do passive aggressive silence."

"I'm sorry if you think I kept something from you," she says, her large eyes downcast.

"It's not your fault," I tell her. "When I can get that mangy wolf alone, he better have something to say though."

"Finished," she announces, patting the back of my elaborate hairdo. "You look lovely. We'd better go… Edi…"

"I'm fine," I tell her. "Let's get through the dinner."

I'm already in the hallway when she catches my hand.

"Edi, you know I love you."

"Course I do," I reply, pulling her into a girly hug. "I love you too."

Unfortunately, we manage to get our hairdos caught up and spend the next few minutes trying to extricate ourselves without ruining the scaffolding. The result is that the guests are all in place at the table when we rush down the stairs in a flurry of skirts.

It's not hard to tell how the dynamic will be playing out this evening, as one glance at the two empty chairs displays. Dulcis sweeps into the chair next to her father, glancing from wolf to wolf as it dawns on her they're all seated at the top end of the table. Fidus smiles at her encouragingly and she returns the grin, despite his brother's frown.

When I do my best to glide past Curt, he smiles at me in apology, mouthing, 'You look lovely.'

My chair is about as far down the other end of the hall as it's possible to go, directly underneath Frozen Hell's ripped portrait. I park my ever expanding posterior, leaving me staring down the length of the table at our scowling Alpha. On my left, sit Serpen and Anguis, facing Adamo and Ursid. Wings is perched in the middle like a feathered buffer zone. The only missing face belongs to the infamous messenger. I've no idea where she is.

Adamo has clearly been at the wine, since he's already refilling his glass, exchanging a pointed stare with his general. I can't say I blame him. Fortification and numbing sounds pretty reasonable right now, even if he is a bit young to be drinking himself under the table. He peers at Dulcis, sat opposite smiling Fidus and ramrod Stinky, and scowls.

To everyone's eternal relief the food arrives. A plate of freshly caught and fried fish is inserted under my nose, its beady eye staring up at me in accusation. Where's the wine? I'm peering through the bottom of a rapidly emptying glass, when I spot the ghoulishly pale Big Wolf turning green at the sight of food. He's the only one who isn't hungry.

That horrible Howling made the wolves ravenous and the rest of us uncomfortable. The upshot is the odd quiet word and tinkling cutlery dropping like pins into rigid silence, made even more excruciating when we all labour to eat without making a sound. Have you ever tried to silently slurp, chew and swallow? It sounds like broken toilet plumbing.

Big Wolf grinds out another round of terminal coughing and massages his temples with both hands as though propping up his head.

"You need more rest, Father," Fidus says, under his breath, but, in the quiet, his words carry to my twitching ears. "Let me help you. I can take more responsibility."

Big Wolf glances up at him with pain filled eyes, but doesn't reply.

Stinky glances at his brother and father before whispering, "Fidus was with you when you toured the packs. Surely…"

"Not now," Big Wolf snaps.

Audira pats her youngest son's hand in an attempt to reassure him, but he snatches his fingers away.

Silence returns.

I'm so busy eyeing up the southern dynamic, I barely pay attention to the food I'm shovelling into my mouth. When a sharp pain spears my throat, I'm forced to open wide to extract a fishbone before I choke on it. From the look on Yelena's face, I guess she'd applaud if I did the latter.

"Are you alright?" Anguis whispers.

"Yes, thank you."

Adamo downs another glass of wine and burps. "Excuse me."

A stone faced Ursid holds out a napkin without looking at him. Curt glances down our end of the table, catching my eye. The ridiculous nature of this whole set up hits us both like a yeti's side swipe. Fighting not to guffaw, I snatch the napkin and bury my nose and mouth in it. A stray snort escapes Curt's nose which he tries to smother with a cough, ending up honking in harmonious counterpoint with the sickly Big Wolf.

I catch Yelena's gaze shifting from Curt to me and back. That sobers me up fairly quickly and I take to poking the corpse of the fish around the plate.

"That's a lovely dress, Dulcis," Yelena remarks, slightly too loud.

"Thank you…" Dulcis begins, but her grandmother isn't finished.

"Edith's dress is a rather unusual shade," she continues, staring straight at me with venom.

I don't bother to reply; I can sense there's more coming and I'd just be wasting my breath.

"I prefer a shade more flattering for my age and shape." She delicately swipes at her immaculately tailored navy dress, removing a stray speck of dust. "More muted perhaps."

"I don't do muted," I reply, immediately kicking myself for playing her game.

"Indeed, you don't," she responds.

"Don't react," Anguis whispers, too late.

"Wings helps me with my clothes, ever since I was little," Dulcis inserts, with forced jollity, trying to protect me. "And he does my hair."

She beams at the old bird, whose smile looks like rigor mortis has set in. I can see the exact moment Dulcis realises she's unwittingly redirected the firing line from me to Wings.

"Yes, I'm surprised to see you still here," Yelena says, skewering Wings with her gaze. "Surely my family no longer needs an eagle nanny these days. Did you not wish to return to your own people when the snakes' little empire crumbled?"

Serpen glances at Anguis, who shakes his head, as if to say 'don't respond.'

"I'm already with my own people," Wings replies. "This is as much my family as it is yours."

"Good for you," I mean to say, but it comes out as a bellow. All attention's now back on the trumpeting Human. "We're blessed to have him. Wings was a true hero last year."

"Indeed, he was," says Anguis, delivered with perfect volume and tone. "He saved many lives."

"Really? Whose?" Yelena replies.

"Grandmother," Fidus whispers, in admonition.

"The lives of my people who had yet to crumble," Serpen replies to her question, his sapphire gaze meeting hers.

She quickly looks away, muttering, "I wonder what your father would have done?"

"Clearly not enough," he replies.

We're thankfully saved by the arrival of the dessert course. Adamo sways in his chair and Ursid pokes him to sit up straight before he nosedives into the plate of carrot cake. The honey bear hammers at it with a fork, turning it into mash.

"I think it's already dead," I whisper at him.

"So, Edi, where are you from?"

"What, sorry?"

"Over here." Fidus waves at me, grinning. "I asked where you're from."

"It's a long story and a long way from here," I reply, principally because this is so not the time for magic books and portals.

"Perhaps your family miss you," states Yelena.

"I doubt it, since they're dead," I reply. She's really pissing me off.

"All of them?"

"Yes. I didn't kill them by the way."

"Her cooking's not that bad," says Curt.

Thank you, mangewit. Very funny.

Dulcis kicks him under the table. Adamo snorts cake up his nose and chokes. Dulcis glares at him, whilst Ursid thrusts another napkin into his face.

"Perhaps you would find it easier living amongst humans?"

Yellfire's off again and my mouth has a will of its own.

"Perhaps we could start a sentence with something other than perhaps?"

"Maybe," she quips.

"I like living here. I love them and they love me."

"Edi," Anguis whispers, trying to warn me.

Yelena rests her chin on raised fingers. "Do they? You don't have fur or fang. If you had fur, you'd be a wolf."

"And if I had gills, I'd be a trout. What's your point?"

"Being a wolf..." she begins. "It's hard to explain. You could be raised from childhood amongst wolves and still not understand what it is to be one of us. I'm not trying to hurt you, but you're living in a fantasy. All of you. Eventually you'll wake up and you'll be hurt."

"I don't agree with your cynicism," I snap.

"Yes, you do," she replies, almost sounding sad. "You all do. Every attempt to befriend other species has ended in betrayal and bloodbath." She glances at Serpen. "You can pretend friendship if you wish, but this will end in war. It always does. Ask my slaughtered baby brother."

Adamo smacks his fist on the table, pulverising the remains of his cake. "You forget what your wolves did to..."

"I am the only one here..." Wings interrupts, with more steel in his tone than I've ever heard, "who witnessed both attacks from that time." Yelena's face flushes with anger at that remark. "None of us should want to go back, ever," he continues. "This may be a fantasy, but it's worth the risk."

"Bravo," I say.

The silence that follows is hardly a stunning display of comradeship.

Dulcis' face drops as she glances at a sozzled Adamo. Curt just stares at the remains of his cake.

"Curt, what do you...?" I'm asking, when Big Wolf's perpetual cough escalates into an all out fight for breath and his mate leaps off her chair to catch him as he crumples sideways.

"Surdi!" Audira cries out, clutching him to her.

"Fetch the healers," Yelena tells a nearby wolf, who promptly scampers off. "Sit him on the floor, leaning forward, so he can catch his breath."

"Should we get Mama Bear?" I ask Ursid.

"They won't let her near him," he replies.

Fidus rushes around the table. "There's no way we can leave tomorrow."

"Alpha," says Audira, barely audible over her mate's distress. "May we stay longer? I don't want him to travel like this."

Big Wolf tries to wave his hands to get her attention, but he's straining too hard to breathe.

"He can travel in the carriage, as before," Yelena offers, exhibiting a bucket load of compassion for her own son.

"Grandmother, no," pleads Stinky Primus, kneeling by his father's side. "Alpha, my mother's right. Please. Until he recovers a little, at least?"

All eyes are on our Alpha, who peers at Yelena.

"You could take the majority of your pack home," he decides, "and leave your Alpha here, to follow when he's feeling better."

"Under no circumstances would this united pack ever leave their Alpha," she responds. "They are entirely loyal."

"If you're concerned about feeding us all," Fidus interrupts, "I can lead hunting parties."

"Thank you, but you will not be hunting in my territory," Alpha states. "Take your father to his room for the healers."

Whilst Big Wolf gets heaved onto a stretcher and hauled away, I head over to Curt. He shakes his head and follows his family upstairs, leaving me behind as though I've never been part of it.

The sound of the closing door echoes one in my heart.

CHAPTER 12

Put A Ring On It

An overwhelming urge to flee the premises sweeps over me, but I'm not stupid enough to freeze to death for any man, no matter how cute or mangy. I head back to our room, disrobe and fling the gorgeous, non muted, blue dress on the bed and pile on wool and leather layers, ready for an arctic jaunt in the middle of the night.

I really don't want to talk to anyone right now and I'm too riled up for sympathy or comfort so, after poking my nose out into the corridor, I intend to sneak down the back staircase and out the door without attracting a stray bear or snake. Unfortunately, I nearly step on the missing messenger, who's sat on the stairs, filling her greasy face with leftover fish.

"What are you doing?" I splutter, grabbing a banister to prevent myself from falling on her head.

"None of your business," she snarls, tearing off her next bite like she's killing it herself.

"You are allowed to eat at a table with the rest of us."

Her eyes widen with barely contained rage. "I am the Official Messenger. I eat where I like." She leaps down the stairs and flounces along the corridor, muttering, "Yelena should have ripped your head off," before disappearing.

I used to like wolves.

Winding my way through the patchwork of tiny, torchlit chalets and makeshift wolf tents, I head up the mountain, aiming for the only home I know: Curt's lodge. It's a ridiculous idea, since every step in my overweighted padding pulls on screaming sciatica and overwrought nerves. The lodge perches a long way up that mountain in sub zero temperatures, my teary eyes freezing in their sockets.

If I had any sense, I could have barricaded my bedroom door in the mansion, refusing the miserable miscreant entry, if he ever decided to show up. Instead, hours later, I'm barely half way, exhausted, cold, stumbling through snow in the dark and three steps off beginning to howl in misery.

It's then that the Good Lord intervenes for poor old grey Edi.

A chalet door opens and a familiar face hovers into view, her head scraping the top of the doorway as she ducks.

"Who's out there? Edi, what the Grojat are you doing out here in the middle of the night?"

I'm hauling in breath, but still can't get a coherent word out, so she rushes over and envelops me in the greatest bear hug in living memory. I'm so overwhelmed with relief, I want to weep, but tears are dammed somewhere in the region of my heart.

"Come inside, right now," Mama Bear coos. The tone sharpens to an order. "Friddie, heat up some broth; it's Edi and she's frozen."

"Yes, dear," a disembodied voice replies from inside.

* * *

Smothered beneath lovely warm covers, I can't yet force my eyes to open, though I'm pretty sure it's nearly morning. Last night went the way of broth, blankets, stoic advice on my love life and an order to sleep. I felt so exhausted, even a cracked heart couldn't keep me awake. I dropped off, knowing for a fact that Yelena's cynical judgement was wrong. Mama Bear and her Friddie prove we are better united.

My eyelids flicker and open to find shiny eyes and a huge black nose filling my view. Homicidal cub stares at me from the vantage point of sitting on my chest and begins bouncing up and down, using my ample bosom as a trampoline.

"Get off, you little horror," I say, giving him a shove.

He amuses himself by taking a few boxing swipes at my nose, then slides off the bed, pulling all my blankets with him and trailing one out the door. I wash in a cold bowl of water and swiftly dress.

"Are you up?" Mama calls.

"Yes. Thank you," I reply, shuffling into view.

"I'd have given you hot water," she tells me, poking at a frying pan.

The tiny table already carries a toasty breakfast, with Friddie busy catching his errant cub underneath.

"Sit and eat," Mama orders, plopping something that resembles egg and bacon onto a plate.

"I should go," I reply.

"Not until you've had a hot meal," she orders, pressing me into a chair with one hand and sliding a cup of broth onto the table with the other.

"You've been really kind," I tell her, after swallowing my first glorious sip.

"Are you continuing up to the lodge?" she asks. I nod. "Don't you think you should go back and talk to Curt? It wasn't always this good between me and Friddie, you know."

Her mate flings their cub off his shoulder and into a high chair, admitting, "I was rather timid."

Stifling a smile, I take another sip of broth, before replying. "I will, guys, but I need some alone time first." My heart sinks at my own words. I spent most of my old life in alone time. In truth, it's the last thing I need. "Besides, I think he's too busy to talk to me right now."

I'm squeezing into my final coat, having first been wrapped up in one of Mama's long scarves like a mummy, when I ask her the question that's been haunting me since Yelena spoke her poison. "Mama, have I been living a fantasy?"

Mama frowns. "Who said that?"

"Yelena."

"Hmmm," she says, "that wolf has a messed up heart. Don't let her mess up yours or that mangy idiot's."

Cub flings himself off his high chair and makes for my padded leg.

"Don't you bite me," I tell him, hustling out the door. "Thank you, Mama, Friddie."

"Always here," she calls out, as I start back on my pilgrimage up the mountain, plodding under the glorious rays of the rising sun.

The warm chalet and a hearty breakfast are a distant memory by the time I haul my aching body up to the lodge, to see smoke pouring forth from the chimney, melting snow dripping from the edge. Someone's started a fire to heat it through. I don't know whether I want them to be Curt or not, so I find myself grinding to a halt in the snow, staring at the front door.

I've barely gathered my chaotic thoughts when the door flies open with a terminal crash and a highly livid, red faced wolfman limp marches out, yelling, "Where the frulk have you been?"

"What do you care?" I holler back. I actually want to throw myself into his arms and snivel, but buggered if I'm doing that.

"I only went into the room to make sure their Alpha isn't dying," he says, getting right up in my face. "When I come out, you're nowhere to be found. Do you know your smell's everywhere in this frulking place? How am I supposed to find you?"

"I bet they ordered you out of the room," I lob, shoving past him and heading for the lodge.

"That's not the point," he bellows.

I sprint into the lodge and slam the door in his fast arriving mush. That achieves nothing, since he can open it from the outside, but it makes me feel better.

"That was childish," he remarks, flinging it shut behind him.

"I'm mad at you," I shout, squeezing my bulk into the rocking chair and staring at the blazing fire.

"I get that," he says, tapping his fingernails on the dining table. "Perhaps you can take the scarf off your face and tell me why."

"Don't you perhaps me," I snarl. "I got enough of that from her."

"Fine. No perhaps. Give me your coat."

Getting it off is like trying to fight a shark in a tyre. He tries to help me as I struggle, but only ends up getting a padded fist in his eye. When I finally rip the arms off and pitch my coat across the room, he retrieves it from the floor and tidily hangs it up. That annoys me even more.

"Food's cooked," he tells me.

"Don't want any," I snap, though we can both hear my stomach rumbling. He sighs. "Don't you dare sigh at me."

"Great. Per... can you talk to me without biting my head off?"

"Mating ceremony," I announce.

"What?" he stutters, wide-eyed.

"Mating ceremony," I repeat, with slow emphasis.

"What about it?" Fingers head straight for his hip.

"You're scratching and you look shifty," I point out, flinging myself back into the chair so hard, it nearly upends. "Why didn't you tell me there was such a thing?"

"It didn't occur to me," he replies, shuffling on the spot.

"Seriously? That's your story?"

"Edi."

"If you were living in here with anyone else for a year, would you have had one?" I regret asking as soon as the words leave my mouth because I already suspect the answer.

"If they were a wolf, probably."

I'm out of the chair and heading for my coat like lightning. He gets there first.

"Edi, give me a chance to speak."

"Why?" I shout at him. "So you can tell me I'm not your mate? What am I then?"

"You're everything to me," he replies, reaching for me, but I don't want to be touched.

"Everything except your mate."

"It's not like that," he insists. "We couldn't do it as it's a wolf thing. In a wolf mating ceremony, we change, fight and bite one another on the nose. Hard."

"What the hell for?"

"I don't know," he hollers. "We just do."

"That's bloody ridiculous!"

"I know!" he positively screeches at soprano level.

"You didn't think I could punch your lights out and bite your mangy nose?"

He snorts with laughter, which really ends up lighting blue touchpaper. Stand well back.

"It's not funny!" I bellow, like an ogre.

"Sorry," he says, choking back giggles. "If any human could best me, it'd be you. And I don't have mange."

"SHUT UP or I'll punch you right now." I glare at him, sheer stubbornness preventing me crying. I lean back against the wall before my legs give way. "Did you not think we have ceremonies where I come from?" I mutter, breathing heavily. "That I might like that instead?"

"You never said anything," he says, scratching so hard, he'll take a lump out of his leg.

"Stop scratching, you're making me itch," I snap, nails raking under my hat. I lob the woolly beanie into the fire in a fit of pique. He wisely ignores it.

"So, what's this ceremony of yours?" he asks, sinking into a chair beside the table, bones creaking. It reminds me so much of the traditional romcom position for a marriage proposal that misery sweeps over my disappointed imagination.

"Too late now," I mumble, face dropping into my boots.

"Why?"

"Do you agree with your dear auntie? Do you think we're living in a fantasy and it'll all come crashing down?"

"No," he states, staring me straight in the eye.

"Then why didn't you say anything to her?"

He leans forward with a groan, resting his chin on his palms. "She's my aunt. Kallosa's mother. We're taught to have respect as wolves."

Give me a break.

"Since when? And what does auntie think I am to you? Has that crossed your mind? What do they all think of me?"

"What does it matter what any of them think?" he asks, grasping at my hand.

I extract my fingers. "Really? You didn't tell me about your mating ceremony? I wonder why?"

He opens his mouth to reply, but a solid knock at the front door replaces his words. He's still struggling to get up when I march over and fling it open. I'm so not up for visitors right now.

Hovering on the threshold stand Fidus and his stinky brother.

CHAPTER 13

What's That Godawful Smell?

I must be staring like I'm peering in a shop window because Fidus cheerily pipes up with "May we come in?"

"Er, yes," I mutter, still staring.

"You probably need to move then, sweetheart," says Curt, coming up from behind, shuffling me sideways and smiling at them so hard, it's a grimace. "Come in. Welcome."

As they pass me, stepping inside, I glare at Curt.

"I invited them last night," he whispers. "Before you decided to bite my face off."

I hiss back, "You really are dense sometimes."

"We can come another time, if it's not convenient?" Stinky offers from within, picking up the vibes. Not that it's difficult.

"It's fine," I reply with all the welcome of an ice cold shower.

Stinky begins lowering his backside, aiming to park it in my rocking chair, when he sees my resting bitch face and decides against it.

"I'm glad you invited us, Curtus, Curt," Stinky says, correcting himself. "I think it's good for someone other than my grandmother or the Alphas to talk."

"Is that a hat in the fire?" Fidus asks.

I don't bother to reply.

"Er, it was mouldy," says Curt.

Stinky nods as though that explains everything. Wolves.

"Please take a seat at the table," Curt continues. "Food's ready."

For the first time since I sailed into the lodge, I notice that the table's set for four. Annoyed, I drag a chair around to one end, so I don't have to sit next to anyone, and move my cutlery with a clatter. The performance ends with my backside thumping into the chair.

That's not very mature, I hear you say.

I. Don't. Care.

Exhibiting more of a diplomatic disposition in the absence of their granny, the brothers decide to sit either side of the table, facing one another.

"This lodge is very cosy," Stinky remarks, when the silence gets too oppressive. "Beautiful workmanship. The carving is stunning."

"Thank you," Curt calls from the kitchen area. "We like it."

I grunt.

I can tell he's made my favourite beef style stew from the beguiling smell, which may be cancelling out any pong from Stinky Primus, although I admit I haven't noticed anything. I just don't like him.

Curt heads over, carrying two plates heaving with stew, and spots my new position. I fold my arms and glare at him. He ignores me and delivers the food to the brothers, before sliding his cutlery into position at the other end of the table.

"This smells lovely," Stinky remarks, inhaling with pleasure.

Fidus catches my eye and looks away with a grin. I unfold my arms, telling myself to relax. Not everyone is my enemy. Just mangy wolves and acidic Yellfire.

Curt whips my food in front of me like he's expecting me to bite him, before he retires to his chair. We all ignore the crack of his hip as he sits.

I grab my fork and commence skewering the innocent pieces of meat. The taste of Mangy's cooking is always fantastic, but I refuse to moan in pleasure and entertain myself by chewing loudly and swallowing like an industrial disposal unit.

"Wonderful," Fidus remarks, after politely swallowing first.

"Thanks," says Curt, with a grin.

"So," Stinky begins, "how did you two meet?"

"I found her staggering around in the snow, lost," Curt mumbles, his mouth full. "I was her hero."

I grimace at that, but he's not finished.

"Then she pretty much saved us all from a war. So, she's my hero."

Stop it. I don't want to like you right now.

"And I keep the bed warm," I add.

That was uncalled for and now everyone's uncomfortable, the male contingent all busy examining half empty plates.

A rather acrid smell wafts into my nostrils, making my nose tingle as though I'm about to sneeze. Is that Stinky? Maybe I've frazzled him and he's stress reeking.

"How's your father?" I ask, trying to redeem myself and ending up sounding like a stand up comedian.

"Not good," he replies, resting his fork on the plate. "I'm afraid there's not much more to be done for him."

He looks devastated and I feel really guilty now, mumbling, "I'm very sorry to hear that."

He looks up at me, holding my gaze. "I may have to be Alpha long before I thought. I hope I'm up to that task."

I glance from him to his brother and back. "I've not been very polite today. Forgive me. I'm struggling a bit with not being a wolf."

"Don't worry. I struggle all the time," Fidus replies. "Nobody trusts me."

"That's not true," his brother says.

"You don't," Fidus adds, with a huge grin. "You've never forgiven me for your hair."

"It took a year to grow back," Stinky replies, mock glaring at his brother.

Oh man, that smell is getting bad, plunging headlong into rancid stench territory. I'm fighting not to gag.

"We're sorry too," Fidus says, his hand wafting in front of his face. "Which is why we wanted to come and talk to you. I think my grandmother has caused a problem where there was none."

"We came here, to the town I mean, to check on your safety," his brother continues, "not cause trouble between any of you. You have to understand, we've spent a year fighting bears and losing our cubs, so it's hard to…" He breaks off and coughs. "Really sorry to ask, but what is that terrible smell?"

"I thought it was…" I start. "Never mind."

"It smells rather like gumwhat urine," Fidus offers.

What? That stink can't be Mr G.

"It's not my gumwhat," I announce, offended.

Whatever it is, it's definitely getting stronger by the second. Curt levers himself out of the chair and heads for the front door.

"Let me check," he says, opening the door.

The stench hurtles through the gap in such an overpowering rush it makes my eyes stream. I spring out of my chair and grab Mama Bear's loaned scarf, jamming it over my nose and mouth.

"Ooft, Grojat frulk," Fidus exclaims.

Curt hares through the doorway and disappears from view.

"Be careful," Stinky yells, rushing out after him, Fidus on his heels.

"Wha ur bluud harl uh ii," I yell, which is muffled garble for "What the bloody hell is it?"

Trying to jam my arms into my coat whilst simultaneously holding the scarf over my nose delays my exit, but I fling myself out into the snow to find the three men round the back of the lodge, pointing at yellow oily liquid dripping from the entire log wall. There's a shed load of hollering going on as they gesticulate.

"I'll grab snow."

"Where's the fresh water?"

"Call for help."

"Put your fire out, now."

"Would someone like to tell me what the hell's going on?" I holler as Fidus legs it past me, haring down the mountain to hammer on the nearest chalet door. I can hear him yelling as he scampers from house to house, doors flying open in his wake.

"Gumwhat pee is highly inflammable," Curt tells me, as him and Stinky struggle up with our fresh water vat and heave the contents over the back wall.

"You tell me this now?" I shriek, allowing the scarf to drop in order to make my point more painfully to wolf ears.

"Why did you think I didn't want it on the roof?" Curt hollers.

"I don't know these things," I yell back at him. "I'm not from here."

Talking of wolves, a few just vacated their chalets and are sprinting down the mountain at top speed, threading through the people heading towards us, carrying water and brooms. I've no idea what they plan on sweeping up.

"The fire," Stinky coughs, throat straining against the fumes of pee. "I'll grab the water."

Curt shouts, "Stay outside," in my face, showering my nose with spit, and hurtles back inside the lodge.

I, of course, ignore him. "What can I do?" I ask, tripping over the threshold in my panic and landing on my knees.

"Can't you ever do as I tell you?" he bellows, going red in the face.

I get as far as "Don't talk to …" when there's a violent whoosh and our open fire place explodes, spraying flames across the back wall and catching light to the curtains and the blankets covering my rocking chair.

"Out, now!" he cries.

A thundering blast drowns his voice and he disappears behind billowing black smoke and falling logs.

CHAPTER 14

Douse My Fire

"Curt! Curt!"

My voice barely penetrates the wall of smoke, words swallowed up with lacerating choking. I'm forging ahead, arms outstretched in the hope I'll feel my way to my wolf, when strong hands hook beneath my armpits, dragging me away from the flames towards the open door. I kick backwards, freeing myself from captivity, fists flailing in the fight to get back to Curt.

"Edi," Stinky hollers, between coughs. "We have to get out. It's too late."

I'm not leaving, I want to scream, but my throat constricts to a pinpoint, wheezing pulses of breath. My arms fly back and forth trying to clear smoke as dense as night, despite the tornado of soot and fire whirling up through the hole in the roof.

Where is he? Where's my wolf?

The flames take hold of everything, eating at drapes, burning through the walls, lapping across the ceiling. The heat sears a flaming tattoo into my skin, but I'll never leave him to burn. Never.

Stinky grabs my wrist and hauls, but I swing round to punch his face, forcing him to clutch at my other wrist, struggling in the epicentre of a raging furnace. A soot caked Curt materialises through the smoke, bends, grabs my legs and upends me, flinging my limp body over his shoulder with a grunt.

"Out! Now," he rasps at Stinky, shoving him towards escape.

The young wolf leaps through the flames, Curt staggering after him, weighed down by my deadweight. Hanging down his back, I catch my last glimpse of what has been my home for a year: my beloved rocking chair as it cracks and splinters under the intense heat, wolf carving dissolving into ash.

Outside, in the melting snow surrounding the inferno, Curt stomps clear of the flames and hurls my sorry backside into a dune, yelling, "Are you mad, woman?" before clutching at his hip and groaning.

I'm back on my feet like a flash, well more like a creaking mess, swivelling him around and thumping away at his back, which happens to be on fire. A bucket of water does the trick, courtesy of an arriving bear, leaving a miserably bedraggled Curt dripping.

"Don't ever do that again," he honks at me, hauling in breath. "You could have died in there."

"So could you," I holler back, dragging him into my arms for a crushing embrace and getting a mouthful of ash for my trouble.

Over his filthy shoulder, I spot a crowd of people chucking snow and water at the flames, with all the effect of peeing on a volcanic eruption. One brave diehard smacks at the inferno with his broom which promptly catches light and ends up being thrown on the fire.

"It's gone," Fidus cries, legging it back up the slope towards us. "We have to stop it spreading."

Right on cue, a resounding bang tears a log from what remains of the roof and hurls it clear over my head, peppering the surrounding people with fiery wood splinters. Curt shoves my face into his chest and leans over me as the arrows hit. I pull clear in time to witness the flaming log roll down the slope and slam into a chalet, where a deluge of water and snow puts it out, just in time. A volley of handy brooms slap away at the splinters, beating them into submission, but it's only a matter of time before the situation escalates.

More and more people dash up the mountain, hurling snow and water as fast as they can, but it's a losing battle with nature's furnace and gumwhat accelerant.

A shadow swoops overhead, drawing my gaze upwards, and a plummeting drop of water splashes me in the eye. A blurry eagle soars through the sky, a huge vat swinging beneath his straining body. His beak pulls a string and the bottom opens, dropping the deluge straight onto the fire, which spits and hisses, drawing back as though in fear. As Wings flies back to the river, the town's people redouble their efforts to end the crisis.

Two more water dumps by our flying hero finally succeeds in putting out the fire in a cloud of steam and smoke. The people understandably cheer, their homes safe, but I want to yell my anger at all of them. With a mighty groan, the listing lodge finally gives up its fight and collapses into a smouldering ruin, thus neatly completing the metaphor on my life. Curt's grip on my shoulders tightens. Whether that's meant to be a comfort or simply a reflex reaction to the disaster, I'm not sure. The only thing left standing of our idyllic year together is a wooden toilet. How apt.

A hysterical volley of chatter flies out of a singed tree and a mildly smoking, chubby gumwhat scarpers into the forest with the air of someone emigrating for life.

"Did Mr G start the fire?" I ask Curt, shivering.

"Only if he drank half the river," he replies, slipping his arm further round my shoulders. "It was all over the entire back wall."

"Then it's arson," states a soot stained, soaked Stinky. "Someone wanted to hurt you, or…"

I cut him off before he can start speculating. "Curt, can you smell them?"

"What?"

"Wolf nose. Can you smell who did this?"

"Over that lot?" he says, waving a hand towards the reeking ruin. "Gumwhat pee and smoke…" He takes a breath, staring as though noticing the wreck for the first time. "It's gone. My home's gone."

I want to correct him with 'our home,' but what's the point? It's still gone.

"I'm sorry," Fidus says, gently.

I peer at him, as soaked and filthy as his brother, as are the town's folk. They all did their best for us. It wasn't enough, but it was still their best. I should say something, but the words won't come. Not even thank you. With the fire now out, the aching duo of cold and shock sink into my bones.

Three wolves and two bears bound into view, followed by furry clothes carriers, backpacks strapped to their torsos. Alpha, Dulcis and, to my horror, Yelena, soon change to human form and dress, just ahead of Adamo and Ursid. A flapping downdraft precedes Wings' return as he gently places Serpen and Anguis in the snow before landing.

Anguis strides towards the chaos, carrying one of Serpen's kingly fur coats in one hand and matching hat in the other. As they're both already fully kitted out, I can't make my muffled thinking figure out why, until he drapes it around me, with empathy pouring from his gaze. Now we both know what it is to lose our home. Curt glares at him and he takes a step back.

"I hear this was gumwhat arson," Yelena broadcasts at the top of her ghastly voice, shoving her way through the milling, soot stained crowd.

"Good news travels fast," I mutter, and then announce more loudly, "I don't think the gumwhat did it alone."

"No. It's clearly the bears," she brazenly states, her words hanging in the air like poisonous fog.

"How do you figure that?" I shout at her. "Psychic?"

Curt yanks me closer to his side, worried that I'm about to take off.

"You have no proof it's us," launches Mama Bear, thundering into my eyeline, Friddie bustling in her wake, swinging a broom. "There was no trouble 'til you and your wolves arrived."

Too right.

"You were obviously trying to kill the Alpha heirs, my grandsons," Yelena insists, now surrounded by a snarling posse of wolf bodyguards.

"You don't know that, Grandmother," says Fidus.

"When I need your opinion, I'll ask for it," Yelena snaps at him.

"What about me and Curt?" I point out. "We were in there too."

"Why would anyone need to kill you?" she replies. "He's a reject and you're irrelevant."

Curt lifts me off the floor as I fight to get at her, fists swinging.

"Grandmother, enough," growls Stinky.

"They tried to murder you," she hollers into her grandson's face. Pointing at Mama Bear, she adds, "And this one did her utmost to get close to your father, pretending to help him. They want us all dead, like my poor brother and my little girl."

"Shut your lying mouth," bellows Friddie, face flushed with rage. "My mate is the most honourable person in this whole damn country."

I'm taken aback, never having heard him so much as raise his voice to anyone or even look miffed. Not even as a kidnapped guest at the snakes' castle.

"Friddie, it's alright. It's actually me she's accusing." Adamo steps in front of the besieged couple, Ursid quivering within reach.

"Put me down," I hiss at Curt; his rigid grip is making me feel sick.

"Not a chance," he replies, pretty much tucking me under his armpit.

"I tried to warn you," Yelena says, skewering our own stunned Alpha with a glacial stare. "That bear has treachery in his blood." Her gaze swings to Adamo. "What did you learn from your filthy bloodline, princeling?"

"General Ursid taught me never to attack the innocent or accuse without proof," Adamo replies, staying remarkably calm for a teenager. "Which is more than I can say for you."

"Really?" Her laugh is the poster child for sarcasm. "Perhaps the former Alpha would like to comment on your honour? How about it, Curtus? Are the bears to be trusted?"

Curt's grip tightens, shoving my stomach into my throat as he growls back, "What happened to me had nothing to do with him."

"General," Yelena continues, pointing a digit at the bear, "weren't you there when your prince lied, betrayed his honour and nearly killed Curtus?"

"He can't answer for my father…" Adamo starts.

"Your father was a liar, why not the son?"

Her bodyguard of wolves growl so loudly, I can barely hear her words. Still, she holds the attention of every ear with her poison.

"Your grandfather stole an Alpha wolf cub from his sick mother, to hold hostage for prisoners of war. When we delivered them, we got back a terrified child who never spoke again."

"None of this was me," Adamo insists. "But what did your wolves do? Your wolves killed my grandmother and her cubs. My father became Alpha heir because of you."

"I wonder what you planned, when you came here to negotiate under the snakes?" she asks. "Who did you come for?"

Wait, Adamo looked away. It was only a moment, but he couldn't hold her gaze. I feel cold. Something is about to happen and no singing will prevent it.

"Put me down," I whisper to Curt. "Please."

He glances at me, reads my face and gently sets me on my feet. "Don't move without me," he insists and I nod.

Yelena strides forward and grasps Dulcis' hand. "Did Adamo get close to you, when he arrived? Charmed you straight away?"

Dulcis' gaze passes from Yelena to Adamo, confusion obvious. She shakes her head, not wanting to understand Yelena's implication.

"Do you honestly think they came to negotiate?" her grandmother says, twisting the knife of suspicion. "They came to kidnap you, and would have done so, if the snakes hadn't beaten them to it."

"And I went to that castle to rescue her," Adamo growls, scowling at Dulcis and her silent lack of support. "Curt and Wings grabbed me to exchange for her. The wolf and the eagle would have sold me to the snakes for her. Who's the liar here?"

Curt shuffles in the snow, but Wings stands as still as a statue, feathers wafting in the freezing wind.

"Oh, please," Yelena laughs. "You're trying to convince us that you never even discussed taking her? You and your general?"

"We discussed a lot of things," Adamo shouts. "Our bears were missing."

The voices cease, as though the whole world suddenly mutes.

Dulcis turns to her ginger prince of bears. "Then you did come to kidnap me."

CHAPTER 15

The Short Goodbye

"No. Not really." He heads straight for her, arms wide, expression begging her to listen, but she shifts backwards.

"Get away from me."

He stalls, stunned by her reaction. "Dulcis?"

"You came here, grabbed my hand, fell all over my feet," she yells, "and all the time you were planning on tearing me from my father?"

"There was no plan," he insists. "How good a plan do you think I'd come up with?"

He has a point, but Ursid's eyelid flutters since this is hardly time for levity.

"I didn't know you before I got here," Adamo continues. "I'd only met you as a cub. And you were mean to me." He gestures towards Ursid. "We talked about it. Once. But we both said no. I'm not my father. You know this. Come on, we're friends now."

"Friends?" she bellows. "Is that what we are?"

Oh brother. Pear-shaped isn't the word. Alpha glares at his daughter and the bear, gaze ricocheting back and forth as he begins to understand.

"I meant the wolves and bears. The pack. All of us. And the snakes," he stutters, digging the hole deeper with every word.

"We're all friends. We are, right?" He peers at all of us, one at a time.

Wind whistles through burnt branches, the only sound penetrating ominous silence. I almost expect tumbleweed to waft across the snow. I want to speak, but my voice has disappeared.

"How can I ever trust you?" Dulcis whispers, her anger swallowed up by burgeoning grief.

Adamo frowns. "You know how I feel about…"

"I don't know anything about you. It's all a lie."

He stares at her until she shuffles behind her father's arm, like a little girl hiding from a bully.

"If you don't trust me by now," he says, a pleading hand dropping to his side, "you never will."

"Prince, I have to ask you, on your honour…" Alpha begins.

Nothing good ever started with those words.

"…did your bears try to hurt them?" He's pointing at Stinky and Fidus. "Did you start the fire?"

"Why would we want that?" Ursid interjects. "They were supposed to be leaving soon."

"I can speak for myself," Adamo snaps at his general. "Edi and Curt were in their lodge." He glances at me. "I'd never hurt them."

Good to know.

"That doesn't answer my question," Alpha points out.

True, but still good to know.

"No bear had anything to do with this," Adamo insists, his face a scowling mask of warning.

"How do you know?" Yelena inserts. "You can't speak for all of them."

"I can and I do."

"You've hated wolves for years," says Alpha. "Can you be sure none of your bears did this?"

I own to finding that question shocking. Why is no-one trying to diffuse the situation? Enough fuel's been thrown on this fire.

"Their homes should be searched for gumwhat urine and other evidence," Yelena states. "They may have other plans. Let me question them…"

"You are not entering the homes of my bears," Adamo thunders, his growling words barely human. "Nor will a single one talk to you. You deal with me. I am their prince."

"We should take this back to the mansion," Curt says, stepping between them. "Deal with this calmly, as leaders."

"You aren't Alpha," his brother reminds him, gaze fixed on Adamo.

The prince takes a step towards him and the half-hiding Dulcis. "Don't let her do this. Please."

"Step away from my daughter," Alpha responds.

"Dulcis?" Adamo whispers, but she meets his questioning gaze with an angry glare. He gestures at Yelena. "You believe her insinuations over me?"

"She's my aunt," Alpha states.

"And a wolf." Adamo peers at Mama Bear, Ursid and his shuffling people before turning back to Alpha. "You're saying you'll never trust us, no matter what we do?"

Alpha glances at Yelena before replying. "I don't know if I can afford to trust you."

"Then your daughter's right. We're not friends and never will be. It's best if we leave."

"Yes," Dulcis whispers.

What? Is she bonkers? I clutch at Curt's hand.

Adamo's eyes widen and his body goes rigid. I don't think he thought it would come to this. You and me, both.

"Truly?" he says, gazing at her.

"You should go," she replies, the words trembling on the freezing air. "I'm the Alpha daughter. I should have a wolf mate."

I don't know if she means it, or is begging him to fight for her.

"Then I wish you every happiness," he snarls, glaring at Primus and Fidus. "We'll go as soon as we're packed."

I turn to Curt, but he looks as stunned as I feel.

"Prince Adamo," says Serpen, using his deepest serpent voice, "swift reactions are not always wise. It would be best if..."

"This isn't snake business," says Yelena, cutting him off.

"Your Highness..." Mama Bear rushes to the prince, ignoring Ursid's shake of the head. Adamo prevents her advancing any further with the force of his scowl.

"Am I your prince?" he growls.

After a brief pause, she bows her head. "You are."

"We're leaving this place and returning home. Ursid."

The general turns to him. "Your Highness?"

"Give the order to pack. We are leaving this mess."

A few of his men and women glance at one another, shock and misery written across their faces, but most stare at their feet, as though they'll find an answer in the snow.

"Now," Adamo bellows.

"Return to your houses," Ursid cries, stung into action, "retrieve the tents and make ready to leave."

Friddie gently takes Mama's hand and draws her away. I can't believe they're all just giving up. I refuse to simply stand here, useless.

"Adamo, please don't do this." I take two steps towards him before Curt wraps his arms around my waist, restraining me.

"You have no say in this," Alpha snaps at me.

Like hell.

"You're letting her get in your head," I shout at him. "What's the matter with you? Go back to the mansion and talk. You've done it for a year."

"She's right," Curt agrees. "Alpha, Prince. You lose nothing by waiting. Decisions need to be made with clear heads."

We might be triggering something in Alpha because he turns to Adamo.

"Maybe we..."

"My thinking is clear," Adamo states, glaring at Yelena. "My bears aren't safe here because you no longer lead this pack. She's taken all the fight and the power from you. Look out for your own safety, *Alpha*."

And with that, he turns his back on us all and walks away, heading down the mountain. For once, he doesn't trip over his own marching feet.

CHAPTER 16

Bear Hug

Everyone left me.

It's so very cold, sitting here, staring at the wreckage of my home, contemplating the ruin of a dream. They didn't all leave at once but, one by one, they melted away, unable to convince me to move or even speak. Alpha didn't try. Dulcis looked at me for a long while - I could feel her stare scratching at the side of my face - but, in the end, she had no words of comfort to give me. I suppose I should be there for her, acting like the mature adult in her life, but I no longer have the energy to follow her home.

I lied just now. Not everyone abandoned me. My wolf is still here, yet he doesn't quite feel like *my* wolf anymore, as though an invisible wall of doubt has come between us. That's not fair, I know, but still…

The warming sun disappears behind thick grey cloud, weeping snowflakes. I tug Serpen's fur coat across my chest and hide my chin in the folds. I want to disappear, yet I'm afraid I'll vanish into misery.

"We have to go now," Curt says, his voice hard. He tried the soft tone of reconciliation, but it didn't work. "We can't stay here any longer. You're too cold."

"I want my lodge," I whimper, throat sore from the smoke and glacial air.

"I know," he replies, with a huge sigh, puffing out steamy breath which floats away on the breeze.

"It's gone." The pile of half burnt logs and ash ceases to smoulder, but I can't stop staring at it, as though acceptance will make the nightmare real.

Curt sits beside me and shuffles closer. "I know it's gone, but I'm still here."

"I know," I tell him. But I don't. Not really.

He understands me well enough to read the look in my eyes.

"Edi…"

I don't want to discuss anything right now, so I peer down the slope, through all those soon to be emptied chalets, at the mansion. It seems so distant. I can almost feel it shrinking further and further away as I watch.

Curt follows my gaze. "Go to one of the houses and wait in the warm. I'll change and fetch a cart.

He's right, of course. I need to get warm before hypothermia makes me ill, but the thought of sitting in one of those chalets, swamped with pity, fills me with horror. I'm saved by the arrival of a giant bird, swooping over the roof tops and zeroing in on my feet. I disappear under a cloud of feathers as he lands. In my entire life, I've never felt more grateful to anyone.

Wings delivers a plaintive caw as he glances at what's left of the lodge, followed by a full-throated squawk as claws wrap around my body and Curt's.

"Just a moment…" Curt gets out, before we both lift off the snow and head skyward.

The freezing flight reminds me of my kidnapping by another eagle – was it only a year ago? - and shock finally sets in. The old bird feels the shivers passing through my body and he gently tightens his claw, trying to shield me from the wind. We pass over the chalets, confused wolves milling around the streets, watching their once friends gathering their belongings. I close my eyes as we soar over Mama Bear's warm little home. I can't bear to see them leaving.

Wings slowly glides in to land, dropping Curt and myself directly at the door of the mansion. He's never put me down this gently. Last year he purposely dumped me in a snow drift and, during the summer, in the river. I refused to fly with him after that. Now, I want to cling to his legs and beg him to take me away.

Curt wraps his arm around my waist and heaves me through the mansion's doorway. A wall of heat from the blazing fireplace hits me like a suffocating blanket. I stand there, a shop store dummy staring aimlessly at nothing, until I notice the torn painting of Frozen Hell, directly in my eyeline. I want to rip it off the wall and toss it in the fire, along with her poisonous sister.

The hall stands empty, tables and chairs the only recipient of the cloying warmth. All the usual occupants are probably skulking in their rooms. The rocking chair, sitting by the fireplace, reminds me of my loss and I can't bring myself to settle into it, no matter how tired I feel. Curt watches as I turn my back on the fireplace and decides to take matters into his own hands. He sweeps me into his arms and proceeds to stagger up the stairs, hip cracking with every step. For once, I let him do it without protest.

Once back in our borrowed room, he peels off my padded layers and kneels in front of me, rubbing life into numb limbs.

"Come back to me, Edi," he says, forcing me to take his gaze. "Don't you dare give up on us."

I hear you. I do.

Say it, Edi. Say the words. You have to speak or the silence will set in.

You're an oldish, grey haired, cantankerous, British woman; you're made of stronger stuff than this. My old nan would have wiped the floor with this lot and she was tiny. She certainly wouldn't have sat stupefied.

"Do something," I broadcast, in the voice of a football tannoy.

Curt jumps from the shock and topples forward on his knees, landing with his nose in my cleavage, from whence comes a muffled, "You gave me a fright, Big Bum."

"Get your mange off my girls, thank you," I retort, lifting his head by his silver hair. "And it's no good us sitting here just letting this happen."

"I agree, but what do we do?" Curt asks, turning and leaning back against my legs. "I'd smash some sense into them, but they're bigger than me."

"Especially Yelena."

He chuckles. "You were right, by the way. I should have spoken up before."

"You tried. No-one wanted to listen."

"I'll build you another lodge. A better one, with all sorts of carving. I'll even put a snake in there. You'll love it."

I lean forwards, wrapping my arms around his torso and resting my chin on the top of his head.

"I'm sorry. Though I'd like a statue of Roger, please."

"Frulking ram," he mutters. "You talk to him more than me."

"He makes more sense and doesn't set fire to anything." I sit upright and bounce my fist off his noddle. "You go talk to your brother and I'll try the ginger twit."

"Best of luck. He's in a right mood."

"We call it a strop where I come from. And he's never faced the wrath of a middle-aged woman." I turn his chin towards me, so I can read his eyes. "Do you think a bear did it? Tried to hurt the Stinky Brothers?"

"I don't know. I hope not." He thinks for a moment. "No, I don't think they did."

"Me neither. And I can't see Adamo kidnapping Dulcis either."

He grunts and hauls himself to his feet. There goes the hip.

"Are you going to talk to Dulcis as well?" he asks.

"Adamo first," I reply. "Then I'll tackle Her Highness. Give her a chance to miss him."

He holds out a hand and I clasp it, levering myself up.

"Here's to us," he says, and plants the kiss to end all kisses on my lips. "We're not done yet."

We part on the landing, sealing our joint mission with another kiss, and I head off in search of Adamo, beginning with his room at the front of the mansion, nestling in the far corner. I suspect he was given that location by Alpha, probably to keep some distance between the bear and Dulcis. That didn't work, but her father wasn't to know. Teenagers can be mightily resourceful and sneaky when they need to.

Tapping politely on gingertop's door gets me nothing, so I resort to a sustained thumping by way of my fist.

"Adamo, open this door," I demand, in counterpoint with the thuds. "Don't you dare ignore me. I'm not giving up."

When my fist turns red, I try rattling the wolf's head door knob and, sure enough, it turns. I thunder into his room, bold as brass. Unfortunately, it's empty, though boxes and bags stuffed full of his clothes and belongings litter the room.

"He's not here," Ursid announces, appearing in the doorway behind me.

"Obviously," I reply. "Where is the idiot?"

Ursid gives me his long suffering general face. "He changed and dashed into the woods. He'll come back, eventually. When he's run it off. I hope."

"Don't let him take the bears away," I plead.

"What do you think I can do?" he asks.

"Talk. Someone's got to talk to him. He'll listen to you."

"I did talk to him."

"Did he listen?"

Ursid grunts before replying, "He did more yelling than listening."

"What did he say?"

"You don't want to know." Ursid sits on the edge of the bed, peering up at me. "I don't think he'll change his mind, whatever anyone says. Even Dulcis, if she deigned to speak to him. Adamo's father was also stubborn when he set his mind. He thinks we're in danger here…"

"And?"

"And I'm not sure he's wrong. The Southern Alpha is too sick to move and his wolves aren't going anywhere. What if they stay permanently? Their anger runs deep. It would only be a matter of time before a fight broke out."

"Do you think this is what she planned all along?" I ask. "Yelena?"

"I think she wants us all gone." He stands and grasps my shoulders in his huge hands. "Be careful, Edi. If I'm right, the snakes will be next and the eagle, then…"

"I'll be alone with wolves."

He nods and gently pulls me into a bear hug. I want to cry, but my eyes are dry.

"I'll try to convince Adamo not to take us too far away," Ursid whispers into my forehead. "We won't go back up the mountain again. If you need me, send Wings to find me."

"Are we having a group hug?" asks the voice of charm.

I look up from the general's shoulder, but I already know the owner.

"Snakes," Ursid rumbles, with a chuckle.

Anguis enters the room and closes the door behind him. He couldn't look more conspiratorial if he tried.

"You're up to something," I state.

"Me? How dare you suggest such a thing?" he replies, the humour already leaching out of his words. "To be honest, I don't have a plan. I hate to admit that I feel outmanoeuvred by a better strategist."

"You and me both," Ursid agrees, releasing me from his grip. "I'm trusting you to watch out for this one."

"Always," Anguis replies.

"I'm still in the room," I point out. "And I haven't given up on this united pack. Not yet. Ursid, you keep the bears close by, if you can, like you said. Anguis, you and I are going to sit and plan and strategise til we drop, if needs be. I want my family back together."

Anguis catches the tremble in my voice. "Yes, My Lady." He holds out his hand to Ursid, who grasps it warmly. "I'm glad to know you, General. I'll be a happy snake on the day you return."

"Silver tongued wretch," Ursid replies, with a sad smile. "I won't miss you at all."

The sound of a raised voice sails down the corridor before it coalesces into harsh words.

"...you expect me to do? This is my pack. I'm Alpha because you didn't want the job. I will not be undermined by him, or you."

"I'm not trying to undermine you, or anyone," Curt replies as I open the door. Alpha thunders past, nearly removing my nose. "Does nobody else think this is happening too fast?"

"Perhaps it was always going to happen," his brother offers up, stomping down the stairs.

Now Alpha's sounding like Yelena. I hate that wolf and her bleedin' 'perhaps.'

"You're listening to Yelena now?" Curt says, leaning over the banister. "To me, she sounds a lot like our mother, and nothing good ever came out of her mouth, as you well remember. Please tell me Adamo's not right about you."

Alpha peers up at him, a thundercloud hovering over his head. "She's right, Curt. Bears and wolves don't belong together. Nor snakes, for that matter."

That statement can't be lost on the former ambassador, standing behind me. I daren't look back to see.

Four men enter the mansion and the argument ceases. They head upstairs, pass me in the doorway and retrieve Adamo's packs, all too aware of the thick atmosphere. Ursid silently follows them downstairs.

Still lurking on the balcony, Curt catches my eye and I shake my head in answer to his unspoken question. I've not faired any better with my assignment.

On my way downstairs, I glance out of the window and catch sight of Adamo racing across the snow, before the huge honey bear opens his maw and roars with such anger that the glass shakes in its frame.

CHAPTER 17

Cubheart

The clarion cry goes forth and, from all over town, bears assemble behind their prince, laden down with packs or heaving sledges through the snow.

When I reach the bottom of the staircase, Ursid turns to deliver one swift hug to my trembling body, before a nod to Curt and the newly returned birdman, Wings. The front door opens and the general leaves without looking back at us again. I'm about to follow him when I catch a glimpse of Dulcis hovering at the rear of the hall, as though unable to decide whether she should leap or hide.

I rush over to her, bypassing her scowling father. "Dulcis, come on. Is this really what you want? Think. Adamo is leaving and taking our friends with him. You have to speak up, girl, or it's over."

"It's already over, Edi," she replies, breaking my heart with her cold gaze. "The fantasy's over. It was a nice dream, but this is real life."

"Real life is what you make it," I tell her, staring back at Alpha. "And you're making it poorer."

"I'm not going out there," Dulcis states, with absolute finality.

Glancing up at Anguis, peering down at us from the balcony,

my face tells him our plan will be a hard one to fulfil. He nods as though reading my mind. I head outside, Alpha's voice echoing after me, "Don't you dare follow her." I don't know to whom he was speaking, but Curt, Wings and Anguis defy him anyway.

We're not alone in our minor rebellion.

As the bears assemble, so do the wolves. Maybe not Yelena's growling minions, but a good half of Alpha's wolves, human and lupine, form two lines either side of the bears as an honour guard for their friends. All the snakes join them, slotting in between, led by Serpen. Holding tightly to his hand trips little Sospa, her face scrunching up with the effort not to cry.

Mama Bear trundles through the snow, trailing Friddie and their strangely subdued cub in her wake. The little monster weaves in and out of his father's stride, sticking to him like glue. Mama sidles over to Wings and I, glancing at her livid prince, but his gaze remains fixed on the route to the valley.

Mama flings her arms around the birdman and myself in a rib crushing group hug and whispers into the gap between our trio, "I've left a list of all the wolves and snakes I've being treating, along with the medicine dosage, in my chalet. The potions and treatments are bottled and labelled in the top cabinet with a red flower on it. I've left you as much as I can." She squeezes even tighter and I let loose a wheeze. "I love you both. Take care of yourselves." She releases the crush before we can reply and bounds back to her family.

Adamo's bear roars into the darkening sky and thus begins the long march to their new home, wherever that may be.

"He's not going to change," I mutter, mainly to myself.

"No," Wings replies. "He has nothing to say to us."

The bears trundle through the snow, heaving their loads. The strain on their faces isn't just for the weight they carry. I would swear they don't want to leave any more than I want them to go. Cubs whimper and snuggle down into blankets or cling to their parents, all joy at bouncing in the snow curtailed. Bears and people glance back at the warm chalets they're leaving behind and their once friends lining the route, wolf pups yowling their goodbyes to their playmates.

As the honour guard lift their heads and howl into the wind, they're joined by myself, Curt, Wings and Anguis, taking up position beside Serpen. I can't trust my voice to howl without breaking so I applaud, every clap an echo of despair. I thought we created a family, but it's all falling apart so fast.

Despite the thunderous noise around him, Adamo's gaze remains locked straight ahead, refusing to acknowledge any of us. A slight movement, caught at the edge of my vision, reveals Dulcis, standing at the mansion's window, watching her lover pass by. For the first time, the honey bear's rigid mask breaks and his mouth turns down with loss. She places a palm on the glass, whether wishing him goodbye or begging for him to turn back, I don't know. His pace slows and he hesitates, fur rustling in the snow laden wind.

Yelena looms up behind her, peering over her granddaughter's shoulder at the sad procession. She says something, but her words are lost behind the glass barrier. Dulcis breaks Adamo's gaze, peering down at her feet before turning away. The corner of Yelena's mouth rises in a tiny smile as her form fills the window.

Adamo turns back, setting his face in stone and the cold, broken future in motion.

"Adamo, no!" screams a little girl, sprinting through the snow. "Don't leave me!"

Serpen catches up with Sospa, swinging her kicking body up into his embrace, murmuring words of comfort. Adamo glances back, but keeps moving forward.

My vision's blurring from freezing tears when a sharp sting pierces my calf. I look down to find that furry monster digging his claws into my leg as though clinging to a tree in terror. He peers up at me with those huge watery eyes and bleats in misery, resting his head on my knee and pleading with me to do something.

"I don't know what to do, Beetus," I tell him, stroking furry ears. It's the first time I've ever used his little boy name.

This tiny scrap gets to my heart more than all the posturing and howling surrounding me. I'm wiping away a stray tear when Mama Bear kneels to disconnect desperate claws and carry away her errant cub.

I can't make myself look away as he peers over Mama's shoulder, still whining and reaching out for me with one tiny paw.

"I love you!" I cry out. My knees crumble and Curt catches me before I collapse into the snow.

CHAPTER 18

Musical Mates

I don't stay down there very long. It's way too cold, for one, and heartbreak's boiling up a head of steam for another. Curt gets an elbow in the eye as I throw myself out of his arms, stagger once, recover and sprint for the mansion. Curt catches up just as I fling open the door with such venom it slams against its hinges and flies straight back in my face, nearly breaking my nose. No-one inside or out laughs.

A swift nostril check reveals no blood, whilst I screech, "Why did you let this happen?" even before my gaze finds Alpha.

"You're not a wolf," says Yelena, gliding into the room like the Grim Reaper, ready to wield her axe. "You don't understand the responsibility of an Alpha."

"Please let me deal with this," the namesake tells her. I locate his voice coming from a chair at the back of the hall. What's he doing hiding in the shadows when we need him most?

"Everything was fine before you got here," I holler at his poisonous auntie. "You came here just so you could ruin everything."

Alpha shoots to his feet and advances on me, eyes glaring. I take an involuntary step back.

"Do not speak to the widow of an Alpha in that disrespectful manner," he growls. "You are not one of us."

I stare at him, tongue sticking to the roof of a bone dry mouth as adrenaline lacerates my veins. His anger slowly morphs into regret as the import of his own words resonates in the room.

"Alpha," Curt begins.

I hold out my palm to stop him intervening. "Then what am I?" I ask his brother. "If I'm not one of you."

"A guest of this pack," he replies, his tone softening. "A very well loved guest."

That's it then. I just lost my family.

"No-one is saying you're not welcome here," Yelena offers in her most conciliatory tone. "Only that you don't understand our ways."

The patronising weight of her words makes me want to vomit.

"Edi."

I didn't realise Dulcis was still here. She looks so sad. I ought to comfort her, but I've nothing left to say. Yelena takes her hand and peers at her father.

"Alpha, with no heir in place and my son gravely ill, you must decide how to proceed to protect both our packs."

"What?" exclaims Curt. "How is this the time…?"

"You were Alpha once," Yelena interrupts, "and, as I recall, said the same thing to my mate, asking for our daughter."

"That was a long time ago," Curt insists, "and everything's changed."

"We're wolves," she snaps. "Nothing ever changes. That's how we survive. This pack needs an heir."

"What about Dulcis?" My own voice surprises me, since my crushed brain switched to mute.

"You make my point entirely," sneers Yelena. "Knowing nothing of our ways. We require an Alpha Alpha."

"A male?" I clarify.

"Of course."

"That's ridiculously out of date," I snarl back. "What are you, medieval?"

"Your words make you a fool," Yelena replies, turning her back on me and facing Dulcis and her father. "You must now see it would be safest to unite our packs in a mating."

"Grandmother, Dulcis already made her wishes clear," Stinky says. "We must respect that."

I didn't even notice the brothers arriving, but he just rose in my estimation.

"That was seasons ago," Yelena replies, scowling at her grandson for getting in the way of her rampant ambition.

"Nevertheless…"

"Fine," Yelena snaps, turning on Dulcis. "If he's not to your liking, and you don't wish to come south, then take Fidus as your mate. He can stay here and become Alpha heir."

Loving grannies are us.

"Wait a moment," Fidus splutters, taken by surprise. "I'm not stomping all over my brother's paws here. Not to mention Dulcis." He gives her a little wave. "Not that I wouldn't be honoured."

"Our father would have something to say about that outcome," growls Primus.

Wow, way to undermine your own brother. I can guess how Fidus feels.

"My daugh…" Alpha stutters, choking on his words. He coughs once and continues, an octave down the scale. "My daughter has her own mind and will be allowed to choose for herself."

"Allowed?" I snarl, the word coming out laden with feminism, before I pass it through my floundering brain cells.

"I don't want to talk about this now," gushes Dulcis and flees up the stairs in a flurry of legs and stress.

Habit has me following. Curt grabs my hand to restrain me, nearly yanking my arm off.

"Leave her alone," Alpha commands, in a tone that brooks no argument.

I don't think I like him anymore. I don't like any of them.

"I want to leave this house," I announce, not meaning to voice my thoughts with such venom.

"As you wish," Alpha replies, far too quickly. He sounds relieved.

"I'll go to Mama Bear's chalet," I decide. It's the only place I can think of, now the lodge has gone. I climb the first two steps, heading upstairs to pack my things. Curt follows. "Are you coming with me?" I ask.

"Of course," he replies, seemingly stunned I'm asking. "I'll always go with you. You know that."

I can only hope it's true. Sorry, I didn't mean that. My heart hurts.

We're entering our soon to be vacated room when we catch wind of Yelena's next manoeuvre.

"As the bears have left," she says, "may our wolves take up the vacant chalets, temporarily of course?"

I turn back and peer over the balcony at our Alpha, whose hesitation is obvious.

"It's very cold for our people in those tents," Yelena adds, ladling on the guilt.

Whilst I know he's left with little choice but to agree, Alpha's simple words hammer the final nail into the coffin of our united family.

"You may. Temporarily."

Curt pulls me back into our room and closes the door. I disappear into his arms, fighting not to howl my heart out.

"Just pack your things," he whispers into my hair before letting me go. "It'll be alright."

'No, it won't' echoes around my mind, but I won't speak those words into being. To voice it is to make it real.

It barely takes a few minutes to randomly stuff my things into a pack, stretching the stitching to breaking point. Most of what mattered to me went up in flames with the lodge and I'm too angry to bother folding clothes neatly. Hoisting my pack over my shoulder like a miserable Father Christmas, I stagger out onto the balcony, only to catch a flash of Yelena disappearing into Dulcis' room. I don't want to abandon my girl, but I'm no longer welcome here.

I clomp down the stairs and stand, staring at the front door as though it'll open on its own. A glance back reveals the empty main hall, memory filling its chairs and tables with fun, laughter and warmth. Curt opens the front door, its traumatised hinges creaking into the silence. Frozen air rushes through the widening gap, jabbing icy knives into my face. I step over the threshold, wondering whether I'll ever feel warm again.

Staggering through the snow under the weight of my accumulated clothes, I'm calculating whether I should have left most of it behind, when Curt swings his pack off his shoulder with a grunt.

"I'll be with you in a moment," he says, offloading his pack into my aching arms. "Can you take this for a bit."

"What? Where are you…?" I grumble, calling out to his back as he limps off. "Fine."

Since he's decided to do a runner, I drag our packs through the snow, managing to dig a couple of short troughs before exhaustion sets in.

"What do I do now?" I ask frosty emptiness. The icicles hanging from abandoned chalets have no reply to offer.

I'm sat on Curt's pack, commiserating with myself, when a familiar swish lets me know what my wolf is up to. Sure enough, there he is, changed into his mangy self, teeth clamped on a rope, dragging a sledge. He trots up beside me, tongue spraying saliva over my feet. The sledge slides into his tail, making him wince.

Those soft yellow eyes draw me in, begging for approval from his Edi, whether or not I'm his mate. My fingers stroke his tufty ears as I lean forward, pressing my forehead to his. The answering whine makes me want to hug him and never let go, but time will not stop, for human or wolf.

I heave our bags into the sledge, like shoving rocks up a hill, and climb in after them, using his pack as a back rest.

"I'm in," I announce, bracing myself.

He slobbers on the rope, getting a good grip before pulling. I still end up on my back, feet in the air.

My wolf weaves in and out of silent chalets, empty homes crying out for the families who once filled their rooms with noise. As we approach the former sanctuary of Mama and Friddie, I glance back down the slope to see an army of wolves creeping through the streets like invading bacteria, slinking into homes not their own.

As am I.

CHAPTER 19

Whimpering Queue

"This is nice."

I suppose Curt feels obliged to say something. He's had time to change and dress, whilst I dumped my pack in the middle of the floor and stared at nothing.

What can I say? I'm tired, frozen and thoroughly cheesed off. He's right though; it is nice, with its neat furniture and embroidered curtains. Unfortunately, the last time I saw it, Mama, Friddie and their fluffy junior filled the space with vibrant love. Now it's just cold and empty.

On the table where I ate my breakfast sits a pristine sheet of paper. A quick look confirms Mama's directive: a list of the sick and the treatments they were receiving when she left. I'll give it to the wolf healers, I suppose. Although I doubt they'll care about the poorly snakes. Maybe I'm being too cynical, too quickly.

"I'll start a fire," Curt says, dropping the remains of his pack on a chair. "It's too cold in here."

Mama and Friddie, being kindly bears, left a basket of chopped wood beside the fire, almost as though they knew I'd need it. It doesn't take my wolf very long to get a roaring fire going in the tiny fireplace.

"Sit," he says, guiding my stiff limbs over to a small loveseat, flickering flames reflecting in its polished wood. "Get yourself warm."

I slowly lower onto one half of the seat without removing my hat or coat. I watch him twitch, but he decides to say nothing. My gaze returns to the hearth, searching for some kind of vision in the flames, but finding only ash.

"Curt?"

"Yes."

I drag my gaze away, not wanting to watch anything else burn. My brain's full of questions, the answers having fled.

"What are we going to do?" I ask him.

"Wait," he replies, giving the fire an unnecessary poke with iron tongs.

"For what? It's only going to get worse with Yelena here."

"I know." He sits beside me with a sigh.

I pull off my hat and let my head collapse onto his shoulder. "I don't feel safe anymore."

"Don't you trust me to protect you?" he asks, draping his arm around me.

"I never needed protection before. Not here."

That's not true, of course. It just seems true. The fire quickly warms the room, but the cold still aches inside my bones. I grasp the edges of Serpen's coat and pull them together, as though trying to shield myself from the truth.

"What if she wants me to go?" There. I've voiced the question which scares me the most. Or maybe it's the answer I fear.

"I won't let you go," Curt growls, his grip tightening to a vice.

"You may not get a choice," I whisper.

"Alpha won't let that happen, or Dulcis."

"I never thought they'd make Adamo go, either."

"Whatever happens, whatever they say, we stay together."

I feel the warmth of chapped lips on my forehead and raise my head to look him in the eyes.

"You'll come with me? If I have to go?"

"I will," he states, emphatically. "Always."

"Where could we go?"

He thinks for a moment. "We'd find the bears."

"Good answer," I comment, a smile cracking my mask of misery.

He kisses the end of my nose.

"Ow. That hurts."

He grins. "That's what you get for slamming doors. Now, are you ever going to take your coat off?"

I'm struggling out of my padding when the sound of scratching fills the room.

"You'll take a lump out of yourself, scratching like that."

"It's the door," he points out, giving me the raised eyebrow treatment.

He's right. Someone's claws are giving the front door a right going over. That'll ruin the paintwork.

"Stop scratching," I announce, opening the door.

Dulcis' sleek wolf howls and pads into the room, shaking the snow off her fur in a shower of freezing drips.

"Lovely. Thanks," I mutter as she heads straight for the fire and plops down in front of it. Her head lays flat on her front paws, huge dark eyes staring at Curt, unblinking.

He takes the unsubtle hint.

"I'll be going for a trot then," he grumbles, eyes rising to heaven as he steps outside.

My fatigued backside is settling back into the loveseat when the door opens a smidgeon and a naked arm chucks his clothes and boots inside. A moment later, a mangy wolf mashes his nose against the window, leaving behind a slobbering tongue and nostril stain, making me laugh. He turns, tail waving back and forth as he limps for the trees.

I'm collecting his clothes when a high pitched whine draws my gaze back to the young wolf. She's peering at me, eyes watery, so I dump his trousers on a chair and grab the loveseat's blanket, holding it out. As soon as teen Dulcis reappears, I swiftly wrap it around her and she curls next to me on the seat.

"Are you alright?" I ask. It's a naff question, but I feel obliged to say something.

She glances up at me through a curtain of wavy hair and the recent cold veneer shatters. I open my arms and she flings herself into my embrace, sobbing her heart out as I gently rock her.

"I'm so sorry, Edi," she gulps out, between howls. "I didn't want you to leave. Please come home."

"It's alright, my girl," I whisper, stroking her hair out of her sodden face. She just cries all the harder.

"I don't want to mate with a wolf."

"I know."

"I want them all to go away."

"I know."

"He left me. I want him to come back."

She's speaking of Adamo, of course. "I know."

"It's all gone wrong."

"I'll make this right," I tell her. "Somehow." In truth, I've no idea how. I need Anguis; he'll have a plan. Maybe.

"You can't make it right," she whimpers, the energy draining from her grief. "It's too late."

"It's never too late for a big bummed woman," I retort. Where did that come from?

Dulcis laughs and gulps.

"You need to get more clothes on," I insist, grabbing my bulging pack and emptying its contents onto the table.

She goes quiet again, sniffing as she shuffles up and rifles through my clothes. Layered up in my oversize sweater and trousers, she reminds me of a toddler playing dress-up.

"Edi?" She glances sideways at me, her gaze sliding down the scale from heartbroken to shifty.

"What?" I'm pretty certain there's something she's not telling me, which is unacceptable. "Out with it, petal."

Her mouth opens and closes, since a firm knock at the door just ended any opportunity for her to confide. Annoyed, I greet my next visitor, who turns out to be the last person I expect to see. Well, with the exception of Yellfire.

Alpha shuffles on the threshold, a leather doggy backpack discarded in the snow behind him. "Erm, can I come in?"

"I don't know, can you?"

Alright, it's a pedantic, irritating response from the grammar police, but he's not sitting highest in my estimation right now.

"Please. I've come to make peace."

Oh for goodness sake. He looks like someone shot his dog. Sorry. I won't bother to rephrase that.

"Erm, I know you might not want to talk to me," he witters, staring at his boots, the soggy laces coiled in the snow. "You're probably not inclined to be my friend at..."

"Oh, give over." I yank him into the biggest hug I can manage, rocking back and forth.

"Come in, Daddy," Dulcis calls, curled up in the loveseat, feet held out to the fire, swamped in my woolly socks. "You're letting the cold in."

"I wondered where you'd gone," he says, marching over to the fire, exercising a one hundred and eighty degree spin and proceeding to warm his backside perilously close to the flames.

"I'll shut the door then," I announce, about to give it a swinging good slam when I catch movement outside in the darkness. "Curt, is that you?" I call, but there's no reply. I don't know why I'm so jumpy; any of the wolves could be out there. Do I feel so unsafe now? I can't shake the feeling someone's watching me.

Telling myself to stop shivering like a coward, I close the door and settle back beside Dulcis.

"I'm sorry," Alpha tells me, eyes huge like a puppy.

"Me too," I reply.

"For what?"

I think about that and you know what...?

"I'm not actually. I wish I'd shouted louder, before the bears left. I should have made you and Adamo talk. And sue me, but I really don't like Auntie Yelena. If that gets me chucked out then so be it. Those bears did not burn down my lodge and didn't deserve to...."

"Who's Sue?"

"What?"

"You said something about Sue?"

"No, it means... never mind about that. What are you going to do now? Apart from throw me out of the mansion."

The wolf huffs, stretching his fingers behind his roasting bum. "Adamo put me in an impossible position and so did you."

"And for your information, Alpha or not, I'm not your bloody guest."

"I know," he shouts. He draws in a huge breath and lets it out with a whistling wheeze like a wilting balloon. "I know," he repeats, more softly. "But I needed you out of there."

"Thanks very much," I growl, crossing my arms like I'm channelling the spirit of Adamo.

"I didn't mean it like that," he says, scowling.

"Then what? And step away from the fire before you smoke your arse. Not that I care."

He feels the ambient temperature of his behind and shuffles forwards.

"The truth is… Edi…" he says, stumbling over the right words.

"Just out with it already."

"I wanted you somewhere safe."

Oh, fabulous. Just what I need to hear.

"So, you think someone's trying to hurt me?" I ask.

"Not if you're with Curt and away from their wolves," he adds.

With perfect theatrical timing, a batch of said wolves choose that exact moment to traipse past the window, on the way to claiming another chalet not their own. Every one of them stops to stare in at us. I make a cross-eyed face at one of Yelena's scruffy guards who lingers too long.

Dulcis' eyebrows meet and she looks pained, as though she's racking her tender brain. "Wouldn't she be safer in the mansion with us? Their wolves are everywhere, now that they've grabbed the bears' homes."

"Yes, I know that now," he mumbles, sweeping Curt's clothes back onto the floor and drooping into the vacated chair. "I'm not doing a very good job as Alpha, am I?"

"I wouldn't say that," I offer.

"You wouldn't say it, but everyone thinks it. Adamo announced to everyone I'd lost control to Yelena. If I lose any more face in front of my pack, I'll be ousted."

"Did she say that to you?"

"Not in those words."

"She said it to me," says Dulcis. Two pairs of eyes dart to her in shock. "Well, pretty much. When she came to my room, she said if I don't take a wolf mate, then Daddy may be in a precarious position. I'm not sure, but I think it was a threat. Maybe."

"No kidding." Did I say that out loud?

"You are not mating with anyone," Alpha growls.

Dulcis and I glance at one another and swiftly look away. Now is so not the time for daddy wake up calls.

He bangs his fist on the table. "I'll have an Alpha fight first."

"I don't think it'd be much of a fight with their Alpha," I point out. "He's half dead already. Oh wait, maybe..."

"I meant the son."

"Stinky?" I ask, incredulous. Father and daughter snigger. "He seems like a fair lad to me. And he doesn't smell at all."

Dulcis snorts. "Not anymore."

"Can we try talking first?" I ask. "Before anyone goes tearing the place up. Maths wasn't my best subject, but I'm pretty certain we're massively outnumbered."

"Not as badly if I get the bears back," Alpha says, making Dulcis and I sit up.

"I'm having a brainwave," I state, a lightbulb dinging to life above my head.

"A what?"

"An idea. Send Anguis or one of his snakes to fetch the bears. The wolves won't notice they're gone. Mind you, what do you do if they do agree to return? We'll be back where we started, facing off for a fight."

"We just need to convince Granny to go home," Dulcis offers. "But don't ask me how. Not now."

"Alpha, I wasn't joking about Stink... Primus," I say. "You should talk to both the sons. They might listen."

"Hmmm. I've a lot to think about," he mutters, scowling. "I'm going to do a walk of the perimeter, like Ursid used to do. It always helped him make decisions. Dulcis, can you take my backpack and clothes home?"

She nods as he heads for the door.

He opens it and glances back. "I will send one of the snakes to fetch the bears though, soon as I'm back. Letting them go was a mistake. It feels wrong without them."

"Curt's also out there," I add. "You might want to find him first."

A few moments later, his massive wolf slinks past the window and lopes into the forest. I still can't shake the notion we're being watched, despite no wolf following on his tail. Alpha's a big wolf, he can take care of himself. Speaking of paranoia, I turn back to Dulcis. "Right. What were you going to tell me before?"

Yet another freaking knock echoes through the chalet. More truthfully, there's a tap tapping like a woodpecker interspersed with knuckles rapping out a musical beat.

"Now what?" I holler, flinging open the door to find a giant eagle, wings spread wide, shielding Anguis from falling snow. The fur coated snake carries a gigantic metal pot perched between two woolly mittens. I peer over their shoulders. "Is there a queue out there?"

Wings drops his bald head and pecks the lid of Anguis' pot with an almighty dong, reminding me of the Hunchback of Notre Dame and his bells.

A swift peek inside the lid gives my eyes a steam bath and wafts a glorious smell up my nose that would wake the dead. It's hot, tasty and it's supper. I wrap my arms around the bird's body and bury my face in his feathers, muffled muttering, "I love you, Wings."

Wings briefly engulfs me in those appendages, delivers a raucous squawk and takes off into the darkening sky. I'm watching him merge with the shadows when a voice in my ear brings my attention back to earth.

"I came to talk to you," Anguis says, pushing the pot into my arms. "And to eat."

"How do you know I haven't already cooked?"

"You're still alive," the cheeky blighter replies, heading inside.

I follow him in, but he's already spotted Dulcis curled up on the loveseat.

"Would you rather I left?" he offers.

Dulcis shakes her head. "No, we need you. But I won't hear plotting against my father."

"Never occurred to me for a moment," Anguis replies, standing even closer to the fire than the wolf did. He sighs with pleasure. "But we do need to do something. Are you both alright?"

"I will be, once I've had some of this," I reply, sliding the pot onto the table.

Our ravenous trio attacks the gifted stew with abandon, leaving very little room for plotting or analysing our situation. Once forks clatter onto empty plates, the debate begins in earnest.

"So, have you got any ideas, Ambassador?" I ask, pushing my chair away from the table's edge.

"Former Ambassador," he replies. "I've been thinking, but none of it seems good. The main problem, to my mind, is that our wolves are outnumbered, especially without the bears."

"That's what Daddy said," Dulcis interjects.

"And I can't quite tell what Yelena might do if he forces them to leave."

I rest my knee against the table, propping myself up. "I don't think their Alpha or his sons would try to oust ours."

"Really? Why not?" Dulcis asks.

"Instinct. The father's too sick and the sons don't seem to want to take over. But you're right," I say, glancing at Anguis, "Yelena is another kettle of fish entirely. And don't ask me why I'd put fish in a kettle. It's a phrase."

Anguis chuckles. "You come from a very odd place."

"You have no idea."

"We still have Serpen," Dulcis points out. "He's more than a match for her."

Anguis leans forward, resting his elbows on the table. "He's not changed into his serpent since we left the castle and I can't help thinking threats would just lead to violence."

I thump my feet onto the table, making the plates rattle. "Although I can't say I'd cry if he swallowed her whole."

"She's also my granny," says Dulcis. "And she loved my mother."

"Yes. Sorry," I agree, suitably chastened. "No eating Granny. Got it."

"No, I mean, maybe I'm the one who should be talking to her. Though if she tries to make me mate with Fidus again, I'll stick this fork somewhere nasty."

I'm snorting with laughter when Anguis adds, "Maybe we should pack up and leave them to it. Go join the bears. Watch Adamo fall over something. I could do with a good laugh."

"Make him dance," I splutter.

"His dancing is almost as bad as your cooking," says Dulcis, and Anguis guffaws.

"I miss that great idiot," Anguis splutters, when he can get the words out.

"I miss Ursid." The old general is so real in my mind's eye, I almost reach out for my bear hug. "How his eyelid used to twitch when Adamo said something weird."

It's then I catch sight of a scowling grey wolf peering through the window, pointedly glaring at the laughing ambassador. Whoops.

"I miss…" Dulcis leans forward, resting her forehead on the table. "Urgh, I feel sick. I'm so stressed with it all."

Anguis pats her on the head. "You sound just like your Auntie Edi these days."

"Anguis, take her home. We all need to rest." I collect the plates and drop them in the kitchen, waving at my wolf en route.

"Edi are you coming back to the mansion?" Dulcis asks.

"Not tonight. I also need to think."

The snake opens the door to find a mangy grey wolf sat in the snow, giving him the squint eye.

"Good evening, Curt."

The wolf rumbles, ominously, as Anguis skirts around him.

"Wings!" I holler into the now night sky, making them all judder. "WINGS!"

A whistling flurry swoops low over the chalet and I disappear into feathery darkness. When the old bird whips his wing off my head, I catch Dulcis collecting her father's clothes and back pack.

"Please fly them both home," I request.

Dulcis and Anguis cringe as his claws tighten around them and they take flight with a whoosh. He swoops low over the chalets, barely missing the roofs, and their cries of horror fade into the distance.

Laughing, I give Curt a beckoning finger.

"Come inside."

My wolf immediately pads into the chalet, claws skittering across the wooden floor, to receive his customary homecoming cuddle.

"You're cold and soggy," I say, giving his sodden ears a rub, being careful to avoid the scar. "Did you see your brother out there?"

He delivers a head shake in the negative. Cuddle received, he's padding over to the fire when his sensitive nose takes a huge sniff and points him in the direction of the kitchen, zeroing in on the pot.

"Sorry. All gone," I warble. "We ate it all. Didn't know when you were coming back."

His face drops like I just put his favourite chew toy in a washing machine. His desperate whine is pitiful.

"Oh stop. Of course I saved you some. You better change."

I've barely finished the word when a naked old bloke flings a blanket around himself and parks his bony backside on the end of the loveseat, nearest the fire. The plate's no sooner in his grasping hands before the stew gets shovelled into his mouth and all talking ceases.

"Thees es gud."

I spoke too soon.

"I assume you're saying, 'This is good,' and your manners are awful."

He proves me right with a gigantic burp, having finished in record time.

"Sorry. Hungry," he apologises, wiping his stew stained mouth with the back of his hand. "You didn't make that. Obviously."

I whip the blanket from around him as payment for that joke, accidentally frisbeeing the plate across the room.

"Cold. Cold. Cold bits. Very cold bits," he sings, sidling up to me and rubbing those bits against me until I wrap the blanket around him once more.

"Randy old wolf," I announce.

"Just as you like me."

He frees his massive biceps from the blanket, because he knows how the sight of them affects me. Hands grasp my face and pull me in for one of his special kisses. The one with the suction of a hoover and the rotating tongue of a whisk. There goes all rational thought for the night.

Sometime and a lot of creaking bones later, we crawl into bed, wishing we had gone rampant on cushioned springs, not the wooden floor in front of the fire. It sounds romantic, but yanking out splinters is no fun. Sorry if that's too much information for the youth amongst us, but you weren't found under a bush by your parents.

Anyway, once safely curled up in his arms, I relay Yelena's veiled threats to his brother and niece.

"No wolf is replacing my brother," Curt growls, drawing me tightly against his hip with a grunt. "The pack would never accept it and I don't think my aunt wants a fight. Wolves don't fight wolves, remember."

"I had hoped our fighting days were over," I murmur into his neck.

His fingers run up and down the flabby folds of skin lurking around my stomach. "It'll be alright, old girl. I promise. I'll think of something... Or that snake will."

"He was barely here. Go to sleep."

"He was laughing. With you."

"Go to sleep, Mange."

"Big Bum?"

"What?"

"About being mates..."

"We're friends; it's fine."

He flips over to stare down at me. "You know I mean..."

"Course I know and you're squashing my breasts."

"Don't try to distract me. They're comfy, by the way. You said you have a ceremony, where you come from?"

"It's called a wedding."

"Which is?"

"We promise to stay true to each other for the rest of our lives, in front of all our family and friends."

"Yep, that's a mating."

"And we exchange rings."

His face drops.

"What's the matter?"

"Can't wear a ring because I, well, wolf claws."

"You can give me one. Ring, I mean."

The puff of his guffaw bounces off my face.

"And you'll need to make mushy vows to me," I add, for the fun of it. Serves him right. "Like how you adore the very snow I walk on."

"Ergh. Yuck."

"Get off my chest."

"Alright. Fine. I'll be as mushy as you want."

He rolls onto his side, allowing me to breathe properly again.

"Your auntie won't like it," I point out.

"I don't care," he growls and plants another of those special kisses.

Sigh.

"Edi?"

"Now what?" I ask, my eyes still closed in delirium.

"How tired are you?"

* * *

He gives it a shot, but it's far too soon for a repeat performance, as you might have guessed. Still, I admire his pluck, and those biceps, as I snuggle down and relax into sleep. It feels odd spending the night in a strange house, with its unfamiliar creaks and groans. The wind gets up, howling and whistling around the rattling chalet in a wintery serenade, but my wolf's chunky arms soon lull me into dreamland.

I'm not sure how long I've been dancing through the summer woodland, like an elf, with a flower adorned wolf on my tail, before a horrendous crash wakes me with a terrifying start. We both fling ourselves out of bed as the rampant hammering on the front door gains speed and intensity.

Grabbing a few clothes to at least be decent, we sprint to a door currently bending on its traumatised hinges.

"Stay back," Curt warns me and, for once, I listen.

Freezing air rushes through the gap as he opens the door to a snow drenched bald eagle and a trembling young woman with red raw fists.

"Daddy's still not back!" Dulcis wails.

CHAPTER 20

Broken

Flakes of white swirl fiercely around our tableau, as though trapped inside a shaken snow globe. I wrap my arms around my girl, trying to draw her into the safety of the chalet, but she digs in her heels, refusing to budge.

"When did he go?" Curt asks, shouting over the howling wind.

"Last night," I answer for her. "Just before Anguis arrived. He said he was doing Ursid's circuit. Couldn't he just be spending a long time thinking?"

"No, he would have come home by now," Curt replies. "The Alpha always returns to the pack, especially in this weather."

"What if he's hurt?" Dulcis wails. "He'll die out there."

Wings squawks and wraps a wing around us both, blessedly blocking out the icy wind. Gathering snowfall barely allows tepid lights from neighbouring chalets to pierce its fierce curtain and blocks the mansion from view entirely.

"Did you tell the pack?" Curt asks.

"Yes. Granny's calling out her best trackers, led by Decipa," Dulcis replies. "Ours too, but…"

"I'm our best tracker," Curt finishes. "We'll change and go together. Edi, you are staying here. You're not following me into this."

"You're right; I'm not," I reply.

He looks stunned at my compliance. "Great. Good. Start a fire. Don't burn down the chalet."

"I didn't cause the last fire and I'm not staying here." The last being flung over my shoulder as I head for my clothes.

"You just said…"

"I said I'm not following you," I repeat, layering up three pairs of woollen socks and two trousers as a prelude to jumper Armageddon. "I'm going with Wings."

The old bird lets out a mild squawk, but he's not wearing his 'scowling eyebrows roast me where I stand' expression, so it looks like he's going along with it.

"You can't fly around in this weather," Curt splutters, disrobing as quickly as I dress.

"Who can't?" I retort, heaving an enormous woollen beanie onto my head as the piece de resistance of arctic attire. "He's done it before."

"He's also got better eyesight than you," Curt points out, stark naked, "so there's no reason for you to go."

I can't argue with that, so I don't bother.

"Let's go, Wings." I hold out my arms in a crucifix and stare straight at the old bird.

He shuffles twice and takes off, straight up, like a Harrier jump jet.

"Don't you dare leave me beh…" I'm hollering when a giant claw looms out of swirling snow and grabs my padded torso, squeezing all the air out of my lungs.

"Edi! Wings! Get back here, now!" Curt bellows. We ignore him. "Frulk you both!" he hollers as his final expletive before giving up.

Two flabbergasted, newly changed wolves stare up at us as Wings opens out and swoops over the chalets. Even given four tyres worth of layers, it's still a freezing ride, the inch of exposed skin on my face stripped of all feeling. I could do with goggles, but it's still easier to spy what's happening from the air. Whilst the mansion remains shrouded in snow, we see a swarm of wolves haring up the mountain, weaving between chalets.

Wings dips his right wing and we swing out, heading for the forest and an aerial loop of Ursid's old perimeter guard duty. Far below, I catch a brief glimpse of Curt's grey wolf, nose to the snow, following his brother's fading scent, before the white curtain closes over him, once more. Barks and yelps filter up from the ground search, but not the howling of a solid lead.

My dangling feet skim the treetops as I strain to see anything through the snow storm. Curt was right: I'm next to useless up here. That great soppy eagle carries a deadweight because he couldn't bear to leave the stupid woman behind.

Wings floats around, straining to glide on the storm wind current as he completes the search circle, bringing us back to where we started. If his eagle eyes can't locate our missing Alpha, then he was never on that route, or veered from it for some reason.

Wings squawks and I look up to see him peering at me with sympathy in his beady eyes. His wings dip and we turn into the full force of the wind, heading back to the chalet. There's nothing I can do out here, except hold Wings back in his search.

"Not yet," I call out, but my words are stolen by the wind and my own conscience.

A sharp pain slices through my temple, as though stabbed by an ice pick, and a memory floods my mind. Something forgotten. Something left behind to burn. Something about to rise from the ashes.

A book.

A magic book, tainted with poisonous mould, that I destroyed, removing any possibility of leaving this world.

A world I may have created in my imagination and brought to life, whose pages told my story before it came into being.

But without the book, without those lines unfolding in ink, I have no connection to the narrative, and even less control.

Or do I?

If this was my story, where would Alpha be?

What would be the twist in the tale, or the set-up duly paid off?

Kallosa. The dying wife and mother. The mystery.

'She ran towards the most dangerous drop at night,' her mother said.

No. Please, no.

"Wings!" I holler. "Take me to the drop, where Kallosa died."

He stares down at me, wide-eyed with shock, and squawks furiously.

"Trust me. Please, Wings. Please. He's there. I know it."

Wings shakes his head, gives a final squawk and turns, gliding away from the forest towards an area of the mountain I've never explored. We fly above the steep slope, its angle providing a fatally panoramic view of the entire mountain range on a clear day. For a brief moment, as we rise above storm clouds, the swirling curtain parts and the pointed turrets of a distant castle rise through the gloom, abandoned to the clutches of its creeping mould. It calls to me as an omen of death.

Wings drops below the clouds and the view falls away, replaced by rock piercing the carpet of snow, all jagged edges and steep angles: a playground for the reckless, or the suicidal.

Why would Alpha come here? I know he did, but my writer brain has yet to discern why. Leave that for later. It only matters that I find him.

A terrifying screech rends the air and I only have time to glance up at Wings before the eagle dives at such speed that rock whistles past in a grey blur.

"Stop!" I scream, as snow coated rock looms up. I'm about to become a red stain in the pristine whiteness. The eagle lands on one claw with a bone juddering thud, flinging me onto a ledge below the infamous drop.

And beside the naked body of a man.

He's lying face down in the snow, seemingly unconscious, blood leaking from a huge gash in the back of his head and freezing into his hair. A glance at the rest of him reveals his leg, lying at an unnatural angle, broken at the knee. I haul off my gloves and press numb fingers to his neck. I think I feel a pulse at his jugular, but it's weak and thready. His skin is ice cold and already turning blue at his fingers and toes. How long has he been out here? I've no idea what I'm doing, but he's going to die if he stays like this for much longer.

My freezing fingers struggle with buttons as I fight to remove my outer coat, desperation making me clumsy. I wrap it around his body as best I can, fighting to stretch the fabric over his larger frame. I slip my hat onto his head, cover his blue fingers with one pair of gloves and haul off my boots to relinquish woollen socks. His broken knee grinds horribly as I heave them over his feet and lower legs, but Alpha neither moves nor groans.

"Hold on, Alpha," I yell into his ear. "Don't give up. Please. Think of Dulcis. She needs you. Don't you dare leave her alone. She can't lose both parents out here." I cry out to Wings, hollering over the howling wind. "We have to go, now!"

We're airborne in a flash, swooping over the terrifying drop and falling down, down, towards the town, leaving my abandoned boots teetering on the ledge. I stare at Alpha, draped in Wings' other claw, eyes closed, so pale, so vulnerable.

So… broken.

CHAPTER 21

Flying Accusations

The storm rages with such force that Wings clips the roof of the mansion in his haste to bring us in to land. The world spirals in a white blur and my stomach spins up my throat in a burn of nearly digested stew. Wings opens his claw and I plummet into a cushioning snow drift up against the wall, spitting and honking snow out of my lungs. He squawks as he regains flight control, still holding Alpha clear of the jarring ground.

Not waiting for him to land, I stagger over the mansion's threshold in my bare feet, the door wrenched out of my grasp by the sheer force of the wind.

"Help!" I rasp, my raw throat still defrosting. "Help us. We need a healer. NOW."

A naked old eagleman follows me inside, buckling under the weight of his unconscious pup, slung over his shoulder. He lurches over to the fire as I heave shut the door, mercifully reducing the wind's ominous shrieking and freezing gusts. As though in faint echo, a door opens and quietly closes in the long hallway above.

"What is it?" a high-pitched, soft feminine voice asks.

Audira, whose face I've not seen since her mate was taken ill, peers down at me over the balcony. Her eyes widen as she takes in the tableau.

"Please help him," I cry. "It's Alpha. He's injured and frozen."

She looks me in the eyes, turns her back and glides away.

I'm about to scream in rage and despair, when she opens her bedroom door and calls out, "Healers, I need you. Hurry. Downstairs, now." As two men rush past her, she adds, "Their Alpha is injured. I'm going to see what can be done."

A soft grunt in reply reveals she was speaking to her ailing husband. Audira hurries downstairs, coming to stand beside me and gently pushing on my arm, wanting me to give the healers room.

"Let them do their work," she says. "Wings, clothe yourself. This may be a long night."

"No." I intervene, grabbing his bare arm. "Fetch Curt and Dulcis. Please."

Wings doesn't reply, except to grasp my cold fingers before flinging open the door. He morphs into his eagle as he passes through the gap in a flurry of feathers. His wild take off scrapes the heads of Anguis and Serpen, arriving on the doorstep.

"We saw you land." Anguis rushes over, flinging his fur coat around my shoulders and leaving his once king to close the door behind them. "How is he? Where did you find him?"

"He was at The Drop, where Dulcis' mother died," I croak, welcoming the coat's comforting bulk, despite the roaring fire. "He must have fallen. Hit his head. I don't know. His leg's broken and he was so cold, Anguis."

"You found him like this? Human?"

"Yes."

"Not a wolf?"

"No. I just said… what are you getting at?"

"This isn't the time for this discussion," Serpen interrupts, glancing at Audira. He asks one of the healers, "What can we do?"

"Let me do my job," the wolf snaps at him.

"Hot water," his colleague replies, looking up at us with more sympathy. "He's far too cold and we have to warm him. We'll need hot water in a bath?"

"Right," says Audira, clapping her hands, twice. Wolves lurking in the background snap to attention. "Do as he said," she orders and they rush off.

"Thank you," I tell her.

She gives me a swift smile before her worried gaze returns to Alpha.

"The head wound will need stitching," Snarky Healer Number One says, "and his knee and lower leg setting. But I'm most concerned about how cold he is and that he's still unconscious."

"Let's get him upstairs to the bath," Marginally Nicer Healer Two adds. "Carefully."

Anguis gives Healer One a none too gentle shove to shift him out of the way and slips his arms beneath Alpha. With barely a strain showing on his graceful frame, the snake carries his friend upstairs, with such precise gentleness, it's as though he's transporting the treasure of the universe. Tears fill my wind burned eyes as I follow him.

Audira's flood of servants are already pouring steaming water into Alpha's bath and testing the temperature with bony elbows. I wonder how they got here that fast, but then, the kitchen always has water on the go, especially in emergencies. They've always reminded me of my old nan, putting the kettle on for tea whenever anyone shed a tear.

As Anguis slowly lowers Alpha's limp body into the water, I hear scraping coming along the hallway and peep out, to see Big Wolf clinging to the banister on one side and a servant on the other as he drags himself along. He looks at death's door, but still not as pale as my poor Alpha.

"How is he?" he whispers.

Audira's face briefly flexes with grief, but she's a true Alpha Mate and swiftly covers her own fears. "They're trying to warm him, but he's unconscious from a head wound and has broken his leg."

"Is it bad?" he asks.

Healer Two replies, "Yes, My Alpha. Very bad, I'm afraid. If we don't wake him soon…"

I desperately want to drop where I stand. All my strength leaves with the speaking of those words, as though he's enacting a curse.

Stop it, Edi. Alpha's not dead and, until he is, I have to fight.

And if he…

If he…

Curt and Dulcis will need me.

"Come back to bed, my love," Audira tells her Big Wolf Mate, taking the place of the servant beneath his shoulder. "They'll do the best they can for him."

As they limp back to their room, I hear him whisper to her, "Stay with them. Let me know what's happening."

She returns to my wilting side, glancing down at my bare feet. A muffled shriek and the flapping of giant wings comes from the roof. Two wolf barks later, the front door bangs and two pairs of human feet pound up the stairs, one with a clear limp.

"Fetch clothes," Audira tells her servants, as a naked Dulcis barrels into the room, her mangy uncle close on her heels. "And shoes for Edi."

"Daddy!" Dulcis screams, plunging her arms into the bathwater with a terminal splash. Curt catches her around the waist, lifting her clear. "Let me go," she hollers, her hand slapping the water, reaching for her father.

My shocked paralysis finally breaks and I fling Anguis' fur coat around her shaking body, heaving her into my embrace.

"What's happened to him?" Curt demands, wearing his most frightening scowl.

Healer One, growing ever more snarky, repeats himself, yet again, unmoved by the look of horror marring Dulcis' beautiful features.

"No, Daddy. Please. Please wake up."

Audira's servants arrive with the clothes and shoes. Dulcis pushes me away, tearing into her clothes as though they're to blame for her father's injuries.

I'm gratefully pushing numb feet into borrowed shoes, when a strong hand grips my elbow and I glance back to see a clothed Wings standing behind me. I lean against him, thankful for the support as his arm encircles my shoulders. I reach up to grasp his hand, clutching at his strength, whilst the healers test Alpha's temperature, stitch the head wound and set his knee. He's still unconscious, eyes tight shut against the pleas of his daughter and the pain of his injuries.

The eerie, echoing yowls of hundreds of wolves seep into the room, growing ever louder, seemingly coming from every direction and converging on the mansion. They'll be here in moments.

Anguis steps towards us, turning his back to the room. "I'll greet them at the door," he announces, taking my hand and guiding me into the hallway. He drops his voice to a whisper. "Did anyone else know Alpha planned to recover the bears?"

I shake my head. "Just us... Although the door was open when he left. He could have been overheard."

He nods, as though getting the answer he expected, before heading downstairs, leaving questions thundering inside my brain. I don't want the answers. They might be the end of me.

I peer over the balcony as raucous howls summon a legion of servants to the door, laden down with clothes. Decipa, Stinky and Fidus all finish robing before Yellfire, but they wait, fidgeting, for her seal of approval to move. I glance at Audira, whose face seems set in stone as she peers down at her family.

"Lady Yelena, perhaps I could..." Anguis begins.

"What's going on, Eagle?" Yelena grinds out, staring up at Wings, ignoring the ambassador. "You just flew off. I don't appreciate your leaving us out there."

"It was more important to bring the family here, before wasting time explaining to you," Wings snaps.

"You forget to whom you speak," she bellows, sweeping upstairs, Anguis on her tail.

A crowd of wolves creep after her, snarling in defence of their Lady. As I feared, this situation is rapidly deteriorating. Out of the corner of my eye, I catch a wide-eyed Audira briefly shaking her head at her eldest son.

"Guards, stay downstairs," Stinky orders.

They snarl and snap their teeth in response. Yelena turns to stare him down, but he holds his ground, gaze for gaze. Good for him.

"Edi, what's happening?" Fidus asks, sliding past his brother and taking the stairs two at a time with that loping stride, shoving the wolves out of his way.

"My father fell," Dulcis hollers from inside the room. "I need Mama."

"Of course, you do," Yelena replies, her gravel laden voice suddenly softening. She pushes past me, ramming my spine into the door jamb. "I know your mother's gone, but Granny's here." She's about to stroke Dulcis' forehead when her granddaughter jerks clear of her grasp and leans towards her floating father.

"She's referring to Mama Bear," I point out, rubbing my bruised back. "The healer you sent away, who might have been able to help him."

"I'm quite capable of treating any wolf injuries," snarls Healer One.

"Shut your maw," Yelena spits at him.

He wilts away from that extraordinary vote of confidence. I catch Healer Two smirking to himself. Nice lot, these wolves.

"Did *you* find him?" she demands, looming up at Wings.

"I flew him back," he replies.

"With those injuries?"

"He was freezing to death," I interject. "Wings saved his life."

"What have you got to do with this? You left this house."

"She's the one who found him," Wings blurts out, then peers at me as though caught stealing.

"Where?" Yellfire demands.

It's about now the reason for Wings' guilty expression starts to dawn on me. There's no point in lying.

"On a ledge. Under The Drop," I reply, catching Curt's look of concern as he shuffles closer to me.

"The what?"

"The Drop… where…"

"Where my daughter died," Yelena finishes. She hauls in a huge breath, as though she's about to detonate. "How did you know where to find him?"

"A hunch," I mutter.

"A hunch? A hunch?" she repeats, rising in volume. "You had a hunch that he'd go to the one place he's banned his wolves from visiting because of the danger?"

Any response to that will bring up magic books and I doubt this is the time.

"Did you send him there?" Yelena gets right up in my face and, with my back to the wall, I've nowhere to go. "Did you try to kill him?"

"You're more likely to kill him than I am," I yell back at her.

"Did you kill my daughter too?"

"What? That was years ago. I wasn't even here then."

"So you say, but you're old enough to have been here."

"So are you. I never met your daughter and I love Alpha. Like a brother," I finish, before anyone leaps to more false conclusions.

"She didn't send him anywhere," Dulcis insists. "I was with her tonight. Unless you think I'd hurt my father."

Stinky rocks up with, "Not everyone loves their father."

Yelena casts a withering look at him, before turning back to Dulcis. "She was with you all night?"

"Dulcis, or me," Curt says, shoving his large bicep between me and his auntie. "Please step back. Edi didn't do this."

Yelena moves back, all of an inch. "*Edi* hasn't answered my question. How did she know where he was?"

They all stare at me, eyes full of confusion, questions... and suspicion. Even Curt and he knows better.

Here goes. I'm about to commit literary suicide.

"A year ago, I was given a magic book for secret..." Nope, don't need that bit of info. "It brought me here from my own world. I discovered that its pages were filling with my story on its own. After I got rid of the book, it occurred to me that I might have been creating my own story, from my imagination. If I'm still doing that now, as in writing this one, with you all as characters, the most likely place for Alpha to be found would be the one with all the unanswered questions: The Drop, where... well, you know."

As I say it, we all realise it makes no sense. Fabulous.

The Southern mob stare at me like I've gone bonkers. The room is so quiet, you can hear the shutters rattling in the window frame.

Curt coughs. "Erm, I know how it sounds, but..."

"She's entirely insane," Yelena pronounces. "This is what you choose to live with?"

"It's a challenge," Curt replies, with the most inappropriate display of levity I've ever heard.

"Get her out of here. Mad woman. Get her away from the Alpha. She could attack anyone in her insanity."

"Oh, give it a rest," I tell her. "I'm no more mad than you are homicidal."

And I just joined Wings and Curt in the 'not the best thing to say' club.

"Get her out," Yellfire hollers, followed by the sound of multiple sets of claws hammering up the stairs.

"We're leaving," says Wings, pretty much launching me off my feet and sweeping out the door.

"You stay with her," I call to Curt, pointing at Dulcis, as the door slams shut behind us.

"And the snakes," Yelena hollers.

The door opens again and Anguis and Serpen step through under their own steam, just before the door slams shut, scraping the former king's posterior. Abandoned on the balcony, the four of us turn, to find a sea of snarling wolves packing the staircase and hallway. The snakes probably aren't scared, given their DNA, but I certainly am.

"I'm not mad," I stutter. "The book. It was real, you know. Curt saw it and the wolves have a legend about it. You know that, Wings."

"Yes," the eagleman replies, eyes fixed on rows of slavering teeth. "Legend."

"What did you do with it?" Serpen asks, shuffling to the front of our little group and braving the first step. "Excuse me, please."

"I threw it on the fire," I reply, inserting myself between Serpen and Wings, leaving Anguis to bring up the rear.

"Why?"

"Er, it had mould... and I didn't want it to take me home."

"Interesting," Serpen announces, moving his hands in the sea of wolves as though doing the breaststroke. "Excuse me, please."

"No, I will not allow this." That's Curt's muffled voice coming from the bedroom.

"Listen very carefully, Curtus," Yelena replies, but I can't hear what follows.

Drool dribbles from a stinking wolf maw, forming a little wet pile on my shoulder as I squeeze past. I've not seen a trembling epiglottis this close since peering in the dentist's tiny mirror.

We've thrust our way to the bottom of the stairs, when the door opens and Yelena sweeps onto the balcony, Audira, Stinky and Fidus standing behind her.

She places both hands on the banister and stares down her imperious nose. "The Alpha remains unconscious and it is not known whether he will waken or recover from his injuries. The Alpha Daughter is too young to take responsibility and our own Alpha of Alphas is currently ill. In this circumstance, his eldest son, the Alpha Alpha, will temporarily take over leadership of both packs, under the guidance of myself as senior wolf."

Stinky's horrified face tells me he wasn't expecting that speech. The wolves turn up their heads and howl, so loudly, my ears ring with the noise. The sudden silence is almost as shocking. Every head, bar our little band of rebels, bows low, though I can't tell to whom they deliver their obeisance, Stinky or his granny.

"No!" I holler. "Curt leads here. If Alpha's hurt, his brother leads this pack."

I feel Anguis' arms trying to shield me as all the snarling teeth turn towards their one, unbending enemy.

"Curtus," Yelena cries out, her eyes never leaving mine. "What say you?"

My Curt, my Mangy Wolf, strides onto the balcony, eyes blazing with rage, yet defeat written across his face.

And before my horrified gaze…

He bows before her.

I punch my way through the crowd of wolves and out into the snow.

CHAPTER 22

I Don't Care About The Frulking Wolf Way

He must have launched himself down the stairs because that idiot wolf catches up with me as I stomp through the snow in a fit of rage, decorated with drool, bits of wolf hair and the odd punctured hole in my jumper.

"Edi. Edi, stop," he pants, grabbing my arm.

Inertia spins me round and smacks my already bruised nose against his shoulder.

"Ow. Get off me," I screech, yanking my arm free. "You just let them take your pack. My family. Your frulking family. What's the matter with you? You scared? Me too, but I'd never give up on my people like that."

"You think I'm a coward?" he replies, voice ominously low, eyes raging a warning.

I don't care.

"You were their Alpha once."

"Once," he bellows, and I feel the force of the word spraying into my face. "Once. That's the point. The pack won't follow me as their Alpha. They can't. I gave up that right when I handed it over to my brother. There's never any going back on that."

"Why not?" I shout. "That's stupid. You know they'd follow you. I've seen them follow you."

"Only with my brother as Alpha."

"He's not dead," I holler.

"But he can't lead. And I can't lead in his place. It's not the wolf way."

A red mist drops in front of my eyes. The bears are gone. Alpha's gone. Now this.

"I don't care about the frulking wolf way. You can't let this happen. You're responsible for them all. For me, damn you."

"Listen to me, for once," he snarls, his face flushing.

"No. This time I'm not listening."

He hauls me into his arms and whispers in my ear, "If I don't agree, I'll be removed by weight of numbers anyway. If my pack follows me and we fight, we lose. And you're not a wolf. Understand?"

I do. I'm under threat.

"What if this is what she planned all along? What if she tried to kill us in that fire and didn't know her grandsons were there? What if she just tried to kill Alpha?"

His whole body stiffens, eyes darting around the vicinity. "Keep your voice down…"

"Someone has to stop her."

"You have my sympathy," interjects a calm voice. I glare at Anguis as he steps between us. "And my support, but this isn't the place. Not here. Edi, you need to come with me. Now."

I glance over his shoulder. Hundreds of pairs of eyes blink in the darkness and light reflects off the snow, glinting on white teeth. I rotate. Wolves surround me in a giant circle, some in their human form, but all creeping ever closer and glaring straight at me, teeth gnashing as though I'm traitorous supper. Two steps inside of the circle pads a wolf I know well, but haven't seen recently. Where has she been hiding, the messenger for the Alpha of Alphas?

"He's right," says Wings, hurtling up to the little group.

"Edi, get between us." Anguis shoves me behind him as Serpen and Wings step up to cover my back. "Send them away, Decipa," he calls out, glaring at her. She growls, saliva dripping from her teeth. "Don't come any closer, any of you. Believe me, none should wish to be the first to face a snake."

"She doesn't need you to protect her," Curt snarls, his face turning an unholy shade of puce.

"Oh, I think she does," Anguis throws back at him. "You just told us all no wolf is going to listen to you. Pardon me if they might find myself and my king a little more convincing."

"You're making this worse," my mangy wolf growls.

"How can it be worse?" I ask, hiding between the two snakes and the eagle.

"I've always taken care of you," Curt insists, peering at me over Anguis' shoulder.

"That's great. But I think I'm going with them," I decide. "Just for now."

Curt's face drops and I immediately rethink that decision. Actually, he looks like he's about to... He turns his back on Anguis and vomits what's left of that stew into the snow with a gut wrenching bleurgh.

"Lovely," I mutter. "Are you alright?"

"No, I'm frulking not," he replies, still gagging.

I step around Anguis, to his surprise, and rub Curt on the back. "You're getting yourself in a tiz. Calm down."

"What have you been eating?" Wings asks, scowling at me.

"Just the stew you brought," I snap.

"I don't feel so well," Curt whimpers.

"Nor I," says Serpen, glancing over his shoulder at us. "Can we get inside, please? Anywhere with a door. Nobody's safe here. Least of all my snakes. Warn these wolves to stop, before I have to change and scare everyone."

"Curt," I whisper in his ear. "I'm scared, my wolf. Please."

"Sospa?" Serpen says, shock in his voice. He swiftly gets it under control, forcing calm into his next words. "Go inside, please. Take the children with you."

Curt and I peer behind us, spotting a gaggle of snake children, huddling together near one of the larger chalets. Sospa's head is on a swivel, staring at the ring of snarling wolves creeping through the snow. She's never seen them do this before, having spent her time in the castle and a year in the new town being cared for by her furry lupine friends. The trembling fear in her eyes finally sets Curt off.

"Go back," he bellows, his order punctuated with another retch. "Decipa, Lady Yelena has not commanded you to do this."

Wonderful. Now he's using Yellfire's name. It seems to be working though, since they're holding position. For now.

"Lady Yelena rules now?" a voice calls out. It's one of Alpha's men, stunned by the scene in his once peaceful little town. "Is our Alpha dead?"

"No, of course not," Curt yells. "He's injured and the Southern Alpha Alpha leads temporarily... with his grandmother."

"Sospa?"

That's Serpen again. I glance back at the children, who are all still frozen in place. All except the king's niece. There's an empty patch of ice where she stood a moment ago. I scan the vicinity.

"I can't see her," I call back to Serpen.

He runs over to the children, leaving Anguis to yank me to his side. Curt glares, but says nothing.

"Did she go inside your house?" the snake king asks, dropping to one knee in front of a terrified small boy. The tiny snake shakes his head. "Where did she go? Where?" Serpen's eyes dart from one child to another, pleading for an answer.

A skinny arm, swamped in an oversized coat, rises up in his eyeline and he follows the girl's pointing finger to the rear of the mansion.

"Oh no," Wings murmurs, his eyes widening.

What's she up to? That feisty little snake doesn't know when to give in. Much like me.

The answer comes with a chilling wolf howl, emanating from the mansion. Self preservation screams at me to run in the opposite direction, but instinct tells me a little girl is in terrible trouble and needs her Auntie Edi. I take off at a sprint, jumping the gun on everyone else. They've all caught up by the time I barrel through the mansion's rear door, heaving in breath and coughing it out again.

"Sospa," I wheeze as Serpen dashes past, yelling his niece's name at far greater volume.

A child's high pitched scream lacerates my ears and sends my heartrate through the ceiling.

"The study," Curt yells, his wolf hearing locating the source of the scream.

I sprint after Serpen, ignoring Curt and Anguis both hollering at me to wait.

Not a chance.

The door to that tiny study, where Sospa hid a mesmerised Wings, stands wide open, a huge wolf backside poking through the gap into the hallway, the tail lashing back and forth from wall to ceiling. The shattering racket coming from inside the room sounds like the furniture giving way under attack.

Serpen drops to his hands and knees, crawling under the wolf, and I immediately follow him. No sooner do my creaky knees reach floor level than I spot Sospa cowering under the desk, tears of terror pouring down her face as wolf teeth shred the wooden shelter above her.

"Uncle!" she screams as he scrambles towards her, wolf limbs crashing around him, saliva spraying the room. He punches the rabid wolf in the throat and her head shoots up, gagging and choking, giving him a moment to reach the little girl. Shoving her further under the desk, he plasters himself across the gap, directly in front of her.

"Grandmother, stop!" yells a voice from the corridor. "She's just a child."

Looking back, I catch a glimpse of Fidus, desperately heaving on Yelena's tail, but she's not listening to anyone. Still choking from the punch, she turns a homicidal gaze on Serpen and I have no doubt she's about to rip his head off.

His sapphire eyes focus on the wolf and his face goes taught. I've seen him try this on me, unsuccessfully as it turned out. He's attempting to mesmerise her. Unfortunately, she's way ahead of him and it just sends her into a greater rage. Keeping her gaze from his, she claws and tears, her body whipping back and forth in a frenzy. Wood snaps, windows shatter and books shred in a shower of torn paper.

I know why he does it. He has little choice, if he's going to save their lives. But, deep inside, I understand there's no going back from this moment. Here is where the dream of my found family ends.

His faces rips open, shedding his human skin, and the Serpent arises, pouring blood across the floor. Those horrendous ridges scrape the ceiling, the gigantic tail smashing through the tattered window frame and collapsing part of the log wall. His mouth opens so wide it blocks out the room, those fangs glistening as they whip down and he swallows Yelena's head and half her body.

"No!" someone yells. No idea who, since I'm too shocked to move.

"Serpen, don't eat her!" Anguis hollers, stomping on my hand as he forces himself into the room.

The gigantic serpent slithers backwards, straight out the crumbling window and landing in the snow with a plop, Yelena's furry back legs kicking outside his closed mouth.

Anguis launches himself through the gap and I follow, grunting and heaving with far less grace, leaving a shrieking mob behind us. Unfortunately, we're now outside, in full view of a wide-eyed wolf battalion, currently too stunned to attack anyone.

Thumps and bumps shift and ripple the serpent's scales, accompanied by muffled snarling and howling. She's putting up a fight in there, but my money's on him.

"Serpen, don't," Anguis cries. "My king. Please put her down. She can't hurt Sospa now."

Serpen shakes his head and the wolf tail and legs swing from side to side. I think the fight's beginning to leach out of her as her kicks grow less manic.

"Don't change," Wings hollers at Anguis, stumbling through the hole in the wall.

"I'll have to change," Anguis says, glancing at me. I grab his arm as Fidus leads the others outside.

"No, Anguis. It'll get worse. Let me try."

"Serpen. King," I shout, shuffling as close as I dare without being crushed. "You are not a killer. Don't let her make you one. Please."

The serpent peers down at me.

"You don't want to do this. Please. You know me. Please."

His head gradually lowers until the toes on Yelena's back paws just touch the snow. I find his eyes, eyes that can't mesmerise an unchanging human.

"Spit her out now, please," I beg, holding his gaze, "There's a good snake."

A glint of humour shines back at me and he turns his head away. Suction followed by an almighty bleurgh heralds the return of the swallowed wolf, covered in green glop, her slimy backside bouncing across the snow.

"She doesn't look happy," I mutter.

Yelena's eyes uncross and she shakes her head, spraying her wolf mob with goo. The rising snarl matches the homicidal rage, until she suddenly changes into her human form, clamping down on her feelings as an eerie calm sweeps over her features. Personally, I find the latter more frightening than the wolf.

"So, just like your father, after all," she says, staring above the serpent's ridges, avoiding his eyes.

Her servants sprint across the snow, wiping the spit from her hair as she dons a huge fur coat. The circle has spread until every wolf now stands in the snow, those I know as family and the interlopers. They wait, shoulder to shoulder, tail to tail, glaring at the wavering serpent. The snakes huddle together, horrified by the turn of events and the resurgence of their serpent king.

"Uncle," Sospa yells, haring across the snow.

The serpent shrinks, fangs and scales dissolving into flesh as my friend returns. Anguis wraps his long jacket around the shivering, naked king. If he keeps giving his clothes away, he'll be naked himself. I catch Sospa on her way past and lift her into my arms.

"He's fine," I tell her. "Look. He's back again."

Wings dashes over and throws both arms around us. "Stay still with Uncle Wings," he says, grip tightening.

Anguis pleads with Yelena. "The king was afraid for his niece. You were violent and left him no choice, but to protect her. She's just a child."

"That *child* tried to take my mind," Yelena replies, "and when I fought her mind trick, she refused to let go until I became wolf."

I stare at Sospa, but she hides her head in my shoulder, hoping to disappear, like the little girl she is. Princess, heir to the defunct Snake Empire and feisty to a fault, but a girl nonetheless. A girl unable to fight a full grown wolf.

"She was wrong," Serpen begins, his voice trembling from the change, "and will be punished. She should not have…"

"Had I been of a lesser mind, she would have taken my will from me," Yelena continues. "I will not be a slave to anyone. Least of all a snake. Nor will I allow my wolves to be endangered."

I know what's coming. It's inevitable. Yet I can't help but fight.

"She's a child and thinks like a child," I insist. "You won't be in any danger from her again. She can stay with me."

"And the so called king?" Yelena replies, her gaze flicking to Serpen and away.

"This is my fault." Serpen staggers as he takes a step towards her. The wolves rumble and growl an ominous backdrop. All of them, even ours. "I take responsibility."

"You tried to reach my mind," she says, her voice building in volume and tempo, "and when you couldn't, you changed into that monster." She rotates, her arms rising, playing to the gallery. "This was ever the snake way. Steal our freedom and enslave our wolves. No more." She spins on her heel and points at Serpen. "I want you gone. I demand you leave this pack. Take your snakes and leave, unless you plan to fight."

Yelena's people and her wolves holler and howl in response. My wolf friends don't join the cacophony, but neither do they object. Only one man moves: Curt paces through the snow until he joins Wings and I, his hand gently stroking Sospa's hair.

"Don't let this happen," I whisper.

"It already has," he replies, eyes full of sadness. "They're not safe here anymore."

"We will not fight," Serpen tells the wolf witch. "We will leave, as you wish. May we have until morning to pack?"

"You have 'til sunrise to be out of here," Yelena snaps. "All of you."

Her wolves howl in agreement, filling the air with hatred. Alpha's wolves remain silent, avoiding the gaze of their once friends. The snakes glance at one another, hands clasping hands in comfort, stunned by the speed of their eviction.

Sospa's head pops up from my shoulder and her arms fly around my neck in a stranglehold. "No. We can't go. I won't leave Auntie Edi, or Uncle Wings."

I hear Curt draw in a ragged breath. He knows, as do I, what must follow.

"No *child,* you won't need to leave them, for they're going with you," Yelena yells, triumph oozing through every goo coated pore. "This pack is for wolves and only wolves. The human and the eagle must leave and go back to their own kind."

"Aunt, please," Curt cries out, rushing towards her. He's stopped by six snarling wolves leaping into his path. "Edi's our friend. Wings has been here since before I was a cub. This is their home."

"Not anymore," she replies and smiles at him. "They don't belong with our wolves, Curtus. You know that."

"She's my... love," he says, as though he can't bring himself to call me his mate.

"You've always known it would come to this," Yelena says, hammering home her victory. "You're just hurting the woman."

I want to hate her, but I'm too tired. It seems I don't have a family after all.

Curt stares at his wolves. They were his wolves, once. Then they were Alpha's. Now they just hang their heads.

"Aren't you going to say anything?" I yell at them. "No-one?"

Not an eye meets mine. The wind howls in the silence, singing a final lament for a lost dream.

Clutching Sospa in my arms, I turn my back on them all.

CHAPTER 23

Let Me Go

Just keep walking. One foot after another, pushing through the snow, leaning against the wind, sheltering the child, until my legs and arms scream in agony, my broken heart bleeding inside my chest. Curt, Serpen, Anguis and Wings crowd around me, hands waving, all speaking at once as I keep climbing the slope. I can see their mouths moving, but I can't hear the words over the throbbing heartbeat filling my ears.

Whump, whump. Whump, whump.

"That's enough," someone says. I don't know who.

Curt shoves a hand beneath my knees, wanting to carry me, but I pull away from him, staggering into Anguis. Sospa's head emerges from beneath my chin, whimpering, snowflakes catching in her hair. She would look magical, if I wasn't dying inside.

"I'll take her," Anguis yells at Curt, but my eyes don't find him in the chaos.

"I can do it," the wolf hollers back.

I don't want either of you. Just leave me be. I want to walk. To get away from it all.

My right knee gives way and I collapse into the snow, the child tumbling from my arms with a scream. I scramble on my hands and knees, desperately reaching for her, but Serpen kneels beside me and gathers her up.

"I have her," he says, one hand gripping my wrist. "It's fine. I have her."

He lets go and both my hands fall onto my knees, burdened by their own weight. I don't think I can move. Not anymore. He rises, leaving me staring at his feet, boots half buried in the snow.

Anguis' face takes their place as he kneels in front of me, cupping his hands around my face. "It's going to be alright, Edi," he says, and I look up into those emerald eyes. "We'll be together. You're not alone. Never alone."

Curt shoves him so hard, he tips sideways, landing on his shoulder, anger flashing in his eyes.

"No more fighting," I scream, shredding my lungs and throat. My whole body starts to spasm and I can't make it stop.

"Go and pack. It'll be sunrise soon," Wings says to Serpen. "Get your people ready."

Anguis gracefully rises, his gaze still spearing the manwolf, even though the question is aimed at the eagle. "You're coming with us?"

"Yes. For now," Wings replies, nodding at me. "She needs shelter."

"She'll have it," Anguis says, finally breaking eyelock with Curt. "I promise you."

"We'll meet you at the mansion," Wings tells him.

"Sospa?" I cry out in fear, suddenly understanding she's no longer in my arms.

"I'm alright, Auntie Edi," she calls, clinging to her uncle.

"Go," Wings tells them. "I'll deal with her."

I barely feel Curt place an arm around me and pull me against his chest, or the melting snow soaking through my trousers, or the claws of a giant eagle as he gently shuffles me into his grip. The land falls away as I rise upward, body limp, my town disappearing into the night's shroud. Held tightly in the other claw, Curt stares at me, willing me to fight, but I haven't the energy to give him what he needs.

It takes barely a moment for the wind to carry my eagle to Mama Bear's chalet, where he places his passengers and lets loose a plaintiff squawk, before taking off in a flurry of feathers.

"Don't forget your clothes," I murmur, if only to myself.

Curt turns my body away from the surrounding houses, ushering me inside the chalet.

"I'll light the fire," he says.

"No point." I stare at the barely cold ashes, wondering how it could have all burnt so very fast. "Just give me enough light to pack."

It won't take long. I lost most of my things in the lodge fire and the little I brought from the mansion will return to those discarded packs.

"But you're too cold." He rubs my arms, eyes begging me to respond.

"It won't help," I reply. "I have to go now."

"We. We have to go." He heaves me into a hug, his grip so tight I can barely breathe, tucking my head beneath his chin and rocking me back and forth, much as I did Sospa. "It'll be alright. We'll go with the snakes, for now. If that's what you want. Until we can find the bears, at least. I'll track them. I'll find Adamo and Ursid. We'll be fine with them."

"I'm leaving with Anguis," I tell him, not to hurt him or make him jealous, but because I have no choice.

"Yes, I said I agree," Curt insists, that grip tightening even further as his wonderful bicep presses against my neck. "The snakes, for now. Then, then the bears." He stutters as the acid truth begins to eat through his wall of fantasy. "We'll be fine. We'll find somewhere warm and I'll build you a new lodge. Just as you want it. With that carving of the ram, or the gumwhat, if you want."

A pain-filled laugh escapes my lips, but I feel like I'm choking.

"You can't, Curt."

"Of course, I can. I've carved much harder things than that. We'll have another ivy staircase, but bigger this time, and better. I'll make you an enormous bathhouse, and a nicer toilet, and a kitchen for me. And a really big table, so we can all eat together without elbowing each other in the eye. And a library. You've always wanted a library. I can find you books, from somewhere. I'll go back to that castle and steal what's left up there."

"Curt…"

"It'll be spring soon. It won't be so cold and we can find somewhere in the trees. You love the trees, and the sky, and the stars. So you need to see the stars. That's fine. I can do that. It'll have a view, our new lodge. You'll be able to see everything."

"Curt, you have to listen to me now…"

"And we'll have the mating ceremony. However you want it. As many times as you like. We'll invite everyone. Even Anguis. It'll be a great day, you'll see. I'll be so mushy, you'll cry."

"Listen to me, Mange." I pull back my head, trying to reach his eyes.

"No. I won't. I won't listen. I won't let you say it."

"You have to let me go, my love."

He grips me so tightly, I hear my bones creaking.

"Never. It took me my whole life to find you. We're going together. I don't care where. Anywhere. But you're coming with me."

"I can't."

I hear his breath hauling in and out of his lungs, the tempo wavering as tears well up to steal his words.

"You… want to go… with that snake?"

"No, my wolf. I want to stay with you, but I can't stay here… and you have to." His gaze finally drops to meet mine as a tear tracks down his cheek. "You know you have to."

"No… I…"

I free my hands and lift both palms to his face, smoothing away the flowing tears with my thumbs.

"You can't leave your brother or your pack. It's not in you. When you gave up being Alpha, you went up the mountain, but you could still see them all. I know you couldn't bring yourself to desert them then, and you won't now."

"I can't…" He chokes on the words.

"And my girl needs you. She's too young for this; Adamo's gone and her father can't protect her. She has only you now. Do you understand? You can't leave them, not for me. You'll never survive it, and I won't let you."

I lift my mouth to his, searing our desperate kiss into my memory. Soon, it'll be all I have.

"Let me go."

His eyes turn dark, filled with passion and fury, and he crushes me against him. "When my brother recovers, I'll find you."

"I love you," I tell him. "And I'll never love another."
"You better not," he replies. "I'll bite his frulking head off."
The tears flow freely then.
His tears.
I have none, when my heart's as dry as desert sand.

CHAPTER 24

Our Story Is Over

We packed my things in silence, except for Curt's occasional sniff and a pronounced bout of scratching. I couldn't bring myself to tell him off, since it was comforting in some strange way. As our darkest night sky threatens to fade to pastel blue, Wings flies my packs to the waiting convoy, assembling outside the mansion, and returns for myself and Curt.

The storm has already passed as I step out onto the blue tinged, pristine carpet of snow, leaving the air crystal clear. In the freezing silence, every step crunches beneath my feet as though crushing my fantasy. The town spreads out before me, a sea of wood and regret, a few lights twinkling through the windows in the rapidly rising dawn.

Not a soul has come to witness my leaving.

Surprisingly, I'm allowed to enter the mansion unhindered, but I'm no sooner inside the door than four snarling wolf guards insert themselves between me and the staircase. I don't care what they try to do, I'm not leaving without saying goodbye to my girl. I ignore the gnashing teeth nipping at my neck as I climb each step, the stench of their breath filling my nostrils.

"Get away from her, or you'll answer to me," Curt delivers with such venom they believe him. The wolves don't back away, but they cease to harass me as he follows in my wake, step for step. I can feel the heat of him behind me, radiating through my clothes, and I fight the urge to turn and wrap my whole self around him, begging for time to stand still.

But the false god Chronos bows to no woman and my time has already run out.

I stare at Alpha's bedroom door, paralysed on the threshold, as though knocking asks permission to abandon him and his daughter.

"Edi?"

I must have been frozen for a long time, since a fully clothed Wings takes my hand in his bony fingers.

"Come with me," he says, turning the carved wolf doorknob and opening the door.

Dulcis' head lifts from her crossed forearms, her wavy hair parting and falling away from her face. Both hands still clutch her father's fingers as she leans forward in her chair. Her face is deadly pale, those glorious eyes sunken into dark circles of fear and grief. Has she been here all night, not eating, not sleeping? Who will care for her now?

"You've come to say goodbye," she states, her voice so very small, retreating to that of her childhood. She doesn't move.

"For now," I reply.

"Uncle Curt is going with you?" she asks, her gaze flicking to his face and back to me. She tries so hard to hide it, but fear rages behind her eyes.

I crouch beside her, one hand resting on her arm. I can feel her trembling beneath my fingers. "No. He's staying here with you. When your father recovers, he'll come and find me."

"Don't lie to the girl."

That voice cuts through the air like a sword. She stands behind me, her poisonous presence filling the doorway. I refuse to give Yelena the satisfaction of a reply or my gaze, so she glides to my side, peering through the window at the golden edge of sunrise.

"It's time," she states. "You should leave. Delay does nothing but hurt her more."

She's right, but I hate her for it.

Wings skirts around our nemesis and leans over the bed, peering down at his charge, his boy. Wrapped in a blood stained bandage, Alpha's head lies eerily still on his pillow, his eyes closed as though rehearsing eternal rest. I never realised how long and dark his eyelashes were before. I may never see them again.

"You wake up; you hear me?" Wings whispers into Alpha's ear. "No pup of mine ever gives up. I taught you better than that. You wouldn't want to disappoint old Wings, now, would you?"

"He'll sing if you don't wake up," I add.

Dulcis lets out a yelp of laughter that dissolves into a gulp of grief. She flies out of her seat and thunders into my embrace, crying my name.

I'm terrified that my heartbreak runs so deep, it'll send me back to my own world, magic book or no.

"This isn't over, little girl," I speak into her ear, not caring if her grandmother hears every word. "You keep your eyes and your heart open. Your Auntie Edi is coming home, and I'll be bringing our family with me."

The glare of the rising sun, streaming through the window, blinds my eyes, but I hear Yelena's pronouncement. "You must leave. Now."

I try to move, but Dulcis clings tighter, refusing to let me go.

"Don't be afraid," I tell her. "This isn't forever. You're the strongest of women and your father's daughter."

Yelena's face darkens, but she doesn't respond, simply looking away.

Dulcis' tear stained face pulls back, meeting me eye to eye, and I'm proud to recognise the moment steel returns to her gaze. Yelena has not won, not yet. Her granddaughter is too much like her.

As I step nearer to Alpha, one of the guard wolves snarls and twitches. Yelena waves him away and he shuffles backwards, stepping on Curt, who shoves him. "Get off me."

Their mutual growls and annoyance draw Yelena's attention, allowing me to sit on the bed beside my friend. I lay a gentle kiss on Alpha's forehead and whisper into his ear. "I love you, brother. Curt will take care of you all now. I'll be back. I promise."

Wings embraces Dulcis and I hear him humming some off key tune, which makes her smile. "You keep eating and drinking properly," he orders.

"Yes, Wings," she replies.

"And get some sleep. You can't help him if you're exhausted."

"I will."

He leans in closer. "And sing to him. He can still hear you."

She chokes up again.

Wings turns to Curt and, stiff as a board, thrusts out his hand. Curt stares at the hand, then up into Wings' face, before grasping his fingers firmly. The old eagle yanks on the hand, pulling his oldest pup into his arms for a manly hug. They both deliver a hefty thump on the back and promptly burst into tears.

I can't bear to watch, rushing out onto the balcony and peering down into the hall below, grasping at the banister to steady my legs. Someone has put out the fire and the creeping cold makes my bones ache.

Yelena follows me out, tossing her head at the exhibition of grief. "It's for the best."

"Leave me alone," I snap. "You've got what you wanted. Broken everyone's heart. Have the grace to go away."

"You think I make decisions to torture you?" She snorts a cold, sharp laugh. "You honestly consider yourself that important?"

"You really are a nasty piece of work, you know that? Your world must be a dark place to live in."

"I live in the real world, Edith. Any other will be the death of you."

I turn to face her, all fear gone, for once. "You honestly believe that, don't you? What did someone do to you, to make you like this?"

Her gaze shifts from my face, and I know I'm right. She recovers quickly, her heart being made of iron, not flesh.

"I know you think you love him," she says, tipping her head to one side as though sorry for me, "but being with the wrong tribe is a worse torture than anything you feel now." She leans close to me and I resist the urge to jerk my head away. "Believe me, I know. And don't go with the snakes. I knew a snake, once. Even thought I loved him. He mesmerised, enslaved me and gave me away." She takes a step back and half turns, done with me now. "Go back to the humans. There's no peace allying yourself with the wrong kind."

"Have you ever thought that the real world is what you make it?" I ask.

"I tried," she replies, with a laugh. "It was just another lie."

"Edi."

We both look down. Anguis stands in the hall, wrapped in fur from head to toe. She glances at me and laughs, nose crinkling with the joy of cynicism. He ignores her, fixing those emerald eyes on me.

"It's time."

"Yes, it is," she says. "More than time. I wish you all well, whether you believe that or not."

Curt rustles past me and marches downstairs, his limp becoming more pronounced with the speed and force of each step. Stomping across the hall, he approaches Anguis as though he's about to murder him.

"Curt, don't," I call out, rushing down the stairs after him, but my wolf doesn't attack the former ambassador. Grinding to a halt directly in front of him, Curt leans in and whispers something, I'm not yet close enough to hear. Their eyes meet and Anguis delivers a single nod.

"Wings," I whimper, glancing behind me.

"I'm here," he replies, touching my back as he passes by and heads outside. "Give them a moment," he tells Anguis, and the snake duly follows him, leaving Curt standing beside the cold ashes of a dead fireplace.

Dulcis slowly emerges onto the balcony, leaving an obvious gap between herself and her grandmother.

"Go back to your father," I tell my girl. "Don't watch anymore."

She nods and backs away, closing the bedroom door behind her. My gaze shifts to Yelena, staring at her until she grants a modicum of mercy and walks away, leaving me alone with my mangy wolf.

"I can't..." he begins, but I place my fingers on his lips to make him stop.

No more words.

One final kiss to remember when I'm alone. One to hold in my head until I'm no longer able to remember anything of my fantasy. Our lips meet and tongues entwine, but the passion sinks beneath the weight of desperation. And, to be honest, he doesn't taste all that well.

Yep, he's gagging again.

"Mange, you need to have some weak broth and a good sleep," I tell him, sounding like Mama Bear. I miss her.

"How am I supposed to do that?" he whimpers.

"Because I say so."

Clutching his head to my chest, I feel both of his hands grab my backside and squeeze. With a final kiss to the top of his tatty grey locks, I pull clear and head for the door. He grasps for my hand, but I pull my fingers clear.

"Edi."

I ignore him. If I don't, I think I'll just collapse and die.

"Edi."

The snakes are huddled together in the snow, shivering beneath multiple layers of fur and wool. They don't like the winter, not without their friends. Sledges and carts are packed with their meagre possessions, much of their own, mould tainted things having been left at the castle or burned. It didn't matter whilst they lived here, part of our glorious pack, everything they needed freely given. They are leaving it all behind, once more.

I pull my coat and scarf higher on my neck and my woollen hat down over my ears. Wings waits beside our cart and I join him at the rope, ready to drag my life down the valley, following in the footsteps of the bears, and a beloved woolly ram.

I was wrong though, when I said none had come to see me leave. They're all here now, all the wolves I've lived beside for this blessed year, all changed into wolf form, their cubs sheltering beneath furry legs. There's no snarling, nor howling to rend the air, only the tears of a little girl.

Sospa looks around her, at her gathered people, and wails, "I'm so sorry. It's all my fault." Serpen lifts her into his arms, hiding her beneath his outer coat as he gently rocks and shushes her.

"Thank you for your shelter, my friends," the once king cries out, drawing every wolf eye to his face. "We wish you nothing but happiness and health." He nods at Anguis.

"Set off," Anguis announces and the little convoy heaves its way forward.

The sun rises above the mountain top, flooding the valley with golden rays and casting deep shadows across the town. Wings pulls ahead of me, purposely lifting the majority of the strain from my shoulders. He could fly, but he knows I need him by my side.

Keep walking and don't look back, I command myself, over and over.

Don't look back.

I look back.

My wolf's following, padding through the snow, his shadow limping alongside. He staggers sideways, retching into the snow.

Go home, I tell him, shouting in my mind. Go home to our lodge, to your wonderful stew and the carved rocking chair.

But they're gone.

He follows, falling further and further behind, but, still, he follows.

Until he doesn't.

I hear a single plaintive howl…

And our story is over...

CHAPTER 25

The Voice

Where am I?

One foot in front of the other. I think my feet are moving, but I'm trapped in my head. It's so quiet in here. How much time has gone by?

Edith.

I'm so tired. I want to lie down and sleep forever.

Edith.

It's all over. I lost him.

Edith Breaker-Smith stop ignoring me.

Go away. I can't hear you.

That's very silly and I'm ashamed of you.

That's nasty. Who are you?

You know very well who this is. You promised me, when I left, you wouldn't give up and now look at you, pretending you're done.

You died a long time ago. It can't be you.

I'm dead, not erased.

Please don't start. I'm not up for profound right now.

Hogwash. You always fancied yourself Queen Fairy of the Mystical.

Excuse me? I conjured with a magic book, I'll have you know.

Yes, you did. Portal/portaloo, very amusing.

Go away. I'm too tired for brain wrestling.

One little blip and you're throwing in the towel. Some fighter you are. Your father and I had mountains to face in our day.

Here we go.

Listen carefully, Edith.

Do I have a choice?

Do you love this Curt?

It's not that simple.

Of course, it's simple. Everything's simple. You just don't like how hard you have to work to get it. And even harder to keep it.

They threw me out.

Are you still alive?

Mostly.

Then it's not over. You read enough books to know that.

I don't know what to do.

What's the next step? Do that. And for Pete's sake Squirt, wake the heck up. Your wolf's relying on you.

"I hear you, Mum."

Did I say that out loud?

Oh. Apparently, I'm back in the present. Gosh, I've just realised it's cold out here. Numb despair was so much warmer. Don't panic; I'm not going back.

So I should think. You're a Breaker-Smith. Jivvy up now. They're all waiting on you.

Who?

Your readers. They think you left them alone in the snow. Not to mention, I like that wolf.

Me too. Alright. I'm back. Thanks, Mum.

Mum?

I miss you.

Right. Readers. Chapter 25.

You don't honestly think I'm giving up that easily, do you? I'm British for God's sake. I don't do shrinking violet. Not to mention it's all got far too morbid recently. People have scraped their way out of much worse situations in loads of stories. Heck, I've even written worse scenarios than this one. I just need to do a bit of thinking, after I've managed to have a good cry, which currently eludes me. My imagination is bunged up in my swelling brain, waiting for a snotty, dam breaking flood.

I'm not thinking about Curt at all.

I'm not.

If I do, my plot wrangling narrative faculties will completely implode and book two would end right here. That's not happening. Suffice it to say, I didn't wait countless decades for those biceps, only to give up at the first hurdle. I'm not giving Yellfire the satisfaction.

But I refuse to get bogged down worrying about Curt. He's a grown wolf and well able to take care of himself, once he's had a good meal and a good scratch.

Sigh.

That's enough. I need to start pulling my weight on this cart, since that old bird's been bearing the brunt all along the valley. Once we turn the corner and head into the woods, I step up and heave on the rope. My resolve lasts for a few hundred yards before sciatica starts hollering in protest and I begin wheezing.

"Have a rest before you pass out," Wings tells me, barely straining.

"You're not having a rest," I point out, though it takes me five minutes to sound the words.

"I'll be even more tired if I have to drag your sorry padding, as well as our packs."

"May I offer my services?" a fur drenched angel pipes up, lifting the rope over my head. I'm too pooped to thank him.

Wings promptly hands Anguis his loop of rope as well. "Thank you, very much. You won't mind if I lay in the cart whilst you pull, will you?" He promptly flakes out on our stacked packs and I can't help but laugh. It feels good, but fleeting, like pushing back the darkness with candlelight, only for the shadows to form flickering monsters.

"Actually, Wings," says Anguis, adjusting the jaunty angle of his hat after looping the rope over his head, "Serpen wonders if you might like to take flight?"

Wings' head pops up, glaring at the snake. "I'm not pulling everyone's carts."

Anguis raises an eyebrow. "Actually, he's more inclined to request an aerial search."

"Oh, recon," I blurt.

"Excuse me?"

"Reconnaissance. Scouting out the terrain. Flying a spy…"

"Or finding the bears," Anguis qualifies.

"Great idea." I grab hold of Wings' arm and pull.

"I can get up on my own," the bird whinges. "I'm not that old."

"Never said you were, Crowface."

He scowls at me, doing his best to hide the affection in his eyes. "We should have let that wolf eat you."

"Charming. Besides we'd both be gristle or fat."

"I'll leave the irritating madam in your capable hands," Wings tells Anguis, dropping his trousers around his ankles with a whoosh.

I love that bird. He's lost the only home he's ever really known and the two pups he effectively raised and yet he still instinctively understands what everyone else needs in order to keep going.

He's soon sailing over our little band of brothers, tipping his wings like a fighter plane before heading out with those eagle eyes. Happy hunting and hurry, Wings, it's cold out here now. What will it be like when night falls?

It feels lonely without my feathered friend. The snakes began the journey chatting amongst themselves with forced bravado, endeavouring to raise their spirits, but as the day wears on and morning turns to afternoon, the stark nature of their fate looms larger and larger in their mind's eye.

We stop to eat and the pots hanging above impromptu fires provide a modicum of warmth to shivering refugees, swathed in whatever blankets they can muster.

Forcing Curt's fate, and my own, from my mind, I allow a recent memory to trigger a new curiosity. One which the former king may be able to satisfy, if he's willing to air some ancient dirty laundry.

I quietly shuffle over, doing my best to seem nonchalant and unconcerned. Serpen stares straight at me, so I park myself beside him on a fallen tree trunk.

"What?" he asks, with the glimmer of a smile, handing me a steaming mug of broth.

"Thanks," I reply, taking a welcome sip and sighing as the hot liquid soothes its way down my aching throat. "And, erm, a couple of things. Starting with, I never asked if it's alright my being here, with you all. Not that I'd have a clue where to go if you said no."

He briefly laughs. "You don't need to ask my permission. I'm not your king. We wouldn't have been safe this past year, if it hadn't been for you. I would have died in that castle. Sospa may not have survived."

"I'm sorry for where we are now," I reply, peering at his people, huddled together around the fires.

"Not your fault," he replies.

"It feels like it's partly my fault."

"Yelena wanted us all gone from the beginning. If it wasn't one thing, it would have been another. If anyone's to blame, it's me, for changing into the serpent."

"From where I stood, you didn't have much choice."

"I had a choice whether to half eat her. No changer does that to another."

"Made me happy though. Seeing her drenched in snake spit."

He smiles again, his gaze taken up with his blue eyed niece, sitting on Anguis' knee, swamped in one of his coats, chewing on a leg of fried gumwhat. I don't care to think about that too much, since I've no idea what happened to my bucktoothed friend.

"What else did you want to ask?" Serpen says, glancing at me. "You said you had a couple of things?"

"Yes," I reply, taking another deep swig of that glorious broth. "Yelena said something to me and I wanted to ask you about it."

"Not sure I'd listen to anything she had to say to you."

"I'd agree, but this was about the snakes."

Those stunning sapphire eyes swivel to take in my face. "Such as?"

"She said she once loved a snake and thought he loved her, but he mesmerised her and gave her away. Did you ever hear anything like that?"

"She's the daughter of an Alpha, albeit the younger one, so she would have had status, even then. Not enough for a mating though. There would have been no chance at all of a snake being with a wolf. They were considered little more than slaves at that time. I'm not saying that was right, it's just how it was."

"I understand, but you just gracefully sidestepped my question." I'm a middle-aged woman; you don't get past me that easily.

Serpen looks directly ahead, pursing his lips.

"From the look on your face, I guess you know who she referred to," I probe.

He finally glances at me. "No-one else knows. Except maybe your eagle. He was around back then."

"I'm not going to repeat it," I insist. "I think you know you can trust me."

"It was my father," he tells me, leaning forward, elbows on his knees.

"He told you?"

"To warn me." He delivers a huge sigh before launching into the explanation. "The bears attacked the wolves, killing Yelena's brother. Not long after, the wolves planned their revenge. Yelena and my father were lovers in secret and she confided in him. He didn't want her to join the revenge attack, afraid for her, but she defied him. He mesmerised her to keep her away. She never forgave him. After she left, he became like his father. Cruel. Violent. He taught me never to trust or care for wolves, or bears." He leans back to look at me. "I learned that lesson too well and it nearly wiped out my people."

No wonder she hates Serpen. In another world, Yelena could have been his mother.

He slaps his palms against his legs and rises, proclaiming, "We need to move on. We have to find somewhere with more shelter before nightfall."

Making our way through the trees only gets harder as fatigue and cold sink into weary bones. If I'm cold, the Menopausal Madam with her built in hot flushes, the snakes must be suffering horribly. We need to locate the bears and soon.

What if they don't want to help us?

No, I can't believe Adamo would turn us away and the Ursid I love would never let him. Right now, I'd give anything for one of his legendary bear hugs. At least I'd be warm whilst I'm crushed to death.

I pull on that blasted rope for as long as I can before gravity shows me who's boss and my knees give out. Two men replace me, looking barely more stable than myself as their limbs succumb to the freeze and blood turns to ice water in their veins.

Twilight casts its deathly hue over the snow and sparkles in Sospa's blond locks. She's so pale she gleams like a ghost in

Serpen's arms, her tiny gloved hands gripping his collar as shivers wrack her body. He tries to rub some warmth into her limbs, but I can hear her teeth chattering. His people are all exhausted, but we can't stop in this exposed location, with its thinning treeline and merciless chill.

Serpen catches his foot on an exposed tree root and staggers, clutching at Sospa as she falls from his grasp.

"Let me take her," I yell, over the whistling wind. "My body's warmer than yours."

I assume that's true, though I've never actually asked. He must believe it's true, since he shuffles her into my embrace. I undo my outer layers and snuggle her against the wool beneath. Anguis helps me button up two layers of coats over her head and body, engulfing the child. I feel her arms and legs gripping on to me tightly.

"Can you do this?" he asks.

I nod at him and take my first burdened steps. My back bends under the strain and pain shoots down my legs, but I cover it as best I can, hiding a grimace inside my collar and scarf. Every step comes laden with a prayer for strength and a miracle for my friends.

Anguis supports his former king over to a cart. "Just for a while, Your Majesty. Please. We need you and you need to rest a little."

His people echo their ambassador's plea, adding their own. Serpen sits on the cart, calling to me, "Thank you. I'll take her back soon," as a woman wraps a blanket around his legs and shoulders.

"I'm fine," I grind out, through gritted teeth, but I'm not. Ahead the trees seem to thicken once more, but it might as well be a marathon for this ageing athlete.

"I know you need shelter. As soon as I can, I'll call a halt," Anguis tells me, wrapping his arm around my waist and lifting, oh so slightly. I try not to groan with that minor relief. "Yet again you're saving my people."

"Just Sospa," I pant. "I love her."

"I know you do. And she loves you, and Wings," he replies, glancing up at the darkening skies for any sign of the eagle. His gaze drops to my face, smothered beneath hat, hood and scarf. "She's not the only one who loves you. We all do… I do."

"Anguis," I whisper. "I'm so..."

His grip around my waist tightens for a moment. "If you were free, I'd tell you much you don't know about me, my life, my family. Who I am. Who I want to be."

His emerald eyes sparkle in the twilight and the temptation to embrace him, to bury my anguish in his arms and affection is so fierce, I conjure my beloved wolf from memory, letting the pain keep him at bay.

"But not now," Anguis continues. "Not with your heart still back in that town. A snake must be loved completely, or not at all."

"That sounds a bit obsessive," I mutter, heaving in breath through the scarf, Yelena's words echoing in my mind.

He laughs. "I'm a snake; it's in my blood and scales."

I don't know whether to be flattered or afraid. Maybe both.

"Anguis, in the mansion, what did Curt say to you?" I ask.

His smile disappears as he answers. "He said, if anything happens to you, he'll hunt me down and kill me."

That's my wolf. I can almost hear him scratching.

Everything hurts, body and mind. I don't know how much farther I can go, yet there are still no tears from my desert heart.

A screech blasts across the snow, echoing from tree to tree like a triumphant bugle call. Every eye turns upward, straining to see the silhouette of a giant eagle swooping overhead. The few snakes with enough energy let loose a feeble cheer as Wings comes in to land, his feathers showering me with snow.

And, as twilight fades to night, a suddenly naked old man proclaims, "I've found the bears. They're coming for us."

CHAPTER 26

The Dam Breaker

Night falls, its frozen edge threatening to end what's left of the Snake Empire for good. We keep moving, every step closing the gap between the flagging refugees and the bears, every step preventing the ailing from succumbing to their personal hell.

A thousand miles back, I could no longer walk and carry Sospa, so Anguis lifted me onto his sledge, pulling on the rope himself. I'd be racked with guilt, if I couldn't feel the child's movement growing ever more sluggish, despite my body heat.

Hurry Adamo. We need you.

Much as he did before, our air ambulance flies the most desperate straight to the bear camp, wherever that might be. Each trip he returns carrying more blankets and lukewarm food, once piping hot, but swiftly cooling in the frigid air. I almost insist on him taking Sospa, but a desperate scan reveals other children in far worse condition. Wings squawks in my face, those eagle eyes squinting with worry.

"I'm fine," I croak. "Go. The bears will be here soon, right?"

He squawks an affirmative and stares at me.

"Go," I insist and force my arm to wave as he takes off with two more children held tightly in his claws.

He's barely disappeared into the inky sky when Anguis staggers at the front of the cart. He can't keep pulling my weight and Sospa's or he'll collapse for good, with me beside him.

Get up, I command my legs, but they refuse to comply.

I conjure the voice of my wolf and shout inside my head, 'Get up, now, Big Bum, you lazy old gumwhat.'

That annoys me enough to get off the cart and take a step.

Now another.

And another.

Keep moving. Left. Right. Left. Right.

It might be a thousand steps, or ten, I can't remember anymore.

Left. Right.

What's that strange set of lights?

I peer through the darkness, straining to focus. That's odd. Two pale lights, flashing on and off in the shadows.

It's not lights…

It's eyes.

Blinking.

Staring straight at me.

A predator has me in his sights.

I try to scream, but my voice won't come, frozen in my throat. If that thing wants to eat me, he'll have to defrost me first.

A terrifying roar echoes through the trees and Sospa wakes with a start and a tiny scream. Arms tighten around my neck as her head pops clear of my coat and I instinctively turn, swinging her away from the monster in the night.

"Edi," she screams, eyes wide with terror as she stares over my shoulder.

The roar sounds again, this time accompanied by the pounding rhythm of mighty feet, rapidly closing the gap between the forest and the vulnerable. I have nowhere left to run, and no way to defend us, yet my eyes refuse to close in defeat.

"Get away from her," I rasp.

"Grrrrr," the monster replies.

Wait a minute.

I know that growl.

Praise the Living God, I know that growl.

"Ursid?" I croak as a ruddy great brown bear demolishes a tree in his haste to get to me. "Sospa, look, it's General Ursid."

The girl fights her way out of my layers, ripping a hole in the side panel of my coat and dropping into the snow with a plop.

"Adamo?!" she positively hollers, with far more volume than the rest of us can muster.

Arrrrrrgggggghhhhh.

If you haven't guessed, that's the ginger prince of bears letting rip with a lung buster as he side butts his general and thunders into our midst, raising both paws above his head like he's scored a rugby try (or a touchdown if you're from the good old US of A).

Sospa's legging it towards the honey bear, suddenly rejuvenated, when Ursid reaches me and the world goes pitch dark as I disappear into a smothering, full on, bone creaking, fur laden bear hug.

And that's when the dam decides to give way and I sob like the world's coming to an end. Every loss bubbles to the surface in a never ending, slurred, snotty litany of woe, punctuated by half my bodyweight in tears and my furry friend's limited vocabulary of comfort.

"The lodge burned down," I wail. "The only thing left was the toilet."

"Grrrrow," and a squeeze (translates to *I know*).

"Alpha had an accident."

"Ruh?(*Huh?*) Grrrad? (*Bad?*)"

"He broke his leg, hit his head and won't wake up."

Squeeze, gentle rocking side to side.

"Curt let Yelena take over everything," I howl, sucking in breath and bits of fur.

"Grrrooo (*No!*)."

I turn my head and spit out fluff. "Serpen nearly ate Yelena."

"Grah, grah, grah (*Ha, ha, ha). Groood grror grimmm (Good for him)."*

"They threw me and Wings out."

A giant paw strokes my head.

"Curt doesn't want to be my mate."

"Grrro, grsssh (*No, shhh*)."

"I had to leave him behind. And Dulcis. I want my Curt," the last delivered as a resounding wail.

The general heaves me off my feet and pats my back like he's nursing a baby with croup. Funnily enough, it makes me feel so much better.

"I missed you... and you're lovely and warm."

"Grawwww (*Awwww*)."

When he finally lowers me back to the floor and I emerge from the walking carpet, recovering my muffled hearing, it dawns on me there's a lot of grunting, chattering and rustling going on. Peering over Ursid's furry paw, I follow everyone's gaze up to a tree branch, from whence Sospa is hanging by her hood, little legs kicking in rage.

"Stop fighting and hold still," Serpen calls up to her, from the base of the tree.

Meanwhile, Anguis teeters on Adamo's bear shoulders, delivering their best circus balancing act, straining to unhook her hood.

"What the heck happened?" I ask, mesmerised by the swaying, swinging performance.

"Adamo lifted Sospa onto his shoulders," Serpen answers, trying not to laugh in the face of his dangling niece's thunderous scowl. "He then stood upright, smacking her head on the branch. She hollered, he dropped, leaving her hanging."

Oh, for pity's sake. Old Big Bum to the rescue.

"Oi," I shout, rediscovering my loud voice after a good cry. "Since the idiot brothers here are about to break their necks, why doesn't Adamo just rise back up beneath her and lift her off the branch."

Have you ever had one of those moments when everyone realises you're the only person in the room with brain cells still functioning? Gratifying, isn't it?

Serpen very rarely laughs, let alone given these dire circumstances, yet he suddenly lets rip with a snorting guffaw that almost makes his former ambassador faint with shock. Anguis gracefully leaps from Adamo's furry shoulders and smiles at the amused snake.

"Not funny," a disgruntled girl snarls down at her uncle whilst Adamo manoeuvres his bulk beneath her dangling feet.

"Going up," I announce, as though I'm a lift attendant, and Adamo starts to rise up on his back legs.

"Go right," Anguis commands.

Face to face with the snake, Adamo heads towards his right.

"The other right," Anguis orders, rolling his eyes in mockery and waving a hand in the appropriate direction from his point of view.

"Grarrr Greffff," growls the honey bear.

"Beg your pardon?" says the polite ambassador, set on winding up the bear.

"That's left," I translate.

"Grrry grran grell grry greff grrrm grry gggrt."

"Er, I can tell my left from my right, I think." Apparently, I'm turning into a Doolittle.

Serpen laughs so hard, tears stream from those sapphire eyes, setting off the rest of the snakes. Adamo positively roars at them, the vibration dumping a pile of snow on his head from the offending tree. He shakes it off, sneezing repeatedly.

"Leave him be, the pair of you," I tell the cackling king, elbowing Anguis in the arm. "I want to go back to their camp, but you can stay out here if you want."

"GRRROO GRRRRT."

"Too right," I translate, waving the bear upwards. "You're almost there. Bit more."

Sospa wraps her swinging knees around Adamo's neck as he stands on bear tippy toes, letting her hood drop free. A resounding round of applause issues from the snakes and a chorus of growls from the pack of bears that have caught up to their prince, since none of us were looking.

Adamo very carefully lowers himself back onto four paws, leaving Sospa riding on his back, grasping handfuls of fur to keep herself steady. The ginger prince pads up and down on his paws until we all get the hint.

Ursid drops low and nudges me in the knees. I don't need telling twice, hauling myself onto his back with a sigh of relief and a hefty snap in my lumbar region. I'm so going to pay for all this stomping about in the undergrowth, but not right now.

All around me, the snakes mount up on their impromptu bear transport, some hugging their old friends with total abandon as other bears take their place at the carts and sledges. I'd be touched by the reunion, if it wasn't so cold.

"Arrggghh," roars Adamo.

"Arrrrrggggh," hollers Sospa in her best grown up, bear simulation voice and she waves her arm forwards like Boadicea leading a charge. Serpen's proud grin is a sight to behold.

Ursid sets off with a sudden jerk that nearly unseats me and I grab hold of his fur and grip on with my legs for dear life, ungratefully wishing he'd come with a saddle. Trees whip by as the general picks up the pace, swerving around knobbly trunks looming up out of the darkness, until I decide that leaning forward and putting my head down is the best way to ride, if not the bravest. A sideways glance at Sospa reveals the feisty princess, head held high, mouth moving as she yells with glee. I'm glad she's having fun. Bear riding may not be my favourite sport, but he's getting me closer to a nice warm tent with every stride, so I'm good with it.

On my other side, Anguis' long legs dangle so close to the ground he's forced to lift and grasp his knees to avoid broken ankles. Even so, he's looking a lot better than he did a few minutes ago. The bear rescue came at exactly the right moment and their thundering charge through the undergrowth raises everyone's spirits.

An echoing screech above our heads tells me that Wings is circling overhead, but I'm clinging on too tightly to look up. When he delivers the most triumphant of squawks, we all sit up as one, risking a smack in the eye from low lying branches, to get the first view of the camp.

I strain my ageing eyes, hoping to catch a glimpse of the colourful tents that made up the bear camp from last year, but I can't see the slightest glint piercing the thick darkness. Is Wings wrong? Is there much farther to go?

Ursid's deep bellow reverberates through his body and mine as he races up to a wall of pale night, which seems to lighten with every bound. We're almost upon it when I realise it's an uneven wall of snow and ice, and brace for impact. Ursid slides to a halt, turning to parallel park himself alongside the wall. He lowers onto his stomach allowing his rider to drop off his back and plop into the snow.

Leaning on his nose, I drag myself upright, staring at the wall looming just above my head, dirt and stones pebbledashing impacted snow and clumps of ice. "Where are we?"

Ursid's nose pokes me in the side, shoving me along, until I see where he's guiding me. A small, two person width hole in the wall marks the entrance to the makeshift fortress. Inside, a line of heavyweight grizzlies dig with front and back paws, showering snow and ice into the air, leaving smaller bears to slap it into the wall like pat-a-cake. It only takes a few steps to feel the wall's partial windbreak effect.

Clumped together in the centre stand those colourful tents I remember so well, probably because I once mowed them down in a runaway cart. Each outer skin is set at a sharper angle, mitigating the weight of falling snow. I know from experience how wonderfully toasty they are inside and I need no encouragement from Ursid to start jogging towards them.

Depositing their riders, the rescue party nudges the snakes in the direction of the biggest tent, before padding off to a smaller one at the edge of the village.

"Come back here!" floats on the wind.

I turn in the direction of the familiar voice and, sure enough, wrapped up in his arctic kit, Friddie sprints between the tents, in full pursuit of a whirling dervish of fluff, making a beeline for yours truly. I've barely a second to brace myself before it wallops me full in the face and down I go.

CHAPTER 27

The Unexpected Return

A cavernous mouth opens wide, revealing a marvellous set of sharp choppers, aiming directly for my nose.

"Don't you dare bite me, you little horror," I yell, giving the monster my best 'don't mess with nanny' squint eyed face.

The open maw freezes in position, with the exception of the odd twitch as cubface tries to decide whether he wants to risk it.

"Don't. You. Dare," I reiterate, dropping my voice to a growl and leaning nose to nose with the pest, which is a risky manoeuvre, given how excited he is. Four legs wave in the air like he's about to take off, reaching for me, and I decide to risk a cuddle. The horror wraps himself around my neck and squeezes until I'm in danger of asphyxiation, his teeth worrying at my hat in a joyous shredding frenzy.

"Sorry," pants Friddie, catching up with his wayward cub. "Come here you."

He tries to peel tiny claws off my padding, but no sooner does he remove one than another snaps back into place. Monster lets out a plaintive howl straight down my newly exposed ear canal and squeezes even tighter. Tapping on his paws and squeaking eventually loosens the grip.

"Alright, alright," I soothe, until the fluffball stops whining, carrying him inside the tent with me.

"Welcome. It's good to see you," says Friddie, following me in.

A ring of happily defrosting snake children, most likely delivered by Wings earlier, surround a central fire, chattering away to each other and filling their mouths from bowls of steaming meat and vegetables, ladled from a half full cauldron of stew hanging over the fire, burping bubbles with puffs of gloriously meaty steam. The tent curtain moves to one side as two men shuffle past the arriving snakes and place a second caldron near the fire, ready to swop with its rapidly emptying twin.

My clingy fur scarf sniffs the air and makes a scruffy bid for the pot, his father catching him by the hind legs before he dives in.

"You've already eaten," Friddie tells his offspring, "and it's time for bed. You can play with Auntie Edi tomorrow."

"Lovely," I croak, giving fluffball a good bonce ruffle.

"Come in. Come in the warm," another familiar voice says. "I'm just going to give you a quick check and then there's food aplenty."

I spin on my heel and, sure enough, Mama Bear is greeting the shivering snakes and ushering them close to the fire. Her eyes meet mine and both sets fill with tears as she rushes to hug me.

"Mama," I wail, in a repeat performance of the Ursid incident. "I left Curt behind."

She crushes my head into her ample chest. "I know, my sweet. Wings told me bits each time he flapped in. Let me look at you. Get the coat off; you're fine in here."

My cub trashed ensemble gets peeled away and Mama pushes my eyelids into my eyebrows, looming so close I can see her nasal hair.

"Tongue out," she orders.

"What?"

"Urrgh," she demonstrates.

I stick my tongue out and she peers down my throat, before feeling around my neck, pumping my arms up and down, poking my stomach and pinching my nose between her knuckles.

"Far too cold, but I was expecting that," she pronounces. "Get some good hot stew into you first and we'll chat afterwards." Her eye falls on her wayward offspring, who shrinks back behind his father's neck, peeping out at angry mummy. "Friddie, he's supposed to be in bed."

"I know, dear," Friddie replies, with a deep sigh, "but he loves her."

"Don't we all," says Mama, giving me and then Tufty Beetus a good squeeze before heading back to accost the line of arriving snakes with the tongue flapping routine. Even Anguis and Serpen are subjected to those indignities before being allowed to collapse by the fire.

"You're far too thin these days," she pronounces, lifting up the former king's arm and squeezing his bicep. A massive family size bowl zaps under his nose. "Get that inside you."

Sospa, squeezing into the ring of children, sniggers, but Serpen meekly replies, "Thank you, Mama Bear. It's good to be here, and thank you for your concern."

"Where else should you go?" she announces and unleashes a smile that outburns the fire.

I'm scraping the bottom of my own bowl with a wooden spoon, wondering whether my poked belly would process another helping, when Adamo and Ursid arrive in fully dressed human form.

The ginger prince of bears spies the snake king, delicately sipping a spoonful of stew, and thrusts his hands on his hips as though posing for a statue. "Now then, about you two laughing at me."

"Well, yes," Anguis replies, having politely swallowed his own mouthful of food first. "I'd rather like to stay by this gratifying fire, so I apologise profusely."

Adamo beams, reminding me of why Dulcis fell for him so hard. "That's fine then. Where's my..." Mama shoves a bowl into his hands, "...bowl?"

"Prince Adamo," Serpen begins, standing up to deliver his official request, "I thank you for your great kindness and, on behalf of my people, humbly request sanctuary with your bears."

"Well, I'm not throwing you out," Adamo replies, with a snort. "Ursid would bore me to death with his wittering."

That fabulous eye twitch arrives with the general's sigh. "Your people are welcome, Serpen. We still consider ourselves one pack, whatever the wolves might think."

"That's what I said, sort of," Adamo mumbles, mouth already full. He points at me with his spoon, dripping stew on Ursid's foot. "Talk to you, please."

I smile in response as Mama Bear ladles the second helping into my bowl with an, "Eat more," command.

Adamo grabs my arm and leads me over to a pile of cushions where we plop down, side by side, fully aware of glances being cast our way. No sooner is my aching posterior happily cushioned than the freckled teenager flings the arm that isn't ladling stew around my shoulders and squeezes until my teeth rattle.

Finishing his first course, he holds out the bowl and shouts, "More! I'm a growing bear."

Mama gives him a speciality stare. "Please."

"Please may I have some more?" says Adamo, fluttering his eyelashes. It works, of course. "How was Alpha when you left?"

"Not good," I reply, face downcast. "His knee was broken and he'd hit his head badly. He hadn't woken when I left, which isn't great."

"No," Adamo whispers.

He glances at me from beneath his drooping ginger hair. It doesn't take a genius to guess what, or who, is on his mind.

"And how was Dulcis?" he eventually asks.

"Scared for her father," I reply. "Shocked with what's happened."

Adamo puts his bowl on the ground and starts picking holes in his fingers. "You're safe with me."

"I know."

"Was she well though?"

"She misses you, if that's what you're really asking."

"You think?" he probes, his eyes flicking up to meet mine.

"Do you miss her?"

"I assumed she'd be safe with you. Sorry, I sound like I'm blaming you."

"I hated leaving her, but she still has Curt."

His massive frame slumps in on itself as his face droops. "I'm a rubbish mate."

"Aren't we all?" I reply, a flash of anger accompanying a longing for my wolf.

"I think I might have made a mistake."

"Probably. Anything in particular?" I ask, giving him a sideways nudge.

"I don't think we should have left." He sits up straight and slaps his knee in frustration.

"Well to be fair," I reply, "they weren't giving you a lot of choice, but I hear what you're saying. I can't help feeling I shouldn't have let them throw me out either."

"Maybe I should have stood my ground, but I was concerned for my people. They weren't safe and I wasn't sure our wolves would back me."

We both sigh in harmony and it's so pathetic, we can't help but chuckle, drawing a glance from Anguis. My gaze wanders around the tent, watching the bears minister to the snakes with such grace that the pain of loss cuts me to the bone. I can't let this happen. We all belong together, snakes, bears, wolves and eagle, wherever he's flown off to.

I belong with Curt.

"I'm going back," I announce.

"We all have to go back," Adamo replies.

"It might mean a fight and loyalties will be all over the place," I mutter, defrosting brain cells firing randomly. "A few of us could go back quietly, at first, to see what's happening. Maybe Curt will lead a rebellion. Maybe."

I catch sight of Adamo and Ursid exchanging what could only be described as shifty, up to no good glances. I'm not having it. I'm done with secrets.

"What are you two plotting?" I ask.

"Erm, we all *have* to go back," Adamo replies, still looking at his nodding general.

"Yes, I know," I reply, glaring at Ursid. "Why are you nodding like a car windscreen toy?"

"What?"

"Never mind. Tell me what's going on. Right now."

Anguis delicately raises a hand. "As a matter of interest, I'd also like to know."

Ursid shuffles up and kneels beside me, clutching my fingers. Now I'm really suspicious.

"Edi, you need to be calm for me," he pleads.

"Why?" I ask, in a voice like crushed gravel, eyes barely slits in my head.

"Calm. Please."

"I've very calm. I'm so calm, I'm almost asleep. I will, however, smack you on the nose if you don't get on with it."

"Bring him in, Wings," Adamo calls.

I've just noticed the sea of bears loitering in front of the tent entrance. Are they there to rubberneck or protect someone? And why are they all staring at me?

The inner lining and the outer skin sweep to one side and Wings enters the tent alongside someone I can't yet identify. The bears part like water around a rock and I finally get a good look at…

No. No way.

What's that miserable bird dropping doing back here?

"Gulid?" Serpen blurts out, popping upright. Anguis slowly rises next to him. "What are you doing with the bears?"

My question exactly. Well, actually, it's a lot more visceral than that.

"Broken Beak? You miserable vulture," I shout, to the surprise of the highly entertained children's gallery.

They're having even more fun when I take a swing at him.

CHAPTER 28

The Snakes In The North

Unfortunately, Ursid got to me first, restraining my arms in a hug from behind, leaving my legs kicking regardless.

"Don't you hit me," Broken Beak hollers. "Not in the face, again. There are children here."

"That's rich coming from you," I yell back. "You punched me in the face. Not to mention locked me in a tower to freeze to death, you homicidal maniac."

My heel accidentally connects with Ursid's knee.

"Ow," he bellows. "That hurt."

"Sorry."

"I forgive you. Stop kicking me."

I plant my feet firmly on the ground. "Alright, you can let me go."

"You promise you'll be calm now?"

"Can I calmly whack him over the head with a bowl?"

"No."

"You're no fun."

"We need the bowls to eat."

Broken Beak scowls at the general.

"And you don't give a sack of bird seed about the children," I fling at my castle nemesis, whilst calmly twitching.

Looking mightily unimpressed, he points at his face. "You smacked me in the beak with a plank. Look at my nose."

That's true, his septum is a tad deviated; however, I will point out, "You were trying to kidnap Dulcis."

"I was ordered to do it."

Anguis raises his hand, again. "He was, to be fair."

"Erm. Yes. Apologies," adds Serpen, sheepishly.

Broken Beak half bows to the former king, like the dutiful servant he was. Not that that excuses him from chucking me in a freezing shower and dressing me in a fluorescent circus outfit. (Read the first book. It's too traumatic for me to recall here.)

"You have no need to bow to me any longer, Gulid," says Serpen, exercising humble magnanimity.

"I know," replies the eagle, "but I've met the Northern Snake King. Briefly. I just about got out with my life and a wing full of singed feathers, without being mesmerised. He makes you look like the height of benevolence."

"Thanks," Serpen mutters. "I think."

"Hello, Gulid," pipes up Sospa, with a little wave. Traitor.

"Hello, Princess," Deviated Septum replies with a grin. "You've grown."

Not so you'd notice, and her beaming reaction annoys me. I decide to pour out my ire on the other eagle pontificating in a corner. (And yes I know that's the wrong word, and that round tents don't have corners.)

"You didn't tell me he was here," I growl, glaring at the offending old bird.

"I was an eagle when I discovered his presence," he points out. "I wasn't capable of much of a conversation whilst flying back and forth. What did you want? Caw, squawk?"

"Don't give me attitude. One of you could have warned me he was here, rather than just flinging him at me."

"I'm not flinging myself anywhere," Broken Beak insists. "I won't so much as touch you."

Yeah, right. "Because you've become such a sweet and kind person? Pardon me if I'm suspicious."

"Can't we put this behind us?" he asks, taking a step towards me.

I step back in unison and stand on Ursid's foot.

"Ow."

"Sorry. Stop lurking behind me."

The general takes a huge step to my right and grimaces at me.

"Don't you start. This isn't funny. It wasn't you he tried to kill."

"Look, I knew the king would order someone to get you out of the tower," Broken Beak explains. "He wasn't much of a murderer. Unlike the rest of his family."

"That's true," says Serpen. "Mostly. I was such a disappointment to them."

I sense we're veering away from the point. "But you told me I'd die up…"

"I didn't like you," Broken Beak states. Like that will endear him. "You smashed me in the face and got me into trouble. But now we've all got worse trouble."

"Such as?" I ask, because I'm curious, despite myself.

"Do you want to know why I'm here?"

"I do," says Anguis.

If he raises his freaking hand one more time, I'm going to snap his fingers off. Serpen must have read my mind because he gently tugs on Anguis' wrist. They both sit at exactly the same time and tempo.

"Sit," orders Adamo, dropping like a rock beside the still bubbling pot, before realising he's about to set fire to himself. He shuffles away without bumping into anyone else, which is a minor miracle.

Tell a lie, there go the bowls.

Bears, snakes and Wings all find comfortable spots to absorb the, no doubt, thrilling narrative about to pour forth from the lying lips of the rancid Beak. As a show of stunning maturity, I'm the only one still standing. You don't get me hanging on your every word. No sirree. I'm a storyteller. I know how this works.

"Edi. Sit down," delivers Anguis in a stage whisper.

"No." So there.

Broken Beak floats into a lotus legged guru pose. "You'll want to hear this, I promise."

"He's going to tell it anyway," says Adamo, building a tower on his lap by stacking empty bowls. "You'll just get tired standing up."

He's got a point.

"Fine. But I don't have to believe a word he says." I plonk myself down in a fit of pique, straight on my spoon. Wonderful. Now I've got a bruised coccyx and a snapped utensil, which I gradually slide out from beneath me when I don't think anyone's looking.

"Let me describe the Northern Empire," says Broken Beak, launching into his epic prologue.

Yawn. Nobody ever reads those.

Mama Bear gently relieves Adamo of the teetering tower of bowls before he breaks something.

"Whilst it took forever to fly there," the miserable eagle continues, "and the weather is worse than at the castle, at least there's no mould. When I first saw their huge city, I thought it looked wonderful. They've got so much room, with rows upon rows of clean houses, wide open spaces and large numbers of livestock. We were all welcomed with open arms by a few fellow eagles. We thought we'd found eagle paradise. So much space for all of us. Not like that castle."

His face drops and a deep sadness enters his eyes. I almost feel sorry for him, but I'm not that much of a soft touch.

"All we ever wanted was a place of our own," Gulid continues, "with no servants and no Oath of Protection keeping us enslaved."

To his credit, Serpen doesn't twitch at that pronouncement.

"I went to sleep on that first night in a warm cabin, all of my own, and woke feeling something I'd never known."

"The Pox?" I suggest.

Come on, that was funny.

"Hope," he says, glaring at me. "High in the hills, sparkling with more beauty than I've ever seen, stood the Citadel. They told us the magnificent structure was a memorial to their eagle ancestors, with an artwork for every loved one that had passed, and that we could visit in the spring during the remembrance festival. As the days passed, they asked questions about where we came from and about all of you. They seemed innocent and interested and we were so grateful to be there, we told them everything."

Oh, boy. Like you, I'm sensing where this is going.

"It was hardly dangerous since there was so few of them. Then one morning, I left my new home, heading for the market, when I came face to face with a snake. All white hair and shiny eyes.

Turns out the sparkling citadel wasn't quite what they'd told us. The eagle memorial stood behind it, apparently. I never did see it. If it even exists."

"They lied. What a shocker," I mutter, feeling suitably chastened when Ursid looks at me with disappointment.

"I didn't know that," Gulid continues. "Not then. I met four snakes and they spoke to me politely, with consideration. They had a king and their rules were tough, but I could leave at any time. I wasn't a prisoner or made to vow anything. I think a few friends even flew back to visit you."

"They did," Serpen agrees.

"It wasn't the same, I kept telling myself. This time I could leave."

He swallows and clams up.

"When did it go wrong?" I prompt, endeavouring to keep snark out of my tone.

He glances up at me. "We talked, but my friends all wanted to stay in the warm city, with its lovely cabins, rather than build another home from scratch on our own. Gradually, I noticed all opposition leaving them, one by one. I could barely get them to talk to me and I felt more and more alone. My friend Revol and I spoke about leaving, even hid some clothes and supplies away from the city, but we just… didn't… Not soon enough.

"One cloudless night, I couldn't sleep and went for a flight. From above, I saw three of my estranged friends enter Revol's cabin. They had a snake with them and I was suspicious, so I hovered until they closed the door, then landed and listened at the window."

"A great brown eagle loitering outside a window, nicely silhouetted against white snow," I describe. "Bet no-one saw you do it."

Broken Beak decides to ignore me. Wings, however, slaps the back of my head.

"I peeped through the window and saw…" The words catch in his throat and he swallows with a loud gulp.

"Saw what?" I prompt, leaning forward. Alright, so he's got me.

"My former friends held Revol down, holding his eyelids open whilst the snake mesmerised him."

"Why?" I ask.

"I'm getting to that," he snaps with the air of an interrupted influencer.

"What good is it to have frozen birds cluttering up the place?"

Sospa snorts, but Wings glares at me.

"Edi, let him finish," Anguis says, blasting me with his most charming smile.

"He wasn't frozen," Broken Beak says. "Well, he was, then."

"What are you talking about?"

A hand winds around my head and briefly covers my mouth.

"Hush," insists Mama Bear.

"The snake mesmerised Revol, then cut him loose, before mesmerising him again. He did that over and over, each time ordering him to sit on the floor when he was frozen, but he couldn't move, of course."

I open my mouth, catch Mama's eye and slowly close it again.

"I lost count how many times it happened, when Revol suddenly sat when ordered. I could see his face through that window. He was dead inside, yet he now followed every single order the snake gave. Sit, stand, spin round… burn your hand."

Broken Beak's head drops with grief. No-one pushes him to continue, not even me.

"He was told not to remember that night, but do as ordered. Snakes are your masters, that thing told him. You belong with your king and will die if you leave him."

"I didn't know I can do that," says Sospa, jumping up and bouncing with glee. "Make eagles do what I say."

"Neither did I," Serpen adds, resting his chin on his knuckles, deep in thought.

I seriously hope he isn't wondering what might have happened to his empire if he did.

"Don't you dare try it out on me," mutters Wings.

"I'm with baldy," I venture, before turning back to my old nemesis. "What happened next?"

Gulid glares at me. "I was spotted, of course. A feathered idiot staring in a window. They came for me…" He pauses as a frisson of terror takes him.

"The eagles?" I ask.

"No. I wish it was…" He hauls in a huge breath. "A great swarm of snakes, slithering through the streets and, swaying at their lead, the most gigantic serpent I've ever seen, covered in scales that shone like metal, spikes the length of my wing. Their king is, three, four times the size of Your Majesty." Gulid nods at Serpen.

"I flew, cawing like crazy for what was left of my friends to follow me. Two might have tried, but the other eagles swamped them. I managed to get in the air when that, that, monster opened his mouth and made a sound like... urrrrggh."

For those having this story read to them, you probably feel nauseated about now. For those reading, it sounds like a dragon regurgitating a steaming pile of brussels sprouts.

"A great stream of fire shot out of his mouth, heading straight for me."

"Can we do that?" Sospa asks her uncle.

"No," he states, wide-eyed with shock.

"I tipped as hard as I could, but the flames caught the edge of my wing. I managed to slap it out on the tops of trees as I flew over. I barely had time to grab the hidden pack before the snakes ordered the eagles in pursuit, but I was strong and too angry to let them catch me.

"I hid, day after day, freezing in caves, flying at night, when it's harder for them to see me. They finally stopped chasing when I got far enough away. I just about made it back to that mouldy castle, warming myself by the king's old fireplace, until I recovered enough to fly here. I was heading for the wolf village, but I saw this camp first."

"Just as well," I mutter.

"He was burned when he flew in," Mama Bear confirms.

"Wearing yellow," Adamo adds.

"Serves you right," I blurt out, and they all stare at me, aghast at my callousness. "I'm referring to the yellow outfit, not the burned wing or the zonked friends. Stop staring at me. So, you're saying one humungous serpent managed to mesmerise and enslave you all?"

"No," Broken Beak replies. "The one who took Revol wasn't the king. All their snakes are able to mesmerise."

"I thought only those who become big ugly serpents could do that." Serpen stares at me, one eyebrow raised. "No offence."

"That's true," Broken Beak agrees. "Or their bloodline."

"Then how?"

"They're all serpents," he replies, his voice squeaking at the end.

Say what?

"They're all like Serpen?" I ask, over the top of a universal intake of breath. "*All* of them?"

"Exactly like him. Their fire breathing king way bigger."

The room erupts with noise as they all speak at once. There is one thing I still need to know.

"Quiet!" I yell, until the racket dies down. "How many of them are there?"

"I'm not sure, but I saw at least fifty whilst I was in the city. There may be hundreds in that citadel. And all of my eagles serving them."

Fabulous can this get any better?

"How could I not know of this?" Serpen pipes up.

Yes, I'd like to know that as well.

"Are you related to them?" Adamo asks our puny king.

"I must be," Serpen replies. "But my family never said anything about any other snakes."

"What about all those crumbling books in your library," I suggest. "Didn't any of them mention other snakes? Especially one who can breathe fire."

"Erm…" mumbles Serpen, not looking me in the eye.

"Anguis?"

I catch the embarrassment painted on the ambassador's face and suddenly understand.

"What a pair of frauds," I say, drawing another of Ursid's looks. "Neither of you read any of them, did you?"

"We were busy," Serpen mumbles, like a naughty schoolboy caught with a cigarette behind the bike sheds.

"You rattled on at that dinner table about your history and biology and wonderful library and you never set foot in it, except to use it as a mouldering highway."

"Is any of this relevant?" Ursid asks, with a gigantic sigh. "We can hit each other over the head with books later. I want to know why none of us have heard of these snakes before?"

"Geography," Broken Beak replies. "It's too cold for them to move in the winter. They'd freeze."

"Spring, summer?" I probe.

"When the snows melt, the river widens and flows faster, and has nasty rocks."

"So, no swimming snakes or on a boat."

"Exactly."

"But..." he begins.

Here it comes: the flaming punchline to this whole narrative.

"They only had a few eagles before. Now they've got all my friends. They could be flown straight here. They won't come 'til spring as they still hate the cold, but come they will."

"Why?" I ask. "What could they possibly want here?"

"You," he replies.

CHAPTER 29

The Revenge Of The Mouldy Book

I had to ask, didn't I? Well now I know.

After the eagle elaborates on his shocking twist, shaking my brain into mush, I absent myself from a crowd of stunned faces and stand shivering outside the tent, trying to calm down and convince myself it's all going to be fine. As if.

Apparently, in these freaking fantasy worlds every Tom, Dick, Harry and Serpent has a Chosen One legend, which all hinges around some poor shmuck getting shafted for the sake of everyone else. In this case, their shmuck is a woman arriving with a magic book, bringing to pass the greatest ever snake kingdom.

Forgive the snark. I've just found out a homicidal, fire breathing dragon mutation needs to drag my sorry backside to his lair for some unspecified legendary reason, having something vague to do with that book I burned. Possibly.

It makes no sense at all, but when does it ever? Now that monster knows I'm here, book formerly in hand, he'll be coming to grab me and expand his slave kingdom, to wit, all my friends, killing two birds with one stone. And I'm not just referring to Wings and Broken Beak.

I can't help thinking that stinking mouldy book is getting its revenge from beyond the ash pile. I could give myself up, but there's no guarantee the serpents won't prefer this balmy climate and head down here anyway. Still, it's worth a try. Maybe I can get the Beak to drop me north, probably from a great height.

"It's too cold out here."

Mama Bear appears beside me, a mug of steaming broth in hand.

"I'm having a hot flush of panic," I reply. "I'm fine."

She pushes the mug into my gloved hands. "You drink that anyway."

"Thanks."

"Don't do anything stupid."

I glance at her. "Like what?"

"Running off to give yourself up," she replies, staring me down. "You're better off staying with us all."

"You're not," I point out. "That monster might leave you alone, if I'm not here."

"Doubt it. He sounds like a frulking bumhole."

I splutter the mouthful of broth into the snow, choking with laughter.

"What's that?" Mama Bear asks, bending down in the snow to take a closer look at a crushed evergreen leaf, I just covered in spit.

"I picked it off my coat," I reply.

"Did you touch it with your bare hands?" Mama asks, peering up at me.

"No. Why?"

"You sure?"

"Yes."

"Good. Don't put your gloves near your mouth. Give them to me to wash."

"What's up?" I ask, handing them over and thrusting my free hand into my pocket.

She holds my woolly friends by her fingertips. "I use a very small dose of those leaves, crushed into food, as a purgative."

"It makes you go?"

"Yes. It's a cure for the badly bunged up," she tells me with a grin. "Downside is, it makes you smell."

That ringing sound is warning bells going off inside your imagination, bringing a certain Stinky Primus to mind.

"Does it kill you?" I venture, conspiracy theories leaping up and down in my head.

"No. It's just very unpleasant. Horrible in bigger doses. You wouldn't feel that bad unless you kept eating it. Even then, eventually the body gets used to it and it doesn't work anymore. Then the bung comes back with a vengeance, far worse than before." She mimes straining, making me laugh again. "Why do you ask?"

"Primus, the Alpha Alpha, was apparently a stink bomb a while back, but he got better."

Right. Let's think about this. If young Primus was stinky for ages, that might mean he kept eating it, or was fed it until it no longer worked. Why? Did someone just not like him?

"Why aren't you with Curt?" Mama asks, dragging my attention back to my newly broken heart.

"Yelena made me leave," I repeat. "I told Curt to stay with Dulcis after Alpha got hurt."

"Hmmm. None of us should have left," says Mama, shuffling in the snow. "And now we need each other."

"I know. We could try talking to Stinky, sorry Alpha Alpha Primus and his brother. They might listen. I'm not holding my breath though. Wouldn't trust the rest as far as I can throw them. Especially Yellfire."

"Decipa's weird too," pipes up a young voice.

"Sospa, what are you doing out here?" Mama asks, swiftly wrapping the skirt of her coat around the girl.

"I want to hear what you're saying," she brazenly admits.

I can't help but laugh. Feels good to be chuckling again. "Why don't you like Decipa?"

"She listens at doors," Sospa replies, ironically.

"Don't we all," rumbles Adamo, from where he's been listening in the dark.

Mama Bear tuts. "You're hardly setting a good example, for a prince."

The ginger prince of bears blows a raspberry at her.

I suddenly clock what Sospa just said.

"What doors exactly?" I ask the girl. "Decipa, I mean."

"Dulcis' room," Sospa begins, before a flood of pocket snakes bounce into view behind her and excitedly offload their undercover information.

"The sickly Alpha's room."

"Alpha Alpha's room."

"Your room in the mansion."

Ewww, that gives me the creeps.

"Adamo in Dulcis' room."

"Dulcis in Adamo's room. She laughed at the funny noises."

Oops. The teens are rumbled.

"And she keeps going in the kitchen when there's no-one there. I think she's stealing food."

"I won't ask what you were all doing creeping around following her," says their former king, gliding into view with his arms crossed, Anguis a step behind. "Not today, anyway. But if I catch any of you stealing food from the kitchen or listening at doors, I'll be an angry snake. Understand?"

The children all nod in unison.

"And she's in lurve with Alpha," a little boy mocks and his spy friends giggle.

Say what?

"Decipa's in love with that dying old wolf?" I blurt. Not that I'm a fabulous catch at my age.

You are to me, Big Bum, I hear the voice of Curt say, and my lip trembles.

"Not the Southern Alpha," Sospa replies. "Our Alpha."

Ok, right. I'm not sure that's any better.

"How do you figure that?" I ask, straining to picture sour faced Decipa panting after Alpha.

"She followed him everywhere, every time he went out."

"Like last night?" I ask.

Sospa nods.

My mind's on a supersonic collision course with suspicion. I turn to Adamo.

"If you were unconscious, would you revert back to human from animal?"

"Eventually," he replies, "but not immediately. Not for a while actually."

"Is that true of wolves too?"

"Yes," states Wings, from right behind me, making me jump. "What are you up to?"

"Alpha," I reply. "When you and I found him unconscious, he was human, not wolf. So he must have been human when he fell. Why would he change out there, where it's so dangerous, without his clothes?"

Anguis wasn't an ambassador for nothing. "You think he changed to talk to someone."

"And that someone hurt him?" Wings adds. "That means I left him there, unconscious, in the house, with his attacker, 'cause I know it wasn't us," he mumbles, blaming himself.

"None of this is your fault. First my lodge burns down," I list on my fingers, trying to make sense of it all, "aiming to kill me and Curt, or Stinky and Fidus? The bears are forced to go. Alpha's accident, or attack. Then we all leave…"

"Who benefits?" Adamo asks. "Decipa?"

"Not for herself," I reply. "Is she spying for Yelena? She now leads the entire pack."

Ursid wraps an arm around me as he appears from wherever he was hiding. Everyone's lurking out here. The tent must be empty.

"What about Curt?" asks Ursid.

"He didn't do it," I snap.

"No, I mean, doesn't he stand between Yelena and the pack if Alpha…?"

"She deposed him and he let her," I growl, anger on that point still red hot, if unfair. "He had to, I suppose."

"I think Curt might have been sick when we left," Wings says, peering at me. "I thought he was upset because of… well, you… but…"

"Are you saying they're poisoning my wolf?" I holler. Ursid's arm tightens around my shoulders, clamping me in place.

"Did he smell?" Mama Bear asks me, trying to divert my panic.

"No worse than usual," I reply, and promptly burst into tears.

"What if their Alpha's also being poisoned?" Adamo offers. "He looked nasty to me."

"He didn't smell," says Mama. "Not when I was there. So it would be some other poison. There's a lot of them to choose from."

"It's not any of us," Serpen inserts. "Their Alpha was sick before he arrived, so it's his own people."

"Or this is all coincidence," Anguis points out.

"I'm going back NOW," I wail, gulping furiously.

"Walking all the way, are you?" asks Wings.

That sass dries up the waterworks a bit.

"Like you're not going," I snap. "You can fly us both."

"We all need to go," says Serpen. "They have to know about the Northern Empire. If we don't unite, we won't be able to defend ourselves."

"By ourselves, I assume you're not joining them," Adamo says.

Serpen bristles. "You're questioning our loyalty?"

Adamo stares at the former king. "No-one said much when we bears got thrown out."

"I understand, but are you really asking me whether I'd join the serpents?" Serpen retorts. "After a year together?"

"No, I suppose not," Adamo sighs.

"And as I recall, you stomped off in a huff, dragging all your bears after you."

"They called me a traitor. What would you…"

"Stop arguing," I wail.

"Don't cry," whispers Ursid, rocking me from side to side, which makes me sob harder.

"I think that wolf got to us all," Adamo says. "She's not going to listen to any of us. Least of all, me."

"And what if Yelena's behind a poisoning plot?" Serpen asks. "We can't just walk up and talk to her, or any of them."

"Curt," offers Anguis.

"What about him?" I ask, mopping my face.

"He needs to make her listen, or at least assume leadership himself. If Alpha's still… not well."

"He won't," I moan. "He told me they won't follow him. And he's afraid for his wolves. And me."

"You'll have to make him," Mama Bear insists. "Tell him we'll all follow him. He'll listen to you."

"I don't know…" I whimper.

"That's enough of that," Mama insists, wrenching me from Ursid's embrace. "Our pack needs you. Now what are you going to do about it?"

All eyes are back on this old girl. I suppose I better dig up the British Grit, even if it's soggy.

"I am going to kick Curt up the mangy arse until he's Alpha again."

"Good answer," Mama replies, giving me a big kiss on the forehead.

"We can't all arrive at once," Adamo points out. "She-wolf will assume it's a battle and we can't count on the loyalty of Curt's wolves without him."

"We also need to avoid hurting any of the wolves," says Anguis, "given the necessity to unite later. Therefore, I propose stealth. A few of us go back to speak to Curt and see what's what. Put the situation to him first."

"I'm going," I state, daring anyone to contradict me.

"So am I," announces Serpen.

"Me too," says Adamo, "and Ursid."

"Of course," mutters the general, giving my shoulders a squeeze.

Anguis raises his hand.

"Are you asking a question or volunteering?" I ask.

"The latter," Anguis replies, with a smile.

"Just try and stop me going," Wings pipes up.

"And me," says Mama Bear, cutting Adamo off in mid breath. "Before you argue, I'm the best one to treat Curt, if he's ill, and I need to get a look at both of the Alphas."

"Thank you, Mama." I'm tearing up again when a flapping great eagle splats into the camp, spraying snow over us all.

"Where have you been?" I yell at the returning Broken Beak.

"I sent - asked - him to take a look at the town," Serpen replies, on the bird's behalf. "Just in case we decided to, well, go back."

Mama Bear wraps the transforming bird man in a blanket, whilst he hops around in the snow on naked feet.

"Cold. My feet are freezing," he groans.

"Get on with it," I holler.

"Charming," he mutters and turns to Serpen. "If you're planning to sneak back in there, you'll need a diversion. The town's surrounded by a wall of grubby wolves and they don't look friendly. I have one question. Why are you all standing out here in the cold?"

CHAPTER 30

Stinking Bears

We all settle back in the nice warm tent, the disappointed children having been unceremoniously ordered to bed. If it wasn't for the nightmare possibility of Curt being poisoned, I'd join them, rather than face a sortie into enemy territory. I exaggerate, since it's hardly likely Yelena would eat or torture me. Feed me deadly nightshade, possibly.

"Gather round," Ursid orders, his back ramrod straight, like the general he is. "I have a plan."

"There's a plan?" chirps Adamo, purposely winding him up. "That makes a change."

"If the prince would like to listen to his wise elder for a moment, he might learn something," Ursid growls, "since I was the one doing a circuit of the town every day and night, whilst he was making noises in his room."

The chorus of guffaws tells me everyone knew of the prince's love life, with the exception of Dulcis' father. I'm praying he lives long enough to find out.

"Go ahead, General," says Adamo, flushing a little. "I know how you love making sneaky plans."

Ursid rumbles and squints at him, before smiling at me encouragingly. He grabs the pile of newly washed spoons (one with a snapped handle) and, laying them end to end, makes a circle on the carpet.

"This is the town, which Gulid says now has a ring of wolves guarding it. We don't know whether they're all Yelena's, but we have to assume they are. If we are going to get inside to secretly talk to Curt without being taken, or starting a war, we have to get past this line."

"Won't they smell and hear us coming anyway?" Adamo asks.

"Exactly, so we can't approach them or try to sneak past."

"I'm not following," I say, since I can't be the only one.

"Our Curt finding team isn't going to enter on the ground," Ursid informs me.

Gulid huffs as he raises an eyebrow. "I sense this is where you expect me to come in."

"Us," qualifies Wings.

"I'm not flying with him," I proclaim, pointing at Broken Beak.

"Get your finger out of my face," he snaps, slapping my hand away. "I refuse to carry this lump anywhere."

"I'll fly Edi," says Wings. "Can we calm down, please?"

"You seem to forget," I point out, "the last time I went on a luxury flight with that vulture, he dropped me from a great height and nearly broke my legs."

Broken Beak scowls right in my face. "Pity it wasn't your neck."

"That attitude isn't helpful," says Mama Bear, inserting her face between ours and staring at us both until we sit back. "The general wasn't finished."

"Thank you," Ursid says to her. "Gulid. Yes, it would be helpful if you join us as part of this plan, but if there's going to be a problem..."

"I'm in," states Gulid, still scowling at me. "If I'm going to stand any chance of getting my friends back, those serpents have to be stopped, and to do that, I need you all, so... I'll fly in whoever you want. Except her."

He gets the joy of my middle finger. "Toerag."

"Baggage," he retorts, lifting up all five fingers.

He's missed the point, but hey, I can be the better person. Stop laughing.

"Around here," Ursid continues, pointing within the circle of spoons, "is the weakest area inside the line of wolves, just outside the town itself, with blind rocks, a steep drop off and thicker tree density. I taught our own wolves and bears how to watch for that location, but Yelena's wolves won't have had time to fully explore the whole area. This is where our eagles will drop us off."

"Surely they'll still see them flying in," Serpen says.

"Not if they dive at speed and the line is all looking outwards, away from the town."

"And how do we achieve that?" I ask.

"Diversion," Ursid replies, with a grin. "We'll send our speediest bears, soaked in every strong smell we can get, to race all around the area, out of view, coating it in so many scents, the wolves can't track anything. Then they'll jump out, one at a time, all around the circle, growling like mad, and race back to hiding spots. We'll set all the wolves going and cause chaos. Wings, you take Edi, because she needs to convince Curt, and Splendia."

Who? He's looking at Mama Bear. So that's her name. It fits.

"Gulid, you'll take myself and Prince Adamo, then you both go back for Serpen and Anguis."

Broken Beak nods, making a point of not looking at me.

"If Curt succeeds in leading his wolves, it may take all of us to convince Yelena not to make a fight of it." Ursid sits back and sighs, running his hand through his hair. "But be aware, this is a one way trip, except for our eagles, who can fly out as soon as we're dropped."

"Not happening," states Wings. "These are my pups. I should never have left them."

I gently lay a hand over his. "Me neither."

"If it goes badly," Ursid continues, "our bears and snakes should not come in after us. We're not having a final battle in this town. Agreed? Your Highness? Your Majesty?"

"Agreed," says Adamo.

"I agree," Serpen says. "And if we can't unite, then our people need to head south, away from the Serpents."

"Your snakes will be taken care of," Adamo tells him. "You have my word."

"When do we go?" Anguis asks.

"It has to be dark, to hide the eagles flying overhead," Ursid answers. "So, we wait until tomorrow, or we go now."

"Now," I blurt. I'm not leaving my family to that she-wolf a moment longer.

"Now," Adamo agrees.

Ursid looks to Serpen, who nods.

"Then I'll round up my best bears," the general states, "and give them the plan. Splendia, can I rely on you to find the smells?"

She laughs. "Oh, I know just the sort of stink you need."

* * *

I look up at the night sky thankful, for once, there are no sparkling stars to enthral me. The Good Lord is on our side tonight, providing a swirling carpet of cloud and falling snow to hide our little incursion. I send up a prayer of protection, that we might all see the morning safely. At the very least, I want to see my wolf again.

The bear diversion squad headed out some time ago, pounding their way back to town. I don't know what Mama Bear used on their fur, but the stench is still making my eyes water. As our group assembles, booted and suited against the cold, I lean towards a suspicious Gulid and whisper. "Are you staying in the town or flying out?"

"I don't know," he replies.

"Look, if you do stay and this goes wrong, and you can escape the town, and can only grab one of us, please take Mama Bear, as she has a cub."

He peers at me and nods. "If I stay."

Anguis steps up beside me, holding out his arms. We embrace for a long, long time, my head on his shoulder.

"Please, don't let anyone get hurt," I whisper.

"We have to go," Ursid announces, clapping his gloved hands together.

"Remember," Anguis says, before he lets go of me. "I'm a snake. If you're afraid, or it turns bad, come to me." He steps back. "I'll see you soon."

I nod my head to Serpen and he tips his in reply.

Adamo slips on a patch of ice and almost bowls us both over in his enthusiasm. I suspect he's covering the fear we all feel.

"Well, erm, good luck then," he bumbles.

I hug him like I'll never let go. "You stay safe, you big bear and, whatever happens, go get Dulcis."

"I will."

Two giant eagles patter in our direction, cawing into the night. Growls from bears echo all through the camp, interspersed with applause from the snakes, rising to a roaring salute.

"Ready?" asks Mama Bear, flipping the strap of her medicine bag over her head. "Let's go find your Curt."

Tears fill my eyes, yet again. I'm getting too soppy for my own good.

Gulid rises into the air, sweeping Ursid and Adamo into his claws. They both squeak like chew toys.

Wings flexes a claw and tips his head, asking the question.

I hold out my arms. "Let's go."

He squawks at full volume, making my ears vibrate beneath my hat. His right claw wraps around Mama as he flaps, rising higher into the wind. I close my eyes and feel the pressure around my torso, just before my feet leave the ground.

CHAPTER 31

Stealth Flight & The Ancient Posse

It's so peaceful up here, without the whistling wind. Below us, clouds undulate like waves in the ocean as we soar, swimming in the realm of stars. Although frozen limbs ache as they dangle from the eagle's claw cage, the simplicity of night remains staggeringly beautiful. Mama Bear waves at me out of the darkness, and I return her gesture. Camouflaged against velvet sky, I catch the shadow spread of Gulid's wings and my friends hanging beneath.

The dim horizon tips as Wings turns, looping around to hover over this place. We can't be far from our destination. The stars dissolve as the pair of eagles drop into roiling clouds and my world turns to dampened darkness, senses suspended in soaking cotton wool. Circling just above discovery, sound filters through as we spiral lower and lower.

A solitary wolf howl pierces the gloom, but silence returns.

Then another yowl.

And another.

Layer upon layer, the air fills with ferocious howling in an escalating chorus of chaos. Through a sudden break in cloud cover, I glimpse a bear leaping into full view of a wolf guard and waving a giant paw, before scarpering into the trees at a sprint. The ring of wolves breaks under the confusion as they chase each insurgent.

My stomach rises up to grab my throat as my feathered pilot streamlines his wings and dives at the speed of light, the world whipping past in a face stretching blur. Despite the terror, neither Mama nor myself make a single gasp of fear. Silence is our friend.

The outskirts of the town, its chalets lit from within, snap into view as we clear the cloud cover. Far below, wolf guards race around, their attention away from the town, just as the general hoped. Ursid's weak spot with its blind rocks, dipping ground and dense group of trees seems exactly as described, which would be comforting if the ground wasn't rising up towards my wide eyes at an alarming rate. A nasty flashback to the castle roof makes me cringe and pull myself into a tight ball, as if that will prevent breakage of all my bones or becoming a fatty stain on the landscape.

At the very last second, my eagle tips his wings, stalling the dive, and drops me exactly in position. I land with a gut wrenching crunch, roll up and over my right shoulder and leap to my feet, just as I learnt in parachute training, when I was a lot younger and far more flexible. I sprint behind those covering rocks as a flapping Wings returns to the air.

Mama Bear arrives with a hefty splat in the snow, rolling on her back to protect the medicine bag she's clutching to her stomach. She lifts her head, scans the area, spots me waving from behind the rock and scrambles over, puffing.

"Dear Lord Almighty what is that smell?" I mutter, as the overpowering stench surrounding us hits my nose and makes my eyes stream in protest. If you mixed skunk whiff with rotten eggs, putrefying cabbage and month old socks, it wouldn't smell as bad as that. Good luck to any wolf trying to pick our smell out of that poison gas cloud.

A self-satisfied Mama beams at me. "Do I know how to bring the stink or what?"

"Tell me that's not gumwhat pee," I mumble.

"Only if you want flaming bears."

Gulid's claws loom out of the darkness, frightening the life out of us both. If anything, he's going even faster than Wings and there's no way he'll stop in time. He swoops low over my head, flapping a wing tip in my face as he pretty much drops Ursid and Adamo in our laps. To their credit the men arrive without a grunt, despite bouncing hard on their backsides. Both glare up at the eagle, but he's already rising above the trees on his way back to Wings' side, probably with a smarmy smile on his broken beak.

The boys dust themselves down as Mama and I peep over the rock. We duck at the sight of a wolf, but he's already sprinting away from us, hot on the tail of a reeking speedy bear.

"So, we wait," whispers Mama.

"We go as soon as the snakes get here," I reply, hiking my scarf over my nose.

"Has it worked?" Adamo breathes down my ear, making every nerve tighten in fear.

"Don't do that," I mouth, scowling him into submission. "Of course, it worked," I tell Ursid, giving him the double thumbs up.

He grins in reply, wrinkling his nose.

Adamo's head tips upwards and his eyes close as a prelude to a trumpeting sneeze. Ursid clamps both hands over his charge's face, muffling the delivery and coating the general's gloves with snot. Ursid peers at his fingers, sighs and wipes the offending glop on the rock. I get the sudden urge to hug him, but I'll hold off until this is all over. If there is such an outcome.

I peer up at thick clouds, straining to spot the returning eagles, but the rolling camouflage is perfect. They only appear out of thick darkness when they're almost on top of us. Anguis and Serpen sail free of opening claws, gracefully running across the snow like a ballet pas de deux, whilst the birds land between the trees, each dropping a bag of clothes from their other claw. I look away whilst two naked blokes maniacally tug on their kit.

"We're here," Anguis whispers, embracing me from behind. I wish that hug didn't feel so good, especially since Curt is close and needs me.

"Fabulous stench," whispers Serpen, nodding at Mama Bear. "Well done."

"Are you staying?" I ask Gulid.

"What do you think?" he snaps, pointing at his trousers. "I'm here to fly you out of trouble. Well, some of you."

"Remember Mama," I remind him, ignoring that last remark.

Ursid peers around the rock, giving the area a thorough scan before gesturing for us to follow him on a stealth creep into town. This place has been my home for over a year, but I confess to being a bundle of nerves as I step out from hiding and tiptoe after Adamo. Have you any idea how ridiculous a grown woman looks trying to tiptoe through thick snow? I keep bending my knees as I shift, as though being three inches lower will make me invisible to Yelena's homicidal wolves.

I breathe a premature sigh of relief when we're across the short open field from trees to town, even though we're far more likely to run into someone, or be spotted, as we approach the chalets. The flitting from house to house, hiding behind walls feels better than outright exposure. If anyone's looking down on us, we must resemble a stream of shifty ants in welly boots.

It's about now the ludicrous notion of eight full grown adults trying to sneak about as a group without being rumbled, dark clothes standing out against the white snow like a sore thumb, begins to hit us all. It's only a matter of time before someone raises the alarm, or Adamo trips over his own feet and nosedives through a front door.

As it turns out, I have even less time than I thought when a wolf streaks straight across my path in a blur of grey fur. I know all the wolves in my pack. This isn't one of them, which is just my luck. I'm exposed with nowhere to go and he's about to turn around and clamp eyes, and probably teeth, on me. Adamo and Ursid tense from behind a chalet wall, gearing up to change, and Anguis arrives by my side, which is comforting, but really stupid. How is the both of us getting mauled going to help? I could do with a handy eagle right about now, but they're both fiddling with their ill-fitting breeches.

"Keep your mangy tail away from my home," an elderly man bellows, flinging open his door and brandishing a log at the wolf, who turns to stare the old man down, snarling. Luckily, for me, this manoeuvre means he's turned tail on Anguis and myself.

The ambassador shoves me sideways, pointing. I follow his sign to an ancient lady waving a bony arm through a crack in her own doorway, gesturing for us to hurry. I clump through the snow and bundle inside her house, Anguis following so closely, he steps on me in his haste to shut the door. Through the closing gap, I spot our brave diversion lobbing a handful of snow at the wolf, hitting it straight between the eyes. He hollers in triumph, before leaping back inside his own home and slamming the door in the angry wolf's face.

Kneeling on the floor, my eyes rise clear of the window sill as I scan for my friends. Six relieved faces peer through a window from the house opposite. Ursid raises a palm to indicate that we should stay put for a while, so I sit back, leaning against the wall to catch my breath.

Apparently, some of my old pack aren't as fond of Yelena's rule as I thought. I still have wolf friends in this town and that warms my chilled heart, if not my toes.

"Thank you," I whisper to my aged saviour. "And the others. You didn't need to do this. I don't know how Yelena will react if she finds out."

"Oh, I think we do need to help," the old lady replies. Luva, if I remember rightly. "None of us think what's going on here is right. They tell us our Alpha's dying and our former Alpha's sick too. We haven't been allowed to see Curt since you left. I tried, but a great brute of a wolf's guarding him now and wouldn't let me pass. No respect for their elders these mangy creatures."

I beckon her over and point through the window. "You see the tall lady?"

"I know Mama Bear," she croaks. "I'm old, not stupid."

"I need to get her to Curt and Alpha, to see if she can treat them." I turn to peer into her eyes. "And I need to convince Curt, sick or not, he should take over as Alpha, because something bad's coming for us, Luva, from the north, and if we're not all together, wolves, bears and our snakes…"

"More snakes?" Luva asks. My surprise must be evident because she nods at Anguis. "I guessed from the look on his face."

He laughs. "Some ambassador, I am."

"I'm just a very old wolf and I've seen a lot," Luva tells him, sitting back in a rocking chair, whose familiar design informs me she's known Curt a long, long time. As she heaves on her boots, creaking as she bends, her slightly milky gaze swings to me. "You go get Curt and tell him he's always been our Alpha, no matter what Frozen Hell or Yellfire say about it."

Boots in place, she rises and strides unsteadily across the room, grabbing her coat on the way. "You let us old wolves have some fun keeping those scrag end of dogs out of your way. It's been too long since I had a good scrap." A skeletal fist shoots out in a boxing jab.

Oh, I like her. Very much.

"If you can help us get to the mansion, we'll deal with Curt's guard," I tell her, although I've no idea how.

"Deal," says Luva, grabbing her walking stick. That wolf's head carving looks like Curt's work too. There's a story here, I'm sure.

A tap at the door strips another layer of nerves. Anguis and I hide under the table as Luva slowly opens to the old man from the chalet opposite.

"It's clear for now," he says.

"Go grab who you can," Luva tells him, waving her stick at his nose. "We're going to keep the way clear to the mansion."

He glances at the human and snake, squidged together under the table and a huge grin lights his face. He takes off at a wobbly jog. Luva waves at the window of the other house and my friends all creep out to join me.

"Wings," says Luva, giving him the eye. "Come back to rescue your pups?"

"Luva," he squeaks in reply, and coughs.

Definitely a story. Remind me to ask later.

Adamo laughs. One look from her beady eye silences that.

"General," Luva says, nodding at Ursid.

"My Lady Wolf," he replies.

"Silver tongued bear," she titters. "Get this rabble to our Alpha. Here come my friends."

The ancient posse tottering through the snow deserve a story unto themselves. The Magnificent Lupine. What an inspiration. It's never too late to be epic.

"Most of Yelena's scraggies are chasing after reeking bears," says Monk. That's not his real name, but a ring of grey hair around a bald patch gives him the nickname in my mind. "But there's still a few sneaking around, up to no good. We'll go on ahead. Stay back 'til we tell you."

"Thank you," I whisper. "I'm so grateful for..."

"Enough, girly," Monk replies. "You're family," and heads off, creeping like a cold war spy.

A tear rolls down my cheek and I furiously brush it away, poking myself in the eye with a woolly glove. Ursid gives my arm a squeeze as he passes, following behind Monk. Broken Beak mimes gagging, which is charming.

"Best in two groups," Luva suggests. "Just in case. You bears come with me. Eagles and snakes go left."

Monk beckons to Serpen's group and they follow him, Wings tossing me an encouraging smile. Mama hugs my shoulder and nods at Luva to lead off.

Thus begins a nerve shredding creep and hide performance, to the howling musical accompaniment of a wolf hunting bear circus and the smell of blocked drains. The elderly posse spread out, covering the ground ahead and behind our two groups. Considering the shaky knees, walking sticks and limps, they're shifting across the ground at a fair rate. In a few years I might join them; they seem like a fun group of reprobates. In my opinion, nobody should ever grow old gracefully.

"Watch where you're going," Luva croaks, at the top of her voice.

Duly warned, we duck behind the nearest chalet. I peep out to catch one of Yelena's wolves snarling at the old lady and, for a moment, consider defending her, until she raps her walking stick on the wolf's nose with a muffled thump.

"Don't you be snarling at me, pup. I'm old enough to be your great grandwolf."

He whines, rubbing a paw over his sore snout, snaps at her and slinks off, apparently unwilling to confront an elder with attitude. At least he has that to his credit, if nothing else. Once his drooping tail disappears around a corner, I pop into view, my expression asking her if she's alright. She laughs and swipes the air, as if to say, 'that's nothing.'

To our left, another wolf pads into view, heading straight for Serpen's group. Monk jogs into her path and trips her up, pretending to fall on her tail with an exaggerated 'ooft'. As she barks at him, yanking on her trapped rudder, he struggles to rise, apologising profusely for his 'knobbly old knees,' neatly pinning her in position as my friends tiptoe past.

Our path veers further to the right and we lose sight of the other group. I swing around a chalet to find a wolf standing right there, back towards me, but already turning. Before he can catch sight of me, an avalanche of snow slides off the chalet's roof and dumps straight on top of him, burying my adversary. We race past the spluttering wolf, claws flying as he digs himself out. I glance up and catch a young boy leaning out of the window, clutching an iron poker. He smiles and waves at me, pointing the poker at the roof, from whence he just dislodged the deluge of snow. I blow him a kiss and sprint to the next cover.

With every step, more and more people flood into the streets, drawn by the howling racket. Any one of them would know us by sight, but not a soul from my pack gives us away, instead purposely blocking our movements from enemy wolves. I love them all and feel ashamed I ever questioned their loyalty.

We're closing in on the mansion, the gaping hole in its side patched up with newly hewn logs, when the front door opens and Yelena emerges, guard wolves behind her. Ursid, Adamo, Mama Bear and I swing right, snuggling close to the side wall. I glance back to see the crumbly posse busy tripping, poking and slowing down any wolf they see. They look like they're having the time of their lives.

"Go back to your homes!" Yelena bellows in the voice of a foghorn.

"Alpha Widow?" Luva croaks, wobbling towards her.

"What are you doing out here, Old Wolf?" Yelena asks.

Staggering into her, Luva leans right into her face, hollering, "What you say?" as though deaf.

Yelena takes a step backwards before shouting, "Why are you out here?"

"Same as you," the old lady scoffs. "What's all this racket? And that smell? Is that you?"

"No, it's not…" Yelena begins, before taking a deep breath. "Everything's fine. Go home now."

"Don't seem fine to me," Luva says. The crowd all mutter in agreement. "Did I see a bear running about?"

"You're fine. There's no…"

"What? What you say?"

She's absolutely priceless. I could watch this performance all day, but Ursid yanks on my arm and I move on. We arrive at the rear of the lodge to find the snakes and eagles have beaten us to it, Wings' head already poking inside the back door.

"Nobody," he whispers, and slips into the mansion.

"There should be guards patrolling this door," Ursid grumbles. "I'll have words with Alpha about his sloppy…"

"Not now," says Adamo. "Hush up and get inside."

Ursid gives his oversized prince the squint eye and shoves him through the doorway first.

I follow them into the rear corridor, scanning left and right as I arrive. Not that I can see much in the dark, except my breath, because it's freezing in here. I hope they've got Curt somewhere warmer than this, or he'll definitely be ill. My heart twists at that thought.

Hold on Curt, I'm coming for you.

"I'll go first," Adamo whispers, heading for the staircase.

"Not a chance," Anguis says, slipping through to block his way. "You'll trip up the stairs and announce our presence to every wolf in the town. I'll go, since I'm the lightest."

"Excuse me?" I hiss, staggeringly insulted, even if it's true.

Anguis kisses the top of my head as he glides past. He mounts the stairs without the slightest creak from the wood, as though weighing less than a feather. At the top, he turns the corner, disappearing from view.

Serpen shivers and Mama Bear proceeds to rub his arms, like he's a small boy. He lets her, being as he remembers her kindness when he arrived here from that foul castle. It's hard to recall how broken he was, back then.

Anguis returns, flowing down the stairs like a bubbling brook. He beckons us into a huddle.

"Luva was right. There's only one guard, but he's huge, sat directly outside Curt and Edi's room." He glances at me. "We can take him, but it'll be noisy. If you want time to talk to Curt before Yelena gets wind of us being here, then we need a plan to move him."

"Probably should have thought of that before we got here," Broken Beak whispers, despite the continuing racket outside.

"Not helpful," I tell him, glaring. He's right though.

"We don't need a plan," says Mama Bear, loosing a teeth laden grin. She delves in her medicine bag and holds up a small brown bottle of some unknown liquid. "I've got this."

And up the stairs she goes.

"No way I'm missing this," I mutter and follow.

CHAPTER 32

Mama Versus The Guard

Have you ever tried climbing a wooden staircase without it creaking like a gothic haunted house? I shift my weight at the first eeek, only to add a grating racccck, followed by a resounding crack. Hopefully it just sounds like a wooden house shrinking in the cold to any hearers, but I don't expect to be that lucky.

Mama Bear reaches the top stair and ties a scarf around her lower face, coming across like a love child of a highwayman and a pirate. When she glances down at me, I mime 'What are you doing?' and she lifts the scarf to mouth back, 'Trust me.'

Nothing bad ever followed that statement, right?

"I'm here," she announces, rushing along the hallway. "Where's my patient?"

I leg it up the remaining steps and poke one eye around the corner, to spot Mama right up in the surprised guard's face, since she's easily as tall as he is, although he's twice the width, with the air of a thumb screwing mafia hitman.

Behind me, two bears, two snakes and two eagles squidge up the stairs, jostling for prime position with a dozen flying elbows, whilst simultaneously staying silent. I'd laugh if it wasn't so counter-productive. I wave at them to stay still and they freeze in a screwball tableau.

Back with Mama, the ruffled guard's spluttering, "Who are you?"

"Fallofal," she replies, her voice purposely muffled.

"What?"

"Sorry, mask," she mumbles, pointing at her face. "In case what he's got spreads. I've heard it makes you vomit and gives you nasty big boils. I don't want a dose of that, no thank you. And it's worse for the men, since they get it on their... you know..." she nods at his nether regions.

"Oh," says the guard, turning green as he stares at his crotch, then his fingers. "Can I catch it from the door knob?"

"It's alright," says Mama, whipping the bottle from her pocket like a magician's rabbit. "This will help." With a flourish, she pulls the stopper and holds out the bottle at arm's length. "Sniff that."

We would all do it. It's stupid, but it's a human reflex to sniff something waved under our nose and, sure enough, the guard draws in a humungous whiff. His eyes cross and he wobbles a couple of steps.

"I don't feel..." he gets out, before his knees buckle and he sits down with a fleshy thud.

"Hurry up, but hold your nose," she stage whispers to me, holding hers with finger and thumb. She yanks off her scarf and pours a few more drops of the liquid onto it, slapping it over the guard's nose and mouth. His eyes roll up in his head.

Complying with her order, I tell the others, "Leth's go. Hold your dose," and run along the balcony, glancing down into the empty hall, below. A pile of ash sits where a roaring fire used to be. They must all be outside with the ruckus, or asleep. I hope.

Exchanging a look with Mama, I tap gently on the door of what used to be my bedroom.

"Go away," a very grumpy wolf growls.

That's *my* grumpy wolf. I could cry, but sobbing is hard whilst holding your nose. I try turning the door knob, but the door's locked.

"It's locked, idiot," Curt grumbles, followed by a honking retch.

"Mama, does the guard have the key?" I whisper.

As she rifles through his pockets, coming up empty, there's a scuffle from the room. A thud tells me Curt's leaning against the door as I hear a key turning in the lock from the inside. That's weird.

"Big Bum?" Curt asks.

"It's me. Open the door."

"Drag him inside," Mama tells the arriving Adamo, pointing at the guard. "He'll wake up with a headache fairly soon, so we have to be quick."

The door opens, but before I can lay eyes on my mangy wolf, Adamo grabs the unconscious guard underneath his armpits and heaves him across the threshold, smacking the door into my wolf's ear. He staggers, his back towards me, moaning.

Not having a free hand, Adamo tries holding his breath, but after turning a shade of puce, still gets a nostril full of Mama's potion. He drops the guard, whose head bounces off the floorboards with a dong. He'll wake to even more of a headache now.

Anguis and Serpen catch the woozy ginger prince and haul him over to the window. Gulid flings it open and sticks his head into the freezing air to revive him. A few lungfuls of that clears his mind, not to mention freezing his face. I'm grateful for the icy fresh draft, since this room smells like baby sick, even if it feels like the inside of a fridge in here. Ursid closes the door behind us all.

Curt turns, shaking his head, hand over his ear. "That hurt," he groans, glaring at Adamo's back, before swinging around to face me.

"You look awful," I blurt, because he does. I've only been gone twenty four hours. One solitary day and he looks like death warmed up, skin all pasty with dark circles under his eyes, greasy grey hair plastered against his forehead and vomit all down the front of his jumper. My arms open wide and I rush towards him.

Wings gets there first, hauling his pup into the hug of a lifetime. If the wolf wasn't feeling sick before, he will be now. Curt's eyes fill up with tears and he lays his head on the eagle's shoulder.

"I don't feel well," he half wails.

"I know. Wings is here," the eagle coos.

Mama Bear creeps up behind Curt and takes a sniff, her nose crinkling with distaste.

Oh for goodness sake, I didn't come all this way to stand here like a twit.

"Excuse me," I say, tapping the old bird on the shoulder. He scowls at me and stays right where he is. "Don't make me ask you again," I warn. He tuts and lets go, a twinkle in his eye.

"You left me," Curt rumbles, scowling at me.

"Keep your voice down," Ursid pleads. "It's chaos outside, but there may still be wolves in these rooms."

"You left me for the snake," Curt delivers at half volume.

"I didn't have a choice," I reply, over the top of Anguis' exasperated theatrical sigh. "I didn't want to go."

"I missed you," he whines, his bottom lip trembling.

"I've only been gone a day."

"Worst day of my life."

"Worse than that?" I ask, pointing at his injured hip.

"That hurt less," he whimpers, eyes the size of saucers.

Aww.

We fling ourselves at one another and crunch foreheads as arms wrap around my padded bulk and his reeking jumper.

Curt launches into, "I'm so sorry. You are so my mate. I love you. I've missed you so much, I wanted to howl 'til I die."

"You had me at Big Bum, Mange," I reply and burst into tears. And it all floods out of me. "I'm so scared. I lost my lodge and my rocking chair. I lost you. What if I zap back where I came from, because I'm so miserable?"

"Never happen," he tells me, kissing my face over and over. "You're stuck here with me. I'm sorry I let you go. Never again. Never."

Over his shoulder I catch sight of eye rolling and gagging signs from the others. I don't much care. I plant a kiss on his lips and he opens his mouth to mine. Unfortunately, even industrial strength peppermint toothpaste wouldn't deal with that.

"Curt, eeew," I exclaim, gagging and spitting.

"Did I say I don't feel well?" he adds, before spotting Broken Beak lurking by the window. "What's he doing here?"

"I came to rescue you, you ungrateful wolf," the recalcitrant eagle snaps.

"Rescue me from what?" Curt asks.

"Whom," I correct.

"What?"

"Rescue you from whom," I explain.

"Does it matter?" Mange snaps.

"Aren't you a prisoner in here?" I suggest, pointing at the zonked out guard.

"I locked them all out because I'd had enough. They said they didn't want my illness spreading, anyway," Curt explains. "He was here to fetch things for me."

"Oh."

Mama Bear gives Curt another hefty sniff.

"Will you stop doing that," he growls, shuffling away from her.

"He doesn't smell," is Mama's verdict. "Well, no worse than vomit."

"Thanks," Curt mutters, sarcastically.

"But he looks awful, so…"

"Adamo, if you feel better, perhaps you should come inside before someone sees you," Serpen says. "Why is it so cold in here?"

"My aunt had them put the fires out early. She said we were too soft, not like true wolves." Curt finally registers a room full of banned friends. "What are you all doing back here?"

"That gumwhat looks rubbish," says Adamo as his head reappears from outside.

"What? What gumwhat?"

I rush over to the window and, sure enough, Mr G's lying on the window sill, flat on his back, legs in the air, looking horrendously green. I scoop my old friend into my arms and he promptly hurls a stream of sick down my coat.

"What's the matter with Mr G? Did you feed him?"

"You weren't here, remember?" barks Curt. "Of course, I fed him. You weren't going to. And he kept tapping on the frulking window."

"From your own food?" I probe, laying my old friend on the bedside table.

"Just a bit." Curt's expression darkens when the penny drops. "You're saying there's something wrong with my food."

"That something probably being poison," says Mama Bear, "since the Alpha of Alphas is also ill. How's he doing?"

"Last thing I heard, he's dying," Curt replies and sits down heavily on the bed. "Oh, frulk."

"We could be wrong," I offer. "I could just be paranoid."

"Yes," Curt agrees, "but you never are."

"Is it the berries?" I ask Mama.

"No, I don't think so," she replies. "Curt doesn't smell."

"Can you treat it?" Curt asks, swallowing hard. "Or is it too late?"

Mama slaps him across the back of the head. "That's enough of that whining. We'll find out what it is and I'll treat it." She rustles in her medicine bag, producing a small, squidgy ball that looks like chewing gum mixed with grass. "Here, chew that. It counteracts a few nasty things I know of and it'll build you up."

Curt pops it in his mouth and chews. A non stop torrent of coughing, eye-watering and snot pours forth.

Mama claps a hand over his mouth. "It tastes horrible, but finish it anyway. Swallow. Go on, swallow."

Curt duly swallows and dry retches repeatedly.

"Wolves," Mama sighs.

"Curt, how's your brother?" I ask, sitting beside him on the bed.

He takes my hand. "He still hasn't woken. Dulcis stays with him as long as she can."

"Is she in my, er, her room?" Adamo asks, catching himself out.

Curt scowls at him, until I turn his face back to me.

"I'm sorry," I tell him. "And I know you don't feel well, but you have to listen to me carefully."

"This isn't going to be good, is it?" he asks.

"I, we, all need you to take this pack back from Yelena. All of us; wolves, bears, snakes, eagles and little old human me. One pack."

"I agree, but why particularly?" he probes, gaze boring into mine.

"The northern snakes are coming. And they're all serpents."

CHAPTER 33

The Fidus Touch

I deliver my story as succinctly as I can. He's sitting there, stunned, staring as though waiting for me to reveal the joke's on him. I'm afraid not.

"How long do we have?" he asks, finally.

"Soon as the snows break," Gulid replies. "They'll come for her and the rest of us."

Curt clutches my hand to his vomit stained chest. "Don't you be thinking about giving yourself up. I know you."

"Much as I'd like to hand her over," Gulid interjects, "they'll still come, soon as they feel how much warmer it is down here. I could drop her up north."

"I could feed you to my aunt," Curt replies. "As fried eagle."

"Thanks a lot," Wings mutters. "I took care of you when…"

"Not you, old man," his pup replies. "You'd be stringy anyway."

I can't help but snort.

"We need to stop that poison first," says Mama, ever the sensible one. "And find out who's behind this, if we're ever going to unite behind you."

"Is it your auntie?" asks Adamo, leaping on the bed and bouncing me and Curt into the air.

The guard groans once, beginning to come round. Adamo leans over me and thumps his fist on the top of the guard's head. That deals with that, although he draws an admonishing look from Mama.

"I don't know if it's Yelena," Curt replies to Adamo's question. "I hope not. But it's possible."

"She is the one in charge now," I point out.

Curt frowns. "Yes, but she, and my mother come to that, were always so stuck on wolf tradition. She'd rip your head off in a fight for leader, maybe, but sneaking around like this, poisoning me, or her own son... No-one will believe it, especially not her wolves, not without proof. Then there's our lodge burning down. Who did that?"

Adamo suddenly stands bolt upright, as though he's having a painful brainwave, crying out, "Dulcis!"

"Sshhhh," everyone choruses.

Ursid listens at the door whilst we wait for any sign of reaction along the hallway, holding our breath. He shakes his head and we all relax. All except the ginger prince, who frantically grabs a hold of Mama and yanks her up to his nostrils.

"You have to help Dulcis," he hisses. "They're poisoning people."

"Calm down, Your Highness," soothes Mama, peeling his rigid fingers from her coat, one at a time. "No-one's said she's ill. Right?" She glances at Curt.

"Not that I know of," he agrees, picking grass out of his teeth.

"I need to see her. Now," Adamo demands, tripping over Gulid's feet and landing on his knees by the door with an almighty thud, shaking the furniture and just missing the prostrate guard.

"Wait," I stage whisper, leaping after him, but he's already staggered to his feet, flung the door open and scooted into the corridor.

I arrive at his shoulder, just as a door opens further along the hallway and the teen princess herself emerges, resplendent in a bright red woollen dressing gown and gumwhat fur slippers. Dulcis falters when she lays eyes on us both.

"I'm just checking on my uncle after that thud," she calls over her shoulder. "He wasn't well earlier." She steps clear of her door, out of sight of whoever is in the room, and jerks her head, clearly telling us both to get back in Curt's room. We bump into one another in our haste to comply and end up doing the tango back through the doorway.

"I'll come with you," states a young man, emerging from her room as we close our door.

"Who's that?" Adamo snarls at me, frowning so hard his eyebrows meet in the middle.

"How should I know?" I mouth back.

I do know, actually. It's Fidus, but now's not the time for homicidal displays of jealousy. Not to mention there's all manner of innocent reasons why he'd be in her room, notwithstanding the dressing gown. Friendship, for one.

There's a knock on Curt's door. "Uncle Curt, are you alright?" asks Dulcis.

Nobody moves or speaks, including Curt, so I elbow him in the shoulder.

"Right. No. Er, I'm fine," Curt yells, way too far up the tonal scale, managing to sound both suspicious and insane. "I fell down, but I'm up. Again. Standing."

The usually miserable Broken Beak suddenly gets an attack of the vapours and starts giggling. Unfortunately, it spreads through the snakes and heads straight for the bears.

Good grief, I'm surrounded by idiots.

"Well, if you're sure you're fine," says Dulcis.

"Yes. Fine," squeaks Curt and Serpen nearly wets himself.

"What about you?" Fidus asks her. "You must get some rest, Dulcis. You've been sat with your father all day."

"I know, but I can't bear to leave him," she replies, her steps flopping down the hallway.

"He's well looked after. I checked on him myself."

"I know. Thank you. You've been kind."

"I'm not my grandmother," he states, following her, by the sound of his footsteps.

Adamo's face screws up as though he's chewing on hot chilli.

"I wonder what happened to Bogi?" asks Fidus.

Now they've got me sniggering.

"What?" replies Dulcis.

"Bogi. He was supposed to wait outside your uncle's room in case he needed anything."

We all glance at poor prostrate Bogi and silent hysteria nears eruption point.

"Then he's probably gone to get something for my uncle," Dulcis answers, thinking on her slippered feet. "Aren't you supposed to be outside with your guard wolves?"

"There's enough of them out there, running around with their tails on fire. My grandmother enjoys organising them into oblivion. I wanted to make sure you were fine."

"Thank you, Fidus. You've been so kind, but I'm not feeling too well. I just need to get some sleep now."

Adamo stares at Mama, mouthing, 'she's sick.'

"Rest well," Fidus says, in the voice of an angel. "If you need anything, just send anyone to get me."

"I will. Thank you."

"I'm always here for you," he adds.

Ok, not so innocent, it seems. Adamo's face turns salmon as his rival's footsteps patter along the hallway and down the main staircase.

We wait inside, listening to the chorus of distant wolf howls, until a door opens and light footsteps run along the hallway. Our door creaks open and Dulcis slips into the room, with a finger to her lips. She listens at the gap for a few moments before breathing a sigh of relief.

"They've left me alone. Finally," she whispers, turning to face me.

"Sounds like you're happy enough to talk with the floppy wolf," whinges Adamo, like the teenager he still is. "And what are you wearing?"

"What's it got to do with you?" she snarks back. "You left."

"You made me."

"Oh, shut up. I hate you."

She suddenly grabs and squeezes me so hard, I fart. Only Broken Beak wafts the air. Like he can smell anything after the bear stink, Mama's potion and this sickly room.

"I'm so glad you're back," Dulcis whimpers, clinging to me. "Daddy still won't wake up."

"I know," I reply. "Mama Bear's here. She'll help him, if she can."

Dulcis peers at our medicinal bear. "Thank you, Mama. I'm so sorry about what happened to you. And you too, General. I never believed you had anything to do with that fire."

"What about me?" growls Adamo.

"Still hate you," she replies, but her bottom lip's quivering. "You lot are terrible at hiding. Urgh, I feel sick."

She barely sways, but Adamo leaps up like a jack in the box and sweeps her off her feet.

"Put me down, fool," she insists. "I only feel queasy and you're making it worse."

He gently places her on the bed, having glared at Curt until the grizzled wolf levers himself to his feet. Mama starts her normal routine of invasive eye and throat examination.

"Have they poisoned her?" Adamo demands.

Dulcis' eyes open wide with shock. "What? What are you talking about?"

"I'll rip them limb from limb," Adamo rattles, now on a roll, "and pummel them with the limbs."

Ursid's eyelid flickers. Broken Beak snorts and honks with laughter.

"Carry on, Bendy Beak," Adamo growls. "I'll snap it off for you."

"Children," warns Wings.

"We think both me and the Alpha of Alphas might have been poisoned," Curt explains.

"Then you think someone hurt Daddy and caused that fire?" asks Dulcis, catching on fast.

"Maybe," I answer. "Probably."

"Why's he here?" she asks, nodding at Gulid.

"Welcoming lot, aren't you?" the eagle snaps. "For your information, I flew them in."

"With me," Wings qualifies, taking umbrage.

"Never said you didn't," the Beak chunters.

"I'm sorry, Gulid. Of course, you're welcome," says Dulcis, smiling at him. "Since you're not here to kidnap me. And thank you, except for bringing the mangy fool."

That last was aimed at Adamo, of course, not Curt.

"I do not have mange," Adamo growls in his lowest voice.

"Give it up," Curt advises, with a sigh. "Not worth it."

Mama moves on to prodding and poking at the patient's belly.

Her right eyebrow shoots skyward as she glances at Dulcis' face, but she says nothing.

Hmmm.

"Is it poison?" Adamo asks.

He's persistent, given the previous mange quip.

"No, I don't think she's poisoned," Mama replies. "She's just got an upset tummy. Probably from being upset."

"Because I left?" he ventures, never knowing when to leave things alone.

"Not everything's about you," Dulcis snaps. "My Daddy's dying."

"I came back for you," the ginger prince whines.

"I thought we were here for Curt," says Broken Beak, with impeccable timing.

"I'm throwing you out that window," Adamo threatens.

"I can fly, you moron," Beak counters.

"What is going on?" Dulcis demands. "What are any of you doing back? Not that I didn't miss you. Some of you, anyway."

"We're here to represent our people," Serpen answers, "once Curt confronts your grandmother and we unite to defend ourselves from the serpents from the north."

"What?"

Dulcis is getting more confused by the moment, so I enlighten her. Rather than put you through the previous chapter all over again, suffice it to say I describe the impending serpent apocalypse and the need for unity. Good luck with that.

"So now what?" Dulcis asks, after being hit with a torrent of angst and Curt retching in her ear.

Everyone suddenly looks at me. I've no idea why.

"Well," I start, having cleared my throat. "If we're going to have any chance with the serpents, we need unity. If we're going to get that, we need to oust Yelena. To do that we need to find out who's behind the poisonings, arson and probably Alpha's accident. So, we best start looking for proof."

"I'm with her," announces Anguis, beaming at me like a superhero's sidekick.

"Looking for what?" asks a stumped Adamo.

Dulcis tuts, with an added huff for effect. "The poison, you twit."

CHAPTER 34

The Denials of Stinky

Given that it's only a matter of time before Yelena and her wolves grow tired of chasing reeking bears, we all decide to do what no sane person ever does in a dark mansion:

Split up.

Even though Mama Bear is the only one who might have a clue what she's looking for, and ten adults sneaking around at night is a recipe for getting caught, or murdered by a serial killer in a mask, we're going to do it anyway. Only the resting place of dying Big Wolf and his mate is off limits.

"Edi, come with me," says Mama. "You've got some sense, at least."

"Thank you. I think."

"Shouldn't Edi…" Anguis begins.

"Sit down, Snake. I'm going with Edi," growls Curt. "I'll be the one protecting her."

"Mama's a full on grizzly bear," I tell him. "You better believe she can protect me, if it comes to it."

"I'm not grizzly," Mama insists, insulted. "I'm very amiable."

"It's a type of bear where I come from. Very big and scary and never mind."

After a whispered, but heated debate, during which everyone airs their prejudices, refusing to pair up with everyone else, my patience gives out.

"Enough," I hiss. "They'll be back and we'll be stuck in this smelly room for life. Mama and me, Anguis and Serpen, Wings and Gulid, Adamo and Ursid, Curt and Dulcis. Don't argue with me. Go."

Five scowling, shuffling pairs despatch to search the bedrooms in the mansion in the hope of unearthing the poison, or something else fishy. Goodness knows what; I'm not a detective. I'm doing the best I can.

Anguis checks the corridor, signalling all clear on his way out with Serpen. "There's no reason to believe it's in here. It could be anywhere in the town."

"We have to start somewhere," I point out, even though he's most likely right. To be honest, I'm going on my gut, which tells me the culprit is close. "Meet back here after you've searched. Don't take chances and don't get caught."

"Yes, General," says Ursid, with a smile.

Broken Beak follows after Wings, slouching like a wet blanket. "I've no idea what I'm looking for."

"A new face?" Adamo quips. Ursid digs him in the back, encouraging him to move faster.

Curt's the last one out of the room, glaring at me as though I just asked for a divorce, before purposely retching in my ear.

"Hush. I'll see you in a moment," I tell him. "Search fast. I don't like being apart." He allows a tiny smile to slip past the scowl as he follows Dulcis.

I'm sneaking along the corridor, peeking down at that empty hall, when I realise we left poor old Bogi laid out on the floor. Let's hope he doesn't come round any time soon. The others disappear into rooms farther along, or down the back corridor, leaving Mama and I lurking outside Yelena's room. I'm about to try the door, when I hear scraping and muffled thuds emanating from inside.

"Is she back?" Mama whispers.

"Don't think so," I reply.

We stare at one another, neither moving.

"Do we leave?" she asks me.

I shake my head and point at my ear. "Listen. Whoever's inside is trying to be quiet, even with all that racket outside. It's not her."

"Then we need to see who it is," Mama insists, eyes fierce. "Get behind me. If I change to bear, run."

She silently turns the door knob and pushes the door open an inch, peeping through the gap. I scoot beneath her, one eye against the opening and, low and behold, spot someone I didn't expect.

So much for my judgement.

Inside her drawers, rifling through his grandmother's clothes, is the Alpha Alpha Primus, young Stinky himself. What a disappointment. I rather liked him.

He looks up, catches sight of a line of eyes at the door, reflected in a mirror, and spins around. Mama pushes me back and prepares to change, but he leaps across the room, flings open the door, grabs one arm from us both and yanks us into the room. He's stronger than he looks, this young wolf.

"Don't scream, please," he whispers, letting us go and holding up his palms.

"I'm not screaming," Mama replies. "I may rip your head off, but I'm not screaming."

"I'm just closing the door," he says, skirting around us, peeping down the hallway and closing it with barely a click.

Mama manoeuvres me behind her every time he moves.

"What are you doing back?" he asks.

"What are you doing going through your granny's knickers?" is my question.

He glances at the drawer, then back at me. "Looking for something."

"Such as?"

He stares at me for a moment, then relents, given the awkward situation. "Poison. I think someone's poisoning my father."

"And you think Granny hides it in her knickers?"

"Can you stop saying knickers, please? I have searched other places."

"Wasn't your dad sick before you got here?" I broach.

"Yes, but now Curt's ill. And maybe someone hurt your Alpha."

"From where I stand, it looks like you. You're the one who'll inherit, even given Granny taking over."

He puffs out a breath and parks himself on the end of her bed. "It's not me. I know it looks like it should be me, but it's not me."

Mama crosses her arms and glares down at him. "But you would say that, wouldn't you?"

"Yes, I suppose so. But it's not me. I promise. What am I doing in here searching, if it's me?"

Good point. I believe him. Maybe.

Mama takes a huge sniff at the top of his head, to his surprise. "No smell now. Are you constipated?"

"None of your business," he snaps, leaping to his feet.

"It's important," I tell him. "Seriously."

"Yes, I am, as a matter of fact," he replies, his face falling. "Badly."

"Fartleleaf," states Mama. "Crushed in your food it makes you go, and smell. Eventually you get immune, but then you're…"

"Blocked," he finishes. "I'll kill whoever gave me that, when I find them, or feed them 'til they explode. Is that what my father has?"

"Did he ever smell?" Mama asks.

"No. Never. Far as I know."

"Then it's something else. The fartleleaf makes you suffer, but this poison is a slow killer."

"So, you think it's your Granny?" I venture.

"I hope not," he replies. "I honestly thought she loved us, in her own way. But then she just took over here and your Alpha…"

"But you haven't found anything?"

"Not in here, no. I've looked everywhere. Is that why you're back?"

Insert another recap of the story thus far. Previously on A Song of Mange, the impending Attack of the Serpents…

"Yelena will take all the wolves, ours and yours, back down south," is Primus's verdict on the news.

"Won't matter," I tell him. "They'll just keep coming, according to the eagle, Gulid. We best leave this room, in case she comes back. Are you sure you looked everywhere?"

"I left her underwear to last," he mumbles.

"We were also supposed to check your room," Mama says.

"You can if you want," he agrees, peeping into the hallway.

"No, back to Curt's room," I whisper.

Cue the three of us, legging it back. We arrive in Curt's room to find Bogi still out cold and Mr G lying across his chest, using the guard as a giant hot water bottle.

"Yes, sorry about that," I venture, when Primus stares at them.

The other pairs gradually return, resulting in the exact same conversation four times over, beginning with, "We found him looking for the poison, like us."

Adamo and Ursid are the last ones to return, having searched the farthest bedroom.

"What's he doing?" growls the ginger prince, sensing yet another rival, especially since he's clearly not stinky these days. Dulcis rolls her eyes and wraps herself in a blanket.

"We found him looking for the poison, like us," I repeat, with chronic deja vu.

"And you just believe him?" asks Adamo.

"I'm not shouting for help," Primus offers.

Adamo points at Serpen. "He can swallow you before you do."

"Did anyone find anything?" I ask, getting back to the point.

The chorus of negatives is highly disappointing.

Bogi groans, drawing everyone's attention. Mr G doesn't bother to move.

"No hitting," warns Mama, glaring at Adamo before wafting another potion under her victim's nose.

A quick spying reccy reiterates that we couldn't search Big Wolf's room as his mate Audira was in there, nor our own Alpha's room with his current nurse in place.

"I can relieve her soon," Dulcis offers. "I'll look around, but I doubt there's anything there." She bends forward, head drooping. "Urgh, I feel sick."

"Me too," Curt whines, resting his head on my shoulder.

I'd be more accommodating if there wasn't something rattling around in the back of my overtaxed mind, like a pebble in a shoe. What is it?

In the silence, Adamo's teenage digestive system unleashes a rolling rumble, like bottled thunder.

"You sick?" Ursid asks, feeling his forehead.

"No, I'm starving," the prince replies. "Got any food, that hasn't been poisoned?"

"You know where the kitchen is," Dulcis snaps.

Bingo. That's it.

The snake kids.

They said that Decipa is forever sneaking around the kitchen when there's no-one there.

"Get up," I command. "We're going to the kitchen."

CHAPTER 35

The Slimy Pot

Eleven hulking adults sneaking down the back stairs is hardly what I had in mind, but here we are, since they all point blank refuse to stay behind and I don't have time to argue. By some miracle, we make it to the kitchen without creaking, stomping or the uncle/niece wolf duo's retching giving us away. The wolves' howling growing louder outside might have something to do with masking our collective noise, but if the guards and Yelena are returning, we're also running out of time.

Curt ventures into the kitchen first, since he's got a right to be there and wouldn't be accosted if he's caught.

"Clear," whispers Curt, beckoning to our mob, squeezed into the corridor.

With all the fires out, including the ovens, it's as dark as a cellar and my eyes take a moment to adjust to what little light penetrates the raised windows.

"It's colder down here than out in the snow," Serpen mutters, with a shiver.

We scatter around the giant room, rummaging through pots, pans, cupboards and shelving full of bottles and various squat and skinny containers. Every time one of us opens something suspicious, Mama peers at it, rubs a pinch of the offending stuff between her fingertips and takes a wary sniff, only to pronounce it a herb, spice or condiment.

"What if the poisoner's got it on them?" Dulcis asks. An intelligent question for a furry slippered teen.

"They might," I reply, "but probably wouldn't want to walk around with it on them all the time."

When we're forced to move on to upper shelving, our travelling circus reveals its tightrope walkers, with the snakes teetering on the ovens, since they can balance. Adamo, being a huffing great twassock, slips off a cupboard, staggers and backs straight into Anguis, knocking Serpen off his shoulders. Adamo promptly catches the king on the way down, earning a silent round of applause from me.

Dulcis is not so sympathetic. "Idiot."

"What's that?" he replies, setting Serpen back on his feet with a bow.

"It's a brainless fool."

"No. That," he says, dropping to one knee, peering underneath the cupboard he just fell off. "I must have dislodged it."

Sure enough, a small pot sits, tipped on its side, the edge shining in the dim light. He inserts his hand under the wood, rummages a little and frees it. Stepping in to the shaft of light from the window, he holds up a circular metal container, about half the size of his palm, and hands it to Mama Bear.

"Let's see what we have," she tells us, unscrewing the lid.

The terrible stench coming from the contents triggers nasty flashback memories and not just for me. I can't tell the true colour, but I'd lay money on that slimy glop being deep brown.

Mama grabs a spoon from a drawer and gives it a poke, then a full on stir, making everyone gag from the rising cloud of stink.

"It looks like a sort of mould," comes her verdict, "ground into a paste."

"Don't bother Mama, I'm pretty sure I know what that is," I venture. "Anguis?"

The frowning ambassador simply nods, leaving his king to pronounce the sentence. "That's the mould from our castle, but we burnt everything before we arrived. I've no idea what it's doing here."

"Likely going in certain people's food," says Ursid, his eyelid fluttering.

"That would explain the sickness," Mama suggests. "Ingested, not inhaled, like before."

"I've been eating that?" Curt stammers, turns olive and retches, over and over.

The others, excepting the ever fussing Wings, take a sensible step back, leaving me to deal with Curt's acid attack. I grab his shoulders and slap a hand over his mouth in an attempt to silence him. He promptly deposits a lovely wet dose of bile in my hand.

Mama grabs a towel from a rack and wipes the offending slime off my palm, while I try to cuddle my wolf back from mould panic.

"It's inside me," he wheezes, hyperventilating. "I ate that mould. It's crawling in my stomach."

In the end it takes a kiss to break into his terror which, given he just upchucked, is a sterling display of adoration on my part. I deserve a medal.

"What if I just poisoned you?" he whimpers.

Right. Didn't think of that.

"She's too leathery to poison," says Wings.

"You can talk, Great Tit. I'm fine," I coo to my wolf, swallowing the urge to spit. "And so are you. There's no mould growing that can take you in a fight."

"I missed you," Mange sighs, resting his forehead against mine. "I don't feel well."

"I know, Poppet."

"Just to mention," Primus interjects. "I've no idea what anyone's talking about."

"You've never seen this mould before?" Anguis asks.

"I've seen mould, but not that type or with that stink," he replies, peering inside the container. "Is it crawling up the side?"

Mama slams the lid back into place with a terminal ding and swiftly screws it shut.

"It's the reason for the fall of the empire," Serpen tells him. "And why we left our infested castle. It kills."

"You think they gave that slime to my father?" asks Primus.

"Yes, and are probably still feeding it to him," I reply, adding, "Sorry."

"How did they get hold of it?" Adamo asks, turning to Anguis and Serpen. "Is the poisoner a snake? No offence to you both."

"It's not a snake," Anguis states. "We got thrown out. Our people were happy staying right here with the wolves and a long way from that horror."

"Well," Adamo starts, squinting as he exercises his straining brain cells, "either it came from the castle or…"

"It's spread south," Curt finishes. "This just keeps getting better."

"Can you treat my father?" Primus asks Mama Bear.

"I can try," she agrees, "but it depends how far gone he is. Curt, eat another one of these until I can get to my Mould Throttler." She shoves another grass/gum ball into his dripping mouth and he gags.

All this vomit and stench is making me nauseated. And yes, she does call it Mould Throttler.

"So, now we need to find out who this belongs to," I state, tapping the offending container. "I suggest we put it back and wait to see who comes to fetch it."

"That could be a while," says Primus.

"They can't get at it when the kitchen's working," I reason, "so they'll come at night. We can only hope they haven't already been."

"I like you," Primus states, with a grin. "Clever as Granny, without the snarl."

Aww. That's nice.

"I like you too," I tell him, "and I'd shake your hand, if mine wasn't coated with wolf puke."

"Sorry," Curt mumbles, chewing the last of the grass ball.

"We can't all stand around here waiting to get caught," Ursid remarks, shuffling the mould pot back under the cupboard. "We can watch in pairs whilst the others…"

And right on cue there's footsteps coming down the corridor.

"Someone's coming," Adamo observes, ever the sharp one.

Dulcis rolls her eyes at him.

Eleven sets of eyes scan the kitchen, searching for somewhere to hide and all end up locking on the same store cupboard. Our spy mob neatly packs itself in amongst hanging meat, pickled veggies and sacks of something dried out. I'm the last one in, squeezing backwards into the slimline Anguis as I close the door on us all.

It's a tight fit and pitch dark in here, but I can hear Curt grinding his teeth at the back.

It's now I realise the entire area has been packed in ice to keep the food fresh, so we're literally hiding in a freezer. It's a bet as to whose teeth will start chattering first. My money's on the pair of snakes.

Being closest to the door, I hold a skinned gumwhat out of the way and peer through a tiny gap as footsteps pad across the kitchen floor. I can't see who it is yet. Come on...

A hooded figure places a cup on the table and reaches beneath the cupboard, removing the slimy pot. Using a twig, they scoop a little mould into the cup and stir, before replacing the pot. As they grab the cup and turn towards the light leaking from the window, the poisoner's face briefly glows like a ghoul.

I knew it.

I just knew it. You can't fool a middle-aged woman. No way.

The culprit tiptoes out of the kitchen, clutching their nefarious wares to their cold, grey heart. I open the cupboard door and step to one side, allowing the mob behind me to tumble out.

"We have to follow," I whisper, heading after the poisoner. "Catch them in the act."

Anguis' first on my tail until unceremoniously shoved out of the way by my mangy wolf.

"Who is it?" asks Curt, breathing over my shoulder.

Cue page turning cliffhanger...

CHAPTER 36

The Snake In the Grass

Got you.

Just as I, and a sneaky bunch of snake kids, suspected, our evil villain turns out to be Decipa Longfang, the official messenger wolf of the celebrated southern pack, trusted voice of the Alpha of Alphas, and miserable mouldy poisoner. I hold out very little hope she's alone in this enterprise and my hard earned pounds are on Yellfire herself.

"Who is it?" Curt hisses, again, since the above battle only played out in my cavernous skull.

"Decipa," I whisper, keeping my eye on the edge of her cloak, whipping around the corner. She's heading up the back stairs.

The revelation filters down the line in a murmuring echo of disbelief.

"Where's she going?" Curt asks, puffing out another stinking breath of stomach mould, bile and chewed gumball.

"Not a mind reader," I whisper, using my manky palm to ease his face back a smidgen.

A clonk, coming from behind me, sounds overly loud in the darkness. I can't prove who walked into something, but I have my suspicions. Decipa's footsteps pause on the upper landing and I frantically raise a fist above my head, military style, to signal everyone to freeze. (Hey, I saw it in the movies.)

No-one has a clue what it means, of course, and they each march into the back of the one in front, the thud rippling through the line, shuffling me forward a few inches with each new bump. I resort to waving them back around the corner as she peeps down the stairs. There's a few moments of silence, during which we all hold our breath, then the footsteps resume.

After waiting a few moments, Dulcis edges up to my shoulder and whispers, "Let me follow first. It won't matter if she catches me."

"Nope. I'll go," Curt insists. "You're all my responsibility."

As he sets his foot on the first step, Dulcis glares at his back. "I am an Alpha Daughter."

"I know, dear," I reply. "Just humour him. He doesn't feel well."

Curt reaches the top and peeps around the corner at floor level.

"What's he doing?" Adamo asks, his head poking through the gap between us.

"What's it look like?" Dulcis snaps.

Curt's head reappears and he gives a thumbs up (a gesture he learnt from yours truly). Dulcis and I climb, side by side.

"She's gone into Alpha's room," Curt whispers as we arrive at the top. "Stay here. I'll find out…"

"What?!" shrieks Dulcis, smashing her uncle into the wall and hurtling down the corridor in a flapping whirlwind of slippers and dressing gown.

I take off after her, leaving Curt to shout, "Frulk," in my wake.

Since her siren screech must have alerted anyone left in the mansion, and probably a few outside it, the need for stealth just exited the window. Our rebel mob stampede up the staircase, led by Adamo, getting in everyone's way, such that half of them arrive on the landing in a heap.

I'm reaching out for Dulcis when she kicks the door open, one slipper flying into the air as she bodily hurls herself into her father's room. The splintered door creaks on its hinges, adding a gothic soundtrack to the scene within.

There stands Decipa, leaning over the unconscious Alpha, cup tipped above his lips, the mouldy liquid pouring forth in a poisonous stream.

"You *!***ing *!***er," Dulcis hollers, understandably (redacted for the sensitive souls like myself) and thunders into the shocked villain like a freight train, slapping the cup out of her hands and spraying the nice clean bed with what looks like brown excrement.

There's a horrendous ripping noise and the air fills with strips of shredded nightie and dressing gown as our teen princess turns homicidal wolf, albeit one back paw still wearing a gumwhat slipper.

Decipa swiftly turns wolf and now we've got a massive howling dogfight to contend with. Just in case that isn't bad enough, Adamo busts into the room as full on honey bear, growling and waving his claws like helicopter rotor blades. Curt grabs me by the collar and yanks me down onto the ground as teeth and claws fly over our exposed heads.

Two eagles, taking one glance at flying carnage and deciding feathers aren't going to cut it in that tiny room, press back against the wall. Ursid grabs a chair and smacks Decipa's wolf over the head with it, which only achieves a shower of splinters, since she's got a concrete skull. Her huge teeth clamp shut, just missing his hand.

"Decipa, stop," yells the arriving Primus, ducking her crunching maw. "I am your Alpha Alpha; I command you to stop."

She ignores him. No surprise there.

I crawl across the floor and climb up next to Alpha on the bed, tipping his head to one side to drain as much mould from his mouth as I can, then scraping out what's left with my fingers. His bed now resembles the diarrhoea ward. Curt crawls onto the mattress and leans across both me and his brother, shielding us from the flying free for all.

Furniture and mirrors smash amidst the cacophony of snarling as what sounds like a jackbooted army thunder up the stairs and down the hallway. Primus is still yelling as his mother and brother arrive to a scene of murderous chaos.

I can see Audira's mouth move, but can't hear what she's saying over the racket. Primus pushes them both back into the corridor and must be explaining. Fidus's face registers shock and he waves at me, yelling, "Stay down, Edi!" whilst stupidly leaping into the room.

"I am," I holler from under Curt, howling as a stray claw catches my exposed wrist.

Curt desperately strains to spread himself even wider, but this riot needs to stop. Having no ha'p'orth of sense between them, Primus and his mother rush after the wayward Fidus, only adding more prospective victims to the mess.

"Dulcis, please. You'll get hurt," Fidus cries, fighting to reach her.

The homicidal messenger wolf flies completely out of control with rage and Adamo swipes at her, his claws catching her tail and severing the tip.

"Decipa, stop this right now," Primus hollers. "We can sort this out. General Ursid, control your bear."

"That's my prince," Ursid growls at him. "And your messenger wolf's trying to kill his lady, and our Alpha, and the rest of you."

"That's enough," bellows Curt, giving me a fright. "You will not murder one another in my home!"

And that's when things take a real turn for the worse.

Yellfire, in all her terrifying designer leather glory, thunders onto the scene, takes one look at a massive bear fighting a bleeding wolf and goes into full on battle mode as a teeth, claw and flying saliva warrior. The first of her guards arrive as the fighting intensifies and Ursid has no choice but to turn bear and join the fray to protect his beloved prince.

My family are going to die here if I don't think of something. Curt beats me to it.

"The snake," Curt says, shielding me in a wall of biceps. "He's the only one big enough."

"Serpen!" I yell, my gaze desperately trying to track the king from under Curt's body.

"Here," he cries, from the doorway, ducking as a guard wolf's claws swoop over his head.

"Change. Please."

He kneels, his sapphire eyes scanning the room. "There's no space to fight," he yells back.

"I know. Fill the whole room. Squash them all into the walls."

Serpen briefly smiles, the warmth disappearing as his face splits open in a shower of blood. Behind him, Anguis' lovely features also tear apart as his smaller snake appears, filling the hallway and blocking the arrival of any more reinforcements.

The king steps into the centre of the room as his hideous serpent rapidly expands like an industrial balloon, filling every crevice of the bedroom, blowing out the windows and scraping his ridges on the ceiling. The combatants, swamped by his scales, splatter and slam into the walls or floor.

Yelena's furious wolf takes a hefty snap at his tail, but he uses the pointy end to smack her on the top of the head and press her nose into the ground. The guards manage a few gouges and scrapes, but the muscle behind his reptilian bulk soon pins down their limbs and renders them paralysed, broken furniture tattooing furry skin.

Yet here we lay, me, Curt and his oblivious brother, safe in the bed, which remains a scale free zone. How the engorged serpent retains enough control to keep us from being squashed is a mystery to me and must be painful to him.

A chorus of howling and yips come from the blocked corridor but, inside the room, only the odd whine pierces the silence, until a weak, but firm voice issues a command from outside.

"Someone tell me what is happening here!"

CHAPTER 37

Throne Of Liars

The arrival of Big Wolf (whose imminent demise has apparently been exaggerated) thankfully pours cold water on the raging fire. Since Curt and I are the only ones whose vocal chords aren't squashed flat, and he's busy retching above me, my conversation with the disembodied Alpha of Alphas zips along nicely. To wit,

"They're all trying to kill each other," I holler, "so King Serpen put a stop to it. He's not hurting them."

Just flattening them a little.

"Why are they trying to kill each other?" Big Wolf calls back, sounding nearer to the doorway. Anguis' snake must have let him edge closer.

"Dulcis caught Decipa poisoning her father. They fought. Prince Adamo tried to help. Your mother saw a bear, went mental and everyone else lost it."

A master of the succinct, me.

"Is my mate in there?"

She's currently pressed, face first against the wall.

"Yes, but she's a bit squashed. Serpen, can you let her speak?"

The serpent wriggles and Audira's face pulls clear a couple of inches, her compressed nose and forehead bearing the imprint of a rampant wolf carving from the wall.

"I'm fine, dear," she warbles, remarkably chipper, given the circumstances. If I didn't know better, I'd say she's enjoying herself.

"Would King Serpen please release them all?" Big Wolf asks. "I can hardly sort this out with everyone suffocating."

Which is true.

The serpent's head turns to look at me, one scaly eyebrow, of sorts, rising. Do we trust the Southern Alpha? Possibly not, but this thing has to resolve somehow.

Curt stops retching long enough to announce, "King Serpen will only change back if all parties agree, on their honour, to stand down. He could have killed any one of us, but he's only preventing us from maiming each other."

Silence follows his sensible ultimatum, which isn't encouraging.

"Erm, no-one can agree to your proposal if they can't speak," Audira points out, a smirk on her face. She's staring at her wide-eyed, enraged mother-in-law, whose nose is concertinaed half way up her wolf face.

"Right. Serpen, please loosen your grip," Curt orders, "just a little."

The serpent wheezes and shrinks an inch or two, as though allowing air to escape the balloon, giving the combatants a tiny bit of leeway.

"Do I have your word of honour to cease fighting?" Curt asks, twisting himself in a knot to catch every eye in a speed survey of the mashed room.

"I wasn't the problem in the first place," moans Gulid, rubbing his deviated nose. "You seem obsessed with breaking my face."

Wings smacks the back of his head, stating, "We eagles are in agreement."

"Grrr" and "Rarr" growl Adamo and Ursid, respectively.

"I command all my wolves to comply," Big Wolf orders, squeezing his deathly pale head past Anguis' snake and inside the room. "And that includes you, Mother."

Her furry head rises off the deck and "YARRAR RARRRA ARRRR" blasts forth from her maw.

I take that as a no.

The eardrum shredding racket cuts off when Serpen's tail slaps her nose back into the floor.

"Mother, I'd really like to go back to bed, so that's enough," says her son. "Please. We're not going to get to the bottom of this otherwise."

Yelena blows a puff of air out of her pinched nostrils and rumbles quietly.

"Are we all good? No dissenters?" I venture, taking over from Curt after a particularly visceral retch. "Fabulous. Could we all change back to nice, peaceful humans for a while? And Curt, please get off me."

Anguis, bless him, is the first to comply, shrinking back to his very fetching athletic form, even more impressive sans clothing.

It all goes dark.

I prise Curt's hand off my eyes, insisting, "I wasn't looking."

Well, I wasn't. Much.

Serpen unpins Yellfire and the others from the floor and walls, a chorus of huffs, groans and sighs greeting their return to humanity. We now have a room full of bloody nudists. (As in cut and bruised, not annoying. Although they are.) It's so blasted cold in here they threaten to expire from goosebumps, so they raid the closets and cupboards for blankets and our Alpha's clothes. He won't be happy when he wakes up. If he wakes up.

Despite the padded circus revolving around them, Decipa and Dulcis face one another in quivering stillness, like a naked shootout in the Wild West.

I wrap her father's dressing gown around Dulcis' shoulders, whispering, "Hold off killing anyone, for now."

"That... poisoner... stays away from my father," she commands, in a tone that's anything but teen princess. Seriously, I wouldn't be crossing her right now.

Yellfire yanks a blanket off a guard's back and wraps herself like a mummy, snarling in my face 'til I lean backwards. "I gave my word, so speak, before I kill you."

"Mother," warns Big Wolf, swaying on the spot as his eyes cross.

Audira grabs him, scanning the room for a chair, but all the furniture has been pulverised by a combination of wolf fight and serpent expansion. Primus legs it down the hall and returns dragging an armchair through the debris. His father sits, gently tapping his son's hand with gratitude.

"Now," he begins, holding court from his new throne, "tell me again what you saw."

Just about everyone, except me, starts talking, so all he gets is noise.

"One at a time," he pleads, but no-one can hear him.

I'm about to holler, or possibly sing, to make them shut up, when his horrendous mother lets rip with the loudest and most raucous bellow I've ever had the misfortune to hear. It would shatter glass, if there were any left in the windows.

It sounds like, "Silentyourlipsscum," but it could be my hearing. It does the trick though.

In the open-mouthed silence, Big Wolf coughs genteelly and says, "Dulcis, could you please begin."

"I'm your official messenger and you're going to listen to her lies," Decipa spits, throwing herself at the feet of her Alpha.

"Silence," snarls Yelena. "Dulcis is my granddaughter, the daughter of Kallosa and an Alpha. She will be heard first."

Not sure I admire the hierarchical reasoning, but I'm staying quiet.

Dulcis offloads her story. "Decipa hid some sort of mould in the kitchen. She took a cup of it up here and I caught her pouring it in my father's mouth."

"I was giving him water," the lying minx cries.

"I smacked the cup out of her hand," Dulcis continues, glaring at her nemesis. "The contents are all over the bed. Does that look like water?"

"It's a medicine," Decipa insists.

Yelena dabs a finger in the brown slop on the bedsheets and sniffs, recoiling from the stench. "What is that? It smells like that mould outside the castle garden sheds."

She glances at Serpen and looks away, her face turning red. I'd guess those sheds were the site of a few raunchy assignations with his father.

"Dulcis is lying," Decipa hollers. "The bear's here. If anyone wants to poison the Alpha, it's him. And they're lovers."

"You." Yelena points at Wings, making him jump.

"Not me. I'm too old," the eagle splutters.

"Did you see where this mould is, in the kitchen?"

"Er, yes."

"Go with him and fetch it here," Yelena orders, grabbing a guard by the borrowed collar. "You watch him all the way."

The guard nods and shoves Wings ahead of him, out the door.

"Granny, I wouldn't lie about this," Dulcis insists.

"Why are there bears and snakes back in this town?" Yelena demands. "And are you lovers?"

"We were 'til you got here," Adamo mutters.

Ursid's eyelids flutter like he's just been tasered.

"Mother, perhaps you could let me deal with this?" Big Wolf says, before she goes ballistic.

The look on her face tells me she doesn't like that 'perhaps' any more than I do.

"So," he continues, turning to Adamo and Ursid, "why are you here?"

"It's a long story," Adamo stutters.

"I have the time, well until I die, which granted might not be too long." Audira scowls at her mate for that crack. He takes her hand and presses his lips to her knuckles, before returning his gaze to the bears. "Are you here to poison the Alpha?"

"I'm not here to poison anyone," Adamo insists. "I wouldn't know how. If I wanted to kill you, I'd take your head off with my claws."

There goes Ursid's eyelid again.

Footsteps clump along the hall heralding the return of Wings and the guard, the eagle carrying the pot of mould at arm's length as though it'll jump out and bite him.

"Eagles are immune from the mould," I remind Wings, since Gulid isn't doing it.

Yelena snatches the pot and unscrews the lid.

"Don't touch it," Serpen warns. "It's the same mould that infests our castle and killed so many of my people."

Her eyes shoot up to his. "Then you're the one trying to kill the Alpha."

"That would be a no," I state, since I've had enough of this blame merry-go-round, "which you well know, since your son is clearly very sick and was before he got here. Not to mention Stinky, sorry Primus…"

"The Alpha Alpha, the Alpha son," Yelena corrects me.

"How long do you want to stand here?" I snap. "Your grandson was also sick before, right?"

"So, you're saying they've both been poisoned?" Yelena asks.

"Yes. Well, no. Mama Bear thinks Primus had fartleleaf poisoning, but your father's been given the mould, as well as Curt. And our Alpha didn't have an accident, since Decipa was up here trying to finish him off."

"You had me smelling like gumwhat piss and shiffling in the grass non stop," Primus snarls at Decipa.

"Language," says Yelena, sternly. Once a granny, always a granny.

Primus ignores her, zooming in on Decipa. "Why? What would you gain from hurting me, or my father? Or this pack's Alpha come to that? Are you working for someone else?"

"Is everyone in this room insane?" Yelena cries, throwing her hands up.

"We haven't got to the bit about the serpents yet," Adamo mutters.

Even Anguis' eyelids flutter at that.

Primus forges on. "Did you also try to kill me and Fidus in that fire? Why?"

"That fire wasn't bad enough to kill anyone," Decipa counters. "You all got out easily." I can see the precise moment she realises that she just outed herself, and counters with, "it was an accident."

"Gallons of gumwhat urine were thrown on my home," I snarl. "That was no accident. Let me guess; you did it so the bears would get the blame. What I can't figure out, like Primus, is why."

"I've heard enough," Yelena states. "The Alpha Daughter indicates you tried to poison her father and has provided evidence, and the suspicion of other misdeeds. I submit to the Alpha of Alphas that you be banished from the pack immediately."

"Just a minute," I pipe up. "I want to know why she did it, and for whom."

"As do I," states Curt.

"Me too," mumbles Adamo, ducking to avoid Dulcis' slap.

I'm staring straight at Decipa when her frightened gaze whips to someone in the room, imploring them to intervene.

And it's not Yelena.

"Say something," she cries. "I did it for you."

Every eye locks onto the face of Fidus as his expression morphs from open innocence to raging anger.

"I've no idea what she's talking about," he snarls. "She's trying to deflect her guilt onto me. Get her out of here. We need to deal with father's illness now."

"Fidus?" says Dulcis, glaring at him, eyes wide. "You said you were my friend."

Adamo snorts, which helps no-one.

Fidus reaches for Dulcis' hand. "I am your friend, believe me."

Decipa shoots to her feet, yelling. "I did it for you and you'd throw me over for her?"

"She's clearly obsessed," Fidus snaps, backing away from her. "She's a liar. She'd say anything to get out of this."

"You told me to burn the lodge and give them that mould. You promised I'd be your mate when you ruled this pack."

"I'm an Alpha's son. I would never mate with a messenger," Fidus sneers. "Grandmother, you know this is true."

"You're the liar!"

The Grand Lady Wolf's gaze switches from Decipa to Fidus and back again. "Why would I believe you, a poisoner and an apparent arsonist, over my grandson?"

"Because..." interjects Big Wolf, his face downcast, "I became ill whilst Decipa was away for months on messenger duty with Primus. Whilst I was defending the packs and joining them together."

"She could have got anyone to help her," Fidus insists, forcing the innocent expression back on his face.

Boy that change is creepy.

Big Wolf hauls himself to his feet. "The only one always with me, fetching my food for me, was you. You insisted on it."

"I was being a dutiful son," Fidus hisses, "and now you accuse me? What about your own mate? She was always there."

"Fidus," Audira whispers, shocked at his words. "I'm your mother."

"I would have given you anything," Big Wolf says. "Why would you do this?"

"I wouldn't!" Fidus yells. "Why would I poison you, when my brother stands to become Alpha after you, not me? Why aren't you looking at him?"

Dulcis takes a step forward, right into his path, making Adamo twitch. "But with my father gone, if you became my mate, you would be Alpha here, assuming you got rid of everyone first. Especially a certain bear."

Adamo reaches out and gently pulls her back until she rests inside his arms.

"How long would it have been before I became sick again?" Primus says. "Do you really want to be Alpha that badly, that you'd poison your own family?"

"You're my son," Big Wolf whispers, heartbroken.

"Did you try to kill your own father?" growls Yelena, her words echoing in the silence. "Look at me, boy."

Fire burns in the young man's gaze as he turns on her. "Don't call me boy. You're the one who wants to rule here, not me. You got rid of the bears and the snakes. You. You appointed Decipa as messenger. You tried to kill their Alpha as revenge for your stupid daughter. And now you're turning my parents and brother against me. This is all you!"

"You're trying to blame me?" Yelena bellows.

Stand by for an explosion.

Curt shuffles me behind him, whispering, "Back on the bed." We start inching backwards.

And... it's then that a rather traumatised Dulcis decides to deliver the retch to end all retches.

"Did you poison my granddaughter?" Yellfire hollers, grabbing the last straw.

She flings the blanket to one side, transforming into her hideous wolf, snarling maw so wide, I can see her supper. Fidus takes one look at that monster and turns tail, sprinting out the doorway and down the stairs, turning wolf at the bottom.

I dash over to the smashed windows, just catching the rear end of Yelena's wolf as she chases him through the town and out into the surrounding forest.

"Leave him to my mother," Big Wolf tells us, sinking back into his chair and pulling Audira into his arms.

"Won't she need help?" Curt asks.

"My money's on Yellfire," I answer.

I'm turning back to Curt when I'm shoved to one side, smacking my head against the wall, as Decipa's flurry of fur shoots past my shoulder and flings herself through the window. I poke my head out to see her yelping wolf shake off the landing, before dashing, full pelt, into the trees.

"Let her go," Primus says, helping me up. "She won't be coming back."

"Urgh, I don't feel well," Dulcis whines, allowing Adamo's arms to stay wrapped around her.

"Me neither," Curt adds, parking his dodgy hip on the end of the bed.

His brother sits bolt upright, like a vampire from a coffin, screaming, "She tried to kill me!"

CHAPTER 38

The Alpha Awakening

Thanks for that, Alpha; I nearly had a heart attack.

Curt falls on the floor, grabbing his hip in agony. Everybody else screeching like victims in a horror movie shoots all our nerves to pieces.

"She kicked me in the knee, then smacked me in the head with a rock!" the newly awakened wolf bellows.

"You can stop yelling, Daddy, I can hear you." Dulcis sits on the bed and wraps her arms around him, hanging on to her resurrected parent for dear life.

"Don't cry, my sweet," he soothes, resting his chin on her shoulder.

"I thought you were dying," she whimpers. "You fell and wouldn't wake up."

"She lured me there, the traitor. Said she had information on why Kallosa died and wanted to show me."

"And you went with her, you idiot?" Curt groans from the floor.

"You'll never guess who it was," his brother states. "Go on, guess."

"We know it was Decipa," says Dulcis, sucking all the wind out of his sails. "Hush now. Let Mama treat you."

Mama Bear, whose ample bosom is still recovering from its flattening against the serpent, practically hurls herself at our Alpha. She feels his forehead, pokes various bits of him, examines his knee and the head wound, then insists on peering down his throat to smell his breath.

"Whaa are oo ooing?" he asks, mouth wide open.

"Oh, dear," she mutters, over and over, before releasing his jaw.

"You're all back," he observes, taking us all in.

"We're back because we never should have left," Adamo states, standing tall. "We should have talked it through. So here I am."

"That's good," Alpha says, grinning at him. "Why's everyone wearing my clothes and my blankets?" The battle wreckage dawns on him. "Who broke all the furniture? I liked that table; Curt made it. There's no windows. It's freezing in here. What did I miss? Have we had a war?"

The last question is aimed at his brother, who replies, "Not yet," followed by a delightful retch which, in turn, sets Dulcis off again.

"I've barely been gone a day and you're all falling apart," Mama moans, pressing on Alpha's knee.

"Ow. What's this stuff on the bed?"

"The mould's back," I tell him, slipping down next to Curt and leaning against the bed.

"Why's it on my blankets?"

"She was feeding it to you. Decipa."

"What?!" He duly starts retching, so now we're treated to a disgusting harmony. "How did it get down here from the castle?" he asks, in between. "And where did he come from?" spotting Gulid.

The eagle simply sighs, rubbing his nose.

"It didn't come with us," Anguis replies. "The mould, that is. But only Fidus and Decipa know where they found it."

"Fidus?"

"He put Decipa up to it all," I tell him. "The lodge fire, attacking you, and poisoning Curt and Big Wolf, er, the Alpha of Alphas."

"Curt?" Alpha exclaims, reaching down to grab his brother's shoulder.

"I don't feel well," Curt whines, grabbing his little brother's hand.

"Dulcis?"

"I'm fine," she tells her father, though she looks green to me.

I finish the traitorous tale with, "They both scarpered, your aunt on his tail."

"I don't think much of his chances then." Alpha spots his Southern counterpart and his long-faced family. "Sorry to hear it's your son. That can't be easy to take."

"We'll leave in the morning," Big Wolf tells him, trying to stand on shaky legs. "The sooner we're gone, the quicker you can repair all the damage my family has wrought."

"You can't," Audira exclaims, horrified at the suggestion.

One glance at him proves her right. He'll never make it back south. Not to mention we haven't got to the worst of it yet. I glance at Anguis, who nods. Now is as good a time as any.

"Actually, you can't leave us," Adamo blurts out, beating me to it. "We need you."

"*You* need me?" Big Wolf replies. "This should be good."

"Ssshh dear and sit down," Audira tells him.

I launch into the study notes version of the problem. "In the north there's another Snake Empire that's now acquired a shed load of eagle slaves. They're all serpents, the size of King Serpen here, able to mesmerise and they're coming our way, led by SuperSerpent breathing fire. On our own we don't stand a chance. All of us together, maybe."

"Although probably not," mutters Gulid.

Thank you, idiot. I suppose I better own up...

"I should also add they're after me, because of that magic book I had. Sorry."

Silence.

"Well. Fabulous," says our Alpha. "I'm going back to sleep."

"I don't feel too well either, I'm afraid," Big Wolf whispers, wilting in the armchair.

Audira holds out her hand to Mama Bear. "I'm sorry, I don't know your name."

"Mama Bear will do just fine," our matron replies.

"Can you help my mate? Please."

Mama gives her a smile and kneels at the Alpha's side. "May I?"

He gives her a weak nod.

Mama taps on his chest, peers at his eyes, lifting the eyelids, checks his tongue and throat, with the obligatory 'ahhhh' and listens to his ragged breathing.

"Right," she announces, rising. "All of you, with the exception of the Alpha Alpha Heir, are mould poisoned, and I'm afraid it's not good, especially in your case, Alpha of Alphas."

"No. Curt," I whimper. I thought he would be alright. I'm here. I'm back. He has to get better. He has to. What am I going to do?

Serpen and Anguis glance at each other, sadly. They watched so many of their people succumb to mould sickness and know the drill. Fear grips me like a vice.

"Stop panicking," Curt says, wrapping an arm around me. "I can see it in your face. I'm not going anywhere. Am I, Mama?"

Our bear crosses her arms, thinking. "Well, Decipa was watering it down, which is something. I've been working on a stronger treatment, in case it ever spread from the castle, but it's not been tested."

"Test it on me," Big Wolf offers. "I'm dying anyway. Nothing to lose."

"Do what you can," Primus begs. "Please. I really don't want to be Alpha. Sorry, Dad."

His parents both laugh.

"I didn't either," his father admits. "Don't tell your granny."

"I'll do my best," Mama tells them and turns to Adamo. "Your Highness, we need to fetch everything from the camp."

"We can fly there," Gulid offers, surprising both me and Wings.

"Good. When you get there, tell my Friddie to collect as many fobly bugs as he can, the fatter and slimier the better, and mash them into a paste. It needs to sit and putrefy for a while before I can cook it," she explains, seeing the disgusted looks.

"I've changed my mind," Big Wolf announces.

"Oh, shut up," Audira tells him. "You'll swallow it if I have to choke you first. I'm not losing you."

Her mate and son grin at one another. I don't blame them. I like her.

* * *

The rising sun fills the mansion with golden light as Adamo and Ursid trundle our Alpha into Dulcis' room, since the windows are missing in his. Our exhausted teen crawls into bed beside her father and they're both asleep before the bears and I can clear the room. I drape an extra blanket over the pair and kiss my girl's forehead.

"Sleep well, princess."

The eagles rocked up a while ago, flapping like crazy in a bizarre turn on pigeon racing. Gulid won, which royally peed off old Wings, who stomped off to lie down somewhere, having lobbed Mama's medicines into the snow with a visceral 'caw.'

Mama sent everyone else to rest, insisting she needed silent concentration to cook up her brew. As far as I know, she's been down in that kitchen stirring a bubbling cauldron for hours.

I find Curt leaning against the window in the hallway, watching the dawn. Last night's heavy snow coats the town in a sparkling, pristine carpet, marred only by the paw prints of a huge, dishevelled wolf emerging from the trees, her tongue hanging loose. I can't see any blood though, so I guess Fidus is still in the land of the living.

I jog down the hallway and peek in Big Wolf's room. The parents are also asleep, Mama Bear snoring in a chair beside them, but their son is still awake.

"Primus," I whisper, "your gran is back."

He creeps out of the room and closes the door behind him. "Best I meet her alone."

"No kidding."

"I'll give her the basics on our friends in the north. She might be more inclined to listen, especially after my brother…"

"I'm sorry, Primus. I know you love him."

"I'm sorry I didn't see it coming," he replies. "He was a sneaky wolf when we were cubs. Always taking things and saying I did it. He threw acid on my hair when I was asleep. I thought he'd grown out of it. I could forgive him for making me stink, but what he did to our father… Anyway, I'm glad you're back. All of you. Even the bears. Now I've just got to convince her of it."

Curt joins me on the balcony, watching as Yellfire's wolf nuts the front door until it gives, slams inside the mansion and changes back to human in one violent manoeuvre.

"He outran me," she growls, as Primus wraps a blanket around her.

I suspect she let him go. Even she might baulk at attacking her own grandson.

"He won't be coming back," she continues, "nor that traitorous Longfang. I wish them the joy of each other."

"Grandmother, there's a lot you need to know," Primus ventures, following her into the hall.

"Is there," she states, stopping to stare straight at him. "Then tell me, boy. But first, find someone to light the damn fire; it's freezing in here.

CHAPTER 39

Mould Throttler And The Secret

Exhausted, Curt and I flaked out for the count in our room, me wrapped around his ailing body, my extra layers of blubber keeping him nice and warm. By the time I awake, the sun has slipped by its highest point and a roaring fire brings the ambient temperature nearer toasty than freezing. I've no idea who sneaked in to keep the flames going, but I'm beyond grateful.

I'm actually woken from my dream of lounging beneath a palm tree by some ham footed twit thumping around in the corridor.

"Shhh. Quit stomping."

That sounds like Ursid, so I guess the ogre is…

"Isn't she awake yet? I'm telling you she's ill. Why isn't Mama giving her the Mould Throttler?"

Yep. Adamo. Whispering through a foghorn.

"She's getting it ready. Besides Mama insists Dulcis doesn't need it. She's not got mould sickness."

"What if she's wrong? I'm going in there."

The sound of a scuffle is followed by, "No, you're not. Let them all sleep."

"Fat chance," I hiss, opening my bedroom door to glare at them. "Go away. Curt's asleep."

"Not anymore," my wolf says, with a nose wrinkling yawn.

"How do you feel?" I ask, as the ginger prince peeps around the door and waves at him.

Curt sits up in bed and waves back. "Not good, but not as sick as yesterday. Tired, still."

I swipe my palm over his eyelids and push on his chest. "Go back to sleep."

"Sorry, no," calls Mama Bear, staggering up the stairs. "The medicine's ready."

She's hauling a pot belching thick purple smoke, hands wrapped in woollen oven gloves. I can't tell whether that's protection from the heat or acid splash burns. The concoction smells as though it could strip paint from the walls and dissolve Tupperware.

"Urgh, Yuck," Adamo pronounces, clamping thumb and index finger over his nose.

"Wings!" Mama bellows. "Gulid!"

That will have woken everyone up.

The eagles jog up the stairs, Gulid carrying a goblet, Wings' eyes fixed on a metal plate he's holding at arm's length. Quivering on the top sits a yellow green paste that resembles a heap of snot.

"Fobly bugs, I presume?" I enquire of Mama.

She nods. "Nicely rotting, so we have to use them now. Curt, up you get. Ursid, please bring Alpha."

"Where we going?" Adamo asks.

"In with our southern friends," Mama tells him. "All three boys need to take it at once."

"What about Dulcis?" He hurries after her as she wobbles down the hall, Wings in tow.

I waft the air in front of my face and cough, trying to dispel the drifting purple smoke. "Come on, Curt. Clothes on."

"I want to sleep," he groans, pulling the blanket over his head. "It's nice and warm in here. And what's that smell?"

"Trousers on for Edi."

I coax my mangy wolf into his clothes and guide him along the hall, half-asleep, yawning in my ear. Alpha's just ahead of us, head wound wrapped, leaning on a carved wolf's head crutch and Dulcis. Anguis and Serpen, both looking remarkably dapper after a good rest, stand just outside the open door, deciding not to push their luck with the twitchy Yelena, whose horrified tones thunder forth and echo throughout the mansion.

"You are not giving that filth to my son!"

I gather she's had a good sniff of Mama's brew.

"Trust me. This will deal with the mould growing in their stomachs," our bear insists.

I suspect it would also deal with concrete, but I'm keeping quiet. Mama can defend herself.

"That will kill my boy," Yelena cries, her voice trembling just a smidgen.

Curt suddenly comes too and decides he'd rather go the other way, back to bed. His brother trips him up with his crutch and they both land on the floor, howling.

"Ow." Curt grabbing his hip.

"Ow." Alpha grabbing his knee.

"Why'd you do that?" Curt moans.

"You were running off. Again."

"It stinks."

"Get inside, you big pup," Alpha says. "If I'm taking it, you are."

"You're supposed to be my little brother."

"I am your brother. You are not dying of mould and leaving me here."

"You can take it first," Curt offers. "I'll watch you."

"You're older," his brother bats back.

"You're Alpha."

"You went off and left me as Alpha. Get in that room. And someone help me up."

Serpen and Anguis deal with getting the wolf boys vertical, whilst Dulcis and I venture into the room. I can see why Yelena's still hollering, since the air's so thick with purple smoke I can barely see my own feet and my nose feels like it's been cleaned out with industrial bleach.

"Fobly paste," Mama yells, over the top of Yelena's swearing. Wings hands her the plate.

As the snot passes by her shocked eyes, Yelena's temporarily struck dumb. It doesn't last long. We manage to manhandle Curt and Alpha onto the bed, next to the ghoulish Big Wolf, whose skin now bears a lilac tinge. Three wide-eyed wolf boys stare as Mama kneels to hold the plate over the fire in her oven gloves.

"Once this turns liquid green," Mama hollers, "I'll stir it into the pot, then you have to drink it down straight away. One shot, understand? No dawdling or it'll go off."

"They're not taking that," Yelena shrieks.

"Yes, they are!" Audira bellows, getting right in her mother-in-law's face, nose to nose. "I will deal with the health of my mate and I say he's taking it. Now sit down, Mother!"

Yelena is so surprised at the sudden about turn of the timid wolf that she slowly complies, sinking into the chair. Primus loops an arm around her shoulders, giving her a comforting squeeze.

"You three," says Audira, pointing at the patients, "are doing as you're told."

The two Alphas nod. Curt looks at me.

"What she said," I tell him.

"Ready," Mama announces, pulling the burning snot liquid from the flames and dumping it into the purple brew. She grabs a wooden spoon and stirs like a liquidiser for a few seconds, releasing another cloud of smoke. "Cups."

Wings pulls three metal tankards from his coat and lines them up for Mama to ladle the obnoxious brew. Three pairs of wolf eyes widen to the point of cartoon comedy and they lean away as each gets a cup thrust into their hands.

"Down it, now." Mama tips her head back in demonstration.

None of the three moves.

I leap behind Curt, grab his hands and heave the cup to his lips. "Open wide, right now." I hit his clenched teeth. "Open. Swallow now. For me. Please, Mange." He opens up and gulps, a cloud of smoke going straight up his nose. He gags, but keeps drinking until he hits the bottom of the tankard. "There's my brave wolf." He gets a gentle hug and a kiss on his nose as reward.

"It's not that bad," he tells his brother in a hoarse voice, nodding back at me. "She's cooked worse."

Alpha drinks his medicine, Dulcis rubbing his back in encouragement. "I love you, Daddy. Keep going."

Audira doesn't need to say anything to make her mate drink, but his eyes remain locked on hers throughout the entire ordeal. She gently takes the cup from his hands when he's done.

Alpha finishes and gags repeatedly. "You lied," he honks at Curt, who shrugs.

"Good," pronounces Mama, collecting up the empty tankards. "Alpha of Alphas, plenty of bed rest in this warm room and gallons of weak vegetable broth to build your strength back. The brothers need lots of rest and a little exercise."

Dulcis leans forward, dry retching into her hands. Mama snatches the goblet out of Gulid's grip and gives it to the young woman. "Drink that."

"What is it?" Dulcis asks, frowning.

"It won't hurt you," Mama whispers, stroking her arm.

Dulcis sips and smiles at Mama.

Curt sniffs, that wolf nose twitching. "That smells nice, why can't I have that?"

The ginger prince of bears looms over Dulcis' shoulder, peering into the cup. "Looks like juice. What good is that? Why aren't you giving her the Throttler?"

"I wondered that too," Alpha says.

"I don't need it," Dulcis tells them. "Mind your own business."

"You are my business," Alpha and Adamo say at exactly the same time and glare at each other. "You're clearly sick," Adamo presses.

"It's fine," Mama tells him.

"It's not fine."

Ursid's eyebrow lifts as he stares at Dulcis, then Mama. "It's best to leave it be," he tells his charge, patting the prince's shoulder.

I'd say our general has guessed the secret, as have I, and probably you, too.

"Please take the Throttler," Adamo pleads, crushing Dulcis to his chest. "Decipa might have given it to you. You're sick. Please."

"I've not got the mould," Dulcis insists, pulling free of his embrace.

"You don't know that."

"I do."

"How?" Adamo presses.

"I just feel queasy."

"Exactly. You're sick so…"

"I'm pregnant."

Silence. He looks like he's been hit by a boulder.

"We're having a cub?" he whimpers.

Thank the Lord he said *we*. He's in no doubt he's the puppy daddy.

"Yes, that's what pregnant means, you twit," Dulcis snaps, staring at him. She's doing a good job of seeming feisty, but most of us know her little twitchy giveaways. As does Adamo.

His stunned expression morphs into the sunniest of grins. "I'm a dad," he says. "Ursid, I'm having a princess, or a prince. A little bear. Or maybe a little wolf. Who knows?" He slaps the shellshocked Yelena on the back and gets a hefty snarl for his trouble. "We must be mated, right now. You and me, I mean. Not me and your granny."

"It's a bit late for that," Alpha growls, struggling to his feet. "I'm going to kill you."

"You can't even deal with your medicine right now," Dulcis says. "Sit down. Daddy."

That cackling in harmony comes from Curt and Ursid.

Our Alpha glares at innocent little me. "I blame you for this."

Say what?

"How in the name of all that's holy can this be my fault?" I trumpet. "We'll have a biology chat in private."

"You knew about them being together."

"Everyone knew about them being together, except you." Probably not what he wanted to hear, but hey.

Alpha glares at Wings.

"Don't involve me," the eagle splutters. "I've got enough problems."

"Curt, why didn't you tell me?" Alpha turns to his daughter. "Come to think of it, why didn't you tell me?"

"I just did," she throws at him.

"Forget them," Adamo interrupts, spinning her around to face him. "You should have told me earlier."

"You weren't here."

"Before then. You knew before. Right?" Adamo bends down to look her in the eyes. "Didn't you trust me?"

"Don't bully her," Alpha hollers.

"Keep out of this, Daddy. Don't bully me, you great bear."

Adamo gently nudges her back into his arms. "We'll be mated and very happy. Whatever we have. Is it going to be bear or wolf?"

"I don't know. Does it matter?"

"Not to me."

She tips her head back and peers up at him. "I don't want you to be my mate because of this."

He grins. "It's not because of this. Well, not just because of this. I love you."

"You left me," she states.

"You told me you were mating with a wolf," he points out.

"You didn't put up much of a fight for me."

He grunts. "I was being accused of arson and attempted murder. I could have done with some support."

"Sorry about that," Curt chimes in. His brother glares at him.

"Do you love me?" Adamo asks.

"Do you love *me*?" Dulcis replies.

"Always."

"Fine."

"If you're fine, why are you still making that face?"

He's right; she's still scowling.

"I'm trying to decide whether I'm going to thump you or kiss you."

"You just been sick?" he asks.

"Yes," she whimpers, waiting for a flood of sympathy.

"Maybe not the kiss then."

She thumps him.

CHAPTER 40

Unity. Kind Of

"This is all your fault," Yelena insists.

You know what? I've had enough of this. Even if it is true.

Wings flew off with Mama Bear, carrying the order for the bears and snakes to return home. Where we are going to fit everyone with the southern wolves still here, I don't know, but we've managed before. The debate precipitating my annoyance is a tactical analysis of how screwed we are in relation to the coming serpent apocalypse, united pack or no.

Addressing an avid audience, haphazardly spread throughout the hall, Gulid gives us the low down, as far as he knows, which ends with everyone staring at yours truly, the book toting pariah, none the wiser as to why the coming monster serpent wants me. The fact that I burnt the magic book only makes me more guilty in Yelena's eyes. Bonkers and guilty.

"There may be hundreds of these serpents coming," says Gulid, rolling to a gloomy close, "and the king is a nightmare."

We could all leave," Primus offers. "Head south to our territory."

"They'll just keep coming," Gulid replies, "following her."

I have a name you miserable bird.

"We could let them have her," Yelena offers.

Thanks a lot, but I suppose someone was bound to bring it up.

"I could stay here and let them get me," I suggest, my heart pounding in my ears. "Or Wings drops me north."

"Not a chance," barks my loyal Mange.

"Your mate's wellbeing is more important than the entire pack?" asks Yelena.

I hate her, but she's right. Strangely, it's Broken Beak who comes to my rescue.

"The last thing you should do is give that monster what he wants. If he wants her, it's for a bad reason, and not just for her."

"Besides, who's to say they won't just mesmerise you all and keep spreading?" Anguis points out. "Where's safe to run?"

"So, we must unite to have any chance at all," says Curt.

"That's convenient for you, reject," growls Yelena.

I shoot to my feet, bathed in a wave of red hot rage. "You call my mate a reject again and I'll smash you in the nose with a tray."

"She'll do it too," warns Gulid.

"Mother," says Big Wolf. "Unity, remember?"

"Hmmmph. Violent little human, isn't she?"

Did I really spot a glimmer of respect in auntie's eyes? Curt tugs on my hand and I sit, seething. He gives me a quick nuzzle.

"This is our home," Serpen says. "We either unite or we run."

Our Alpha stands, leaning on his crutch, and lays a hand on Curt's shoulder. "Neither of us is running anywhere, even if we could. Edi, you're my family. Our family doesn't desert or betray one another. That's what you taught Kallosa. Right, Aunt Yelena?"

She looks at him, then her son. He nods.

"Right," she repeats, and leans back in her chair. "I'm too old for this."

"Aren't we all?" I reply.

* * *

A procession of bears and snakes return home to the thundering silence of southern wolves, some milling about in the streets, others doing their Anubis thing in tight formation, making a point. Snakes tend to be genteel, so they ignore their frosty reception, but the amused bears entertain themselves with mutterings of 'Up yours,' 'Up your tail, tufty,' and 'If Sospa comes past, you'll get stuck like that.'

Somewhere around the middle of the returning pack, a great mob of padded out children are unleashed into the snow in an over-excited frenzy, hurling snowballs in all directions. The Anubis mob only get direct hits in the snout a few times before the frozen parade cracks and they take off after their fleeing attackers in a whirlwind of paws, yipping in fun. Apparently, they're not as uptight as they seem and a colossal snow fight might just be a grand way for unity to build. Thank the Lord for children.

A tiny snake girl leaps around, playing with the thankfully recovered Bogi, a wolf ten times her size, until she trips and falls. Bogi gently licks her grazed knee and nudges her to her feet. Giggling, she shoves a handful of snow down his ear and sprints off. He shakes his head, chasing after her with a raucous howl and a tail swish.

"Friddie!" Mama Bear sprints towards her mate, swamping him in her embrace and muffling his response.

I'm smiling indulgently when a flying ball of fluff smacks me in the knees. "Ow. I see you're back, you little horror." He climbs up my body, sticking his claws in my padding, until he can wrap himself around my neck like a scarf. "Alright. I'm glad you're home too," I wheeze, before a slightly tearful Mama retrieves her sprog.

Waving at the laughing Friddie, I turn and catch Yelena standing just outside the mansion, watching the children having fun in the snow. She's as ramrod straight as ever, but the look on her face surprises me; it's a mixture of indulgence and regret. Speaking of which, I'm probably going to regret this, but I head over to stand beside her. She glances at me, saying nothing.

"There's my princess," Serpen calls out, jogging past on his way to swing Sospa into his arms.

Over the king's shoulder, the girl spots Yelena and her eyes widen. "Are we home now?" she asks her uncle, worried the wolf lady might throw them out again.

"Yes, we are," he replies, giving her a big kiss on the nose.

"Ewww," she says, wiping her nose on her sleeve.

"They're not all the same, you know," I tell Yelena. "These snakes, they care for each other and this pack."

Yellfire scowls at me, then swallows, hard. "You don't know them."

"I know these ones. And they're not their fathers or grandfathers."

Yelena shivers, rubbing her hand up and down her arm, trying to warm herself.

"Did you love him, the one who betrayed you?"

It's none of my business and her answering glare repeats that fact. Her gaze goes back to Sospa, leaping from the king's arms to bounce in the snow.

"I did love him," Yelena says, surprising me, again. "He was charming back then. He turned foul later."

"So, probably best you weren't together," I venture.

"Not really."

A pair of complete reprobates appear from around the back of the mansion, probably because they would be waylaid if they came out the front door, not least by me. Curt and his younger brother are supposed to be resting by the fire, but here they come, limp as wet lettuce, determined to do themselves some damage.

Curt lobs a snowball at Alpha and lets fly with a volley of honking coughs. His brother dodges the missile, staggers and almost tumbles off his crutch, making Curt catch him. I'm about to head over, before they're both flat out in the snow, when Dulcis marches out the front door, looking for all the world like her grandmother, stood beside me.

"Get inside, NOW!" she bellows, descending upon the wayward duo, who are holding each other up like bookends.

"Ahhh," Alpha whinges, channelling his inner toddler, "just a bit longer. I can't sit inside anymore. I'm bored. They're all having fun."

"You'll fall down and break your neck," she replies, "to go with your head and your knee."

"He's alright," Curt says. "I've got him."

"Who's got you?" Dulcis asks, hands on hips. "You can play all you like when you're better. Perhaps the Snake King in the north would like to play hide and seek?"

"You're no fun," her father moans, but pride is written all over his face.

"She's like her mother," Yelena remarks, wistfully. "And a little of her father."

I can't tell whether she's speaking to me, but I reply anyway. "I wish I'd met Kallosa. Alpha has done a good job raising Dulcis and her uncle loves her. Wings too."

"Not like my sister," Yelena states.

"Frozen... erm, Helena?" Oops.

"I know your Alpha called her Frozen Hell," Yelena tells me, a slight smile making her eyes briefly twinkle. "And me, Yellfire."

"Tough duo," I say, with a laugh. "But I suppose you had to be."

"She hated me, my sister."

My surprise shows before I can contain it.

"Not everyone's like your Alpha and Curtus," she continues. "I wonder if my sister and I brought this on our family; Kallosa fighting to leave me. Now Fidus..."

"Nothing you did made him a poisoner. Primus is a fine man. Wolf. As is your son."

I expect her to be angry, but she seems miles away in memory.

"I could sing you know, as a child. I loved it. Helena told our father and he made me stop. Not suitable for an Alpha daughter. My sweet girl could sing." Her gaze finds Dulcis, who's ushering the wayward boys towards the mansion. "I miss her."

"They do too," I tell her.

"I think, in their hearts, you've replaced my daughter... and I don't know what to do with that."

Her gaze bores into mine, leaving only room for truth.

"Please know I love that girl," I tell her. "They're the only family I have. I'd do anything for them."

"Just don't get them killed," Yelena replies.

That would be my worst nightmare.

"Do you want to play snowballs?" a chirpy voice pipes up.

Sospa slides in the snow, skidding to a stop in front of a stunned Yelena, who stares at her.

"You don't like me very much, do you?" the mini snake asks, tipping her head.

Yelena glances at Serpen, who hovers nearby, watching.

"I don't like you trying to mesmerise me," the wolf tells the girl.

Sospa lifts her chin and stares Yelena down. "If I promise not to try, will you play then?"

I swear I just saw the old girl smile. Like, full on smile.

"Maybe not right now, since I need to speak to your Alpha, but perhaps later."

"I think we're going to get along," little miss feisty announces before tugging on her uncle's arm, making the frozen king jerk into action.

"Perhaps," Yelena laughs. She catches sight of my face and smothers her giggle with false solemnity. She's not fooling me. The limping duo, however, are another matter entirely. They attempt to speed up as they pass her by, but she's on them like a... wolf, I suppose.

"You need to make a decision," she demands.

"What about?" Alpha squeaks.

"Primus!" she hollers, making us all jump.

"Grandmother." He materialises out of the hallway, carrying a steaming mug of broth, which she promptly whips out of his hand.

"You will have to lead the pack because your father, their alpha and Curtus are all sick."

The former Stinky shakes his head. "This united pack business needs them, not me. And you know it."

"What about Dulcis?" I suggest.

"No thanks," is the teen princess's verdict. "I think Edi should do it."

Very funny.

"Neither of us are dead," Curt points out, leaning on his brother.

"Why don't you all lead?" sings Sospa, flying past on Ursid's back.

You know what, out of the mouth of babes...

"A council," I announce. "A war council of wolves, bears, snakes and eagles."

"And a human," Curt adds.

I smile at my mangy wolf.

"Not necessarily you," says Alpha.

I flounce off, with Alpha's voice echoing after me.

"I was joking."

CHAPTER 41

Bite Me

Everyone loves a good mating, right?

I'm referring to the ceremony, of course.

Chairs of all shapes and sizes, carved wood and twisted metal, armchairs to stools, all borrowed from multiple houses, pack the hall of our mansion, leaving an aisle down the centre and a gap at the front to serve as a stage/altar. Apparently, a mating ceremony normally takes place outside in furry coats, namely as wolves, and involves some rather intimate nasal biting, but not on this occasion.

Oh, by the way, you should probably know this mating is for me and His Furry Mangeness, not the youngsters, which accounts for the flood of furniture and the arriving occupants being dressed like a 1970s psychedelic musical. Who knew there would be an occasion for that monstrous gumwhat eyes yellow that Gulid's nostalgically wearing? He reminds me of a fluorescent banana.

Speaking of gumwhats, Mr G didn't like that Mould Throttler any more than Curt, but it did the trick for both of them. He's lounging on my bedside table – Mr G, not Curt - crunching his way through some far more tasty biscuits in honour of our ceremony, so he's happy.

Frankly, I probably would have gone with the outside biting version, but Curt sent Mama Bear undercover with a bottle of

100% proof 'wine' to wheedle all the details of an ideal earthly wedding out of me. He then set about trying to realise it in the most bizarre manner possible. Bless him, he meant well, but goodness knows what I told Mama under the influence.

Curt spent last night in with his brother and, since they both snore like a sinking ship, neither got much sleep. Still, it warms my heart to see them, twitching side by side, running nervous fingers over cobbled together suits, awaiting my arrival. Ursid, who somehow drew the short straw to officiate this extravaganza, has been gussied up like a fur lined vicar in one of Anguis' coats. I assume Wings let the seams out for him.

I'm peering down at the congregation through a gap in woollen curtains. They've hung yards of the multicoloured stuff, tacked together, stretching from my room to the top of the stairs, so I can have my big reveal as I turn the corner. I'm not convinced of the need. I think it's thirty years too late for all that malarky, but it's my own fault, since I ran my mouth off under the influence of that wine made by snakes. Mama Bear took some away for the preservation of medicinal samples – or so she said.

Curt's obvious choice for his Best Man was his brother, which left this bride in an awkward position. I like to think myself an old school feminist, but, to tell the truth, I also like the idea of being escorted down the aisle, even if I'm not handed off like a sack of spuds at the end of it. Word got around and just about everyone had their own 'word' with me, pitching their case for my escort, with the exception of my final choice, who said nothing, knowing I would pick him.

"You need to get your dress on," Wings whispers in my ear, making me thump him.

"You nearly gave me a heart attack, you old vulture."

He laughs, widening the gap in the curtain to peer at the filling chairs. "Who's down there?"

"Your boys look nervous," I tell him, nodding my head towards the brothers, currently limping in mirror image.

"I'd be nervous, if you were my mate," the bird quips, grinning at me. "Why are they all wearing bright colours? My eyes hurt."

"Didn't Curt try to get you into yellow?" I laugh.

"He said something, but I wasn't listening," Wings replies, adjusting his usual attire, given a special press for the occasion.

In comes Luva, leading her elderly posse, all wearing scarlet, which is appropriate to my mind. Wings smiles, then blushes a similar shade.

"Tell me the story," I insist.

"What story?" he replies, faking wide-eyed innocence.

"Don't give me that. It's my wedding day. Tell me."

Wings sighs, glancing at me. "Luva took care of me when I first came here. She was older than me and…"

"And…?"

"I had a terrible crush on her."

"And…?"

"She's never let me forget it."

"That's not all," I push.

"That's all you'll get," he replies, avoiding my eyes. "Yellfire's here."

He's right. Unlike the primary coloured crowd, she's arrived, classily dressed in a brown leather dress suit, on the arm of her son, Audira being on his other side. Yelena takes her seat as though she's clenching nuts between her buttocks.

"This is not going to work," she mutters, directly below the curtain. "Wolves and humans are not right for each other."

"How would we know?" Big Wolf replies, looking better with every passing day. "Hardly anyone in our family was happy. I was lucky with Audira," he continues, smiling at his mate, "but my father was a beast to you, just like grandfather. Your own sister was a horror. I like it here. People are nice to each other."

"You think I'm not nice to you?" Yelena unleashes a tight lipped glare.

Her son takes her hand. "I love you, Mother."

"So I should think," she mutters, turning away, only to look straight into the face of Sospa.

"Can I sit with you?" the child chirps, not waiting for an answer before parking herself next to the scary monster and imitating her ramrod straight manner. Serpen sits in the row behind, trying not to laugh.

Yelena peers down at her snake miniature. "So, about you mesmerising," she whispers, making a show of glancing around as though checking they're not being overheard. "Perhaps you can show me."

The pair of them grin like wicked kindred spirits. Well, what do you know?

"Where is she?" That sounds like Dulcis. "She should be here by now. I'd better go check on her." Sure enough, she floats into her seat wearing a full length royal blue concoction, covered with yards of green lace. I glance at the eagle, beside me.

"Don't look at me," he whispers. "I didn't make it."

"Stinky, you can sit with us," Dulcis announces, grabbing the poor boy's arm as he walks by, swinging him into Adamo's seat.

"Thank you, Trumpet," Primus replies, getting up again, "but I'll sit with my grandmother, since she's less dangerous than the bear.

Adamo laughs and plonks himself into the vacated seat, beaming at his former rival. Apparently, they're fast becoming friends.

"I'm going upstairs to Edi." Dulcis tries to shuffle past Adamo's bulk. He presses her back into her chair, adjusting the fit of his flamingo pink jacket.

"Leave her be. Wings is in control."

"Yes, I am," Wings agrees, pulling me away from the curtain. "Dress, young lady."

And so, we get to it. The moment you've all been waiting for: The Wedding Dress. Given that the congregation looks ridiculous and the hall is decked out in reams of multicoloured drapes, you would be forgiven for thinking the dress would go down in the annals of rainbow infamy.

You'd be wrong.

The old bird had no hand in the others' dreadful attire, but he did make my dress and it's gorgeous. I cried when I first saw it, actual tears of joy. Where he managed to get white linen and lace from, I've no idea, but it's so light it floats like waves on the beach and clings to my figure in all the right places.

Once I'm laced into his creation, Wings sits me down for one last poke at my elaborately plaited hairdo. He's adding one more pin to tame a wayward lock when there's a gentle tap on the door and Anguis enters, carrying a wad of yellow material. He halts and takes me in, where I'm sat at the dresser.

"You look beautiful," he says, eyes glossing over.

He's going to start me off crying in a minute.

He holds out the throbbing yellow horror, announcing, "I've made you something."

The look on my face would speak for me, but Wings croaks an appalled, "That's yellow."

Anguis rolls his eyes. "It's inside the wrapping."

I peel back the material and, when it gives up its treasure, I can't prevent my own eyes filling with tears. In its yellow nest sits a veil of white lace embroidery, so delicate as to be almost transparent.

"It's stunning," I whimper, moving towards him, arms outstretched for the hug.

He steps back and I pause, confused.

"I can't," he tells me. "Not anymore."

I understand. He's letting me go.

My eyes meet his for a brief exchange of what might have been. "Thank you, Anguis. For everything."

He nods and swiftly leaves the room.

"Mop up," Wings tells me, handing me the yellow material as a hankie. I blow my nose whilst he fixes the new veil to the hairdo, allowing the lace to flow down my back. "There," he pronounces. "Look at you."

I'm reluctant to peer in the full length mirror. I've never been considered a beauty, although I was never the monstrosity that teen years had me believe. I learned not to put too much store in my appearance, yet, this time, just this once, I long to see a beauty staring back at me.

Wings wraps an arm around my bare shoulder, smiling as though he's reading my mind. "Be brave."

Taking a deep breath, I turn towards the mirror, gaze glued to the floor. In my mind, I'm repeating, 'Don't be disappointed. Don't be disappointed,' as I lift my eyes.

Oh.

"Don't cry," Wings commands, dabbing under my eyes. He's too late.

The dress drapes across my breasts and falls into folds of lace in the style of an Ancient Grecian goddess. I can't believe it. I look drop dead gorgeous. My wolf won't know what hit him. Never let them tell you that wedding dresses are for the young.

"Thank you," I stammer. "I love it."

"Good. Right then," the eagle mutters. He grabs my face and kisses my forehead, before holding out his arm. "Like this?"

"Like that," I agree, linking my arm through his.

Out we go, side by side, on a stately march along the balcony. Through the window, we glimpse the bonfire, casting a warm flickering glow on our faces. Hundreds already wait for the Howling, unable to fit inside the packed hall for the ceremony. I wave at them and a muffled cheer swamps the mansion.

Wings glances at me and smiles as we reach the staircase and turn the corner to descend.

Anguis stands at the back of the hall, every inch the formal ambassador as he bows to me.

"Rise," Ursid commands.

Chair legs scrape as a sea of bodies find their feet, peering over their shoulders at the human oddity.

I'm floating down the stairs on Wings' arm when I spot the stunned look on Curt's face. His eyes are so wide they might pop out of his head and his tongue hangs loose from his open mouth as though he's in the process of turning wolf. Alpha laughs and nudges his brother to close his mouth. Curt rallies and tugs on his embroidered jacket.

Down the aisle we tread, the grey-haired siren and her proud eagle, passing Mama Bear, Friddie and Beetus, squirming in his uncomfortable human suit. He'll turn cub and scarper as soon as they look the other way. There's Serpen, Sospa, a teary eyed Dulcis and a grinning Adamo. My family. It's all I can do not to burst into tears and sob.

We glide to Curt's side, where Wings pats my arm. I kiss the old bird on the cheek and he sniffs as he takes his place behind Alpha.

"Please sit," says Ursid, and the congregation duly oblige in a rustle of odd skirts, shirts and jackets. "Greetings wolves, bears, snakes, eagles and human," he announces, smiling at me. "We assemble to witness the mating ceremony of Curtus and Edith, both of this united pack, and to celebrate their Howling with them. Now, er, does anyone know just cause why they shouldn't be joined together?"

Good grief, Mama Bear must have an incredible memory. We'd both had a few tumblers by the time I got to that detail.

Yellfire sucks in a breath and opens her mouth, but her son and Audira lean forward to stare at her until she closes it again. I catch the wink she gives the giggling Sospa.

Adamo's voice carries in the silence. "Why's he asking that?"

"It's part of the law where Edi comes from, I think," Dulcis whispers, shushing him with her hands.

"Strange people," he mutters.

He has no idea.

"So, if you're done," Ursid growls, glaring at his prince, "we'll carry on with the ceremony. Curtus, do you take Edith for your…"

"I do," he blurts, a bundle of nerves.

"…mate?" Ursid finishes.

"Erm. Yes. I do," Curt repeats, giving me a sheepish look.

He's scared of doing something wrong in the ceremony and ruining it for me. Aww. I beam at him and he relaxes a little.

"Edith," says Ursid, turning to me, "do you take Curtus to be your mate?"

"Too right, I do."

Curt snorts and a wave of laughter ripples through the crowd.

"Curt, do you have a ring for Edith?" the general asks.

Now that surprises me. I thought he'd forgotten about that.

Alpha makes a big show of delving in his inside pocket and handing over a gold ring to his brother. They formally shake hands. How twee and sweet.

I hold out the correct finger and Curt slides the ring on. It's a perfect fit: a stylised howling wolf's head in profile. I love it.

"It's now time for your own personal vows," Ursid reminds us. "Curt, you first."

This ought to be good. Curt's been wandering up and down corridors muttering to himself for days. I said I'd help him, but he was so insulted, he turned wolf and flounced off with a swish of his tail. I would tell him not to worry about it, but I'm curious.

He starts by clearing his throat and shuffling on the spot. "I vow that I'll cook for you whenever you want."

"To save his own life," Adamo mutters and Dulcis digs her elbow in his ribs.

Curt scratches his hip so hard, I'm forced to hold his hand. He grips my fingers like a lifeline.

"My wolf will keep you warm when it's cold and keep to himself when you're too hot. I'll fan you instead. I'll always love your face, your big bum and bits that wobble," he says, cupping the free hand to indicate my breasts, "especially naked."

A few people shift in their chairs. Adamo fights to smother his giggles, which sets off Primus.

Curt forges on. "I'll love your voice, your strength, your honour and your loyalty. I promise I'll be right there beside you, night and day, man and wolf, until I howl my last. Even then, within the Forest Vale with my ancestors, I'll howl every night, so you'll know I wait for you to join me. You're my mate and my human wolf."

Wow. I'm so choked I can barely breathe.

The laughing ceases. Wings blows his nose into his hankie.

"Edi, your turn," Ursid prompts.

I thought long and hard about this. All the things I could say, want to say, will say over the coming days.

"Curt, I waited my whole life for you. They could burn it all to the ground and I vow you will still be my home." My voice breaks on the last word and Curt hauls me into his arms and crushes me.

I've never felt more at peace in my life.

"Awww." That sounds like Adamo being soppy.

"United Pack," Ursid begins, "I am honoured to announce that Curtus Furtletooth and Edith Breaker-Smith are now life mates."

Curt gives me one of his special suction kisses and I feel the breath leave my body to the background chorus of cheering and clapping.

"To the Howling!" Ursid hollers.

I come up for air with, "One last thing, General."

Curt's happy face drops into his boots. "I missed something? What did I miss?"

"Just this."

I bite him full on the nose, lift my dress off the floor and leg it down the aisle at full pelt, howling to the heavens, leaving my shocked mate to give chase. I pass Yelena, who's sporting a look of horrified surprise, making everything worth it, and out into the freezing cold I go.

CHAPTER 42

The Final Shocker

I sprint towards that glorious roaring bonfire, being as I'm not stupid and it's sub zero out here. Gammy hip or no, my new mate hunts me down in double quick time, lifting my frozen feet off the snow. My legs hook around his back as two giant hands clasp my chilly buttocks. Slowly he opens his mouth and delivers the world's softest nip to my frost bitten nose.

"Mine," he whispers.

I tend to agree.

Hopping off him, I fling my arms into the air and dance around the flames with total abandon, giving in to my primal side. I probably look like my old dad at a new year's party, but who cares? The hundreds outside need no urging to cut loose.

The congregation stream out of the hall to join us in our own special Howling. In my honour as the lone human, no-one changes to their animal or gets naked, instead letting rip in full fancy dress. Legs and arms fly through the air as they howl and leap with glee, the horrors of the past and fear for the future swept away in one glorious night of jubilation.

As soon as the snakes shiver, feeling the cold, an army of bears start wrapping them in wool and furs, the mini ones being lifting into warm embraces and jiggled around the fire. I'm stunned, as is

Serpen, when Yelena waltzes past, Sospa perched in her arms, both singing off key at the tops of their voices.

Curt nudges me and I follow his gaze to Dulcis and Adamo, clasped together, eyes closed, gently swaying as though hearing their own music. Alpha sports an annoyed dad face until Ursid clasps his shoulder.

"Good evening, Grandwolf," the general says.

"Hmmm," Alpha replies, giving in to the inevitable with a wry smile. "Her mother would have liked him, even if I don't."

Ursid laughs.

Even Big Wolf ventures out into the cold, although Audira makes sure he's smothered from head to foot in wool, his mittened hands clasping a steaming mug of broth. Primus parks a chair behind his father, who gratefully sits.

When we all finally run out of dancing steam, a stream of men and women bring out a table and fill it with bowls, plates, spoons, dishes of meats, vegetables and piping hot stew, with broth or mulled wine to drink. The revellers wrap up in an array of coats, hats, scarves and blankets and descend upon the feast like padded vultures.

Speaking of miserable birds, Wings flaps over to his oldest pup and new mate, hurling an endless supply of coats until he's satisfied we're warm enough, muttering, "wolves," under his breath.

For a brief moment, I remember Anguis, my eyes searching for him amongst the crowd. I find him chatting with Luva. The grand old lady makes him laugh and it warms my heart.

A great crowd of children, led by one shifty looking little boy who's clearly up to no good – no prizes for guessing who – descend upon Serpen, surrounding him with shouts and yells.

"King Serpen, please change," Mama Bear's brown haired little monster pleads. "We want to see the serpent. Please."

"Please change. Please. Change, change," they chant until he raises a palm.

"You'll be scared," he tells them.

"I won't," announces the monstrous cub.

"Change, change," they start up, again.

He stares at the crowd of shiny little faces, until he looks up at Yelena, Sospa still in her arms.

"Do it," his niece tells him, chewing on an unidentifiable meaty bone. "Scare them all."

Yelena shrugs.

Serpen turns his back and walks away. All the children groan their disappointment, but he's only going far enough so they don't see his face splitting in a shower of blood. The full serpent arises, growing taller and taller into the night sky.

The children stare, frozen with shock. His ridged head suddenly drops towards them and they scream, but it's not terror, it's excitement. The crowd of miniatures swarm the scaly serpent. Serpen flattens his tail until the brave can all pile on and off they go, slithering through the snow. Yelena pops Sospa on the tail end as they ride by.

I'm squeezing inside Curt's many coats, snuggling up to his wolf warmth, when I notice the newly freed Yellfire waylaying Gulid as he attempts to tiptoe past. She's been trying to nail him down for a 'chat' for days.

"There you are, eagle. I've been looking for you."

"Have you?" he squeaks.

"You were up there with these coming serpents. You must know more about why they want Edith."

"Auntie, this isn't the time," Curt says. "It's our Howling."

I would agree, only I can see the look on Broken Beak's warped face. Yelena notices it too. Oh no. There's more isn't there? And I'm not going to like it. When do I ever?

"Out with it," Yellfire insists, looming up at him, her intensity drawing the attention of Alpha, Ursid and her family.

Wings steps up beside him. "Gulid, have you told us everything you know?"

Curt sighs and hugs me close, sensing the other shoe is about to drop.

"I didn't want to say," Gulid pleads. "You wouldn't have helped me and I want my friends back."

"Fair enough," I tell him, emerging from Curt's layers. "We understand friendship, but we need to know all of it."

"Well," he begins, eyes darting everywhere, "they said there was a rumour. Something about the snakes having a mage."

"That's fine," I pipe up. "Mama can treat that."

"Mage, not mange," Yelena snaps.

"Yes, I know. I was being humorous. Bit of a stretch for you."

Yelena ignores me. "There are no more mages. They've been gone for centuries."

"Don't believe in magic," Curt states, with finality, notwithstanding a certain mouldy book.

"You're saying they've got a wizard?" I ask Gulid.

"A homicidal, insane, magic wielding mage who can turn you into a gumwhat," Gulid spills. "That's what the eagles said, but I didn't believe them as I never saw anything like that. Their king was bad enough."

"Well then," I start, "just rumour…"

"Although…"

Here it comes. The news we've all been waiting for.

"… I did take one flying pass at that citadel, during the night."

We all lean in.

"What did you see?" Alpha asks.

"Nothing."

We all groan with frustration.

"But I did hear something," the bird continues.

"Like?" I prompt.

"It was an animal, I think, but I've never heard anything like it."

"What did it sound like?" Curt asks.

"Meeeeoooowwww. Purrrrrr."

That sounds remarkably like…

"That's a kitty," I tell them.

"A what?" asks Curt.

"A moggy."

"What?" Yelena snaps.

"A cat," I pronounce. "We had them where I come from."

"A CAT!" Gulid shrieks in utter terror. "They have a mage cat?!"

What? I like cats.

Gulid flees, streaking across the snow, ripping his banana suit to shreds. He takes to the air in a frenzied flapping of wings.

Wolves, bears, snakes, one changed serpent, an aged eagle and a human, all stare into the night sky as a lone feather floats down onto the snow.

And on the far horizon looms the spectre of a trilogy.

ABOUT THE AUTHOR

Caroline Noe lives in London, having earned her living as, amongst other things, a tour guide for Wembley Stadium, shoe salesman, dog walker and keyboard jockey.

Having obtained a drama degree, she became an actor and singer, where she swiftly learnt the difference between dreaming and hard graft.

She is a keen photographer and film buff, having once reviewed film for live radio broadcast.

Caroline loves Science Fiction & Fantasy and would, if she could, live in Hobbiton and work in Gotham. She believes that real life is also epic and mystical, if you work hard enough at seeing it that way.

More information on Caroline's books and photography can be found at:

    Website: carolinenoe.org to sign up for her newsletter

    Instagram: @carrieauthor

    Facebook author page: carrieauthor

If you enjoyed this novel, or even if you didn't, please consider leaving a review. Feedback is helpful to the author and raises the profile of the book.

Printed in Great Britain
by Amazon